WELCOME TO THE GALAXY

OR, HOW I LEARNED TO APPRECIATE THE IMPORTANCE OF A GOOD FLOCKING

M.D. TABAT

Dedicated to my daughter, Rebecca.
Thanks for the inspiration.

PART 1

CHAPTER 1

In the handful of years BQ (Before Quane), the world was a very unhappy place.

The future was bleak. Optimism polled at an all-time low. This global funk was not the result of a world war, lethal pandemic, or threat of an asteroid impact, but simply the wear and tear on human beings surviving the effects of a protracted worldwide recession, social and political upheaval, and the inescapable cacophony of another election cycle.

Ordinary people were afraid for their own and their children's future. They were worried the next missile attack might be on their border, or the next shooting in their local school. Many were especially anxious the next generation of cell phones would lack any new features.

The pessimistic outlook for the future was shared universally on every continent and across every religious and ethnic affiliation.

Humanity was trapped—forced to watch a dismal, decrepit, three-ring circus.

Like a poorly tuned calliope, the news media wheezed a weak song of hope, coloring the pervasive gloom with a watery rosy tint.

The captive audience watched wide-eyed as their raggedy governments walked frayed tightropes over the net-less, unyielding ground of bankruptcy and anarchy.

Dictatorships, like so many mangy, worm-eaten lions, clawed the air against their tamers and trainers, emboldened by the realization that the whips, chairs, and pistols—designed to scare rather than harm—had become limp and feeble.

Candidates for office behaved like feckless clowns, vying for the audience's attention and votes by pummeling their opponents with cottony bats and oversized spongy hammers.

The air under the stained big top tent canvas was stifling. The ice in the thin drinks had all melted. Many concession stands nearest the cheap seats had already closed—no more drink, no more food.

Inept guards chased after rabid, flea-infested rats deliberately chewing the ropes holding the tent upright. The vermin reveled in the terror the tent's teetering created and understood its collapse would take them as well.

The captive audience tried to shift seats: shabby refugees trying to find comfort away from the heat, the lions, the rats, and the clowns.

But no one could leave the show.

Suddenly, under a pale spotlight, a new act—never before seen by human eyes—appeared in the center ring. A devil disguised as a talking dog arrived, flourishing a flimsy piece of barely functioning space junk to sell to the highest bidder: a piece of junk with the power to catapult humans to the stars, and ultimately make Earth one of the most influential and richest planets in the galaxy.

The year was 1 AQ (After Quane.)

CHAPTER 2

Nancy Wahl, a twenty-something third grade teacher from Macon, Georgia, hovered in the cupola, a seven-window observatory on the International Space Station. Six trapezoidal windows angled toward each other like a tank turret without a cannon. A thirty-one-inch round window made the floor. The view from inside the station resembled the *Millennium Falcon's* cockpit. The observatory was five feet deep and nine feet wide where it attached to the bottom of the *Tranquility* module, which constantly faced Earth. The ultimate glass-bottomed boat.

Sometimes Nancy's blond, braided hair curled over her head like a scorpion tail; other times, it would wrap around her neck like a loose hangman's loop. Usually, she kept it tucked in her shirt to keep it from whipping at her face like a cat o' nine tails.

Nancy squeezed a golf ball-sized sphere out of her water-pouch straw. It wobbled and bobbled in weightlessness. She pretended the shimmering orb was a planet and she was a giant space monster—a giant floating head. The monster opened its mouth wide and swallowed the planet whole. The space monster choked, almost sending the watery snack out its nose.

Nancy imagined viewing her school's playground on the green and brown landmass below, but was not quite sure she was even viewing the proper continent. Nancy was a reluctant astronaut by winning, what was to her mind the dubious honor of, passage to the station via a promotional stunt to fuel taxpayer interest in space exploration by sending an ordinary person into space. The other astronauts were respectful, but not inclusive. She had no special scientific experience or technical knowledge useful to the operation of the ISS and was relegated to making *Daily Life on the International Space Station* films for posting on YouTube: "How Earth's Continents Look From Space," "Cooking on the International Space Station," "Going to the Bathroom in Weightlessness."

In less than two weeks, the shuttle, the most expensive limousine on Earth, would arrive to take her home. Her first action was undecided: burying her face into Shemp's schnauzer-soft fur; gorging herself on gooey, drippy cheeseburgers at The Varsity drive-in; or sneaking into her classroom and grounding herself with the smell of chalk dust, fruit-scented crayons, and janitorial disinfectant.

As she squeezed out another lazy wiggly blob, smaller than the first, a shadow suddenly blocked the light from Earth. Between her and the imaginary schoolyard was an alien spaceship a football field away.

Nancy sputtered and reflexively crushed the drink pouch. A water rope squirted from the water straw. Words gargled in her throat. Her crewmates no longer rushed to her aide after her many mundane calls for help—to free her hair from Velcro stays, release her from the claustrophobia of her twisted sleep hammock, or, more recently, assist in the capture of her escaped urine.

Had they seen? What was it?

Risking any remaining crumbs of respect her crewmates might feel for her, she used THE WORD. The word astronauts knew, feared, and if simply whispered would wilt the burliest spacefarer's soul. A word that would bring the entire crew to her instantaneously, but could never, ever be used again.

"Fire!" she yelled loud enough for her Earth-bound students to hear. "Fire!"

Fedor Yashin, a thirty-eight-year-old Russian materials scientist, was the first to arrive, panting and in his sleep attire— a white T-shirt and white boxers. His wild eyes scanned skittishly for flame, his nostrils flared, sniffing for smoke. His hands, the size of baseball mitts, had white-knuckle grips on two fire extinguishers. His thin white hair, washing back and forth, followed his jerking head like seaweed churning in a violent current. Fedor was the image of an escapee from a paranoid-schizophrenic ward.

Miriam Wu, the mission's astrobiologist, arrived close behind Fedor with a fire blanket and first aid kit. A sweaty V soaked her shirt front. Her cheeks were flushed and her brow was raised questioningly. Nancy had interrupted her workout on the stationary bike. The thirty-three-year-old from Beijing floated a foot higher than Nancy and stared down, ready to admonish the misbehaving child.

Richard Winn, a thirty-two-year-old physicist, Canadian, and ISS mission commander, arrived before Miriam could start her sermon. No frenzy. No sweat. Just unblinking brown eyes and a military presence. "I checked the instruments. No sign of fire or any reading outside critical limits." He straightened to his full six-foot-one-inch height with hands on his hips. "Nancy, explain." His medium-length black hair lay, as usual, in the same precise wave. Friends and colleagues joked behind his back that he was so tight and disciplined he clenched his scalp to set his hair. Neither the weightlessness of space, buoyancy of water, or strenuous workout ever seemed powerful enough to dislodge a single strand.

Nancy floated in the middle of the bedroom-sized *Tranquility* module above the entrance to the cupola. Her legs were bent and crossed at the ankle, knees together. Her hands were pressed between her closed, shaking thighs like she was freezing while sitting on an imaginary chair. Pulled a hand from between her legs, she mimed pressing a single invisible

7

typewriter key with her index finger, indicating the emergency was in the observatory below her. Her forehead wrinkled. Her chin vibrated. "I didn't know how else to call you." She sobbed and covered her face.

Fedor and Miriam released their possessions and swam headfirst into the cupola. Richard pulled his closed lips back in dismay, anticipating another false alarm, but followed the others. Through watery eyes, Nancy watched their legs and feet extending en masse from the small room—a strange, low bush with foot-shaped fruit.

From space, the observatory window was a glass enclosed nest with three faces bobbing and turning. Their eyes were wide with anticipation and their mouths flapped open and closed as if begging food from their arriving mother.

"ISS, do you read?" The stationwide intercom echoed. "We have radar confirmation; there is another vessel in your vicinity. Do you have a visual?"

Richard pushed himself out of the cupola. Nancy was dabbing her eyes with her sleeve. "Good work, Nancy." An index finger waggled at her while the other hand was on her shoulder. "But don't ever do that again." He winked, shot her a small grin, turned, and flew off to the nearest communication port.

Nancy smiled; relieved she was not going to be jettisoned into space. "I won't, Richard…I mean, Commander." She wiggled her way into the cupola to see what was going on with the spaceship.

"It's probably Chinese or American," Fedor said. "I know Russia does not have this technology. Besides, we would be ashamed to display such a wreck."

Miriam ignored Fedor's hard-boiled skepticism. "Could we be the first people to make contact with extraterrestrials?"

"You and what army? They'll never let us go."

Above the cupola, Richard relayed Earth's orders: they were to set up cameras for Mission Control to monitor the vessel. Under no circumstances were they to attempt contact without Earth's approval.

CHAPTER 3

Many hours later, Earth's scientists had deduced a few facts.

WELCOME. PLEASE COME ABOARD scrolled in an endless loop on a panel above an open hatch on the alien ship. The display rotated through Mandarin, English, Spanish, Hindi, Arabic, Russian, Japanese, and German, dwelling on each for exactly 321 seconds. NASA's Mission Control Center in Houston confirmed all the languages, grammar, and spelling. Experts agreed the writing was impeccable, down to the calligraphic precision of the Devanagari and Naskh scripts.

The ship was not human-made. At least, no government or group claimed it. And the many launches it would have taken to construct something so massive would certainly have been noticed.

It had been invisible to all human detection capabilities, including visual, until it materialized a football-field length away from the ISS. It had not moved a whisker since. The aliens knew Earth's languages, so they clearly had the technology to intercept and interpret. The boom extending to an arm's length from the ISS indicated they knew humans might need a helping hand to cross to their ship.

Heads of state, generals, and their staffs deliberated on the best method to maximize their nation's stake in the spoils acquired from the alien technology for civilian or military use.

Ordinary people wondered why aliens were here. To enslave us in their mines? Wipe us out and steal our resources? Was this a scout ship to see if humans were tasty or would make fertile hosts to incubate their young? Or was this an unmanned space probe looking for life?

The space visitor's arrival came as the ISS was failing to maintain public interest. Taxpayers demanded that public funds be spent on Earthly projects like roads, bridges, and schools to generate jobs and improve life for Earthlings. Political interest in extraterrestrial adventures was waning. Increased attention and funding was required for terrestrial affairs: the maelstrom in the Middle East was spinning the NATO alliance and Russia ever closer to military conflict; the Islamic State threatened Western civilization with bombings and beheadings; oil, gold, and international stock markets were fluctuating wildly; and the reality television show, also known as the elections, was playing nightly.

Most disconcerting to the ordinary person was the sudden and inexplicable cancellation of the most popular and addictive television show ever made: *Zombies Without Borders*—an inspiring tale about medically trained zombies nursing apprehensive yet ultimately appreciative humans back to health without charge or bloodlust. Their humble and altruistic mission was to become liaisons of zombie goodwill. Inevitably, at some point in every episode, the zombie medic would grunt a request to their patient to please pause before putting a bullet in the skull of the next threatening undead human and listen to their howls, for they might not be shrieking for "brains" but simply and honestly inquiring if anyone has "pains."

Just another day in a fading, dissolving paradise.

Deliberation over the appropriate action might have lasted indefinitely, as politicians and pundits alike behaved as if they were paid by the word rather than the deed, spouting nonsense with authority.

The space station astronauts agreed to take matters into their own hands.

As they saw it, they had proximity; therefore, they had the responsibility to do something. There was no possibility for Earth to cobble together a defense to repulse the visitor by nuclear or other means, or rocket up a delegation of fawning ambassadors. The astronauts feared that by the time Earth acted on the invitation, the visitors might have given up and gone home. They did not want the scrolling message to become TOO LATE. CAN'T WAIT. BYE!

Ignoring pleas from Mission Control to wait until Earthly deciders decided on an action plan, the ISS crew drew straws to see who would climb the pole to answer the alien invitation. Nancy prepared three drinking straws, one shorter than the others, and held them out. She refused to be considered as a possible emissary even if the whole world, Shemp included, barked at her to accept.

Miriam drew the first straw, seeing this as an astounding, not-to-pass-up opportunity to examine real extraterrestrial life—alive, dead, or missing did not matter. The simple nuances of ergonomic furniture design and fixtures would provide clues to physical form, the same as everything from automobiles to laptops hint at how humans look and operate. The straw was long.

Fedor drew second. Despite his cynicism, he viewed this as a possibility to discover new alloys or manufacturing methods applicable for space-equipment manufacturing. His straw was long.

Richard did not have to draw but tugged the last piece from Nancy's fist anyway. The short straw.

They all knew this meeting might be the encounter to propel humanity into space. It also could prove the biggest mistake the human race ever made since the creation of texting.

CHAPTER 4

After fixing his umbilical to the boom extending from the alien ship, Richard tugged once, verified the fastener, tugged again, and nodded. One deep breath steeled him to step off the ISS to start his slow, hand-over-hand crawl into history. Richard was ashamed at his arrogance but thrilled to his core with the prospect of becoming way bigger than Neil Armstrong.

What would he say when he arrived and met the alien? What would be the first words ever spoken to an alien race? He had three microphones and two cameras attached to him, all tested and active. Thousands of engineers, scientists, astrophysicists, exobiologists, philosophers, and theologians, and millions—if not billions—of ordinary people watched behind each receiver. The words had to be powerful, momentous and great enough to be engraved into the base of his statues standing in before countless elementary schools, universities, and shopping malls named after him for this single moment. There would be ribbons cutting ceremonies with mayors, governors, senators, and presidents. He would be the most famous Canadian astronaut, and possibly the most famous human, in history. And possibly might be invited to the president's box at the next State of the Union Address. Or better still—throw out the first pitch at a Blue Jays game.

Unfortunately, the best opening lines his mind could muster were nothing more than inappropriate Bible quotes or weak variations on the already used "This is one small step for man…"

"Greetings from the Human race!" or "We welcome you in peace!" were too trite and had been overused in every science fiction movie he ever watched. All of those movies were scripted dialogue. What if the alien was so horrific he became paralyzed with fear? Could he hold his emotions in check long enough for his mind to catch up and create a statement so profound that everyone from the reality TV crowd to ivory-tower philosophers would quote for years? Or would he choke on his own fear and vomit into his helmet?

"Halfway to the alien ship," he announced to the listening audience while focusing on getting to the alien ship without an accident. The space station, illuminated by Earth's reflected light against a black and starry background. He could just make out the worried faces of Fedor, Miriam, and Nancy pressed against the cupola windows. Richard managed a small salute; careful not to overexaggerate an action that would send him out into space. His crewmates struggled to return the salute in the cramped space.

Richard was oriented with his feet facing Earth and the alien craft, while his head was toward the space station. He climbed the beer can-thick pipe by reaching down with one hand and pulling it up slowly until his hand was near his helmet, then reached down with the other hand for another purchase. His motion was slow and deliberate to control his momentum and allow time to examine the seamless pole. There were menacing holes as big as his hand in the metallic pole with sharp, ragged edges ready to slit his suit, or snag and slice the tether. When he looked between his feet to gauge his progress, he saw he stood astride the Cook Strait. His left foot stood on New Zealand's South Island, his right on North Island—like a modern-day Colossus of Rhodes. "About twenty yards to go—officially in the red zone."

The alien vessel had not moved since it first appeared. It resembled half a dumbbell, or a car axle with only one wheel.

The axle was the size of a 747 fuselage without the tail. The wheel was a solid disk as wide as the axle was thick. Its diameter was half the axle's length. The wheel was situated near one end, making the whole thing look like a lowercase T, or a crucifix.

For lack of better terms, the scientists involved had dubbed the two pieces "Axle" and "Wheel." The pole Richard climbed originated near an open hatch on the outer rim of the Wheel. The opening resembled a square hole cut off-center into the tread of a skinny tire. From there, the boom extended to an arm's reach from the ISS's Quest airlock. The airlock was a bit larger than a phone booth and cycled one person at a time in or out.

There was no longer the question "What if someone else was living out there?" but rather, "From which star did they come?" and "How many more are out there?" Inside his spacesuit, Richard could hear his breath, deep and even, and the circulation motors' tiny whir maintaining his environment. His halitosis reminded him he had forgotten to brush his teeth.

"Richard, you OK?" Mission Control asked.

"Yeah, I'm OK. Just taking a minute to soak it all in."

A booted left foot was the first human extremity to touch the ship's surface. It was real after all. It was not a mirage. It was not a dream. And it was he, Richard Winn, who was stepping on this extraterrestrial construction. *Also Sprach Zarathustra* echoed in his head.

He thanked his god, his luck, and his fortune for allowing him to be the first human to make contact with an alien. All the twists, turns, and random events in his life culminated with him being here, now. Was it coincidence or karma that his life's timeline happened to intersect the timeline of this craft's appearance? Was it more than chance some people won lotteries while others lost sons and daughters to disease or auto accidents? All the people on the blue-green planet beneath his feet spent their lives bouncing into each other like pinballs. Some ambitious people tried to force their way into history, only to find history was not ready for them. Others, modest people, were dragged into history by events beyond their control. If one could believe in the butterfly effect on a meteorological scale, one had also to believe in an analogous "football effect," wherein circumstantial human forces conspire to pass, carry, and kick one's lifeline back and forth across the field of history. If one is lucky, their life becomes the revered relic of some past championship game. Losers pass their lives ignored and forgotten by history, mumbling, "If only..." and "What if..."

There was a long calm moment, almost an out-of-body experience. He was relaxed and ready—no longer Richard Winn, but rather a collection of chemical reactions primed to do the universe's bidding—nothing more or less than an extension of the Human race.

The image of his foot touching the alien craft was broadcast to billions of straining eyes. The video record would be immortalized in every artistic medium known to humankind—from Carrara marble to fetid trash—as the most significant step ever taken by *Homo sapiens*. A step by which humanity would stumble into the galaxy and ultimately force the inhabitants from the ends of the spiral arms to Rebroz and Nilrebwen near the galactic core to learn what it means to deal with Humans: Like befriending an excitable puppy, but realizing soon after bringing him home that his ticks and fleas carry Lyme disease, Rocky Mountain spotted fever, and bubonic plague.

"Mission Control," Richard said, "I'm in physical contact with the ship. Boy, this is really fantastic!" Without removing the tether from the boom, in a slow, tentative motion, he bent down and pressed his open hand gently against the spaceship. A tingle of excitement lifted the hair on the back of his neck. He pressed harder, sensing for vibration and to confirm the extraterrestrial reality. Like a child on Christmas morning, full of wonder and promise, he stood up slowly and held himself at arm's length from the boom with his right arm. His left foot was at the edge of the Wheel's rim and with a lean, he could look straight down the Wheel's sidewall to the Axle.

"I'm standing on the edge of the Wheel I have a good view of the Axle."

The Axle was dull brown and made of overlapping strips a yard wide that ran its length. The surface was scarred by gouges, dents, scrapes, and burns. Faded designs resembled military or corporate logos.

"Any indication of how it works?" Mission Control asked.

"Not that I can see. It looks dead."

Richard strained to lean farther out for a better look at the Wheel's sidewall. There was a hole in the center where the Axle passed through. The two pieces were tied together by cables. There were vicious dents and burns and irregular, discolored areas like structural patches. Some of those repairs were dented and scorched. "I'd say this piece either saw battle, the losing end of a police chase, or was in a galactic parking lot during a Black Friday sale."

"Looks like our image of aliens tooling around space in sleek, unblemished ships needs some serious revision," Mission Control said.

"Agreed. Maybe they're so welcoming because they need our help."

Richard pulled himself back to the boom and held himself at arm's length. His right foot was at the edge of the open hatch. His arm span was roughly equal to his six-foot-one inch height, give or take a little for the spacesuit, so he was about six feet from the Wheel's edge. The opening at his foot was about six feet square. It was another eighteen feet to the other edge of the Wheel. He detached the tether from the boom, took a deep breath, and exhaled slowly. The stars twinkled brighter than ever above him.

"I'm entering the hatch". Gently, he pushed off the pole and slipped into a black unknown: A dream of humankind or a nightmare for a human?

The calm he felt earlier was fading. His heart was pounding so hard, he was sure it could be picked up by the microphones strapped to his suit.

*

"ISS, this is Mission Control, any activity on the outside of the ship?"

Miriam and the others had been watching Richard's every movement at the cupola's windows. "The hatch closed as soon as he entered. The welcome message stopped and the boom retracted."

"I guess we know what they wanted," mumbled Fedor. Houston did not hear the comment.

"Does it look like the ship is preparing to take off?" asked Mission Control.

Miriam was now the ranking officer. "The hatch closed and the message stopped. The ship looks completely dead. I agree they might be shipwrecked and as afraid of us as we are of them."

*

From helmet-mounted lights, Richard saw the square room he had stepped into was slightly larger than the closed hatch door above him. With his feet against one wall, he could not stand up straight or his helmet would bump against the other wall. The walls and floor were nothing but structural bulkhead. Via his helmet and body-mounted cameras, the rest of the world and the ISS crew watched along with him.

Scorched tracer marks on the walls made it look like someone or something ducked a few shots before the hatch closed. For a few frightening moments, he felt trapped, like an insect caught in a bottle.

"Mission Control, any activity on the outside of the alien ship?" Richard asked after a hard swallow.

"The message stopped, is all. It looks dead. Hang in there, Rich."

Nothing happened. Were they watching him? Were they evaluating him as an environmental threat? Were they testing the air for pathogens? Was the ship on autopilot and the crew dead? Was there anyone left to let him in or out? Richard twisted his body to illuminate all corners of his cage. He poked, pressed, and tugged, looking for a latch with one hand while the other kept a tight grip on the framework to detect any vibration. Kicking and knocking, were useless. The boot and glove insulation were too soft to sound the walls.

"Richard, anything happening?" asked Mission Control. "Have you tried to open the hatch? Can you feel any vibrations?"

"I've tried everything but no results."

"Rich, we have contacted the ISS. Fedor is on his way to help open the hatch. The brass is pissed you didn't wait for orders, picked your straws, and now got yourself trapped."

Richard slapped the nearest wall in disgust; his predicament might place someone else in danger. "You don't have to send anyone. I can wait."

"It will take ten minutes for him to suit up and fifteen minutes to get there," Mission Control said.

*

Nancy bustled and fumbled to obey Fedor's gruff commands. A third-generation astronaut, he despised the so-called political intelligence for putting publicity above the safety of the astronauts. Space was not safe. It was not a place for schoolteachers or hairdressers. It was not like a trip to the mall. He would have been more confident about their current dilemma if Nancy had been replaced with a seasoned astronaut. Now she was simply a butler helping him suit up for a spacewalk, and not a very able one.

Miriam ignored Fedor's attitude and Nancy's distress, frowning at the systems checklist on her clipboard. Because the boom had retracted, Fedor would have to use his SAFER: the Simplified Aid For EVA Rescue—a small jet pack fixed to his Extravehicular Mobility Unit, i.e., spacesuit. He would be flying without a tether. If he missed his target, he would become Dead Satellite No. 1501 among the chunks of orbital debris larger than 100 kilograms. The SAFER had to work flawlessly. Protocol for a systems check required a second set of eyes to ensure the first set did not miss something. Miriam glanced at Nancy nervously tucking Fedor into his suit like a new mother unsure about sending her child into the snow. After shaking her head and counting slowly to five with eyes closed; she raised her pen to the checklist and started over.

*

Richard could not pace in his weightless metal box, so he did the next best thing—clenched his jaw and redoubled his efforts to find a way in before Fedor had to leave the station. Mission Control would blame him if this encounter failed and take the credit if it succeeded. Was it was Winston Churchill or John Kennedy who said, "Success has a thousand fathers, but failure is an orphan?" He pulled on some framework he had tested twice before and felt a short but strong rap. Then a sound like poorly greased metal surfaces scraping against each other. A panel lurched and haltingly jerked its way open.

"Mission Control," Richard said, "someone *is* home. You can call off the rescue." His relief would only be complete if he knew Fedor had not already left the station.

"Fedor will remain at standby," said Mission Control. "Reception is positive on all instruments. Be careful."

"Will do." He struggled barely to keep his voice from cracking. He swallowed hard again and swam into the next room. It took a minute for his eyes to adjust and for the room to make sense.

"Richard, we can see everything on our monitors, but we want your description and opinions to reinforce our images."

From a step inside the room, oriented in it as if he was stuck halfway up a Ferris wheel looking toward the wheel's hub, he relayed his impressions. Instrument consoles and stools were bolted to the left-hand wall. Each item on the left wall was mirrored on the right wall as if the occupants sometimes operated the ship with the "floor" on the left-hand side and other times on the right. Not an unusual arrangement in weightless space.

If the outside of the ship was dented and damaged from some gun-blasting scuffle, the inside looked like one missile had penetrated and exploded in this room. Instrument panels had ragged holes; chairs and stools had been ripped out, leaving bent and twisted floor panels in strange, frozen, storm-whipped waves of burnt and melted metal. Shrapnel shards, thick and thin peppered the walls. The aisle ahead was a hopscotch maze of razor blades.

Richard twisted his body to set his feet against the left wall. If he was to walk on this floor in bare feet without stooping, his head would brush the instruments hanging from the ceiling. In his current attire, he would have to stoop to avoid banging his helmet. A simple calculation based on his measurements when he was outside indicated there was another area the same size as this room above the ceiling.

Maintaining his orientation, he panned the camera around the room, starting from his right. The entryway was an arm's length away to his right. The room was round, populated with consoles similar to the ones nearby. The only obstruction was a bare, curved wall at the room's center where he guessed the Axle passed through. It was twenty paces from his position along a narrow aisle to the curved wall. The aisles were narrow and he judged his legs would brush against the instruments on both sides of the aisle. Seven more aisles radiated from the center like spokes on a wagon wheel. The aisles were all the same width, but the area between them became wider the farther one was from the hub. The instruments filling the pie-shaped areas were not more plentiful at the widest portion, where he loitered, they were simply larger.

There was no life, no action—nothing to indicate anything was alive on this ship other than the random blinking of console lights. The nearest displays drew him in. The markings were unintelligible. He feared coming too near the controls. By weightlessly bumping into a console, a button might be accidentally pushed sending the ship crashing into the ISS.

"Mission Control, this appears to be the control room or bridge. Above me must be the engine room, fuel tanks, living quarters... Who knows."

"Any signs of life?" Mission Control asked.

"No. It doesn't look like anyone or anything has been in here for a while. Is there a recommendation? Do I stay put, or do I explore?"

"I wish we knew. You're the boots on the ground now. We are behind you one hundred percent—as long as you don't accidentally send the ship crashing into Milwaukee."

It was Richard's turn to chuckle quietly, releasing some tension. "I think I can wait a few more minutes before I initiate the self-destruct sequence."

Entranced by the blinking lights only a reach away, Richard again wondered if anything was alive on this ship. Perhaps the entire ship was automated, and since it had been damaged, lost its way and drifted aimlessly in space until it beached itself here. If this ship was abandoned space flotsam, Earth would cut it up and distribute it to scientific labs around the world. Humanity might discover new alloys or novel engineering methods; if the other room was the living quarters, maybe even something about how aliens lived. If there were dead bodies, Miriam would have a field day. But that would be a fraction of what could be learned from a single living alien.

A dark, quick motion at the corner of his eye shocked him from his daydream. Turning, he captured a figure in the camera light. It was growing—flying straight at him. His instincts told him to duck the projectile, but his spacesuit would not respond to his body's demand. Lamely he grasped for an anchor to brace against the impact and willed his feet to the floor, but without gravity, he could not create a fighting stance. He stiffened, brought his gloved hands up, defensively, in front of his helmet, shut his eyes, and turned his head away. Something soft hit him and bowled him over. The momentum started Richard spinning backward, head over heels. Something brownish and apparently *furry* was attached to his helmet.

The room was spinning and what appeared to be a paw was planted on his faceguard. Then a face pressed against his helmet at eye level. Richard's brain scrambled to define the unexpected creature on is helmet. When the spinning wheels of cognition clanked to a stop, he had a word: Dog.

The alien dog licked Richard's helmet once with a short, reddish pointed tongue. It pulled back, stared directly into his eyes, and said, "Welcome aboard." Then, in a tone as if he was the last guest to arrive for a barbeque, "I thought you would never come."

CHAPTER 5

Quane, the alien who had been waiting inside the spaceship for the Humans to accept his invitation, was the iconic Human image of the devil. He was three feet tall and crimson from the tips of the small curved horns at his temples to the tip of his barbed, prehensile tail. His face sported a long, pointed chin and even longer and pointier nose. Deep black, polished onyx marbles occupied his eye sockets. Unlike the devil, he did not sport wings, breathe fire, or wear a cape.

The planet Dia'Bolos was a hot, dense, desert planet circling a dying red star called Nilrebwen. His home was located within the star-dense galactic center, but outside the uninhabitable zone defined by the central black hole anchoring the orbits of the hundred billion stars constituting the Milky Way.

Nilrebwen was distant from the artistic, political, and financial hustle-bustle of that cultural nexus, but was still well within the portion of the galaxy considered civilized—in the same way Boston, New York, Philadelphia, Baltimore, and Columbus are within Washington, DC's influence.

Earth and its lonely sun on the galactic periphery were, in comparison, the equivalent of Buford, Wyoming; population, 1. Earth was nothing more than a remote outpost: a gas station, tavern, general store, city hall, and post office—all in one decrepit, collapsing building.

Quane yanked on his sewing. The thread snapped. "Bleen be Flocked," he cursed. The rushed seam on his furry costume was crooked and amateurish. There was no time to waste. He stabbed another thread at the needle's eye with machine-gun urgency. The thread found the target just as a piece of floating trash bumped his head. He tossed his head back, clamped his eyes shut, and exhaled in a burst. His hands were shaking from the sight of these "Humans."

They had an uncanny resemblance to the Smez, the species that nearly murdered him. If it weren't for the gullibility of Earthlings, the trove of riches here, and the pain Wyruk would inflict upon him, he would escape this backwater planet.

"Yeouch!" Quane sucked the pain from his needle-jabbed finger and shuddered at the thought of Smez. A scar above his left horn throbbed—a memento of the metal pipe thrown by an incensed Smez mob. For some unknown reason they had viewed him as an abomination and recoiled at seeing him. Before he could utter a word, they attacked. Costumes were worn to a sale ever since.

As long as he could pass the introductions, pass the irrational fears of an alien invasion, and the ensuing shock of an alien's real appearance. Then all he had to do was prove the customer could travel the ten thousand light years from their boondocks planet to the galactic core, nonrelativistically, in a shorter time than they could explore the limits of their own solar system using their old-fashioned, reaction rockets.

Quane sold stardrive engines. Unfortunately, what the customer usually had to offer in payment—rare minerals, virgins, and country music—were either too bulky for him to carry, impossible for him to keep alive, or made his ears bleed. Hope of ever finding a planetary pot of gold, a jackpot, a one-dollar buy-in to a galactic prize was less than a daydream. He was up to his horns in debt to Wyruk, beyond anything he had in collateral, except his life. Wyruk would blissfully take payment—possibly with Xcrutians. The scar throbbed and he lifted his black eyes from his sewing to gaze at his surroundings.

He was strapped to a rickety iron chaise bolted to the floor in the living quarters inside the Wheel, as the Humans were calling it. If the Humans accepted his invitation, they would enter via the control room. The broken-down pod was all he owned and contained all his possessions. Even the three junk engines he'd brought here to sell were borrowed from Wyruk.

The habitat pod was an old military unit. Most consoles were unused. Some were for weapons-targeting, but had been retired long ago. Others were redundant systems to maintain capabilities in the event of damage to some other part of the ship. Few of those systems were needed now to operate the ship, but he turned them all on during a sale. Yokels were always bedazzled by flashing lights and beeping instruments. He bought the habitat in as-is condition, floating trash included: spent ammunition casings, crumpled food containers, and odd clothing scraps. A magazine floated by, the pages washing back and forth as if casually animated by a ghostly reader. The images depicted giant grasshopper-like creatures in various levels of submersion in leaking tubs of bubbling pea soup: Shnacuoilitian pornography. A fate Wyruk might enthusiastically inflict on him if he could not pay the next time they met.

Quane jerked to attention and returned to sewing; he had to be finished before the Humans arrived. His computers had collated, extrapolated, integrated, and formulated. After weeks spent translating and interpreting deodorant commercials, sarcastic news shows, and reality TV shows, the computer came to a singular recommendation. Sales were all about appearing to be on the customer's side. That meant becoming like them—or something they would like and trust in every possible way. A salesman had to become something nonthreatening and inviting, especially when the salesman was from another planet. Xenophobia had become an occupational hazard for him since the Smez. First impressions were everything.

The buzz of motion sensors indicated a Human had boarded.

"Finally," he said out loud to himself and squeezed into his costume. It was tighter and pricklier than he preferred, but he put his trust in the computer's deciding this disguise was the least threatening and most appealing to Earthlings. He pounced from the broken iron chaise to an imploded cabinet, avoiding the myriad satellites of trash with the dexterity and grace of a tree-hopping squirrel. A cracked monitor, erratic and snowy with static showed the Human standing near the airlock with no weapons drawn and wary but curious about the instruments.

The bulkhead door between his living quarters and the control room was heavy on his shoulder and opened slowly; he could not afford a torn seam now. Costume paws gripped the open bulkhead's edge. He aimed. It had to be a cruel galactic joke that he would have to deal with these Smez clones to save his life.

"Bleen, I'm sorry for wishing you be Flocked. Give me strength. I'll pound my Ballwangt in honor of the Inverted Pisht for an entire month if you help me make this sale." Quane pulled his body out of the hatch, braced, and launched across the control room.

Wearing his raggedy dog costume, he collided with the visitor and licked the stunned Human's helmet. "Welcome aboard." He swallowed his fear with a gulp. It was showtime; time to make a sale. "I thought you would never come."

CHAPTER 6

Denise Ratz clawed her car keys from the bottom of her purse after waitressing second shift at the Crossings Diner in Exeter, New Hampshire. Walking to her car, she noticed a funny scrawl on her left front tire. She squatted in the gravel parking lot to examine the lettering. Half was shadowed by her fender. The other half was visible under the red neon business sign. Her finger traced the yellow chalk lettering which ran in an arc, starting at the one o'clock position on the tire. The childish chicken scratch read: D r A t Z.

She chuckled at forgetting that she had her winter tires removed and these summer tires installed. The lettering was there to assure the warehousemen responsible for storing her tires that they would recover the proper tires and the mechanics would install D rAtZ's tires on Denise Ratz's car. The mechanics simply forgot to wipe the chalk from this one.

Driving home on the dark country road with the windows open, she inhaled deeply the smell of wood and moss dampened by the evening dew and lilac. The olfactory bouquet purged the oily glaze, reeking of deep-fried chicken and oversalted potatoes, from her nose. The high-pitched chirp of spring peepers was a symphony.

She twisted the radio dial from end to end, but every station blared with the same monotonous replay of the space station astronaut's encounter with an alien talking dog so she shut it off. The radio in the diner had droned an endless loop of the story for any new customer to hear. She began to envy the customers. They could eat their fries; drop their crumpled, grease-stained napkins on the counter; pay their bills; and leave the torture of the never-ending story. The newly freed customers could decide for themselves whether they listened to the latest speculation about aliens looking like flying pigs or dancing cows, or surrender to the sounds of a late spring night.

Two miles from the diner on a lonely, unlit, unlined road, Denise was startled by a quick series of white flashes coming from the left front wheel—the same wheel with the lettering. Her initial reaction was to suspect pranksters had secreted some fireworks up in her wheel well, but there were no *bang-cracks*—no sound of any kind. The commotion was more like a flashing lightning storm without the thunder.

The second thought racing through her mind was that a garage mechanic screwed up on the wheel change and his mistake had somehow ignited a fire. Denise pulled hard to the right to get off the road and escape the burning car.

The centrifugal force exerted on the car during this sharp turn demanded the car lean hard on the left front tire. Where Newton's laws expected to find a properly inflated tire firmly attached to a sturdy metal rim, the force found nothing but air. The bare metal rim bit deep into the asphalt and jerked the car off the right shoulder and down a steep embankment. The car rolled over three times, tumbling Denise like a child's tennis shoe in a dryer, before it smashed hard into an unyielding red oak tree.

Passersby and rescue personnel agreed Denise was lucky to be alive in the crumpled mass looking like a child's toy stomped by a giant, thick-lugged hiking boot.

The paramedics shook their heads and shrugged their shoulders when the handful of onlookers asked about her chances. They rammed the gurney into the ambulance and sped off into the night with sirens blaring and lights flashing.

Police waved their flashlights over the ground, searching for the vanished tire. Thoughts of the absent rubber ring subconsciously reminded them that they were overdue for donuts and coffee. The search for the wayward tire would have to wait until morning.

*

"Single car accident," the ambulance driver said to a black-haired scalp. The Emergency Room admissions nurse did not look up from her paperwork. She hunched over the admission form, elbows on the desk, her writing hand moving as if it were a robotic instrument only responding to the ambulance driver's voice. If he talked, she wrote; if he was silent, she stopped.

"Brain damage suspected," the driver said.

"Brain damage? You a doctor?" the nurse asked. The driver had been silently appreciating the backside of a fresh young intern stooping to fill the bottom tray of a printer behind the robot. "A-hem!"

When the driver turned back to answer, he noticed the sarcasm in her remark was meant for him. The nurse glared from under substantial and frowning black eyebrows.

"For the entire thirty-minute drive here," he said, "all she says is, 'Smez, cutie pie. Smez, cutie pie,' over and over."

"How do you spell 'smez'?" the nurse asked, her writing hand paused for the answer.

"How should I know? She's all yours. See you next time." The driver rapped the nurse's counter twice with his knuckles, stuffed his hands in his pockets, and strolled out into the night whistling "Johnny B. Goode."

CHAPTER 7

"A talking dog?" said Mission Control. "What's a dog doing in space?"

"We know nothing about the alien's home planet," Miriam said. "The gravity, the environment... This may be an outstanding demonstration of analogous evolution. What if a parallel evolutionary path, remote from Earth, followed the same development except for a few trips and turns along the way? Mammals evolved, just happen to look like dogs, and develop speech and the intelligence for space travel."

"Skip the lecture, Miriam. Has anything happened to the alien craft since Richard boarded the ship?"

"Nothing since the hatch closed after he boarded."

"Let us know if there are any changes in attitude of the alien vessel," said Mission Control. "Richard's safe return is priority number one."

CHAPTER 8

"Down, boy," Richard said to the alien dog clinging to his helmet.

And so it became that history's first recorded words ever spoken by an Earthling to an alien were no more inspiring or influential than a man's disciplinary response to a dog's exuberant welcome.

Richard had failed to brace himself for the dog's impact and Quane's momentum started the two spinning slowly around an axis at Richard's waist.

"I am Captain Richard Winn." He stiffened his body to attention but could not halt their weightless ballet. "I am a human from the planet Earth. I am here in peace." Richard avoided grabbing the dog with his hands; it might bite, puncture his suit, and give him who-knows-what disease.

"Yeah, yeah," the dog said. "I know who you are. My name is Quane. I'm from the center of the galaxy—a planet named Dia'Bolos. What took you so long to finally decide to come aboard? Did you think I was going to bite?" His gravelly voice had the quality of grinding Styrofoam. The dog's toothless jaws opened and closed out of sync with its words like a poorly operated ventriloquist's dummy.

"No, sir, Mr. Quane." Richard avoided the alien's cold, black eyes. "Our leaders needed some time to evaluate the situation. Our leaders do not always trust foreigners especially if they come from another planet."

"I understand. I'm just glad you finally made it."

"Mr. Quane, sir, how do you speak all our languages so perfectly?"

"I've been watching you for quite some time. I knew from the minute I listened to your broadcasts that you were just the people I wanted to meet. I said to myself, 'Quane,' I said, 'Those are the people you really want to meet.' That's what I said. So I studied your languages in order to meet you properly."

Quane had arrived at Earth a month before he made himself visible. Computers needed the time to ingest, digest, and regurgitate the results from an algorithm created to instantaneously translate all Earth's languages and dialects. The translation algorithm was designed millennia ago. It enabled communication between the plethora of species populating the civilized portion of the galaxy wherever strangers needed to plead their case before a judge, drown their sorrows at the nearest bar, or—as in Quane's case—make a sale. All one needed was a headpiece tied wirelessly to a translation computer. Any *burp, squeak, buzz,* or *guffaw* was given its proper interspecies meaning. A speaker interfaced to the translator allowed him to simply lip-synch the words.

"Rich," Mission Control said quietly, as if the alien was eavesdropping because of its proximity while hanging on to Richard's helmet, "we can't see the dog." The suit-mounted cameras and lights were designed to view objects at least an arm's length away, not something stuck to his helmet.

The acrobats were windmilling, but also drifting. They came to a sudden halt when the back of Richard's helmet collided with a wall. The dog lost its grip, squashed its belly onto the faceplate, and slid off. The crash shocked Richard back into reality and he hustled to verify his spacesuit's integrity. All readings confirmed he was not losing air—his helmet was intact and his suit was not torn.

In weightlessness, an object's motion is continuous until it strikes something; then, if it cannot stick to or hold on, off it flies to the next pinball bumper. Richard's bounce sent him straight toward a blinking console. His helmet was going to crash directly onto a panel full of impressive buttons, switches, and joysticks. There was nothing within reach to grab. He rowed his arms backward in a fruitless effort to slow himself down.

The spacesuited man had a mass of 225 kilograms—a weight of 500 pounds on Earth. Stopping his momentum in the distance from his outstretched hand to the top of his helmet, while moving at several feet per second, would feel like doing a handstand pushup in the gym. Arms were straight out and braced. Hands made contact at the edges of the instrument panel. Muscles atrophied by three months of weightlessness, strained against the load and forced him to grimace. He came to an arm shaking stop with his helmet an inch above a yellow, winking button with a worn symbol looking, oddly, like a duck. Even in his environmentally controlled suit, beads of sweat tickled his temples.

Richard maintained his grip, extended his arms, and pulled his feet to the floor; relieved he had avoided pressing the button that might have activated who-knows-what. The worn marking on the yellow button did indeed look like a duck. The blue button next to it was an alligator's head, and the green button was a turkey. He smiled at his apophenia—identifying patterns in random data—like imagining Elvis's face in the craters of the moon or Einstein on a piece of rye toast. Something as simple as the true meanings of these few symbols—whether they enabled the engines, weapons fire, communications, or plain old light switches—would have sated Richard's curiosity about aliens for the rest of his life.

"Mr. Quane?" The alien had disappeared after they collided with the wall.

"Here I am." The disheveled dog pirouetted expertly onto the console and sat, pressing his haunches on the same buttons he had strained to avoid.

"But," Richard sputtered, "what do those buttons control?"

"These? They're not connected to anything."

Quane was a large-sized, reddish-brown dog of no breed Richard had ever seen. Its coat was a patchwork of different fur types. Some were long and soft, some were short and coarse, and some lay in different directions. A straight scar ran from its chin to its tail. The creature was lumpy, like it was full of tumors, or hastily stuffed. There was no way to determine the dog's sex.

Quane clutched the panel with his feet and stood up. He rubbed his forepaws together. "Let's get down to business, shall we?"

"Rich," Mission Control said, "ask it what it wants—why it's here."

"Mr. Quane, sir," Richard said, "where are you from? Why are you here? What do you want from us?"

The paws stopped rubbing as their owner considered an answer.

He wanted, just once, to toy with a gullible race's emotions.

Play to the Human's worst fears, "The ignorance of your race makes me ill and angry. I am here as vanguard of an all-powerful civilization determined to domesticate you as slaves and food." But they would likely pull out a weapon and kill him before he could admit he was joking.

Incite their megalomania. "I am here because we observed the advanced stage of your technology and civilization. I have come to invite you to join the Galactic Federation of Planets." But they would likely pull out a weapon and kill him when they found out that, too, was a joke.

Or simply test their benevolence. "I'm from the center of the galaxy and have broken down and need help to get back home." But when they realized he was playing on their sympathy to make a sale, they would likely pull out a weapon and kill him.

But he could not afford to blow this sale because these Smez-Humans overreacted. Earth had much to offer.

"You ask why I'm here. I'll tell you why I'm here. I'm here for a very good reason—an excellent reason for you and your planet. Today is your lucky day." A ratty paw poked Richard in the stomach once.

"But first, can you take off your helmet?" The dog tilted his head to one side. "I'm the type who likes to look my customers straight in the eye when making a sale." His jaw bobbed up and down randomly.

"How do I know the air is breathable?"

"Breathable? What do you take me for, some junior-ranked novice salesman? I have tailored the air perfectly for your enjoyment—nitrogen, oxygen, and argon, with a dash of carbon dioxide and a pinch of methane for fragrance. Why you Humans like the smell of methane so much, I won't judge. But you seem to keep making enough of it." He pulled at the skin at his armpit. "Why would I want to harm my new friend and best customer?"

Quane's black-hole eyes seemed to look everywhere and nowhere at the same time. It did not make sense the alien would go to all the trouble to bring him here just to suffocate him. Teeth clenched and cheeks puffed with stored air, he closed his eyes, and carefully removed his helmet. Shallowly, timidly, his lungs inflated.

"It smells a little funny." Richard's nose wrinkled as it sniffed the air. "Smells a little like dry cleaning fluid."

"So, maybe I did get it a little mixed up." Quane shrugged and pulled the fabric on his arm. "So what if I added a few extras to help you relax? You're fine—that's all that matters.

The salesman slowly patted Richard's shoulder, "My friend, how would you feel if you knew your race was forever limited to exploring these few rocks spinning around your sun? And would die out long before you visited even the nearest star?"

"You can predict the future? You can tell we will never develop interstellar space flight?"

"No—" The dog's mouth flapped. "—I cannot see into your future, but I can tell you have a long way to go before you will catch up with the rest of the galaxy with regards to space travel. You asked why I'm here. It's very simple, my friend— today is your lucky day. You and your entire planet are now able to purchase, from me, for a limited time only, the technology to allow you and all the inhabitants of your planet to travel to the stars. No longer will you be planet-locked."

Quane turned his gaze upward. "No longer will your solar system define your space. No longer will your reality be limited by your technology." His paw traced an arc toward the scene he was imagining on some distant screen beyond the ceiling. "The galaxy and all its inhabitants and wonders are at the tips of your fingers, right here, right now." With a flourish, he opened his arms toward Richard, presenting himself as the provenance of humanity's future.

"You came here to sell us spaceships?" His brow pulled down and his cheeks rose as his face screwed up with incredulity.

"Exactly." Quane smiled. "I'm from the civilized part of the galaxy, near its center. I've been making stops along the way. You know how it is—visiting old customers, making sure they're satisfied and enjoying their purchases." A Dia'Bolos' autonomic response to telling a lie was to smile.

"If I would have come here directly, at your gravitational acceleration, it would have taken about ten of your years; one way. Yet, I came here using this engine. This very same one I want to sell to you now. What do you say?"

Richard was stunned. Mission Control was silent. If the earth's collective heart had almost stopped beating at this first encounter with an alien race, it went into full cardiac arrest at the thought that they were being offered the ability to purchase alien technology to fly to the center of the galaxy in a fraction of a lifetime. And all from a floating, talking, lumpy alien dog.

"You mean you have the technology to travel twenty-five thousand light years in ten years? Twenty-five hundred times the speed of light! This will really do that?"

"No, no, no, Richard," Quane shook his head and waved his hands. "Even you should know nothing can go faster than light."

"How is it possible? Wormholes? Time warps?"

Wormholes. Time warps. Quane choked on the naiveté. He had watched some video footage and knew Humans clung to the childish notion that instantaneous acceleration of mega-tonnage of metal and people to many times the speed of light without turning into puddles a few atoms thick was actually possible, energetically favorable, and a really cool idea, even though their computers were barely sufficient to direct airport luggage or keep accurate bank accounts. But if Humans were so backward they believed those things remotely possible, what he had to show them would knock their socks off, even if it was vintage salvage yard.

He regained his composure with a hard swallow. "Richard, may I call you Rich?"

Dumbfounded, Richard nodded listlessly like a bobblehead doll with a slow spring.

"Rich." Quane hooked his arm around Richard's elbow and pulled him close. "I see you are a man I can deal with; a man who can understand and grasp the big concepts. Am I right?"

The dog loosened his grip. "Or am I wrong? Should I be talking to someone else from your suborbital station?"

"Wake up!" Mission control said. "Find out what he is up to or we *will* send someone else."

"No," Richard blurted out, blinked hard, and shook his head awake. "Yes. I mean, I'm the man you want to talk to. I can understand the big concepts." And felt ridiculous the instant the words left his mouth.

"So, you want to sell us this?" He gestured with his hand, indicating the control room.

"No, no, no, Rich. Maybe we should start over. I am here to sell stardrive engines. This is the habitat pod. The engine is the long cylinder—what you have been calling the Axle."

"You mean that beat-up—"

"Whoa," A paw went up to deflect the insult. "Wait a minute. This is a vintage piece of machinery. Yes, it is a little scratched and worn, but that baby has a lot more *oomph* than the new stuff they try to peddle. I can tell you are a man with a critical eye." Quane winked and grinned broadly. "I bet your whole species is smart enough to see past a few scratches to what a fine piece of technology this is." He grabbed a pawful of fabric on the front of Richard's suit. "Tell me, Rich, do you like classic cars? Maybe vintage motorcycles?"

"Yes, I do."

"Really?" Quane feigned interest. "What do you like to drive?"

"Actually, I've been looking to buy a Sunbeam Tiger, like in the old TV show, *Get Smart*."

"Would you believe I have ten of those exact cars, perfectly preserved, in the next room?" His jaw flapped while his computer mimicked a perfect imitation of Maxwell Smart's nasal intonation and did not wait for a response. "Would you believe three partial wrecks? How about one cracked hubcap?"

"What is he talking about, Richard?" Mission Control said.

"What are you talking about, Mr. Quane?" The dog's puppet mouth distracted Richard's concentration. The loosely bobbing jaw was out of rhythm with his words.

"I'm trying to say that this is a perfectly preserved example of a classic stardrive. This baby is a collector's item. What you call 'beat-up,' I, and other collectors, would call 'a natural patina.' There are a lot of folks in the galaxy who would pay a fortune for this. It's a real museum piece." Quane's mouth ached, straining to control his smile.

His engines were not museum pieces. To call them "junk" was a compliment. The engine he was trying to pawn off on Humans was an old military unit he had acquired at a remote scrapyard. It had been first used by one side in a war, then the other, and finally the first again, as each side gained and lost ground. He knew how to clean the contacts, straighten the fibers, and fill in the dents well enough to survive a test drive. Legally, he could not sell these engines; bought from unscrupulous scrap dealers and sold to ignorant species at the galactic periphery—the only region left in the where the inhabitants were totally ignorant of interstellar travel and sales laws.

"I know what you're thinking, '"If this item is such a classic and so valuable, why is this alien wasting his time trying to sell it to a planet that doesn't have a clue about its value? Why doesn't he take this piece of prime merchandise back to the center of the galaxy and sell it to someone who can really appreciate it?"'"

Quane put his arm around Richard's neck, swung around behind him, and pulled close to his ear. "I have to be perfectly honest with you, Rick. I'm only telling you this because I like you, and feel I can trust you. Can I trust you, Rick?"

"Sure," he said, not feeling sure at all.

"Well, Rick..." Quane scanned the empty room to see if anyone else was listening. "I have to admit I am not proud of it, but this baby is hot. As in: stolen. As in: I can't be seen anywhere near civilization with this little baby."

"What the..." Mission Control yelled. "We're dealing with a galactic criminal fencing stolen property?"

"So, you're a galactic criminal fencing stolen property?" Richard repeated.

"No, Rich," Mission Control said. "You weren't supposed to say that. Now he knows we suspect him."

"You're not a galactic criminal fencing stolen property," Richard sputtered, trying to reset the discussion.

"Seriously?" Quane folded his arms, turned his back, and hung his head. "You hurt me, Ricky. You think I'm a cheap crook trying to pawn off stolen goods on you. You think I'm going to take your money and let you get jail time with the galactic police once they catch you with this. Right?"

"I don't know what to think."

"I'll tell you what to think, Ricky. This baby is a real head-turner. I'm guessing you will generate a lot of interest wherever you go. But be careful, my boy," Quane nudged Richard with an elbow. "There are many cheats out there who will try to buy this from you for the equivalent of a fistful of beans."

*

"What is going on?" Fedor yelled. "Why is Richard talking to a puppet? Where is the alien?" Fedor was furious with the crew for leaving him alone to remove his spacesuit, making him late for the show.

Miriam and Nancy were hovering in front the nineteen-inch communications display, engrossed by the video feed from Richard's cameras. They did not acknowledge Fedor's arrival nor apologize for leaving him to undress himself.

"It's not a puppet." Nancy first tilted her head to one side, straightened it, then tilted it to the other side and licked her upper lip. "It's a dog from the center of the galaxy, but I can't tell what kind. I think it's a mutt."

Miriam was jotting notes as fast as she could without looking at her clipboard. The video was being taped, but she did not want to miss recording her first impressions.

Fedor yanked the clipboard from her hands. "What is happening?" he said.

Staring, unblinking, at something beyond Fedor, speaking calmly and robotically, as if she had been drugged and was under a CIA interrogation, Miriam said, "The alien's name is Quane, and he wants to sell Richard a stolen stardrive engine."

Fedor grabbed her by the shoulders to shake her out of her trance. "What are you talking about?"

"It's unbelievable, Fedor. The aliens don't want us as slaves or cattle; they want to sell us secondhand technology to explore the stars."

He sneered. "The alien is nothing more than a used car salesman?"

Fedor found a spot near the communication display to get a better look at the smarmy, talking alien dog. "If he wants to sell us that beat-up thing he's driving, he's more weasel than a dog."

"I think it has mange." Nancy tilted her head back to the other side and scratched behind her ear.

*

Quane floated before Richard with his hands on his hips. "So what do you think now?"

Richard thought it would be great if someone from Mission Control, who knew what he should say, would pipe it up to him. "It sounds like a great opportunity." The dog's flapping mouth was insanely distracting.

"'Great opportunity' is an understatement, Ricky. Think of it: Your planet free from the limits of this solar system—free to explore, free to colonize other worlds, free to achieve your highest aspirations, free to find your place in the galaxy. This day might be remembered forever as the day Humans freed themselves. I'd even be so bold as to call it 'Independence Day!' That has a real nice ring to it, don't you think?"

Quane pulled at the back of his neck and adjusted his headpiece. Crimson appeared around the eyes as the costume shifted. A pointed protrusion snagged the fur near the dog's ear.

"But, I can't waste time revisiting everyone who turns me down the first time, just to see if they changed their minds. Who knows when or if another salesman will come this way?" Quane sniffed and stared into the distance. "You may never thrill to the experience of presenting your posterior to the Nibor of Xof, or enjoy pounding your Ballwangt in honor of the Inverted Pisht, touching the Sanx of the Bleating Galb, or seeing the tricolor dawn over the falls on Shnacuoility." Eyes covered in his elbow, his head shook at the loss.

"If someone else does come, will he be willing to part with such an excellent piece as this, or will he try to pawn off some scrapyard junk on you?"

Quane pulled real close and whispered, "I know some salesmen who do just that. It is illegal, of course. But I don't engage in that kind of behavior. Never. Not me. Some people are just plain dishonest. But not me. Not your old pal, Quane." He slapped Richard on the back and his lie was stretched so large he imagined the corners of his mouth might touch his horns.

Floating around to face the Human, he said, "I got it. I have a great idea. How about a little spin around your solar system—take a couple hours to show you how it all works?" Quane nodded lightly. Richard's head mimicked the nod.

"Since this is one of the engines I'd like to sell you will want to see it works perfectly. Then you can make your decision." Quane nodded deeper.

"You know what I always say—'If you're not on board, you must be the anchor.' You don't want to be an anchor, Ricky, and hold your whole planet back, do you?" The mangy dog shook his head slowly; pleased the Human followed his lead.

Quane almost hoped the Human would refuse the ride and just buy the piece. It was a few clips, strips, and bits of Ursu glue away from unworkable scrap and he didn't know how many more times it would start or how many more light weeks it would last. Two more engines, in even worse shape, were parked near the next outer planet the Humans called Mars. His good stardrive, on loan from Wyruk—which was not for sale and which he needed to return home—was also parked there, but on the other side of the planet...away from the junk engines. In case they accidentally exploded. True, he could never come back to Earth for a follow-up sale after they found out how they had been cheated. But it would be many years in the future before they could ever catch up with him to demand a refund.

Was it an innocent, or spiteful, galactic coincidence that he encountered the Smez on a planet called Mars Lost and Humans, who were nearly identical to Smez, lived near a planet named Mars?

"So, Ricky," Quane nodded his head slowly up and down. "Do you think your friends can live without you for a few hours?"

"Definitely not," Mission Control said. "We know nothing of the possible hazards. It may be a ruse to kidnap you for ransom. What if the interstellar police or whoever are waiting to ambush this thief and pick you up as an accomplice? Wait for further orders."

"Definitely," Richard replied aloud to the alien, his head nodding slowly. There was no way Mission Control was going to stop him from taking the joyride of his life. Nearly half the hairs on his head had freed themselves from his restrictive scalp. They levitated and waved, suddenly alive and free.

"Captain Richa—" Mission Control said before Richard switched off his receiver. Later he would claim the alien blocked his reception. The transmitter he left on so they could verify he was not in distress.

Quane shoved himself to a wrecked instrument console. The side covers were stove in, frayed cables were visible, and only one tiny red button with the image of a baseball eating a chimney flashed intermittently and weakly.

"Here we go," he said and pressed the one button.

Richard braced. No acceleration, no vibration from rockets firing. No hum, sizzle, or snap from high voltage arcs. There was nothing to indicate they were moving. Only silence.

The ISS astronauts watched unblinking at the cupola as the alien craft vanished.

CHAPTER 9

"ISS, this is Mission Control. What happened? The alien ship dropped off our radar. Do you have a visual?"

"The ship with Richard and the alien faded away," Miriam said.

"Try thermal imaging," Mission Control advised. "And LiDAR. All wavelengths. There's a chance they're still there, but hidden."

"I'll get the thermal camera," said Nancy, determined to regain a morsel of respect from her crew mates by proving she could be the tiniest bit useful. "It's in *Kibo*."

Nancy swam out of the cupola. Straight ahead, surrounding the Quest airlock, was the pond: a wall of water made from fifty-gallon plastic bags that held the contingency water supply for drinking, flushing, and oxygen generation. A cargo net held the containers in place against the 14-foot-high wall. Any other day, the wall would have started Nancy singing, "A hundred bags of water on the wall..."

Today, she silently turned left into the United States' lab, *Destiny*, the length of a city bus and twice as wide. After passing the stationary bike, workstations, and sleep chambers, her flight dead-ended at the Pressurized Mating Adapter, the docking hatch for the shuttle and supply ships. Above the hatch were small flags of the fifteen nations partnering in the ISS. It was the most colorful spot on the station and Nancy's private wildflower garden.

Nancy made a left into *Kibo*, the Japanese module larger than *Destiny* and read the sign above the door written in grammatically incorrect English, "Welcome to *Kibo*. Please relax in this brand-new, the most spacious and quietest room in the ISS." Halfway in, on her right, she found the locker with the thermal imaging camera.

"I've got it." She retraced her path to *Tranquility* and the cupola.

Nancy snapped open the lid and pulled the trigger to initialize the test sequence and brought the instrument to her eye. "I don't see anything."

Miriam gently pulled the lens cap off. "Try again."

Blushing, Nancy handed over the camera. "Here, you do it."

"Nothing." Miriam panned the camera up and down to the extent of her vision. "The only thermal signatures are from the ISS."

Fedor had hauled the microwave oven-sized Light Detection and Ranging unit, a laser version of radar, to the Earth-facing observational window in *Destiny*. He affixed it to the specially designed mounts and set it for auto-scan, wide field. "Scanning now," he said.

LiDAR was used to create high-resolution maps of Earth's topography. Different wavelengths of laser light accentuated different features: air, land, water, and vegetation. If the alien spaceship was hovering in the same position but invisible to the naked eye, the LiDAR image would display an image of Earth with a jigsaw piece missing, a piece the same size and shape as the missing spaceship.

Nancy and Miriam floated to Fedor. They bookended him and clung to opposite shoulders. This was their last chance to prove the ship had not moved, Richard had not been kidnapped, and humanity's nightmarish fears about first contact had been exaggerated. A red light flashed, indicating the scan's completion. The image was an uninterrupted picture of the Mariana Trench, the deepest, darkest place on Earth.

"Nothing," mumbled Fedor. "They're gone." Fedor faced his second loss to space. The first was his grandfather, a pioneer cosmonaut. A faulty attitude adjustment valve caused his capsule to re-enter the atmosphere backward. He was ash before his fiery, meteoric trace across the night sky as a shooting star was appended to a sleepless child's secret wish.

Miriam squeezed Fedor's shoulder. "Fedor, do you believe they are going on a test drive?"

"I'd believe anything right now," Fedor said, staring blindly at the fading red LED on the LiDAR box.

CHAPTER 10

"We're on our way," said Quane. The engine ignited on the third try. Richard was oblivious to the desperate attempts get it started.

"Now that the ship is accelerating," Quane said, "we will experience gravity."

Orienting himself to the ship and surroundings, Richard guessed outer space was two feet below him, and the ship was moving in the direction of the short end of the Axle.

"All kidding aside, Ricky, I am obliged and bound by galactic laws regarding the sale of stellar-drive engines to inform you that the ones I have are used and are covered by no warranty, real or implied. Do you understand?"

By the time Earthlings learned they had been sold worthless junk—and if they were lucky enough to reach a sympathetic galactic ear who was not another cheat or pirate before the junk died for good—Quane would be long gone.

"I think so," Richard rubbed his forehead, hoping to massage in some understanding. "The spaceship we are driving now is used, and this—" His arm swept the room. "—is an engine?"

"No, Ricky, this is the habitat pod. What you called the Wheel, is my habitat pod. The *other* piece, what you call the Axle, is the engine. And is, by the way, is one of the finest stardrives ever made: the best and most reliable brand. They are handmade on Otkin Adarab Utaalk, a small rocky planet far, far away, by workers who look something like your lobsters."

Quane did not admit there was only one brand of interstellar engines. The government of the Rebroz system, which funded the original experiments, owned exclusive rights to the theory, application, development, manufacture, sales, and licensing of stardrive technology. The penalty for unauthorized sales or manufacture, new or old, working or not, was life imprisonment.

The Utaalkian planet was deliberately chosen as the sole manufacturing facility because of its remoteness. The principle catalyst for the stardrive reaction, Flock, was a deadly toxin to all known beings in the galaxy except Utaalkians. They were clumsy and dimwitted, but smart enough to lord their genetic accident over all—to the intense exasperation and expense of their managers.

"Let me explain what is happening," Quane said. "Right now, we are moving through the space membrane. The side of the membrane where your station is—what you think of as ordinary space—is what we call light space. On the other side is dark space. In the same way light space is made of light matter and light energy, dark space is made up of dark matter and dark energy."

"Like traveling to another dimension?" Richard asked. His hand was cramped from holding his space helmet like an upright fishbowl since he took it off. The pain was only now starting to reach his brain. He set the helmet down near his foot and massaged his hand.

"That's exactly how we think of it," Quane's tail started to wag slowly at the Human's understanding. "We are crossing from one side of space to the other. The membrane is the barrier between the two spaces. It's not part of light or dark space."

Most customers were confused at first and he was used to the dazed and confused expressions. "Let me start at the beginning.

"A long time ago, it was discovered that gravity is a dimension and space is the representation. Let's start with what you already know. Your space station and satellites keep circling the earth because they are in Earth's gravity well. Your planet bends the space around it. If you do not go fast enough to escape Earth's gravity well, you wind up in orbit around it.

"Your sun bends the space around itself and keeps all of your planets in orbit. And if you want to escape the solar system, you have to travel very fast, or you will wind up in orbit around your sun's gravity well.

"Likewise," Quane continued, "the superdense center of the galaxy bends space so far out that your sun, and billions of other stars, are trapped in its gravity. Space is bent back on itself all over the place. Got it so far?"

"Yes, I understand the concept of gravity." A furtive finger flicked on his transmitter so Earth could hear the lecture. They were about to get a lesson in advanced space travel. But there was nothing, not even static.

"Your device will not work in here. You will not be able to communicate until we return to light space."

"I had full communication when I first boarded," Richard protested.

"Your communication will not work in the space membrane or in dark space," Quane said. "Electromagnetic radiation cannot penetrate the space membrane. The laws of physics are identical on both sides of the membrane—light travels at the same speed in light and dark space—but information cannot cross the membrane from one side to the other. That is why you never discovered this space. It's also why they can't see you anymore."

"We're invisible?" Richard tried to imagine the military implications of a cloaking device.

"Technically, we're hidden while in the membrane. Right now we are operating on battery power. In dark space, it's dark matter which fuels the engine and charges the batteries."

"If your ship runs on dark matter, how did you fly around the space station?"

"My ship did not move after I appeared. I approached your station hidden inside the membrane operating on battery power. You did not see me, either visually or with radar, until I appeared. These engines work well for traveling around dark space, but barely move in light space because there is no dark matter there. It is like your airplanes. They work well traveling through the air, but are inconvenient for commuting on land."

Richard, alerted by a high-pitched whistle, saw Quane hurry to a console two stations away and adjust the angle of a small display. "Welcome to dark space. Pull up a port and I'll try to get you a view."

Quane gestured to a round panel, as wide as the aisle, on the floor near him. When Richard did not move, Quane bent down and slid the blast cover off the panel, revealing a portal to space.

The discussion about light space, dark space, and the barrier membrane led Richard to think dark space was going to be the inverse, or negative, of the normal universe. He expected stars to be black dots on a white background. Actually, it did not look much different from what he was used to—pinpoints of light surrounded by blackness.

"I have to admit, it all looks the same to me."

"Wait a minute, Ricky. You're looking at random stars." Quane punched, twisted, and banged on the controls. "OK, try now. Feast your weary eyes on the Milky Way as seen in dark space."

The Milky Way spread out in a thick, hazy band. Sprinkled randomly, were intense points of light shining with the brilliance of sunlight reflecting off polished chrome pinheads. At the center was a blinding spotlight the size of the sun as seen from Earth.

"Wow. What are all those super bright stars?"

"Those are the tips of the gravitational wells of black holes." Quane got down on all fours next to Richard. A mangy paw scratched on the window. "All the other points are the tips of ordinary stars' gravitational wells. The black holes—the especially bright points—are what we use as guideposts on our maps. The brightest light at the center is the black hole holding the galaxy together."

"I thought you said electromagnetic radiation could not pass across the membrane from one side to the other."

"Paying attention, I see," his scruffy tail wagged harder. "Yes, I did say that. And it is true. But strong gravitational wells can stretch the membrane so thin light can leak through. The more massive the star, the brighter and bigger the image is on this side. Black holes are the brightest. You can't even see planets."

Quane hammered and kicked the controls. "Ahh. Here, let me show you your sun as seen from dark space. Remember, we are still looking from the approximate perspective of Earth."

The sun was something like a distant comet. The light was bright at the narrow end of a thin, horn-shaped cone. The intensity quickly faded to black toward the mouth of the horn. The entire length, from the bright tip to the wide mouth, was the diameter of a full moon as seen from Earth.

"Let me show you how it works." At a desk-sized touch screen, Quane reached underneath the console, yanked on some wires, and the display sparked to life.

"No offense, Ricky, but I think we need to start you with the introductory lesson. This is a little program used to explain how space works to children. It is tough to try to explain four dimensions using only three."

The video started with a wire-mesh plane, crisscrossing yellow lines extending from the foreground to the horizon on a black background. A ball dropped into the middle and created a depression in the mesh. Then several smaller balls dropped onto the mesh at various distances from the first ball, but still within the larger depression.

"Let's start here," Quane said. "Think of the big ball as a star, or your sun, and the smaller balls as planets."

The planets began moving in orbits around the star and the mesh turned so the edge was a horizontal line. A giant cone extended from the star and smaller cones extended from the planets.

"All those cones are gravity wells distorting space. But space isn't two dimensional."

The flat plane in the video bent back around itself and a sphere formed. The sun's gravity well extended to the sphere's center. The planets had shorter wells, which pointed to the tip of the sun's well, like compass needles pointing to a magnet.

"Here is a more accurate depiction of a solar system. The planets' wells point to the well that holds them in orbit. Next, we extend the example."

The wire-mesh sphere expanded and many more gravity wells puckered its surface.

"This is a very simple representation of what's going on. Pretend all of the small wells are the bigger stars in the galaxy. What would hold them in place?"

"A larger gravity well?" Richard asked, tentatively.

"Exactly, Ricky." Quane's wagging tail was banging the console enthusiastically at his customer's growing understanding. A red sliver peeked through a cut along the flailing tail.

On the screen, a cone formed, distorted the sphere, and stopped when its tip was at the sphere's center.

"See this?" said Quane, pointing at the largest cone. "That, my friend, is the gigantic black hole at the center of the galaxy holding everything in place."

After fiddling with a few more knobs, he said, "Now I'll show you the membrane. This is it, Ricky—the thing making it all this possible."

Suddenly, all the gravity wells vanished, leaving an uninterrupted, yellow-lined wire-mesh sphere slowly rotating on a black background. The wire mesh pulled back to create a hemisphere, and Richard was looking into a bowl. A second, smaller hemisphere appeared within the first, giving the bowl's edge a thickness. Gravity wells of all lengths again, one by one, poked their way into the sphere.

While the outer surface maintained its round shape, except for where the gravity wells created dimples, the new, inner sphere stretched maintaining contact with but not allowing the wells to penetrate. It resembled a bizarre circus tent with the canvas stretched between poles of various heights. Where there were no poles, no gravity wells, the thickness of the membrane was thin. Where the poles were long—deep gravity wells—the membrane was thick. The image's cross section resembled an apple that had been partially and irregularly hollowed out by drunken worms.

"There you have it. What do you think?"

"I think this is fantastic." Richard was smiling, giddy with the excitement of being the first person to learn a brand-new set of physical principles.

"Let me get this straight." Richard touched the display outside the hemisphere's area. "You're saying the outside, here, is light space, what I think of as normal space." He then touched the distorted area inside the hemisphere. "What is inside is dark space." He dragged a finger along the irregular boundary between the inside and outside. "The membrane separates the two and you know how to move across it from light space to dark space and back again. And it's in dark space where you can travel faster than light."

"You're getting red hot, Ricky." Quane's tail wagged furiously—strong interest implied a likely sale as long as he could keep his excitement from shaking off his costume. If Humans were related to Smez and shared a common hatred of his real form, the instant they saw him out of costume, they would attack him. He had to make the sale first. "But nothing can travel faster than light."

"So how do you travel faster than light...?" Richard stopped, then he slapped his palm on his forehead with the realization. "I think I get it now. Instead of traveling across the galaxy the long way around, as we have to do in light space to get from here to there..." His index fingers touched two points on opposite sides of the hemisphere's outer edge, then he traced one finger around the outer edge of the hemisphere until it touched the other.

"You cross the membrane into dark space and go straight there." Richard touched the same points on opposite sides of the hemisphere, but this time, he moved a finger on the shortest line to touch his other finger. "Like a shortcut. Right?" He said beaming with pride at his quick understanding. "It's like having to travel the long way around the earth's surface to get someplace instead of taking the shortcut by drilling a path straight through the earth."

"Yes, exactly." Quane's tail wagged, curled, and twisted so violently he could feel his costume starting to rip. "Now add to the analogy the idea that your earth had been hollowed out like an irregular geode. And travel in the thick shell takes almost no time at all. Then your travel time is simply the time it takes to jump the short space between two points on the inside."

Quane used his paws to push Richard's fingers to two points on the inside edge of the membrane pictured on the display.

"We have learned how to enter dark space, hop from one gravitational well to another, and rise back to light space. The membrane is a like a dimension, and travel in it is timeless. Travel time is practically from one inner point of dark space to another. For you to reach the center of the galaxy, at your gravitational acceleration, the shortcut makes the trip a tiny fraction of the twenty-five thousand light years it would take using your best technology."

"And you don't have to travel faster than light?"

"No, Ricky," Quane said, "you don't. Typical speeds of your rockets. And with these engines, we don't have to carry fuel. They run on dark matter, and there is plenty of it in dark space. The engines eat it up and chew their way through space. The faster they eat, the faster you go."

A paw reached back under the console and jiggled some wires. The display blinked off. A plume of smoke curled up from under the console. His paw came out flaming. "Bleen-Flockit," he swore, pounding the flame out with his other paw. Richard stared, open-mouthed.

"Oh, uh, I'll have to get that looked at when I get back."

"Are you OK?" Richard moved toward the dog with more than an animal lover's compassion. His own well-being was at stake. How would he get back to Earth without Quane? "We have full medical facilities on the station."

"I'm fine." Quane deftly flourished his still-smoking paw quickly, in part to assure the Human, but also to see if the costume had burned enough to expose his hand. "See? No pain. No problem. Where were we?"

The brushed off smoking bits of hair reeking of burnt wool. "Oh, yes. Species normally accelerate based on the gravity of their home planet. When they reach the halfway point to their destination, they start decelerating. That's why there is identical instrumentation on both walls. I bet you thought it was because I don't know if I'm coming or going, eh?" Quane slapped Richard on the back with his clean paw.

"At your gravitational acceleration, you could make it to the center of the galaxy in about ten years, more or less. So, what do you think? Is your species interested?"

"This is incredible," Richard whispered. "Most definitely I'm...I mean, we are interested."

"One last thing, in dark space, you do not have to worry about ionizing radiation frying living tissue. Even the most radiation-sensitive life-forms can live in this space indefinitely."

"How come *we* haven't thought of this?" Richard wondered aloud.

"Don't beat yourself up, Ricky, my boy. As is typical with great scientific discoveries, the actual invention of the stardrive engine was an accident. The scientist who invented it, Dr. AtZ, a major scientist from the planet Rebroz I, was simply looking for a way to detect dark matter. On the first test, his device vanished from his lab. The second time, the same thing happened. The third time, he attached a communications cable. The communications stopped working almost instantly. When they winched the cable back, there was nothing at the end but frayed wire. The last time they installed a timer to turn off the device and reverse the process." Quane turned his back to the Human and tugged his sleeve down to cover the fraying, burnt fabric over his paw.

"What happened? Did the device come back?" Richard asked. He loved the lore of scientific discovery and once considered writing a book about the unsung lives of the great discoverers' assistants. The working title was to be *Watson, Come Here!*

"No, and yes. Dr. AtZ never saw it again. He died penniless, homeless—a suicide. The doctor lost every bit of venture capital invested and had borrowed heavily against all of his possessions including his family. When he had no results and the bills came due, he was ridiculed as a charlatan. His possessions were auctioned and his family became indentured servants. An hour before he was to be hauled off to a debtor's prison, he killed himself.

"And, yes, years after he died, the third test device was found orbiting an outlying planet of his solar system. The government, as principal investor and shareholder, as well as owner of his family, claimed possession of the invention and all the rights to license. Rebroz became the richest solar system in the galaxy.

"Time for the switch," Quane announced and yanked at the skin on his legs. "Hang on—the ship is inverting. We'll be standing on the opposite floor as we decelerate to our destination."

Richard lost his weight and started to float. No sound of rocket thrusters. No vibration. The flashing lights continued to flash. Then he was gently attracted to what used to be the ceiling. His palms flattened on the floor and pushed off. Gravity was increasing. He grabbed his knees and somersaulted backward. By the time the ship reached full gravitational deceleration, his legs were straight and he stuck a perfect landing. He had not attempted a backflip since college. Since the instrument consoles were mimicked on floor and ceiling, the only noticeable difference in the room was the window he had been looking out on the floor was now a skylight.

"A perfect ten," Quane said.

In less than a minute, Richard's world turned upside down. He tried to absorb it all for future debriefing: dark matter, governments stealing inventions, an unlimited power source, defamed extraterrestrial scientists who sell their family and commit suicide, exploration of the galaxy in human lifetimes, trade with aliens. He stared at the display.

Quane left Richard to ponder his new reality while he busied himself with fixing busted controls.

CHAPTER 11

One hour after Richard disappeared, Steven Burke, president of the United States, was slouched over his fingers as they rubbed the cool mahogany finish on the Roosevelt desk. The nails were neatly trimmed. He was probing the grain for Wilson's, Truman's, and Eisenhower's spirits, as if he could rub an inspirational genie from the wood. Had they ever rubbed these exact grains for answers to their crises? The desk was picked for his Oval Office on the strength of its understated simplicity. From the front, the desk was two bulky wooden boxes bridged by a mahogany slab. The desk's user saw four drawers on each side with simple brass pulls. It was unadorned by engravings or markings, except for the small shield on the slim center drawer.

Burke's sixty-year-old figure was boney, wiry, and all angles—in contrast to the desk. Even his face was triangular, from the wide, flat-topped forehead to the narrow pointed chin. A pile of unruly salt-and-pepper hair looked more like it was plopped on his head than was part of it, and might decide to fly off in search of a better home in the next stiff breeze.

The Oval Office's east door was ajar. The syrupy sweet perfume of grape hyacinth was cleansed by the light lemon fragrance of magnolia. A catbird was squawking and burbling like an R2D2 robot on crystal meth. Peale's portrait of George Washington on the wall to his left was there to remind Burke where this country had come from. The photograph of Earthrise from Apollo 8 in orbit around the moon hung on the right-hand wall to remind him where this country might go—a prescient choice, considering the current events. The last two items he insisted on were Rodin's sculpture, *The Thinker*, and Remington's *Bronco Buster*. The first he divined for wisdom and patience, the second for the strength to ride the bastards—the press, the Congress, the public—until he or they were tamed.

Steven Burke was the first Independent candidate ever elected president. As such, Democrats and Republicans supported him as one of their own or fought against him as a player for the opposing team, depending on the direction of the swirling political winds. Congress was locked in a stalemate and progressed as much as an impossibly drunk giant wallowing in a gloomy bog.

Lobbyists had been neutralized. The tsunami of cash intended to purchase influence, advocacy, and the reshaping of the economic landscape to the investors' design was ultimately unable to dislodge the smallest pebble or nudge the largest boulder from the unbending, Capitol Hill breakwater. Despite record cash flows to political candidates, not a single congressional seat changed sides. Political influence dried up and receded. The public quit paying attention to the boring sport of politics.

Only three bills arrived at Burke's desk in his first three years. The first law he signed required the rough, grooved edges of quarters be removed for a deficit reduction of $279,842.31 over ten years. The second decided the word "employe" maintained the same legal status as "employee." Not printing that final "e" on the tons of yearly government proclamations netted a ten-year taxpayer savings of $57,079.06. The final and most contentious law to barely pass was the one which made it a misdemeanor, punishable by a $25 fine, to text while walking or while standing and obstruct the normal flow of foot traffic in the middle of a corridor in any federal building. If one had to text, they were required to be touching any wall lining the corridor with a part of their torso—arms and legs did not count.

As circumstances would have it, restricting meddling hands from the levers of power allowed the economy to solve its problems naturally: business gained confidence in the stability of rules and laws, and international trade rebalanced and found its natural level. The domestic result was fat and happy consumers, stable growth, and 70 percent approval ratings for Burke. Burke's genius of governing by not governing promised to sweep him into a second term.

"I'm not sure I agree." Burke lifted his gaze, stopped rubbing his desk, and pushed his blocky, black-rimmed glasses up on his nose. "Why would they deliberately drug him to kidnap him? Richard was already on the ship. Where could he go?"

Donald Gregory, the secretary of defense, was leaning backward with his elbows on the fireplace mantel. In his mid-forties, paunchy, and with a receding hairline, his overlarge ears and droopy-eyed expression reminded Burke of a basset hound. While Burke was a fidgety, nervous wreck, Gregory was comfortable and loose; a twenty-five-year veteran of the confusion and crises that are just another average day at work on Capitol Hill.

"Mr. President." Gregory held up a palm to hold back the president's opinions. "Admittedly, the evidence is thinner than my wife's alibis, but do we dismiss Dr. Wu's concerns and observations outright? She was the one who pointed out that the alien said he 'added a few extras' to Richard's air. Richard said it smelled a little like dry cleaning fluid. Miriam put two and two together, stirred them up with a dash of experience, and came up with the possibility that Richard had been drugged and kidnapped."

Gregory pulled out his cell phone and scrolled to a stored message. While still leaning his elbows on the mantle, he faced the phone toward Burke.

Miriam's voice was strained, damming back an ocean of tears. "I know what anesthetics smell like. I have used them many times to sedate animals before experiments." There was a choking gulp. "Richard's metabolic records displayed a sudden slowdown after taking his helmet off, at the same time he should have displayed a high level of anxiety—humans are hardwired to fight or flee at the unknown."

Burke had listened to the call more than once. Next came three wet coughs.

"I often rationalized experiments on lesser animals," Miriam continued—her words punctuated by gasps, "as necessary to advance and improve human life. Is Richard nothing more than a lab rat now—a subject of some unspeakable alien experiments?" The dam burst. Everyone who heard the message within the next week assumed Miriam would never stop crying.

Gregory pocketed the phone. "The facts are that an alien abducted a human and—"

"A human who," Burke interrupted, "according to the record, went willingly."

"An alien *allegedly* abducted a human." Gregory corrected himself. "We all saw the size of the alien. What if it knew that a larger, physically fit human could easily overpower it? Maybe it feared Richard might run amok and accidentally or deliberately destroy delicate instrumentation."

"You saw the same videos I did." Burke stopped rubbing the desk and looked at Gregory over the top of his glasses. "He never compromised his position; never lost his composure. There was no reason for the alien to feel threatened."

"Mr. President," Gregory said, stepping forward from the mantel. "I have to remind you that we have a hard enough time discerning the motives of our friends and allies, and they are human. How can we possibly have any confidence in fathoming an alien mind?"

"What are you suggesting we do?" Burke flattened both palms on the desk and fanned his fingers.

"Send SCaTS. This is exactly what they were made for—to counter a threat from an alien race."

"What threat?"

"Exactly," said Gregory. "Who knows? But do we sit here like the proverbial frog being slowly boiled because it does not jump out of the pot at the first sign of danger? Or do we act preemptively, even if it is eventually seen as an overreaction? I see several scenarios…" Gregory counted them on his fingers. "One, the alien abducted Richard and we never see either again. Two, the alien abducted Richard to test him for human weakness and returns with an army to enslave us all. Three, he returns Richard safe and sound."

"But how does SCaTS fit in?"

"If it's the first or second," Gregory said, "we may not know for a while, but at least we'll have our frontline guard in place. If it's the third, we do everything to subdue the alien, bring it to justice, and claim its technology for the old 'red, white, and blue.'"

"What?" Burke stood sharply and walked around the desk to face Gregory. "Imprison an alien and steal his technology for taking a human on a joyride?"

"An *alleged* joyride," Gregory returned to the mantel and leaned back on it. He knew the president had lost the argument when he left the bastion of his desk and walked around to his side. "It would be trivial to spin this in our favor…"

"Millions, maybe billions, of people saw everything. Are you going to have them undergo mass hypnosis, or just hit them with a memory-eraser ray from space?"

"We're still working on that," Gregory mumbled, his foot toyed with the nap of the rug.

"Mass hypnosis?" Burke asked.

"No. The memory ray." He waved off further conversation on the topic. "Trust me. We can easily spin it as a diabolical alien plot. The alien lied to Richard and all humanity. We manufacture evidence to support the story. The only real eyewitness is Richard himself. If we can get to him before he talks to the ISS crew…"

"You are proposing to fully discredit Captain Winn's account of what happened on the ship?" Burke leaned his butt against the front of the desk and crossed his arms. "Make a liar out of a good officer—and better man—to get your hands on alien technology?"

"It's not as bad as it sounds," Gregory said. "We'll claim Richard was hypnotized, brainwashed. After our doctors finish with his deprogramming, he will believe he was abducted by the devil himself."

"Why didn't you raise the SCaTS option to me the instant the alien ship appeared if all you really wanted was the technology?" The president was back to sitting at his desk and rubbing for an inspirational genie.

"A janitor accidentally hit the EMO—Emergency Machine Off—button," Gregory said, "with his mop handle, two hours before the alien arrived." Gregory had turned his back to the president and fidgeted with a leaf on the descendant of JFK's Swedish Ivy perched on the mantel. "The entire launch code system was completely powered down. We deliberately overrode many of the restart protocols to bring the system back up ASAP. We were launch-ready thirty minutes ago." Four pulverized ivy leaves littered the mantel. Although the oversight of allowing one emergency button to disable a trillion-dollar project had been his predecessors' responsibility, Gregory would shoulder the blame if this launch delay precipitated the loss of any ISS astronauts or the alien spaceship.

"Ed, your opinion?" The president addressed the only other person in the room, Captain Edmund Sherman, founder and commander of SCaTS, who had been sitting silently, ramrod straight, on an upholstered chair in the corner. Sherman stood and snapped his heels and spine to attention.

"Sir," Sherman said, "the operation is feasible. An *Icarus* is moving to ISS proximity. We can launch roughly an hour after your order and arrive at the ISS a little over two hours after that."

CHAPTER 12

Minutes after the president's launch order, the military was in charge of handling the alien dog.

In letting Quane escape and abduct one of their own, the scientists on the ISS proved they could not be trusted with the responsibility to make first contact with an alien species. They could not balance the social, political, and military importance of the encounter against their personal and scientific curiosity. Dealing with an extraterrestrial species required finesse. Dealing with an unknown foreign power required a firm, yet delicate touch. Real diplomacy required the "speak softly, but carry a big stick" approach. Scientists could be counted on to lose sight of the priorities and become more interested in defining the genus and species of the stick.

This interaction obviously required the skills of an elite, highly trained, space-faring military strike force. Such a team existed. They were the Space Command and Tactics Squad (SCaTS) within the Department of Defense Manned Space Defense Office. SCaTS was a top-secret gray program funded by "lost" money: millions confiscated from major but unpublicized drug busts, billions lost during Iraq's reconstruction, trillions lost in weapons cost overruns. No elected representative involved with SCaTS wanted it publicly revealed that they were wasting taxpayer money on the ludicrous notion that an extraterrestrial visit was a real possibility.

SCaTS soldiers were extraordinarily well trained. The ability to best another human was a basic prerequisite for the job. What set this group apart was prospective candidates also trained barehanded against dangerous animals, large and small—cougars, bears, alligators, crocodiles, komodo dragons, bulls, honey badgers, wild boars, rabid dogs, kangaroos, and anything else their creative, sadistic superiors could find to unleash at them. The logical reasoning behind this extreme training regime was simple: weapons were only useful if they could function. Gunpowder-based weapons were neutralized in oxygen-deprived environments. Projectiles from compressed-gas weapons could puncture a ship's hull. Handheld stun lasers did not exist. A space soldier was expected to capture the unknown barehanded. Only soldiers who survived the test were selected for the team. Winning and losing tactics were recorded, analyzed, evaluated, and used to update training regimens for the next round of candidates.

SCaTS' launch platform was from ultra-high altitude reconnaissance bomber planes code-named *Icarus*. Icarus planes were stealth bombers upgraded with nuclear thermal rocket engines. The nuclear engines propelled the planes to altitudes of 150 miles—roughly the space shuttle's cruising altitude—but only maintained thrust for short periods. Long enough to launch lightweight spy payloads into high orbit, or the SCaTS capsule to the ISS.

Only three secret planes existed. A group of five SCaTS soldiers rode as passengers on one of them at all times and the group changed when the plane landed for routine maintenance. The SCaTS capsule held a maximum of four soldiers. The fifth was an alternate.

What had started in the press as a gala welcome for a being from another planet and grown into the pomp and circumstance of Humans meeting aliens in broad daylight—not on some back road in the middle of nowhere to be probed against their will and summarily discharged with ripped clothing and impaired memories—in two short hours had turned into worldwide suspicion and hatred toward the malevolent invader from outer space.

There was no assurance the alien would ever come back. He was on record saying the trip was a several-hour test drive. If that was not a ruse to abduct Richard permanently and he did return, SCaTS would be ready.

CHAPTER 13

"Can you fly to other galaxies using this principle?" Richard said.

"Not yet. Scientists have been searching for the node that holds the local cluster of galaxies together. Most have given up the search." A bell chimed. "We're here."

"Mars… Jupiter?" Richard scratched his scalp and a few more hairs floated out of place. They had been gone almost two hours and he was hoping they had not arrived at the boring old moon, which takes normal astronauts almost three days to get to.

"No, Uranus. It took two hours of your time. Now we float back up to light space to have a real look."

Richard shook his head. His eyes were wide in disbelief. "We went eighteen astronomical units—eighteen times the distance from the earth to the sun, half the distance from the sun to Pluto—in two hours?"

Another instrument chirped. Quane pulled at the skin on his shoulder. "We are back in light space, your space, but there is not much worth seeing."

The excitement of being the first Human to see another planet as close as if looking at the moon from the earth deflated quickly. From the ice giant's deep blue-green color from an atmosphere of liquid hydrogen, helium, and methane to its thin, vaporous rings to its tiny, insubstantial moons to its swirling storms had all been photographed and videotaped by the procession of satellite probes slingshot out from Earth over the past thirty-plus years.

His impulse was to take samples and collect new data, but he had no tools, no instruments. All of his cameras were useless because they did not record—only transmitted. Mission Control had determined the operational battery life on Richard's suit would be best utilized by maximizing the number of cameras as backups instead of running recorders. Mission Control was responsible for recording. No one could have predicted an alien would take him behind a space curtain that prevented communication. And he could not land on Uranus to collect souvenirs: no gold, no parrots, no Indians.

"Time to head back," Quane was sweating with excitement at the promise of making the sale. The sweat was making the costume itchier than ever.

"Is there anything I can take back to prove I was here?"

"Why? Buy this engine and the others I have and you can come back anytime."

"If I have proof, it will be easier for you to sell your engines to my planet."

The costume was getting scratchy at the waist. He pulled at his costume and scratched his back. "Check out the planet's color and details. That should give you proof enough you were here."

Richard shook his head; a few more hairs swished themselves loose. "Any of my observations will be meaningless without proof. There has to be some other way."

Quane clapped his paws and pointed in the air. "I know! I can angle the ship to reflect your sun directly back to Earth, and at the same time, you will send a message to Earth. When we arrive back at your station, you will predict exactly when and where the message will come from, as well as what the message says." He tweaked the skin on his leg.

"That's it!" His hair was a wild black aura around his head. "The message is sent in light space and has to take the long way around to Earth, but we slip into dark space and take the shortcut. Since we will arrive before the message does," he pounded a fist into his other palm for emphasis, "they'll have to believe me. How much time difference will there be— between when we arrive and the message arrives?"

"About thirty minutes. Is that enough time?"

"I sure as hell hope so."

"I'll set up the reflection." Quane darted back and forth between four consoles twisting, pulling, and pushing knobs on each.

Richard envied Quane's commonality with the ship, his mature understanding of its operation, and his casual urbanity with the galaxy. He pictured himself one day in the future, conversant in the theory and practice of operating stardrives, visiting an uncharted planet, and amazing the wide-eyed, speechless aliens with his own raucous tales of galactic exploits. And Quane had not even left the first aisle of instruments, where he and Richard met. So much to learn.

Quane worked feverishly to enable the Human's request. He tested the primary, secondary, tertiary, quaternary, fifth, sixth, and seventh backup systems to find any still working. Precise attitude adjustment was required for the direct solar reflection and interplanetary communication—and Bleen's banging Ballwangt overflowing with luck.

"Do you know what you want to say?" His voice had an edge; he did not look up from his effort to juggle the control systems to maintain a stable alignment.

"I think so." Would he blow another chance to make a statement that would last throughout history? If it was good enough, the world might forget his "Down, boy," blunder.

Quane slapped a wireless microphone into Richard's hand. The housing was missing so he held the device gingerly to avoid contacting the unshielded circuitry. The head was attached to the handle by three frayed wires and it lolled back and forth in spite of his best efforts to balance it upright.

"Remember," Quane did not raise his attention from the console, "this sale could be the biggest thing to ever happen to your planet since air." And the biggest windfall for him. He clawed at his shoulder. "Let me know when you're ready."

Richard coughed into his hand, hummed the opening notes from Beethoven's ninth symphony, blinked his eyes hard, and licked his suddenly dry, cracked lips. When he nodded, Quane pounded his fist on a large button with an image of a porcupine climbing a Christmas tree. The red, plastic cover sailed off in three pieces, twirling into the bowels of the control room.

"This is Captain Richard Winn from the International Space Station." He struggled to keep his voice composed and steady. "This message is coming from a small spaceship orbiting the planet Uranus. This message is intended as proof that interplanetary and interstellar travel is possible in hours and years instead of lifetimes. The pilot of the alien ship that was parked next to the ISS is here to sell us engines able to take us from the earth to the center of the galaxy in a mere ten years. As proof of the engine's ability, I will be back at the ISS before this message arrives. This is a great day for the peoples of Earth. This is the day we shall look back on and remember as the day humanity became part of the galactic community. We will meet new civilizations, experience new cultures, and go where no one has gone before, and for the price of… Wait. You never said how much it will cost…"

Quane was staring at a display beyond Richard's vision. His paws held two fistfuls of cables that he had wrenched from beneath the console to interrupt the communication and prevent two robotic police drones from homing in on the signal.

"Not now," Quane growled at the display. "Why now?"

"Quane, are you OK?"

"What?" He barked. His body stiffened then relaxed.

"Ricky," Quane said smiling broadly, "I am truly sorry." A paw gripped Richard's bicep. "They lost the last part of the transmission. I thought you were done so I sent us back into the membrane to dark space."

The first oration to the world, pontificating on the reality of interstellar travel, had been interrupted by a technical difficulty.

If the drones caught them with the junk engine they were using, they would be hauled off to the nearest prison with no trial, no chance for a plea. Due process was simple: seek, verify identification numbers, and, if illegal, destroy. If it was attached to a habitat pod, they were both dragged to the nearest prison planet and the travelers were discharged. Fortunately, he had picked up the drones flying beyond Pluto. He kept a nervous eye on the scanner, ready to duck into and hide in the membrane at the first sign of them. It was just his luck that the drones had to be here now, on the verge of his biggest sale.

"I just got shocking news. I was overdue in checking my galactic mail." Quane hung his head and obeyed the translation computer's advice to shed a tear. "My nearest and dearest friend, Wyruk, is seriously ill and has been asking for me." He had neither friends nor relatives. Wyruk was the first name to come to his lying and clownishly happy lips. "I need to return to your station as quickly as possible and see if your planet is interested in purchasing this, and rush to his bedside before it's too late."

Quane ignited the engines and logged in the return trip to Earth. Hopefully, he could avoid an episode like the time he took several giant amoebas for a ride. The stardrive caught fire shortly after entering dark space. When he informed his clients that they might be stranded for a short time, the amoebas became frantic and started vibrating. The vibrations became faster and faster. Their colors flashed through the spectrum. The pulsations became audible as the strobing colors nearly blinded him. Finally, in what was the ultimate act of self-defense against what appeared to them to be a potential rapist running out of gas on a deserted dirt road, they exploded. It took days to clean the sticky ooze off the consoles, walls, and floors, and weeks to air out the acrid smell of rotten eggs.

Quane prayed silently to Bleen that this one did not break down. This was the best of the three. One of the others did not work, and the third was an empty shell. Both were parked near Mars along with his own good engine. All were in danger of being discovered and destroyed.

It could have been a perfect sale. Bleen, Flock the drones! He had to distract his mind from his worries.

"Ricky, my boy, we have some time to kill, so I'll give you a tour of my habitat. If you're going to be tooling around the galaxy, you'll want to know how to pack."

Quane led them down the narrow aisle toward the curved wall at the center. Richard moved slowly to avoid stepping on the threatening bits of razor-sharp metal. Twenty consoles lined both sides of the aisle. Some were flashing randomly while others beeped, buzzed, and burped. Two looked like they had caught fire and the flame retardant had dried and crusted over their surfaces. Richard noted that not only are the laws of physics constant throughout the galaxy, but so is the smell of burnt electronics.

"On the other side is the fine little engine that will soon be yours." Quane stopped and patted the circular wall at the center of the room with his singed paw.

Trotting along with the wall on his left, he waved a paw at the expansive room, "All of this is what we refer to as the control room, or the bridge."

"As you can see, it is well equipped. This old freighter pod was rigged with many redundant systems. Obviously, there are navigation and operational instruments on the acceleration and deceleration walls, which is one redundancy, but there are duplicates elsewhere making many layers of backup. When you're a freighter out moving cargo for years, you don't want to waste time fixing things. The other instruments are for manual operation, loading and unloading cargo, and salvage operations." Quane's grin was so broad that his speech was almost unintelligible.

Only the few systems he had used to pilot the ship were working. Quane had no need for additional instrumentation and no money to have anything fixed. To impress and amaze prospective customers with the level of activity and sophistication, he activated every console and let the machines run their initialization sequences repeatedly. He had lied about the pod and engine's original function. They were for military use, not freight. There was no need to alert the Human to the abuse the engine had endured during battle.

"And here are the living quarters," Quane said. "After you." They had walked nearly all the way around the curved wall. In the floor was a small opening with a fixed ladder leading down.

The room was as expansive and as tall as the one he just left. Like the control room, the floor and ceiling were mirror images. But instead of consoles, they were covered in battered furniture. Some pieces could have been human-style beds, others were shaped like the letter W. Shelves and cabinets of all sizes and shapes crowded the spaces between the beds. Littering the beds and falling haphazardly off the shelves and cabinets were clothing bits, dented containers, and crumpled trash. The room smelled of skunk, garlic, and pine auto freshener.

"The maid's day off. This is the passenger's cabin, where both the freighter crew and interstellar passengers lived and slept. Not much interesting here. You can see the previous owner was a slob and left in a hurry." A single kick skidded a deflated ball across the floor, knocking bits of crushed paper and colored plastic into other trash bits in a junkyard chain reaction. The refuse was the remains of bartered payment for sales to planets that lacked anything of real value.

Quane was anxious to get back to the controls to watch for drones and leave this trophy room of past failures. "How about I give you a basic lesson on controls and operation?"

With a child's excitement at the offering of a new toy, Richard bounced in his step as he followed the tattered dog.

"This button here," Quane's paw hovered above a button with lettering like a butterfly wing, "begins the warm-up sequence for the engine…"

Richard fought to keep his attention on Quane's instructions; his mind was pestered by the question of what Earth could possibly offer as payment. Precious metals, gems, oil, and water all had to be available a thousand times over on other planets, inhabited or not. There was no reason to believe that because these things were valuable to *Homo sapiens* they would be worth anything to the rest of the galaxy. If Quane had seen valuables on any other planet in Earth's solar system, he could have taken them without offering Earth anything in return. Earth would not have been able to mount the slightest defense of a territorial claim anyway.

But he was afraid to ask the price—afraid that he, or Earth, would not be able to scrape up enough to purchase an engine.

"Now, you try," Quane said. Thoughts of the drones distracted Quane from Richard's recitation. The autonomous, robotic drones were programmed by SDEI, to prevent unauthorized stardrive use or sale. If they found the two scrap engines hidden at Mars, they would destroy them and search the area for him. The probes would not spend long looking for him. The loss of the items was punishment enough for an unlucky dealer in unregistered stardrives. Quane feared they might find his good, properly registered engine parked on the other side of Mars. Circumstantial evidence would implicate him with the illegal merchandise. His name and face, from his operator's license, would be broadcast everywhere. Rewards would be posted for his capture. Bounty hunters were relentless at cleaning up the galaxy.

"I think that about covers the operating basics. I can send you a translation of the parameters for your records. There are instructions on how to set up the computer interface to the operating systems and how to get power off the engines for any habitat. You will have to build your own habitat. As much as you might have fallen in love with this one—" Quane patted Richard's shoulder. "—I do have to take it home."

Quane had no plans to stay around and tutor Humans in space technology. He had to move out fast to avoid the drones. He silently begged Bleen to let him be long gone before the Humans found out they had been fleeced.

CHAPTER 14

Stuffed inside the SCaTS capsule—which was barely bigger than a MINI Cooper car—were four soldiers in state-of-the-art space gear that only a top-secret government project could afford. The outfits resembled black scuba wetsuits rather than the balloon-y, Michelin Man-like costumes from the Apollo era and what the current space station astronauts wore. SCaTS uniforms were jumpsuits tailored from a graphene-nylon composite—lightweight, breathable, and impenetrable by knife or claw. The only decoration was the owner's name.

The capsule was stripped to minimize mass and the amount of fuel required for maneuvering. No life support or communication, since those systems were fully contained in their spacesuits. The guidance control computer and display was a ten-inch laptop resting on the pilot's knees. There were two viewports forward and viewports arranged so every passenger had unobstructed vision into space: up, down, left, and right.

The American pilot was Chuck Martin, a three-year, SCaTS veteran. Alex Freytsis, the Russian, and Fan Chan, the Chinese—and only woman representative—had graduated from Chuck's SCaTS class. The latest SCaTS graduate and space rookie was an Iranian, Danel Magarefteh.

Elite foreign national soldiers were encouraged to join SCaTS. The first reason was to keep their home governments quiet in case they hacked their way into the computers of the US secret space squad and blabbed to the world how idiotic the

United States was for actually believing in little green men. It would be hard to scold the United States if they themselves were complicit in the fantasy.

The second reason the United States accepted foreign soldiers into SCaTS was for political cover. If the first encounter with an alien race went badly, propaganda and finger-pointing from all sides would help spread, diffuse, and dilute the blame and liability.

The SCaTS capsule was thirty minutes away from docking with the ISS.

CHAPTER 15

"And here we are," Quane said, "entering the membrane near your station."

Before entering the membrane to cross into light space and Earth's orbit, two blips on his display revealed the drones had dragged his junk engines at Mars into dark space and destroyed them. Quane's tail drooped. A single cough cleared the fear of failure stuck in his throat. The sale should end quickly after the Humans heard proof of this stardrive engine's worthiness via a message from Uranus within thirty minutes.

He shook his body like a dog shedding water to compose himself. *Showtime.*

"Here is your station, right where you left it. Your communications will work again."

"ISS, do you read me?"

"Richard!" screamed Miriam. "We hear you and we see you. Where have you been?" She floated in the cupola, her turn at watch.

"Our alien friend took me on a short trip to Uranus. I can prove it. Can you patch this through to Houston?" Richard squinted to make out her face at the cupola window. His voice was raised as if calling out to a friend a city block away; ignoring the fact that sound could not travel across the void between them.

"Mission Control, this is Miriam Wu. The alien ship is back. We see them. We are in contact."

"We have them on radar as well," Mission Control said. "Open a scrambled communication channel to Richard."

Miriam lifted the toggle switches and enabled the communication. "Richard, you are online." She wiped away tears of relief for his safe return and flew off to wake Fedor and Nancy.

"Captain Winn," Mission Control said, "report. How are you, and where exactly have you been?"

"People of the world, this is Richard Winn calling from the alien craft—"

"Richard," Mission Control said, "this line is scrambled. There is no one listening on this line but us. What is going on? Are you all right?"

"I need to talk to the world. My message is not for any one nation or group of nations. It is for the entire earth."

"Not going to happen," Mission Control said.

"I have been to Uranus and back. In exactly—" he checked his watch "—twenty-six minutes, I will have proof. Turn your telescopes and radio receivers toward Uranus and you will hear a message I sent from the alien ship it orbit there. The message you will receive is meant to prove that the stardrive engines Quane is here to sell us are real. Interstellar travel happens in a way we never could have imagined. This technology will take humanity off Earth and enable human beings to travel to the stars."

There was a long pause. "Richard, this is Mission Control. You were gone a little over four hours. You say you went to Uranus to post an email to Earth and made it back before the message arrived? The message is traveling at the speed of light, but you traveled faster. Is that what you are saying?"

"Not exactly. The message is traveling at the speed of light, but we took a shortcut. We didn't have to travel anywhere near light speed. Sort of a tortoise and hare thing, but the tortoise cheats. Welcome to the galaxy!"

"Is the alien there with you?"

"Yes, obviously, I am on his ship."

"Captain Winn, can you guarantee this communication is secure? Is the alien listening?"

The alien had no headphones on and was half-buried under an instrument console, busily testing and connecting the burnt, broken cables he had ripped out earlier.

"Quane, are you listening to or recording my conversation?"

"I'm not doing either." Quane turned his head to hide his grin; he was doing both.

"Mission Control, we are clear."

"Richard," said Mission Control, quietly, just in case the alien was listening, "we are not certain this alien has our best interests at heart."

"*Our* interests?"

"Earth's, that is. Do you really know where you went? Are you sure you were not subjected to drugs, hypnosis, or some other alien mind control? Were you probed in any way?"

"Quane never touched me." Richard was not feeling the joy he had expected from his return. "We went to Uranus. I saw it. You will have proof, if you watch and listen."

"Not sure we can wait that long," said Mission Control.

"What do you mean?"

"SCaTS was activated after your abduction. They will arrive in about twenty minutes. Your orders are to stand down, get back to the ISS, and let SCaTS take over. They have orders to capture the alien and his ship. If you have any way to lure the alien to the ISS to enable his capture, you are ordered to try. Any action toward ensuring the alien's capture would make you a hero. Any actions preventing his capture might be construed as treason."

Richard froze at the implication. Quane would be captured, interrogated, and eventually dissected. The ship would be seized and disassembled to back engineer the technology. The press cover story would be, "The courageous SCaTS successfully defended the earth against the first attempt to invade our planet. We must redouble our efforts to ensure we are ready for the next invasion, which may be more formidable than this one single invader." But if he helped Quane escape, there would be no engines and no trekking among the stars. The galaxy would be lost to humanity until the next alien salesperson came. If there ever was a next time.

Should he warn Quane now fretting over an instrument panel? Should he obey orders? Did he stand a chance with either decision? Could he really say he visited Uranus? So much had happened in the last two days and could not remember how much sleep he'd had. Was it possible his mind was playing tricks on him? Quane could have easily drugged him by introducing something into the air to overcome his willpower and allow his mind to be manipulated. Some Coué autosuggestion might have made him believe what he was seeing was real. Quane had said something about the air on his ship when Richard first stepped on board. He had encouraged him to remove his helmet and had said something about "tailoring the air" and how he should "breathe deeply." Was that when he was drugged?

No, it *was* real. Why would he bring him back if his intentions were not honorable—or, at the very least, commercial? All Richard had left to believe in, or hope for, was that a message would come soon and prove to everyone it was real. A decision had to be made in less than twenty minutes. Who could he trust?

Richard activated a secondary communication channel.

"Miriam, are you there?"

"Yes, Richard. I'm here. What do you need?"

"How would you like to meet an alien dog named Quane?"

CHAPTER 16

Quane had listened in on the Human conversation. He had been around this block many times before and knew enough not to harm soldiers trying to protect the virginal honor of their planet, yet he could not let them interfere with his sale. His play had to be timed perfectly. The soldiers had to arrive. They had to seize him and his ship. To expedite the situation, he had to go to the space station. If he had the Human astronauts come to his ship, it might appear he had taken more Human hostages. Only after the masters controlling the politicians and soldiers calculated the value of what he had to offer, decided the price was right, and ordered the soldiers to stand down could he finish the sale. He had to be caught willingly and released willingly. The drama had played out many times. Fortunately, none of his many mistakes were fatal. With a bit of luck his costume would remain intact in case the Earthlings reacted to his form like the Smez had. This planet had so much and he was so close. It was worth the risk to stay and finish the deal. Where were the robot drones now?

"Quane, would you like to visit the ISS and meet some other people from my planet? They are quite excited to meet you." Richard suppressed an urge to scratch him behind both ears.

"Absolutely." The enormous grin was buried in his elbow; preferring to be dropped from an orbiting shuttle onto the knife-edged, fungus-covered, vermin-crawling rocks of Attuclac instead of suffering more time among Humans. He activated the boom originally used to invite the ISS astronauts to his ship. "I'd love the opportunity to meet more of your kind."

"Don't you need a spacesuit?" Richard snapped his helmet in place, and ran through the test protocol. There was just enough air to get to the station.

A small compartment sprung open near the airlock and Quane pulled out a limp, transparent piece of fabric, like a thin plastic bag. Opening a seam, he stepped into the plastic, and sealed himself in. The plastic covered him from head to toe like a loose drop cloth over a piece of furniture before painting. Another button above the compartment sprung a plastic tube which was fixed to the thin envelope. As the air was sucked out, the plastic shrank until it conformed perfectly to Quane's dog-shaped body. His paws, claws, and tail were perfectly covered, like shrink-wrapped meat. After the suit fit him like a second skin, the process reversed and the suit filled with enough air to create a thumb-thick space between it and Quane. His paws were fitted with gloves after insertion into another opening. Finally, he attached a small bracelet with a hemisphere the size of a golf ball to his right foreleg.

"Ready for my walk. I hope it's a nice day."

"Quane," Richard pointed at the bracelet. "Is that some kind of weapon?"

"Weapon? Why would I take a weapon to a sales meeting? I know I'm a killer salesman, but I think you're taking it a little too far, Ricky. This is a simple communicator. I need to be in communication with my ship. It's a precaution, really. I mean, what if the toilet overflows, or I forgot to turn off a burner on the stove."

"OK, then. Let's do this." Richard glanced once more at Quane's suit and wondered if Miriam's experiments were onto something. How many generations would it take humanity to become so readily adapted to space they could spacewalk with such a flimsy suit?

This is it, Richard thought once again as he attached his tether to the boom extending from the right side of the open airlock on the alien spaceship. *Déjà vu all over again.* A faint notion that he was going the wrong way worried his thoughts. The future, Quane, and galactic exploration were behind him. The past was ahead of him. He was taking one step backward for a man and one thousand steps forward for humankind.

Quane was so constricted by the dog costume and bubble suit he could hardly move and asked to be towed to the station by a tether secured to his belt.

Richard's skin and soul grew warm in the bright Earth-shine in spite of his environmentally balanced spacesuit. He giggled to himself at the thought of stripping off his suit and floating naked in the void with his hands behind his helmet—which, obviously, he would need to breathe. When Mission Control questioned his sanity, he would reply that he was only trying to get a nice "Earth tan" before facing the cameras.

Richard hovered near the Quest airlock, ready to remove his tether from the boom. "ISS, request permission to come aboard."

"Request granted," said Fedor. All three ISS astronauts had watched the surreal motion of a space-suited man towing a bubble-wrapped, stuffed toy dog as the man made a hand-over-hand walk along a firefighter's pole to the hatch on the ISS. Mission Control had not granted permission for either one to come aboard. Quarantine protocols to protect humans from exposure to an alien pathogen were ignored by the ISS crew.

"Airlock secured," said Fedor. "Pressure equalized."

"Welcome aboard!" Nancy yelled into the microphone in Fedor's hand. He frowned at Nancy, miffed that she scooped his welcome.

Nancy, Fedor, and Miriam floated near the airlock door in breathless, unblinking anticipation of receiving both the first astronaut to make contact with an alien and the first alien the Human race had ever seen. Richard pulled himself out of the airlock and removed his helmet, while Quane floated behind like a balloon on a string.

"Greetings, all," said Richard.

"Hello!" yelled Nancy as she pushed off the nearest wall and sailed toward him with the intention of giving him an enormous welcome-back hug. Her inexperience with weightlessness turned it into a football tackle. She flew into him right shoulder first and grabbed him around the waist. Both slapped into the water bags on the pond with a squeaky plop. The displaced water sloshed back into place like a weak trampoline and bounced them back into the room. Quane saw Nancy coming and deftly somersaulted backward, out of harm's way.

"Wow. What a welcome." Richard's hair was swirling loosely.

"What happened to your hair?" Miriam said. "It's all messed up."

Richard reached up to press it back into place and shrugged. "It finally relaxed, I guess."

Further attention was diverted to his guest. "Members of the International Space Station, please meet Quane, a salesman of stardrive engines from the center of the galaxy." Richard managed an attempt at a weightless bow and flourished his arm in the alien's direction. Extending an upturned palm, he introduced the ISS crew. "Quane, please meet the members of the International Space Station: Nancy, Fedor, and Miriam."

Quane floated at the end of his tether like a talking piñata. "Excuse me, please, if I take a second to get out of this spacesuit." He unhooked the tether, undid the seam, and slipped out. The suit maintained its shape as Quane lightly pushed away the dog-shaped bubble.

"Your paw," Miriam said. "It's burned. Do you need first aid?"

Quane quickly tucked his paw behind his back. "It's nothing."

The talking dog and its marionette-like jaw was an attraction that left the crew speechless.

"We have to get on with this," Richard said. "The message is coming in about ten minutes." The question was would the message or SCaTS arrive first.

"Gotcha, Ricky. OK, group, let's get this over with." He slapped his paws together and a thin puff of soot came off his paw. "I am a stardrive salesman from a planet called Dia'Bolos near the center of the galaxy. In a little less than ten minutes, you will get proof these items can do what I promise in a message Ricky sent from the planet Uranus. I need to emphasize, this is a limited time offer. When I leave, I am not coming back. I will leave no card, phone number, or forwarding address.

"By the way, I think one of your spaceships with a group of soldiers is ready to board this station to take me prisoner and claim my technology."

Richard, Miriam, Nancy, and Fedor all started to speak when Quane held up a paw. "I am going to allow my capture in order for everyone to come to a mutual agreement on the purchase of these engines."

That he knew of the SCaTS' imminent arrival was not too surprising to the astronauts since he was an alien with advanced technology. The surprise was his wish to be taken captive. Four Humans were thrust into negotiations between an alien dog, willing to sell a device more significant to the advancement of human history than the discovery of fire, and the Human military, which needed to conquer the unknown.

"I for one am not going to let them take him," Miriam said, "or his ship." She floated to Quane's side and folded her arms across her chest, tilted her head back, set her jaw, and frowned. It was the first time she'd ever tried to look fierce and hoped it was working. She also wanted to sneak a peek at the dog's backside; there had not been any indication of sex from the front. A red horn was protruding from his fur next to an ear hanging on by a few bits of tendon. Crimson was visible in a separation of fur near his tail. Miriam mentally scrolled through her taxonomic record for examples of asexual mammals that molted; not only their hair but their entire skin.

"I'm with Miriam," Richard said. "I'll leave with Quane, never to return, before I let him be captured." And he would enthusiastically accept being an alien's cabin boy if it meant he could cruise the wonders of the galaxy for the rest of his life. He stared off, trying to remember his exact words at Uranus.

"Count me in," said Fedor. "I have nothing to lose and everything to gain by supporting our new friend." Perhaps this one event would prove how shortsighted and narrow-minded Earth had been in underfunding space exploration.

"I'll agree to whatever you all decide." Nancy could not place her life in a balance against politics, fame, or personal reward. She loved animals and wanted very much to hug and pet the alien dog and assure him everything would be all right. But she was unsure if a scratch behind an ear would be polite, considering he could talk. Would people like being petted by an alien without their consent just because they looked coincidentally like one of their domesticated animals?

"Since we are all on board," Quane said, "I have a plan to get us all out of this situation." He waved his paws to huddle the astronauts close to him. "Here's what I need you to do…"

CHAPTER 17

After being dropped from the belly of *Icarus B*, a booster rocket ignited on the back of the SCaTS capsule, catapulting the crew toward the ISS. The spent rocket dropped away and the capsule coasted toward the space station.

"ISS ETA in five minutes, sir," Chuck Martin said.

"Ladies and gentlemen," Ed Sherman was watching a live feed from Chuck's laptop. "This is what we get paid for, but never thought we might actually see. Every action, every word will be documented, dissected, analyzed, and reviewed. By your positive or negative actions, you and I will effectively write the rules of engagement with an extraterrestrial. I need your full attention. Do I make myself perfectly clear?"

"Sir! Yes, sir!" the SCaTS soldiers chorused. Ed thought he heard several shoe pairs click.

"Anyone want to leave?" Ed asked.

"Sir! No, sir!"

"Five minutes to ISS dock," Chuck informed the SCaTS crew. "ISS, request to commence docking maneuver. I repeat; shuttle to ISS. Request to dock at the Pressurized Mating Adapter, PMA 2."

"ISS here," said Fedor. "Proceed with docking."

The hatch of the PMA opened underneath Nancy's flag garden. Three members of the SCaTS team boarded. Two soldiers advanced with weapons ready. Their suits were ninja black from head to toe. Even their self-contained breathing apparatus face shields were blackened to prevent an enemy from reading or targeting their eyes. Chuck scanned the *Columbus* module on his left. Alex examined the *Kibo* module on his right. They nodded to each other and proceeded. Fan held back to guard the hatch. Danel monitored the group's progress from the shuttle. Despite Ed being 250 miles below, on Earth, the soldiers felt his glare burning on the back of their necks.

CHAPTER 18

Chuck and Alex scoured the four phone booth-sized sleep stations. They floated cautiously along the United States laboratory searching for hidden Humans, aliens, traps, or weapons. They turned the corner to face the ISS crew in *Tranquility*.

"Everyone freeze!" Chuck ordered as he and Alex established positions with their backs against the pond's water bags, their backs covered and padded against the recoil from the weapons.

The astronauts and alien were hovering motionless above the cupola. Nancy and Richard were on Quane's right. Miriam and Fedor were on his left.

The prisoners smiled patiently at the soldiers and the weapons trained on them. The weapons were made of lightweight plastic and resembled a child's Ping-Pong ball-blaster. They shot small, air-filled rubber bladders by the discharge from compressed CO_2 cartridges. The projectiles were designed to impact with distributed force—to stun or injure, but not penetrate. The weapons were nicknamed "Jeremiah" for the strange sound that the bladders made upon impact. Collision with an object forced the bladders to quickly release the trapped air with a deep bellow reminiscent of a bullfrog. Each weapon was fingerprint coded and completely useless unless in the hands of its assignee.

"Commander Richard Winn," Chuck ordered, "stand down. SCaTS is in charge now."

"We surrender." Richard held his hands high and open. "This is the alien. His name is Quane." Following his lead, the other astronauts raised their hands.

"Mr. Quane," Chuck said without lowering his weapon, "you are now in the custody of the Space Command and Tactics Squad. Surrender all arms, your ship, and prepare to come with us as our prisoner." The weapon's laser sight was an unmoving spot on the middle of Quane's chest. Alex ranged his laser site over each astronaut in random order.

"I surrender." He lifted his empty, open paws over his head. "But if I have to leave with you, I request my one phone call first."

Chuck started; he had practiced hundreds of enemy-resistance scenarios. During training, he had captured or killed every wild beast they had sent at him. But there was never an instructional condition where the prisoner surrendered willingly and requested his right for a phone call. Who would an alien call anyway? Reinforcements?

"Mother," Chuck said, "this is Point. Have objective in sight. Subject is not armed. Subject requests a phone call. Advise."

"Point," Ed said, "this is Mother. We heard. Ask it who it wants to call."

"I want to talk to the president of the United States," Quane said loudly enough for all to hear, "and the prime minister of the United Kingdom, as well as the leaders of every country on Earth." Richard nodded ever so slightly.

The nod affirmed he had enabled communication and Quane's message was sent. SCaTS had scrambled all communication from the ISS to Earth in order to prevent any communications from the ISS to Earth. They forgot—or, more appropriately, were not informed—about an emergency channel. A backdoor channel existed in case a rogue Earth government attempted to acquire the ISS for their own interests and block communication in the same way SCaTS did now. Richard had activated the emergency frequency minutes before SCaTS landed. The emergency channel was a hotline to the joint chiefs of staff, the speaker of the House, the vice president, and the president.

"Point," Ed said, "request denied. Take it now."

Chuck began a move toward the alien with Alex covering him.

"Stop." Quane held out his burnt paw. Chuck reached back to grab the cargo netting to halt his motion.

"I started a self-destruct sequence on my ship before I left. Not only will my ship and your station be destroyed, but your planet will suffer the fallout from the explosion. I am not familiar with the biology of your planet, but I have seen other planets use these same engines as weapons of last defense during their wars." This was not a lie and he his face was sober. Flock, the catalyst that enabled the dark matter reaction was the most toxic substance known to galactic-kind.

"I have to be allowed to get back to my ship to disarm the bomb." Quane smiled and nodded. There was no self-destruct device and he had no intention to kill any Humans or himself. He was using their science fiction mythology against them to buy a little time to make the sale.

"Sir," Chuck said, "did you hear that?"

"Affirmative. Stand down, but maintain positions. Wait for further orders."

The SCaTS soldiers lowered their Jeremiahs halfway, but kept their fingers on the triggers.

Quane started a mental countdown. These backwater planets always coveted alien technology, but were afraid of it blowing up in their faces. That fear roughly correlated with how advanced they were technologically. If they were not advanced enough to keep a fertilizer plant from blowing up, how could they safely poke at an alien power source? Even if they decided to poke at it on the backside of a moon, how could they ensure the fallout would not destroy the ozone layer, interfere with military communication, or, worst of all, interrupt their satellite TV signals?

Planets with inhabitants ignorant of atomic power, how to build and launch satellites, and clueless regarding the health effects of exploding excrement were not worth his time. No amount of talk could persuade them to purchase his technology. Earthlings were slightly above that level of galactic imbecile.

It was only a matter of time now. Three, two, one...

CHAPTER 19

"This is the president of the United States," Burke said. "Am I addressing the alien named Quane?" He stared at the speakerphone while still trying to rub the inspirational genie from his desk. The Oval Office was crowded with advisers, campaign managers, lobbyists from the weapons industry, and congressmen and senators from both sides of the aisle. The Rose Garden doors were shut tight and a phalanx of black-suited, sun-glassed, and wired up Secret Service agents blocked most of the light coming in the windows. Burke didn't know which smell was worse; the cheap body sprays on his personal advisers or the expensive cologne on the lobbyists.

The rug Burke picked for the Oval Office displayed the presidential seal in relief instead of color; the pile was cut to different depths to bring out the pattern by the subtle difference in shadows. It was doubtful the pile would ever recover after being trampled by this crowd.

The president had ordered Mission Control to patch his feed to every monitor on the ISS.

"My name is Quane." He bowed formally to no one in particular. The negotiations had finally begun.

"I have all leaders from the major countries of the earth on a conference call with me," the president said. "Please, state your intentions."

"My intentions are very simple, I am here to sell your planet stardrive engines to take your Smez, I mean Human, race into space. You are invited to become involved in the exchange of goods, culture, science, and art that more than ten thousand planets throughout the galaxy already enjoy. This is a quality bit of merchandise. I don't think you can afford to pass it up."

"First, Mr. Quane," the president said, "how can we trust you when you kidnapped a person from our planet? Second, do you really believe we do not have the sophistication to understand your technology and copy it? Third, and most importantly, what assurance do we have that your technology can do what you say?" The president and his chief adviser had a short whispered exchange.

"And what about this self-destruct sequence?" Burke stopped rubbing the desk. The uninformed crowd stared at him dumbfounded.

"Mr. President, sir." Richard addressed the walls of the ISS as if the president's disembodied voice lived somewhere within them. "I went with Quane willingly. I was under no duress. We traveled to Uranus and back."

"Captain Winn," the president said, "there is some concern that you were drugged and taken against your will, and possibly never went anywhere at all."

"That was my fault, sir." Miriam pleaded with the voice coming from the space station walls to understand and forgive her motives. "It was my speculation from watching the tapes before Richard vanished that he might have been drugged. I was trying to account for every contingency."

"I can explain." This was taking too long. He had to be gone before the probes found his good engine, or he would never get to spend any of his profits and might be marooned here forever.

"I am here to negotiate the sale of stardrive technology. As your Human astronaut has witnessed, it works perfectly. We went halfway to the edge of your solar system and back in four hours and it can take you to the center of the galaxy in roughly ten Earth years. Please turn your attention to your planet Uranus. Your astronaut sent a message from there. This unit performs so well we actually arrived here before the message. If you listen and look, you will hear the proof that this high-quality, lightly used, perfectly functioning machine will make all your space faring dreams a reality."

The plan Quane laid out with the ISS crew before SCaTS arrived had them use their cell phones to call astronomical observatories and inform them of the incoming transmission from Uranus. All available observatories recalibrated their instruments to intercept the transmission and informed local television stations of the impending message. Each facility was promised they would be credited with the astronomical scoop of the century.

"Mr. Quane," said the president, "I am afraid there is not enough time to contact all of the observatories before the message arrives... What?" The president covered the telephone speaker with his fingers to listen to an adviser. "Turn on a monitor. No, I don't care what station."

Quane, the ISS astronauts, and the SCaTS members listened in on the news report playing in the background, muffled by the president's hand. Richard winked at Quane, but the alien ignored the contact, occupied with tugging and itching. Several deep scars in his fur revealed dark-red skin underneath.

"We interrupt this program to share breaking news," said the dapper white-haired news anchor. He had a satisfied smirk and tiny crow's feet at the corners of his eyes—this report might become the acme of his illustrious career. "As you know, an alien ship appeared near the ISS three days ago. It flashed a welcome sign until yesterday, when one astronaut, Canadian Richard Winn, made his way to the extraterrestrial craft and was recorded making first contact with an alien civilization. Strangely enough, these aliens look much like man's best friend, the dog.

Shortly after Captain Winn boarded the craft, it disappeared. There was no contact of any kind until recently. Four hours after it disappeared, it just as magically reappeared outside the ISS with Captain Winn and the alien on board. According to anonymous sources, the alien craft was able to fly to Uranus, which is at the edge of the solar system—almost four billion, that's right, *billion,* miles away from Earth—and back in four short hours. To prove the alien technology works, Winn sent Earth a message from Uranus, knowing he would arrive back at the ISS before the message. He predicted when and where to look for the message. Observatories have confirmed the message was received thirty minutes after the craft arrived, and from exactly the point predicted. What you will hear next is the full text of that message, uncensored.

"'This is Captain Richard Winn from the International Space Station…'" The news anchor played the entire message while nodding slowly in solemn contemplation of the speech. Tears welled in eyes, as if awed by a Human future filled with interstellar flight. The anchor was actually straining to maintain his composure while being tortured by a thorny tickle at the back of his throat. Any cough or sip of water would break the spell of pensive reflection he was conveying to his audience. He gathered as much saliva as he could and swallowed hard.

"As incredible as it might seem," said the anchor, "it appears space travel is possible, and Captain Richard Winn has been the first Human to visit Uranus. Other sources, who insist on remaining anonymous, claimed Winn was the first person to see planets outside the solar system. And, on at least one of the newly discovered planets, there are enormous cities with skyscrapers built from solid gold occupied by beings that resemble flying pigs. For more details about this and the other fabulous discoveries, watch our regularly scheduled eleven o'clock report. Now, a message from our sponsor." With the cameras finally off, the anchorman went into a fifteen-minute, gut-wrenching, sweaty coughing spasm.

"Do you believe me now, Mr. President?'" asked Quane.

"All right," said the president. "I admit the evidence supports your statement that you and Captain Winn took a spin around space and your engine is capable of interstellar travel." The president paused to be sure he correctly understood the mimed prompts he was receiving from half the bystanders in his office. "On behalf of the American people, I have to ask you, sir, how many engines do you have to sell, and at what price?" The defense-industry lobbyists elbowed their way nearer to the president's desk.

"I regret I only have this one to sell." The regret that the drones had destroyed his other two engines was real. "My price is trifling. A pittance compared to what your planet has to offer. There is no way you could possibly feel even slightly poorer for the price."

"Try us," said the president. The Oval Office crowd had surrounded the president, silenced their cell phones, and was fixated on the speakerphone. For a split second, Burke thought they all had been frozen by one of Gregory's "nonexistent" memory rays.

"What I would accept for this sound and perfectly functioning item is no less than twenty-five thousand genomes." Quane winced at his brazen stab at wealth.

CHAPTER 20

"Genomes? Like DNA?" The president was startled at the request, expecting to have to negotiate over oil reserves, several tons of rare minerals, virgins, or country music…but *genomes*?

"Exactly," said Quane. "The DNA sequencing of twenty-five thousand individual examples of your plant and animal species. It doesn't matter if you consider them higher or lower forms of life. A variety is preferred. It's only a suggestion, but examples from every kingdom, phylum, class, order, family, genus, and species would be just super."

"What could you possibly want with all that?" The president's advisers were waving their arms wildly, miming at the president to stretch out the conversation. They needed time to work out the moral, philosophical, and political ramifications of giving an alien dog blueprints for life.

"Well," said Quane, "it's simple. You Humans place a high value on diamonds and precious metals. To us, those are useless pieces of crystalized carbon and rock. Vigorous life takes centuries to develop and prove its resistance and adaptability to environmental changes. That kind of life is extremely valuable in the galaxy."

"But what assurances do we have…" the president hesitated so as not to get ahead of his coaches, animatedly signing, waving, and lip-synching to him. "…that what we give you will be used only for the most honorable purposes?"

"Obviously the purposes are most honorable. Ask anyone here on your station if I look like the type that would take advantage of a situation, or even consider placing the tiniest creature in harm's way. Many beings may be profoundly allergic, repulsed, or poisoned by what you give me. Your genomes could possibly annihilate whole planets if not examined first and introduced properly. They will be tested by a team of our best governmental scientists before dissemination." The scientists would only get what was left after Quane filtered out the most profitable black-market items.

"I will have to consult with our top scientists," the president said—meaning campaign managers. "Can you give us forty-eight hours?"

"I can't. I have an important meeting with a delegation of activists promoting the latest laws against cruelty to animals. It seems there are no laws to prevent pet owners who are tired of, or can no longer take care of, their pet from ejecting their unwanted animal into the vacuum of space. It is nothing less than an abomination and must stop. It is quite personal to me." He sniffed and used the action of wiping a forced tear to hide his lie.

"One half hour or I leave and never return." His costume was getting drafty from the opening seams. His identity had to remain hidden until he was paid in case, like the Smez, they reacted violently to his real form. He snuck furtive glances out the cupola's windows and prayed the drones would not arrive until after he left with his loot. Then the drones could destroy his merchandise and Earth. Quane's anxiety made him sweat and itch. Itching ripped more seams, and ripping seams refueled his anxiety.

"Mr. Quane," said the president, "you must realize a decision of this magnitude must be fully—"

The Russian president cut in. "The Russian people will pay thirty thousand genomes for this engine."

The Chinese premier upped the stakes. "The People's Republic of China bids forty thousand genomes for the engine."

"This is the prime minister of Great Britain, fifty thousand—"

"Now wait just a minute," the president interrupted. "We can't go bidding the planet away without a little reasoned thought and—"

"Seventy-five thousand genomes!" said the Russian.

"Eighty-five thousand!" offered the Chinese.

"One hundred thousand!" exclaimed the British.

"Wait! Stop!" yelled the president. "Quane, I'll be right back." Communication stopped.

Quane was giddy from the level of the bidding. He had forgotten what it was like to deal with a planet without a unified, dictatorial government. Few planets were still as fractured as Earth. Knowing that his technology worked, they would overbid its true worth and he would make a fortune.

He would take his time examining the loot. Anything the least bit addictive, he would sell to the black market to be manufactured. There was no end to the venom, saliva, and excrement that some species somewhere would not ingest, inject, or rub in their frake holes to get high. Several new religions would probably grow from this haul.

After the illegal drug industry, the next level of value was the gift industry, which paid well for novel and interesting items for religious sacrifice and offerings of gratitude after a family member finally up and died and left them rich. The remainder he would sell to educational and government scientists to dissect, categorize, theorize upon, and write thesis papers. Nothing much useful came out of the science. Everything important to daily life came from the black market.

Quane stood to make an enormous profit and could pay off Wyruk with a fortune leftover. Depending on how many genomes he received, he might hold some in reserve and release them slowly over the years. There was no sense in flooding the market. For many years to come, he could just lie back and let it happen.

If only he could make his getaway.

The ISS astronauts and SCaTS had listened in silence.

Quane was weightlessly twirling, itching, and scratching like a flea-bitten cur rolling in a raspberry patch. His fur was coming off in clumps. Nancy couldn't stand watching his obvious discomfort and reached out to scratch his head with both hands. Her nails snagged the costume. Before she knew it, a limp dog costume head was dangling from her fingertips. Quane was exposed, a Dia'Bolos: the devil himself.

"You're a devil!" Nancy cried.

Nancy's alarm alerted Chuck and Alex and they fixed their weapons on Quane. He had been concealing his identity; was he also concealing weapons?

The mask was gone. The Humans, the Smez, had seen him. He was naked, with no tricks left; he was at their mercy. Instinctively, he hugged his knees, curled into a ball, and waited to be shot, beaten, and jettisoned into space. "Go suck the vac!" was a common galactic imperative from persons or beings slighted, rightly or wrongly, by other persons or beings, and wanted the galact-hole to be permanently eliminated from the universe by cursing them to inhale the void.

Instead, Nancy tenderly touched the spinning devil dog. "Are you OK?"

Quane unfurled cautiously and faced the Humans. His black marble eyes squinted at the expected assault; he was not smiling.

"Are you molting?" Miriam asked. "Is this some kind of metamorphosis?"

"All of you," Alex said, "move away from the alien slowly. He is obviously in disguise." Chuck and Alex had moved to positions ninety degrees from the alien. Alex was floating high; Chuck was low. Long bayonets had been fixed to the barrels of their Jeremiahs. "Quane, very slowly remove the rest of your uniform. Make no sudden movements."

Quane found the internal zipper and freed himself from the constricting costume. He floated in all his crimson, devilish, Dia'Bolos glory, ready to trade everything: his ship, habitat, and one good engine—he hoped was still at Mars—for his freedom and his life.

Incredibly, the Smez—the Humans—did not attack.

"Amazing," Miriam said. "Tell me more about your planet, your civilization. You look exactly like what we call 'devils.'" Miriam and Richard grabbed for the discarded costume as a souvenir and scientific prize.

"Devils?" Quane's black eyes flitted around the room. If he could keep them talking, maybe he could also find a way to distract the soldiers and escape.

"Devils," Miriam said, "are what we humans consider the personification of evil and the source of all sorrow and tragedy afflicting humanity. It must be pure coincidence that your evolution made you into the perfect caricature of the devil."

CHAPTER 21

The ISS connection to Earth snapped back to life.

"Mr. Quane," President Burke said, "on behalf of all the governments on Earth, I am authorized to pay you two hundred thousand genomes for your engine. But before I do, I need to ask some questions."

"Please do." He almost swooned at the windfall.

"First," said the president, "you mentioned a self-destruct sequence. How do we know you turned it off? And it won't explode after you leave with the genomes?" This was Burke's first foray into a negotiation that resembled an interplanetary drug deal.

"Remember you threatened me with soldiers and weapons first. I was only responding in defense. Since we have an agreement, there is no need for me to destroy this engine. Besides, now that I know you have the genomes to pay, I will return with as many as you want to buy. Why would I want to destroy my newest best customer?" The lying smile appeared totally genuine to the crew and soldiers on the ISS.

The space station speakers rumbled with several minutes of tense, muffled argument. The ISS occupants heard:

"… how to trust…"

"…alien terrorist…"

"…pure extortion!"

"…chance of a lifetime…"

"… got to lose?"

"If we agree to trust you, Quane," said the president, "we need a warranty or guarantee that this engine will perform as tested for a length of time. If it fails before the warranty expires, we expect it to be repaired or replaced with one of equal value without additional cost."

"What is your time period?"

"We think five years is reasonable," the president said firmly.

"That is a standard length of time where I'm from." Quane smiled gleefully. It might not last five Earth days. What did he care? He would never see another Human again. Ever. "Next?"

Richard smiled broadly; his chest was inflated with pride. He had helped negotiate the pivotal sale to define human history for millennia to come. Miriam was frowning as she fingered the shed skin. It seemed to be some type of synthetic fabric instead of biological material. Fedor rubbed his chin, imagining the metallurgical analysis of the engine's metal and experiments to determine its propulsion principles. Nancy hugged herself with her eyes closed. The first thing she would do back on Earth would be to rough and tumble with Shemp until they both passed out from exhaustion.

Chuck and Alex were unmoving and unmoved. They would not let their guard down until the deal was done, the alien gone, and the ISS secured.

"We need the operational manuals to understand how to adapt the engine to our systems," the president said.

"Certainly. The manuals have been translated and are ready for transfer to the station's computers."

"Finally, we need your contact information if we have any concerns, questions, or problems."

"I will add that information as an appendix to the operator's manual." Quane knew further contact was impossible, since communications could not penetrate the membrane. By the time Humans figured out how to interface the engine and travel to dark space, he would be long gone. "Anything else?"

"How would you like payment?"

"Upload the genomes to the computers here on the station. I will take the information from them." Quane suppressed the urge to dance a weightless jig; thoughts of the nearby drones sobered him.

"First detach the engine and anchor it to the ISS." The Oval Office crowd had loosened their ties and removed their suit jackets. Some were sweating with anticipation, some were salivating with desire. President Burke's galactic bucking bronco was tiring; he just might win this rodeo. "When the transfer is complete, we will upload the genomes."

"I will detach my habitat from your engine and anchor it to the ISS. I have a small power supply to get me back to one I have parked at Mars to take me home." He would work slowly, but deliberately, at transferring the stardrive. And also monitor and secretly intercept the upload with the golf ball-sized remote computer on his wrist. The Humans would think he needed to go back to the ISS to physically retrieve his payment.

Long ago, Quane learned from a patron in an out of the way bar that it was imperative to intercept communications on the sly. The stranger was drinking a Kick Your Klaardid cocktail—one part vinegar; two parts fermented goo from the folds of a male Shiel; three parts Sleens: the digested remains of a blind, brainless, weasel-faced creature after passing through the nineteen stomachs of a two-horned Trazom; all shaken and poured over two frozen methane cubes and one frozen ammonia cube.

The story went that one planet's residents had tricked the stranger into transferring a very nice, slightly used, secondhand engine into their possession and then arrogantly denied payment. They flung insults and missiles at him. He made his escape, but had the last laugh.

He never tried to recoup his loss; he simply never submitted the "Official Certificate of Transfer of Registration of a Used Intra-Galactic Engine for Personal Use Only," to the GMVD, the Galactic Motor Vehicle Department. Coincidentally, when this form's bureaucratic title, OCoToRoaUIGEfPUO, was spoken in a slow, guttural voice, it was an insulting reference to hack off a particularly delicate part of one's anatomy, dry it in the hot sun, grind the result to dust, mix it with putrid Grotch flesh, and eat the resulting mix as a dip with nachos. This salesman anonymously reported the stardrive as unregistered and gave an approximate location to the drone police.

That engine, along with the first batch of twenty-seven missionaries who had been sent to spread the divine word of their invisible, only-to-be-known-personally, all-powerful Super-Friend, was captured. The ship was confiscated and the passengers taken to prison. Three galactic novitiates were killed for food by other prisoners before it was discovered that no amount of putrid Grotch flesh could mask their awful taste. Two others died from the olfactory assault of prison stench. The rest were converted to a transcendental cult believing in shouting loudly and continuously without saying anything in particular cleansed the body, mind, and soul. Cult members who were not imprisoned made comfortable livings recording infomercials, or as political pundits.

The stranger laughed so hard at the thought of his payback to his enemies that his glanux fully dilated, depriving him of methane. Before he pass out, his Kick Your Klaardid drink only half finished, he muttered, smiling, "I lost mine, but they got theirs."

CHAPTER 22

"Quane," Richard said, "is there nothing else on Earth to use as payment for an engine? I could cash in my retirement fund and buy whatever you want—jewelry, gold, flower seeds…" He reached into his pants for his wallet, forgetting he still had his spacesuit on.

"No, there is nothing valuable here other than the variety of novel and unique plant and animal species." Humans, like most backward species, did not understand that their highly prized minerals were valueless. There were countless unpopulated planets and moons providing all the elements needed to support building and maintaining a galactic civilization for the simple cost of mining and transport.

"Quane," Miriam said, "you really mean to take blueprints of various Earth species to pollenate the galaxy with Earth's flora and fauna?" Miriam understood the value of what he was getting in payment and knew the true depth of Earth's genome well: almost nine million known plant and animal species living in the air, on land, and under Earth's vast seas. New insects were being discovered daily. Countless undiscovered life-forms lived under polar ice, thrived in volcanic craters, or danced between tectonic plates under crushing ocean pressure.

"Yes," Quane said, "it's true. A fraction of these items will be sold. After all, I do have to make a living." The translator let him avoid an outright lie. He was going to sell a *large* fraction.

"I am a salesman, but I am also an emancipator of life. Believe me when I tell you that life, in all its forms, is the most valuable commodity in the galaxy. Planets consider themselves lucky if their narrow environmental windows can support ten thousand species. Planets with a hundred thousand plant and animal varieties have been made into high-class vacation resorts.

"Life is a limited commodity because of its lifespan, and it's fragile because it can become extinct overnight if an environment goes bad. Life is also a regenerative, renewable, and adaptable commodity. The genomes I take will be guaranteed to live forever. They will be freed from this single environment—which could fail at any moment—and will be ensured a continuity of existence somewhere in the galaxy."

Shortly after the discovery of the stardrive engine principal, life was transplanted in almost every hospitable environment. Local novelty was diluted by cross-pollination. Not only was life valuable for keeping a planet—and the galaxy—vibrant, but new life-forms were valuable in rejuvenating planets made barren because of natural environmental variations, and unintended or deliberate habitat destruction.

"So you really are here with earth's best interests at heart," said Miriam.

"Most definitely." Especially if those interests meant he would make an enormous profit.

"I'm still suited up," Richard said. "Can I help you disconnect the engine? I'd love to see how it is attached to your pod."

"I could use your help." If the Human was with him, Earth would not risk an attack. The transfer was a simple task and the Human would be an effective hostage and bullet shield. Quane sealed himself back in his doggy bubble.

"How will we communicate out there?"

"Come on, Ricky, you must know I can listen in on your communications. All I have to do is broadcast on the same frequency so you and everyone else can hear what we are saying.

I want to assure everyone that everything is on the up and up. Ready?"

"Ready as I'll ever be." Richard opened the Quest airlock. Fedor helped slide him in feetfirst.

"Will we ever see you again?" Miriam said. "I'd love to hear about the evolution of your species, your planet. What is life like in the rest of the galaxy? How much is intelligent?"

The airlock was just big enough for Quane to squeeze in at Richard's chest and allow the human to hug his balloon animal.

"Look me up and we'll have tea," Quane said before the airlock thudded closed.

"Do you have religion? Philosophy?" She yelled at the closed hatch.

The two spacewalkers made their way to the beat-up spaceship via the boom still extended from Quane's ship. The exterior of the habitat pod had recessed handholds to allow an easy hand over hand pull. An arm's length from the engine, Quane opened a recess and retrieved a device the size and shape of a car's steering wheel. He fixed a foot-long shaft with a triangular socket to the wheel's center.

"Use this to loosen the bolts on the shackles. Press this button," Quane touched a rocker switch near Richard's right hand. "Press here to spin right, press this other button to spin left. From what I have translated, you are the only planet in the galaxy that spins right to tighten and left to loosen. Everyone else does the opposite. And don't let the bolts fly off into space. Tighten them back into the pod anchors so I can use them again."

Richard took the instrument and floated to the nearest shackle. The bolts had triangular heads. The first bolt spun off easily. The cable floated away and he replaced the bolt onto the stay. He repeated this for three more cables. Quane had disconnected his three cables from the bar.

"I guess I screwed up. I thought the cables stayed with the engine."

"There's no time to change it back." The robot drones' whereabouts was a great unknown. What if they had already found his working engine? He had to make a run for it as soon as possible. Three stays would be enough to hold the pod to the stardrive at Mars as long as he minimized acceleration.

"Connect the tether from the ISS to any one of the stays," Quane said, "and it's all yours. Last but not least, tie off the command and control cable."

Richard noticed Quane's nervousness. They did not make eye contact the entire time and his attention was not on his hands, but something unseen around him.

Quane rolled up the electrical cable and checked the hemisphere sized golf ball attached to his right foreleg. A single flashing light signified the upload of the genomes to his computer was complete. There was no need to stick around with these Smez reminders a nanosecond longer.

"It's time for me to leave, Ricky."

"What? You're not coming back to the station to get your genomes?"

"How many times do I have to tell you that I can intercept your communications? I downloaded everything while you were uploading. I have my payment and you have your engine. I can't tell you how indebted I am to you for all your help. I really don't think I could have made this sale without you."

Quane extended his glove and bubble-coated hand in friendship. Richard took it and their eyes met. Tears welled in Richard's eyes at the imminent loss of his greatest teacher. Quane's tears were from the joy of success after a lifetime of failure.

Richard grabbed the tether to the ISS and tugged his way back to the station. Quane slithered his way into the open hatch on his pod.

Back at the ISS, Richard admitted to the others, "You know, I think he really likes us and is sad to leave. I know I'm going to miss him."

In his pod, Quane entered the word "devil" into his galactic encyclopedic computer. There was something familiar about the word. Humans were Smez-like idiots and probably would not go far in the galaxy, but at least they had made him incredibly rich. And, Bleen be praised, there was no sign of the drones. He began to believe he might make it out of there alive *and* rich.

Quane retracted the boom and initiated the idling motor. Slowly, the plate slid off the end of the bar. Without streamers, confetti, or fanfare, the ISS crew watched from the cupola as the alien ship slowly decreased in size as it headed to Mars.

The ship's computer identified several hallucinogenic drug secretors from the batch of data. One was called "Bat." Sniffing its dander induced a hallucinogenic high that convinced the user they were driving in an expansive, open-topped transportation device while being attacked by distorted, winged humanoids. Bat alone would make him a fortune.

There were a few medicinal applications. Some promised to be interesting seasonings. But one actually looked like it could do almost anything. It was so developed for survival that its DNA coding enabled near immortality on any and every populated planet. Each part of this creature had value. Quane assumed it was sheer Human stupidity that this ancient, aboriginal species was not exalted.

The galaxy might forever revere the name of this creature. Children would be named for it. Planets and solar systems, once barren before its introduction, would rechristen themselves by adopting variations on the name.

All of the galaxy would know its name: Cockroach.

CHAPTER 23

Mars appeared dull and red. The south polar cap was smaller than when Quane arrived. The top of the planet was smooth and uninterrupted, as if covered by a calm reddish sea. Olympic Mons, the largest volcano in the solar system, pointed a celebratory thumbs-up.

The one functioning engine was exactly where he had left it—in low orbit above the planet. Nothing could ruin his feeling of accomplishment. Wyruk would be paid with interest and enough left over to live like a king, surrounded by servants and sycophants. His pod mated easily and he took a minute to appreciate the view. This solar system had been enormously valuable to him.

In his final glance at Mars before entering the habitat, he saw it. At first, he denied it. He tried his best to refute it. But there it was, without a doubt. Turning his head side to side and twisting his weightless body upside down did not change the image. Cut into the Martian surface was the symbol of the Smez: a perfect circle with an arrow jutting out from one edge. It was smudged and eroded by time, but there it was, definitely and indisputably. The same symbol he saw carved into the Smez planet, Mars Lost, halfway across the galaxy.

Quane entered the habitat and doffed his spacesuit. The encyclopedic computer flashed a confirmation that it had found a historical reference for devil.

Before opening the reference material, he slapped his forehead for his idiocy at not making the connection sooner.

"Mars and Mars Lost." He held out both hands palm up.

"Humans look like Smez and live near Mars." His left hand flipped over. "The Smez live on Mars Lost." The right hand turned over.

"And both——" He clasped his hands together. "——have the same image of a Dia'Bolos as the 'personification of evil and the source of all sorrow and tragedy afflicting humanity' as Miriam said."

The computer display scrolled its findings. D'vil was the name of an ancient Dia'Bolos that lived approximately fifty thousand years ago. His small claim to encyclopedic glory was that he was the first to leave his planet as a stardrive salesman. Little was known about D'vil after StarDrive Engines, Inc. drove all independent dealers out of business. Rumor said he became one of the many black-market stardrive sellers who roamed the galaxy looking for technological suckers.

Quane praised Bleen the engine started on the first try. Mars, Earth, Humans, and Smez vanished. The course for Nilrebwen was plotted and initiated. The gravity in his accelerating habitat forced him to hopscotch his way over the knife-edged shrapnel on the floor to get to the living quarters. Trash bits now grounded scurried away from his kicks. He brushed the Shnacuoilitian pornography off a stained broken cot and flopped down.

Instead of pushing imaginary Smez one by one into a massive black hole while drifting off to sleep, Quane tried to piece the Human-Smez puzzle together. A long time ago, Smez left Mars and made it to Mars Lost, where he met them. They must have had a stardrive engine, but he had not detected any evidence they were space-faring. If D'vil had sold them a junked stardrive at Mars, and it got them as far as Mars Lost before it broke down completely, the marooned Smez would naturally revile anyone that looked like D'vil. Abandoned and exiled on a strange planet, forced to rebuild a civilization from scratch, Smez culture would understandably mythologize the Dia'Bolos as the source of their misery and would attack anyone looking like them at first sight.

Somehow, Martian Smez must have landed on Earth a long time ago and evolved into the Humans Quane met. They also reviled the Dia'Bolos image as the entity that exiled them from their ancestral home, banishing them to another planet with no chance of repatriation. Every time they gazed starward, they saw their paradise lost floating in the night sky.

But Humans had treated him as a curiosity rather than the personification of evil in need of destruction. Perhaps the Earth-bound Smez' hatred of devils was tempered by the knowledge that Earth was more hospitable than their dying Mars.

This brief but inconclusive history lesson was reason enough never to return to this part of the galaxy. His hibernation would last until he reached home, where he could make his fortune. His eyelids drooped. His body felt both heavy as lead and perfectly weightless.

"Flock the Humans," he muttered, "and the Smez." His eyelids flickered. Dreamless sleep enveloped him.

CHAPTER 24

Richard turned around on his way back to the ISS and watched Quane's ship shrink silently away. The emotional loss of both a new friend and the fulcrum with which humanity would leverage its future emptied him more efficiently than if he had opened his helmet and sucked in the vacuum of space. He fumble-bumped out of the Quest air lock.

"Did we get it?" Richard asked anyone who would listen. "The engine?"

"We have it." Fedor turned his head and grimaced at Richard's odor. "And the operator's manual with schematics. Houston was asking if you remember bumping into the Voyager I satellite on your trip to Uranus. For some reason, they lost contact with it. They insisted I ask."

"I don't remember." Exhaustion was tugging his eyelids down. If he had been in full gravity, he could have fallen asleep standing up. "I didn't see anything and we didn't hit anything. Right now, all I can think about is getting to Earth to let them know the potential of what they bought."

"Sir," said Chuck, "Alex and I have been ordered to stay behind on the ISS and give you our seats on the return SCaTS shuttle. Mission Control wants to debrief you as soon as possible." The soldier saluted.

Richard acknowledged the salute with a weak wave. "How soon will the shuttle leave?"

"Fifteen minutes," Chuck said.

Richard conversed with Miriam, Nancy, and Fedor through a dreamy haze. Counting the forty-eight hours before leaving for Quane's ship, he had been awake for over sixty hours. The excitement of meeting a new species and the possibility of humanity's first reach for the stars had sustained him. Now, he was physically and emotionally spent. He felt as old as humanity and twice as exhausted. Richard clambered into the shuttle and buckled himself in. The bulky suit took up both seats and his helmet was so big, he had to lean sideways.

"Sir," Fan said. Richard was already starting to snore. "This engine, is it really a big deal?"

"It's the stuff dreams are made of," he grunted before falling into the abyss of long-overdue sleep.

PART 2

CHAPTER 25

The purchase of the first interstellar drive engine opened wide the door and rolled out a red carpet at humanity's feet to pursue galactic exploration, to identify and lay claim to new resources, to discover and colonize habitable planets, and to interact and trade with who knew what aliens for galactic goods and technology. Every government craved a share of the potential profits from space exploration. Since the engine was purchased with Earth's most abundant natural resource, life, no single country or group of countries could claim sole ownership of the technology; all realized gains would have to be shared. Earth owned the engine; thus, every country was entitled to a base share, but a new habitat had to be built, furnished, and supplied. The size of a share was scaled to the level of participation in the preparation for that first foray into the galactic unknown. If a country could not provide finished parts, they might supply the raw materials to be machined. If they could not supply raw materials, they offered the ores to be refined. If a country had no natural resources or manufacturing base, they donated labor or cash. If they had none of the above, they were relegated to wallflower status—sitting alone on the sidelines while all the cool countries partied.

A shift occurred in international politics. World governments and institutions had to decide whether to continue funding aggressive behaviors and armaments designed to hold neighboring political systems at bay, or realign those resources toward space exploration.

Countries conducted media blitzes rivaling the promotion of a world war. Bonds were sold, rationing was imposed, and posters encouraged sacrifice for the greater good. Neighboring countries once chastised as evil incarnate were soon downgraded to mere nuisances and ignored. Taxes were raised. Defense budgets were slashed. Social programs were reduced. Every redirection of government funds from Earthly concerns to space exploration shared the same argument: every dollar invested in space would have a tenfold, twentyfold, or hundredfold return. Future economic security required a relatively minor sacrifice today. Tens of thousands of jobs were created to support the space effort.

By the year 5 AQ, the International Space Station had grown and changed names to become the International Space Center, but not the stereotypical spaceport of science fiction imaginings. Modules were added hastily and haphazardly to extend the ISC's reach to dock with the engine without the least regard for the most basic of Feng Shui principles. In its final form, the space center resembled a twisted, arthritic, mechanical hand holding a battered pencil by its fingertips. Internally, the ISC was a hamster tunnel maze. Corridors were clogged with new or leftover building materials. The lights, plumbing, and air purification systems failed frequently and unexpectedly. The residents were sleep-deprived, slovenly, and surly.

Scientists from all nations fought mightily for a chance to visit the ISC to investigate the physical principles behind the stardrive reaction, gather information to write papers, and, hopefully, discover a new physical law to hang their name on or, in the secrecy of their private imaginations, for which they might win the Nobel Prize. Engineers came for extended stays to read the operator's manuals left by Quane and learn how to interface the engine's electrical power supply and maintain the life support systems of a Human habitat pod. Technicians came to maintain the existing ISC systems and prepare for the next upgrade.

The weightless environment on the space center station required regular turnover in personnel to prevent debilitating physical damage. Upkeep and buildout meant supply ships and passenger shuttles docked several times a day. Scientists, political liaisons, technicians, janitors, and commercial spies found their way onto the ISC.

The richest nations had either singular or coordinated plans to create individual, traditional-style, wheel-like spinning space stations independent of the ISC. Big money was betting that the next time a stardrive salesman arrived, they would prefer to visit an upscale station and do business with the well-to-do humans who lived there rather than deal with the obviously low-rent rabble inhabiting the ISC.

The Mercedes-Benz Corporation lobbied hard and expensively for a three-spoke model to resemble their logo. In spite of all scientific reasoning that a four- or five-spoke design was superior, the political vote was leaning ever more toward having a giant corporate logo spinning though the night sky. Other carmakers strategized how to morph their logos into circularly symmetric models so they too might be able to get their logo spinning in the starry night sky.

Corporations not only jumped on the bandwagon, they played king of the hill on the wagon to prove who the biggest supporter of the space station was.

Businesses of all sizes offered endorsement money to any government with a presence on the ISC and would listen. Recipients of corporate largesse would have to promise prominent positioning of the company's logo on astronaut's uniforms, internal and external surfaces of the ISC, and any other surface with maximum exposure to news reporters' cameras. Hollywood purchased the rights for staging John McClane blowing up half of the space station in *Die Hard Part IX* and three lovable fools waking up on the ISC after an amnesia-inducing bachelor party in *The Hangover Part VI*.

Dunkin' Donuts was the first franchise to rebrand their product. Their slogan was adapted to "The Galaxy Runs on Dunkin'." Some DD corporate executives thought the jingle was a bit of a reach. They felt it would have been safer to start with something more local such as, "The Solar System Runs on Dunkin'," but "Solar System" did not have quite the panache as "Galaxy." The public relations and advertising directors argued that if they filed for the copyright license to the "Galaxy" slogan today, Dunkin' Donuts would not have to rebrand all of their merchandise and advertising later when humans did get the engine running and finally made their way into the galaxy.

Dunkin' Donuts had already filmed a commercial portraying astronauts with an iced Jupiter Almond Fudge Swirl coffee in the spaceship's cup holder and a chocolate chip Cosmic Muffin on the dash. A second commercial focused the camera frame on two donuts bumping together in a friendly toast, one donut in a tentacle, the other in a claw. When the donuts reappeared in frame, there was a triangular bite out of the tentacle-held donut and a square bite out of the donut held by the claw. It was a subtle nod to the hopefully universal appeal of fried, sugar-laden dough.

A vast, and growing, internet community of science fiction fans and real space scientists lobbied hard for the adoption of a new dating reference: before Quane (BQ) and after Quane (AQ). Their argument for the recalibration of the human time reference was that Quane's arrival and subsequent sale of an instrument to allow humans to freely explore the galaxy and become full members, albeit latecomers, to the galactic community would, in future historical context, prove to be the most significant influence on the direction of human history. Ever.

The BQ-AQ crowd organized an international grassroots fundraiser to pay for bringing the Quest airlock from the ISC to a pedestal on the Washington Mall. They promoted the framework as the portal which admitted the first alien into human history and the door through which humanity took their first step to the stars.

A small but extremely vocal congregation was convinced that Quane's arrival on Earth was not an accident, but the manifestation of God's beneficent hand promoting humanity's survival. Earth was getting too small. Overcrowding, pollution, global warming, and vanishing resources were driving humankind to the brink of extinction. Quane's arrival at this time of upheaval and uncertainty was proof of God's a plan for humans. The godly pointed out that the price paid for the engine was not a product of man's ingenuity. It was God who covered the earth with life. It was God who ponied up and paid humanity's entrance fee to the galaxy.

An alternative group denied the existence of extraterrestrials all together. The Book of Genesis claimed God created life on Earth—not on any other planet. They claimed Quane was nothing more than Satan incarnate, determined to lure humans from their heaven on Earth into the hellish void of space. Humanity's purported imminent demise was nothing more than a ruse to hornswoggle people into believing the falsehood that they had outgrown the earth. God would not allow an asteroid or melting glaciers to destroy his children—those he made in his own image and likeness. The misguided fools who believed and followed the devil's false promises of greener pastures on the other side of the galaxy would all wind up going to hell in a handbasket—a handbasket that just happened to look like a donut on the end of a billy club.

Satirical news programs and late night talk show hosts never tired of lampooning this schizophrenic aspect of God's character; wanting people to leave Earth, but...maybe not.

CHAPTER 26

The year was 5 AQ.

General Richard Winn comfortably reclined on his deck in the backyard of his suburban Washington, D.C., home. Low magnification binoculars rested on his belly. The birds had adapted to his slow-moving presence and had learned to ignore his nonthreatening movements while they feasted at their feeders—and his clothes were usually decorated with their droppings. Red-breasted nuthatches, tufted titmice, catbirds, and finches devoured the seeds his aides poured into the hanging feeders daily. It was a windless, hot, and humid July morning.

By midafternoon, most of the city would be hiding behind air conditioning. Richard wore an insulated ski jacket and knit hat. A thick quilt covered his legs; he had not found a way to be comfortably warm since the accident.

Richard was prematurely gray at the temples, his eyes were sunken, and his face was drawn and gaunt. At thirty-seven years old, he could have easily passed for seventy-something.

A female reporter sat on a small stool on his right, blocking his view of the birds. Her hair was pulled back into a tight bun; her makeup had been applied thickly and in dark shades in a deliberate attempt to add years to her age and a solemn professionalism to her features. Her suit was gray, tight fitting, and bland in its sexless conservatism. Richard thought she looked like an overdone mannequin in a secondhand clothing store if it wasn't for the beads of sweat forming at her hairline.

"How do *you* account for the fact," she asked, "that you were the only one fully incapacitated by contact with the red dust inside the engine?" Even though there was nothing new to tell about the story, a byline on a personal interview with Canadian General Richard Winn would be a highlight on her resume.

"Would you mind going over the events one more time?" She leaned her expressionless, plastic face in close to him and rested a small notepad on her knees and readied her pen.

"No, I don't mind." Richard sighed heavily, leaned back, and closed his eyes. The continuous parade of reporters was a distraction from his pain and brought comforting confirmation that his brain still had not been affected by exposure to the red dust. Richard was completely incapacitated in his lower body and fully functional above the shoulders. His middle third had good and bad days.

"Shortly after Earth purchased the alien stardrive, I led a scientific party to examine it and try to discover the physical principles behind its operation. If we understood how it worked, we might have a chance at building our own without having to rely on an alien selling us another one, or our having to go find a new or used stardrive engine lot to buy another." Richard pushed his elbows on his chaise's armrests to relieve the painful pressure on his back. This was a bad day for his middle.

"I examined the end of the engine closest to Quane's habitat pod. There was a bit of argument about which end was the front or back. Was there an intake and an exhaust? Did it matter?" Richard shrugged loosely. The reporter did not look up from her scribbles. "Anyway, all of the surfaces were covered with a dark-red powder, like rust, but had the consistency of carbon soot."

Richard grunted as he tried to stretch his body to see what the reporter was doodling. The reporter caught him, lifted her pad, and blushed. She was sketching a devil in a dog costume.

"I was poking around," he continued, "and got some of the red dust on my glove and spacesuit."

"When did you start experiencing symptoms?" She had flipped to a new page and was taking notes in earnest.

"About twenty-four hours after the end of the spacewalk. The doctors think some of the dust may have penetrated my glove and gotten on my skin. Or I contacted the dust when I took the gloves off. The original diagnosis was flu. Then they thought it was a tick-borne illness. A month later, they admitted they could not find anything wrong with me. Yet, all the time I felt weaker and weaker and more and more tired, as if I was being drained of energy."

"What about the others you came in contact with?"

"Whatever I had was highly contagious. If someone touched a table where I sat a week earlier or breathed the same air in an elevator I'd been on, they got sick. The only difference was that their symptoms were milder. The severity of their symptoms was related to how distant the contact was from me in both time and space. The people they infected experienced even milder symptoms. Everyone else but me got over it in three to ten days, depending on how many degrees of separation they were from me. The farther they were away from me, the milder the symptoms and the sooner they were cured."

"Is there an update on what happened?" The reporter's eyebrow rose slightly with the hope of a scrap, a tidbit, something new to add to Richard's story. Her pen made baton twirls around her thumb.

"The strangest but most reasonable explanation is my body processed the dust somehow," he said. "What I passed on to others was a type of vaccine. I got the worst of it by being the first exposed. You know how the saying goes, 'If it doesn't kill you…'"

"It only makes you stronger?"

"Not that one; the other one, 'If it doesn't kill you, it only leaves you maimed and permanently disfigured.'" Richard chuckled and winked. "I have stabilized. I'll never be cured, but at least I won't get worse. The doctors finally finished with all their tests and I've been released. I'm heading back to Canada next week."

The reporter probed for some new angle to Richard's story or a new factoid about the dust. "What about plants and other animals—are they resistant, too?"

"A few of the heartiest weeds," he said, "and a handful of insects are—cockroaches especially. But none of the higher animals are. Dogs, cats, and even aquarium fish died while their owners were contagious. After their symptoms cleared up, their new pets were unfazed."

Richard licked his lips and looked at his hands folded in his lap. He was under top-secret orders not to reveal tests had been conducted on every animal species scientists could get their hands on. Every animal species, including humanity's closest evolutionary relatives, chimpanzees and orangutans, failed to develop any immunity to the red dust.

The strange fact that of all life on Earth, only *Homo sapiens* was immune to the red dust was not of any particular significance. But if the People for Ethical Treatment of Animals or the Society for Prevention of Cruelty to Animals ever got wind of the tests, authorized by their elected officials, those officials could kiss their next re-election good-bye.

The medical community's only conclusion was Richard's condition and human resistance to the red dust was a medical curiosity, independent of DNA construction, and an insignificant footnote to the present or future state of humanity.

"I'm really tired now. One last question." He squirmed in his chair and pressed a button on his armrest to summon an aide. The birdfeeders were nearly empty.

The reporter clicked her pen closed, flipped the notebook shut, stood, wiped nonexistent wrinkles off her skirt, and tugged her jacket. She turned and bent to pick her purse off the floor. Her skirt rode up above her knee. Richard stared and daydreamed at the sight of her shapely calves but could not stir any feeling below his belt.

Every question regarding Quane's visit had been asked many times over in the traditional media: Why did he feel he had to wear a costume? Were his motives more commercial or charitable? Will the purchase of the engine prove to be humanity's ultimate success or screw-up in space?

Social media was more immersed in conspiracy theory: Quane wore a costume because—as everyone knows—the aliens have been living here among us for decades and were secretly, patiently waiting to capture him. But were they waiting to collar an über-criminal or an intergalactic spy, or rub out a stool pigeon ready to spill his guts on the operation of the biggest crime syndicate in the galaxy? The answer depended on what movie was currently driving the box office.

An offhand question came to her mind and she cocked her head to one side. Richard saw a bit of the curious ten-year-old girl she most likely used to be and led her into the life of a reporter. She hooked her purse strap on her shoulder.

"Do you think Quane will ever return with more engines?" she said. "And why didn't he bring more? Any self-respecting salesman would normally bring more than one sample."

The question stunned Richard. It ricocheted off every corner of his brain, searching for the answer it knew was there and burrowed and bounced about his gray matter until it bit into and shook what it found up into consciousness.

"Yes!" Richard yelled, his hands pressed against the armrests. If his legs could have responded, he would have launched into a standing position. "I remember now."

The reporter was wide-eyed. "What? What do you remember?"

Richard stared into a not-too-distant past. "I remember that Quane said, 'Buy this engine and the others I have and you can come back anytime,' when we were at Uranus. But he never offered those extra ones to us. Maybe he was saving those for the next planet he visited."

He only glimpsed the shocked expression on the reporter's face before she turned and ran, braking a heel half way to her car. Finally, something new to add to the story, the legend. This new twist would be broadcast continuously on the cable news channels for at least the next twenty-four hours. It would be analyzed and interpreted from every angle using holographic, three-dimensional projections until there were no more words or imagery to wring out of the story.

"Why didn't Quane try to sell us the other engines?" he mumbled absentmindedly, as his aide scooped seeds into the bird feeders.

CHAPTER 27

Lacking even the basic knowledge about the engine's performance limits, from thrust to maximum payload, the designers of the Human habitat pod thought to play it safe and model the pod along the lines of Quane's dwelling. The new Human habitat was designed to resemble that one in nearly every aspect, except size and condition. Richard had estimated the radius at twenty paces—sixty feet. The control room and living quarters were each twice Richard's height—making the total outside thickness roughly twenty-five feet.

The new Human habitat was half the diameter. They did not need as much instrumentation as Quane—they did not need weapons management or battle maneuvering—and making it smaller would require less construction material. A wall divided the habitat in two like a sliced bagel. One half was operations and the other half was living quarters. On each half, the floor and ceiling were mirrored reflections for comfortable operation and living, whether in acceleration or deceleration mode. The control room and living quarters were each four feet taller than Quane's, since Humans were taller and needed the extra headroom. The habitat was a giant donut sixty feet in diameter, thirty-five feet thick, with a twenty-five-foot hole in the middle for the engine.

Unlike the open, barrack-style living arrangement in Quane's pod, the Human living quarters were divided into separate, private rooms for each astronaut, a galley, a laundry, and a common lounge complete with a sixty-inch wall-mounted

LED TV. The TV mount rotated with a fixed weight hanging from the bottom of the monitor. The swivel and weight automatically turned the monitor for proper viewing whether accelerating or decelerating. Food and water lockers were distributed evenly around the pod to prevent a hull rupture—due to accident or a well-targeted pirate's missile—from taking out all of their provisions.

Like the original version, the Human pod was designed to mate to the engine at the same stays, using the same shackles as Quane's, and again reminded onlookers of a wheel on the end of an axle. This time the wheel was shiny and new, even though the axle resembled one from a corroded, junked car after suffering the potholes of too many New England winters.

Simulations were run to decide the optimum number of astronauts to take the trip. Food consumption rates and water storage were measured against the expected trip length. More travelers were better because a larger skill set could be employed to gather the most data. Fewer travelers required less food, thereby lengthening the trip. A longer voyage might enable the crew to reach a destination of real interest; specifically, a used engine lot to buy more.

The primary requirement for the astronauts was the lack of a significant other. It was going to be a long trip, possibly greatly extended. There was no room for homesickness or pining after the one left behind.

If the crew was lucky enough to meet friendlies who would assist them in restocking their consumables, they might be able to continue indefinitely. Miriam lobbied to take all of Earth's nine million genomes to barter for future supplies, services, and, if all went well, engines. The discussion concerning the request was heated.

The first argument against sending so many genomes was a fear the crew might be cheated by creatures less honest than Quane, trading away the cow for a handful of magic beans.

At worst, they might be boarded by pirates and robbed outright. Earth would then be bankrupt and unable to ever trade for stardrives again.

A second argument for sending fewer genomes started with the fact that the galaxy was immense. Quane could not have squandered his payment very far in the five years since he left. It was astronomically unlikely the crew would negotiate with anyone who had seen any of their genomes. Therefore, replicas of the genomes used as payment could be used over and over again with only a statistically insignificant chance of having them being branded as counterfeit. The same dollar could, in essence, be used repeatedly—as long as the businesses were reasonably far apart or not on the same path Quane took when he left.

The great unknown was how much a new, or even slightly used, stardrive engine would cost. The final decision allowed the crew to take five hundred thousand genomes. Two hundred thousand were copies of those given to Quane. The rest were an assortment of dogs, butterflies, songbirds, tulips, roses, and coral reef fish to satisfy the "beautify the galaxy" crowd. The rest were invasive weeds, parasitic insects, and particularly aggressive vermin. One way or the other, Earthly life would gain a solid foothold somewhere in the galaxy.

If the crew encountered pirates or thieves, the crew was authorized to decide the best course of action. The bad guys might follow the Human ship if it went straight back to Earth. If the human crew could not lose them, they would have to draw them away from Earth and possibly never be seen or heard from again. In the event of surrender at gunpoint, the crew was ordered to wipe the computers clean. Thieves could not be allowed to obtain Earth's treasures, nor could they be allowed to deduce where Earth was located.

The anxiety and anticipation surrounding this trip was not unlike the glory days of exploration of the earth's surface.

Humans were embarking into the unknown, unsure of what they would find or how far they had to go. And like explorers of old, the astronauts understood that once they passed across the space membrane—over the horizon, as it were—there would be no contact with their homeport and they would be entirely on their own.

Many names were proposed for the ship. The finalists included: *Enterprise, Titanic, Minnow, Serenity, Jupiter 2, Bellerophon,* and *Tardis.* In the end, the ship was christened *Galaxy Quest.*

Richard was the natural first choice as crew leader, but incapacitated from his brush with the red dust, he had to satisfy himself with breaking the ceremonial bottle of champagne on the end of *Galaxy Quest* from his bed by a remotely controlled robotic arm.

Miriam Wu accepted the offer of *Galaxy Quest* Commander instantly and unconditionally.

Fedor and Nancy both refused offers to crew *Galaxy Quest.* They were quite happy to have their feet on the ground and their names highlighting the lecture circuit.

The second to accept the mission was the SCaTS soldier, Chuck Martin, who was on the ISS during Quane's visit and gave up his return shuttle seat to Richard. He was a natural to do the heavy lifting, spacewalks, and would be the go-to guy if there was trouble making a deal for food or drinks in a galactic equivalent of a Chalmun's Cantina. Chuck's SCaTS training also included intensive field medicine. Since *Galaxy Quest's* crew would have no access to real hospital equipment, he would double as the ship's medic.

The third astronaut, a senior engineering specialist—an absolute necessity to keep all systems operating—was a skinny, twenty-two-year-old genius, Nicholas Danthier, who, in private, fancied the moniker "Nick Danger."

CHAPTER 28

Two years before the launch of *Galaxy Quest*, Nick Danthier was a junior assistant engineer (JAE) assigned to the group responsible to interface the engine's electrical power source to the life support systems on the habitat pod. Graduating from MIT in three years, in the top 5 percent of his class with a double major in electrical engineering and video game design, he bragged to his friends and absorbed the admiration of his family for being the youngest and most successful of the Danthier family tree. But as bright and scholastically successful as he was, he maintained the lowest level of engineer on the space station. His immediate bosses, the assistant engineers (AEs), were the professional and intellectual equivalent of his teachers' teachers and their mentors' mentors. Senior engineers (SEs) were prizewinners or nominees in the fields of physics, chemistry, biology, and engineering. The SEs populated all of the top management positions.

Nick's mundane task on the ISC was to use trial and error to detangle the convoluted schematics as one of six JAEs and three AEs on the space station. The thousands of JAEs—plus the hundreds of SEs and AEs—that remained on the ground had not been able to make the tiniest bit of sense of the schematics or the manuals, in spite of the availability of all of the world's computing power.

Attached to the fifth six-month rotation of scientists, engineers, and technicians, Nick was just another mind on the space station ready to test any idea—no matter how cockamamie—in order to interpret the schematics. Engineers and scientists had battled for years with the senseless drawings: control lines were shorted to instrument relays and those were shorted to power supply lines. There were 512 outlet pins on the main connector to the engine and no way to test which ones to connect to the habitat unless the engine was running. But the engine could not run unless someone could start it. The only way to start it was to connect it to the control systems on the habitat pod, but there were 512 connections! The possible permutations reached way past infinity.

The joke circulating on the ISC went: "How many engineers does it take to translate alien schematics?"

"I give up. How many?"

"Only one, but we haven't found him yet."

Wearing cheap, garish sunglasses to enhanced his contrived alter ego, Nick Danger. Before he was launched into space, he discovered his current pair of shades in a box of breakfast cereal. The white cardboard frames were as wide as a dollar bill and as thick and flimsy as the cereal box they came in. There were small cutouts for the bridge of the nose and the tops of the ears. The lenses were rainbow colored plastic. The glasses made everyone's head look square, and passersby wondered if the wearer suffered from a rare astigmatism, attention deficit disorder, or were just plain fools because no one in their right mind would wear them willingly or without a doctor's order.

Nick thought the glasses made him look dangerous. The lenses were color graded, from red on the top to violet on the bottom; correctly copying the light spectrum: red, orange, yellow, green, blue, indigo, and violet. But he avoided wearing them in public on the ISC.

The JAEs' station was in the module named *Vision*. All six JAEs who slept, worked, ate, and went to the bathroom in the module nicknamed it Tardis; under their breath, they called it

Prison. The nickname was not because of bars on the windows but because every module was overcrowded and whoever was assigned to a module stayed in that module. Privacy was in the toilet—which never lasted long—or the claustrophobic, coffin-sized sleep chambers embedded in the module's walls.

The ISC lights were always on since engineers worked round the clock. The sleep chambers were the only place to find pure darkness. The ISC occupants settled into a circadian rhythm of sleep and wakefulness specific to their personal metabolism. Nick's body had settled into twelve hours on, twelve hours off.

His Nick Danger dream woke him unexpectedly one sleep cycle. It was two hours earlier than usual for him. The dream began the first night of his arrival at the station and repeated with some slight variance—the woman's hair color, the accent of the spy, the patter of the frustrated police captain—every night.

In the dream, he was wrapped in a fog-repelling trench coat with the collar up and a Fedora hat with its brim pulled down over his right eye. Without knowing exactly how or why, he had outfoxed the spies, won the dame, frustrated the police, and saved the free world.

This night, for the first time, the woman in red was unzipping the back of her dress as she pressed her soft, fire engine-red lips on his. He woke to find the dame was a pillow pressed to his face. A shudder at the sudden need for a cold shower and a pee started his left hand spidering along the wall of his sleep chamber, searching for the touch plate to activate the light in his coffin. All he had on were his boxer shorts and the crappy glasses he wore while falling asleep. He undid his harness and opened the sleep chamber lid. Since all of the other JAEs were male, Nick didn't think twice about floating off to the john in his underwear.

Before he made it to the lavatory, an enveloping silence distracted him. The module had never been so empty of life. He removed his glasses and looked down the length of *Vision* to the module straight across—*Ascension*, the AEs' module. It was as empty as *Vision*. Both were cylindrical tubes twice the length of a mobile home and double the diameter.

Nick scratched the thin, scraggly whiskers on his chin trying to remember if he was missing an evacuation drill, birthday party in *Tranquility*, or the circumstantial possibility that everyone's sleep cycle happened to overlap. He didn't worry for long; his curiosity sucked him into *Ascension*.

With the toy glasses were propped on top of his head, he drew his fingers reverently across the enormous blueprint in front of him. The page was five feet wide and three feet tall— an AE's blueprint. JAEs were given subsets of the full schematics expecting smaller pieces of the puzzle to be solved more easily, and when the solved pieces were later assembled, the whole picture would be revealed. So the logic went. Nick had never seen an entire AE schematic.

A different schematic faced him from another table. Nick made a slow weightless somersault, viewing all eight tables, each with a different blueprint covering another table on the circular wall. There were three more sets of tables along the length of *Ascension*. Thirty-two unique alien schematics were on display. The table arrangement was the same in *Vision*, but each table had a blowup of a portion of these originals. The line density on these originals was dizzying. In some areas, the space between lines was the same as the width of the line itself.

The drawings had been printed using a specially formulated ink, as specified in the engineering manual. There had been no attempt to secure them as intellectual property because the world's best minds could not fathom them. Some engineers secretly hoped enemy spies would steal the documents, translate them, solve the mystery, and let the engineers go back to their old ordinary, albeit brilliant, Earthly lives.

Nick was scanning a blueprint when he recognized the section he was currently working on. Seeing the small piece nested in the larger context did not make it any easier to understand. A shiver of danger told him he shouldn't be here looking at the drawings and urged him to hide his identity by pulling his glasses down over his eyes.

Instantly and perfectly, he saw it.

The colored lenses lifted and separated the lines. As Nick tilted his head up and down through the color spectrum, lines moved toward or away from the plane of the paper. Descriptive words and identifiers were now fixed to different planes.

It was so simple. So obvious!

The drawings had been designed to be read in three dimensions. With glasses like his, it would take only a few days to figure it all out.

Nick spun slowly, head over heels, scanning the drawings. The glasses worked on all of them.

He laughed out loud, giddy with excitement, and twisted to orient himself. The AEs' sleep chambers were to his left; he could wake any or all of them, or rush to *Tranquility* and shout the news to anyone awake or interested but caught himself at the door.

Instead of rushing down the center yoke of the station yelling, "Eureka! I have found it!" like a modern-day Archimedes after discovering the concept of displacement, he floated back to his sleep chamber. His need for a cold shower and urination was forgotten. The netted pockets lining his sleep chamber nearly ripped from his rough rifling in search of a notebook and pen. Tossing aside anything unwanted, the refuse bounced and danced in the small space like a trailer park in a tornado.

The implications of this discovery were huge—not only for his personal and professional life, but for the lives of everyone on Earth. Ideas swirled in his brain, whipping his thoughts out of control. He had to write down these ideas—focus, make a plan. If he was the only person on Earth, or in space, who could translate these drawings, they might make him king... Or emperor... Or even an assistant engineer!

Nick spent the next six hours in his sleep chamber, swatting away weightless debris and scribbling, erasing, and modifying pages of logic flow diagrams—full of ovals, diamond, squares, and arrows galore. Assured that he had concocted the best plan, he fell into an eight-hour coma of a sleep and, for the first time since he arrived at the ISC, did not dream of Fedoras, lithe women, and fog; he was hurling himself off the highest, jaggiest Acapulco cliff in a perfect swan dive into a giant, bubbling sausage pizza.

The trickiest part of the plan required him to wear the cheap lenses in public. His excuse would be that his eyes were strained by the intense, detailed work and needed the calming influence of sunglasses.

Nick cut the rainbow lenses from the cardboard frames with the patience and dexterity of a brain surgeon and glued them to an old set of eyeglasses with tortoiseshell frames. The glasses were used on Earth for driving, and on the station, for looking at Earthly details from the cupola. The frames were more comfortable for wearing all day and much less conspicuous.

Fortunately, the simple act of wearing glasses was the biggest change to Nick's behavior. The JAEs were encouraged to spend time at each of the thirty-two tables in *Vision* without spending too much time at any one of the four blown-up portions of the schematics on each table. Before the glasses discovery, his motions from table to table, from section to section, were random. After the discovery, he concentrated on sections of a single drawing and copied what he saw into his notebooks. There were seven levels of wiring and he kept a notebook for each level. If he noticed a lack of AEs in *Ascension*, he would drift in quietly to verify his interpretation of the blueprint he was currently working on and fill in missing pieces. It took him four months to fully recast the drawings and another week to double-checking his work.

Nick knocked gently on Desmond Driscoll's sleep chamber, but no one answered. Driscoll had not been seen for two days and he did not want to disturb him if he was crashing from overwork. A bursting net pouch labeled "IN" floated next to an empty pouch labeled "OUT." Obviously, Desmond was so exhausted, or over-sedated, that he did not have time to check his mail. Nick unhooked the IN bag and wriggled the contents into the OUT bag. He threaded his notebooks into the empty IN bag and flew off to his sleep chamber.

His sleep was fitful and full of cheering hoards carrying him on their shoulders—floating him with their fingers—in a jubilant parade in the ISC, up one module and down another until he had done the queen's wave to every square inch of the center. Humbly waving off their accolades, he modestly admitted that anyone could have seen what he had seen. The best part of the dream was the fistful of phone numbers he collected from the very prettiest of the female admirers.

No one came that morning.

No one came that afternoon.

No one came that evening.

Nick waited impatiently until the next morning before he nervously drifted past his boss's now-open door to see if his manuscript had been read. There it was, untouched. Front and center, still in the IN bag.

"David!" Nick called to the first bleary-eyed, senior scientist he saw. "What happened to Desmond?"

"Heart attack. Last night." David's eyes were red and his voice was dry and raspy with exhaustion. "I just got back from the services and loaded his body onto the next transport to Earth."

"What?" Frantic, Nick grabbed two fistfuls of David's shirt. "Who's going to take his place?"

"I guess I am." David yawned and brought his forearm down to break the grasp.

"In that case," Nick let go of David's shirt and smoothed over the wrinkles. "I have something really, really important to show you." His voice cracked as he led David by the elbow to the notebooks in Desmond's IN bag.

CHAPTER 29

Nick Danthier became an honored and decorated genius and graciously accepted his place as Senior Engineering Specialist on the first flight from Earth to the center of the galaxy.

A story that never made it to public consciousness was that someone else had seen the alien drawings while wearing a similar pair of glasses Nick had used. Six-year-old Tommy Driscoll, son of Desmond Driscoll, Director of Engineering in charge of interpreting the alien schematics—the same Desmond Driscoll who died of a heart attack the same night Nick delivered his interpretation of the schematics—had been visiting his father at the prelaunch facility. That morning, Tommy Driscoll had finished a box of the same cereal Nick had eaten. Tommy brought those glasses with him to his dad's office.

Desmond Driscoll lay stretched out on a cot with his elbow over his eyes. The bottle of premium whiskey he had hoped to break out in celebration of deciphering the drawings before his launch to the space center became the vessel for drowning his failure. None of the higher-ups were pleased that after nearly two years, he and his group had made zero progress on interpreting the alien drawings. He was going to the ISC to personally oversee this last rotation and guarantee, on his professional reputation, a solution to the problem. But had no clue how he was going to fulfill that promise.

Tommy was playing alien and spaceman and tearing around the room pretending to fight off alien dogs, to the annoyance of his father's pounding head. Tommy grew silent for a bit, and Desmond finally drifted off for some welcome sleep.

"Dad!" Tommy shouted. "Dad! You should check out the drawings with these glasses! They look really neat."

Startled awake, Desmond saw his son leaning on the schematics and drawing on them with colored pencils. Desmond bumbled his way off the cot and lunged at his son.

"I thought I told you never to touch those drawings." Desmond shook Tommy by the shoulders. Colored pencils flew everywhere, clattering as they landed on the floor. Desmond reached out to cuff Tommy's head. Tommy ducked the blow but his dad's hand caught the edge of the glasses. They flew across the room and slipped down a ventilation grate. Tommy chased after them and tried to reach his hand into the grate, but they had slid down the duct out of sight and out of reach.

"Aww," said Tommy. "You should have seen the drawings. They looked so cool with the glasses."

"Tommy, go find me some aspirin. My chest hurts." Desmond found his way back to the cot and lay down rubbing his chest. His launch was in six hours.

CHAPTER 30

The year was 7 AQ.

It was deliberately planned—and seemed fitting—that the first day Humans ventured into the galaxy, Launch Day, was the seventh anniversary to the day of purchasing the engine.

No prelaunch tests were conducted. No monkeys, dogs, or dolphins were rocketed into dark space to test the control systems. There was no guarantee an unmanned, unpiloted stardrive would find its way back to Earth. And if it did, like Dr. AtZ's experiment, it might arrive at Jupiter, Neptune, or some location so far away it would be unfeasible to recover. The first mission of *Galaxy Quest* would be fully manned with a trained crew.

Miriam led the group out of the airlock of the ISC. Just like Quane's habitat, a boom extended from an open airlock on *Galaxy Quest*. Above the open hatch, an LED display repeated the phrase, "Welcome Aboard," in every one of the languages Quane had used. If booms and message boards were good enough for the rest of the galaxy, Humans would not argue against the value of such options.

"I wonder if there will be a flower or a mint on the pillow," Chuck joked.

"I hope there is a bottle of champagne to christen the voyage," Nick said.

Miriam smiled inside her helmet, happy her crew's light-heartedness. She was not yet comfortable with the role of Mission Commander and exactly what it meant regarding her comportment toward her crew members, who not only were male, but one was a brawny gladiator and the other a brainy geek.

"OK, boys, enough of that. I promise the champagne's on me when we get back."

Miriam stepped onto the surface of the habitat pod first and paused to make a mental note of everything visible on the engine: every scratch, dent, and patch. The habitat's surface was new, clean, and unblemished. Earth was the brilliant white, blue, and green globe they were leaving to travel into the immense unknown emptiness of the galaxy. *Galaxy Quest* suddenly seemed smaller than the tiniest diatom washed from a warm secluded beach into a cold, infinite ocean full of dark unknowns. She shivered.

"Coming, Mom?" Chuck said, the top of his helmet just visible inside the airlock.

Single and childless, she bristled at first, then paused before she outright refused the title. *Maybe a mother figure is an option. Loving discipline may be what "the boys" need to keep them in line.*

"Right behind you. Don't leave without me."

The habitat's layout replicated Quane's pod: instruments on one side were reflected on the other side; the aisles were wider, but still ran radially like spokes on a wheel—closer together near the hub and farther apart at the edge of the wheel. All of the major command consoles—for navigation, life support, networking, and communication—were the largest and were situated where the aisles were farthest apart. Backup and support systems for each of the major consoles lined the aisles toward the hub.

It even had that new habitat smell: newly extruded plastic and disinfectant.

Everything in the pod had been designed to minimize weight; not because weight mattered in weightless space, but because every nut, bolt, and toilet seat had to be thrust off Earth. Lighter and smaller components meant more space to jam them into cargo bays and, therefore, fewer trips. Every component was preassembled on Earth, then shaved and whittled down until it was structurally sound enough to survive two G's—twice Earth's gravitational force. Then all of it was disassembled, packaged into the smallest volume possible, and shot into space.

Miriam, Nick, and Chuck huddled together at the entrance of their new home, eyes and mouths wide open like three scared and hungry tropical fish dropped into their new aquarium. Mission Control planned on their entrance cueing a sustained, rumbling double low C, then three single trumpet notes, rising like the dawn, and finishing with a two-note soaring crescendo. A tympani pounded as loud and fast as their excited hearts. Mission Control assumed Strauss' *Also Sprach Zarathustra* a fitting welcome and christening of the voyage.

Miriam blinked hard and cleared her throat. "Begin preparations for engine test in ten minutes," she said. "Nick, begin systems check and begin launch sequences. Chuck, ensure that all equipment is stowed and secured."

Neither moved. "Now!"

The two men flew off to comply with the orders. Miriam smirked. Having men jump at her command was much more satisfying than she imagined. *Galaxy Quest* was a civilian ship and, as such, uniform haircuts and dress were not requirements. Her helmet of thick, straight jet-black hair was cut to the shortest length that would still be considered feminine, and would last for who knew how long.

A brand-new wardrobe consisting of five pairs of khaki shorts and five loose-fitting polo shirts, for everyday wear; three pairs of black jeans, three flannel shirts, two hooded fleece sweatshirts, and two wool sweaters—just in case the men decided to turn down the thermostat. Also included was a pair of black silk slacks, a long-sleeved white satin blouse and a pair of black patent leather low heels. She accessorized with a short pearl necklace, single pearl earrings, and pearl cufflinks. One had to be ready for the fingers-crossed possibility of an invitation to a formal state house dinner thrown by alien emperors, presidents, or whoever was in charge—ready and willing to cordially introduce humanity into polite galactic society. Everyday footwear was a pair of lime-green Reebok CrossFit Nanos.

Nick flitted like a hummingbird from console to console, from red-colored button to yellow-colored button to blue, activating the relevant systems. Behind the panels, he pictured individual circuits lighting up one by one, and those circuits stacked vertically on separate, singularly colored planes, pulsing and glowing with the mechanical lifeblood of flowing electrons. These new actuator buttons did not have rabbits, butterflies, or ducks to indicate the button's function, but Human words like "Engine On," "Running Lights," and "Eject Waste."

The EW button guaranteed that even if humankind should suffer the misfortune of extinction, by dotting the galaxy with tight little planetoids of frozen metabolic waste, sometime, somewhere, some alien out for a Sunday drive would encounter the Human legacy. They would resurrect humanity's ghost with their curses: "Flocked be the morons who left these crap bombs floating around free in space. How am I going to clean that off my windshield?"

Nick had not touched the few fingernail-long curlicues on his chin or a lock of his wavy brown hair; he planned to return to Earth sporting a full beard and a rock star's unruly mane. Ten pairs of faded, ripped jeans and ten T-shirts comprised his wardrobe. The shirts ranged from ragged to new, and the displays varied from a portrait of James Dean to a smiling black cartoon face with the caption, "Ask me about my explosive diarrhea." He wore one pair of red Keds that he purchased brand-new for the trip.

Chuck ensured their spacesuits were stored, then went to the living quarters and checked each supply locker. After his formal duties were accomplished, he quietly secreted a non-metallic, CO_2-powered pistol behind a tertiary navigation panel and a second pistol in his living quarters. Chuck had shaved himself bald on head and chin. His ensemble consisted entirely of the same digitally pixilated camouflage designed for the SecOps team in the movie *Avatar*. This trip was nothing more to him than an extended deployment to a foreign country without a line of supply. He had two pair of shoes: jungle boots and a pair of black Air Jordans.

A bevy of digital entertainment, including music from Beethoven to Zappa, and movies from Jolson to Johansson and *Kangaroo Jack* to *Killer Klowns from Outer Space,* were burned into *Galaxy Quest's* computers for the crew's personal enjoyment. None of crew would ever be able to honestly say that there was nothing on.

For the next twenty-four hours, the crew slipped back and forth across the membrane. On the first slip, they waited five minutes in dark space before reversing the process to return to the space they occupied. LiDAR imaging proved they returned to their original position within a millimeter on every axis. On the second slip, they waited fifteen minutes in dark space before they returned. The wait in dark space doubled from there—30, 60, 120, 240, and 480 minutes. The engineers acquiring relative time, absolute position, surface temperature, human life functions, and radiation levels of the ship and crew determined each wait in light space. When they confirmed the data was complete, they authorized the next slip.

These tests also enabled the recording of homeport coordinates into the guidance system. With each slip into dark space, a 360-degree image was taken. Each image was correlated with the previous image. The exact position to enter the membrane was then burned into the guidance system to ensure the accurate return of the ship to Earth orbit. Miriam was the only crew member with life vitals tied to a homing algorithm specifying, in the event of her death, the ship would automatically return to Earth-orbit coordinates.

All of the engineers and scientists were oblivious to the data. This slipping back and forth was irreparably stressing the already weak, overused junk engine. Had Earth engineers had any experience with travel in the membrane, they would have recognized the characteristic trends in the measurements confirming the engine was near total failure.

Each time the ship returned from dark space, the transit time to cross the membrane was different. On each return, timepieces on the ISC, Earth, and *Galaxy Quest* were recalibrated to the National Institute of Science and Technology clock—a timepiece based on the oscillation of strontium atoms and so precise it would not gain or lose a second in fifteen billion years. Earth engineers argued the *GQ's* crew was sloppy in their timekeeping. Miriam was enraged at the intimation that a woman could not tell time, but the time for each slip *was* different. Not by just fraction of seconds, but by minutes. The first slip took 4.0627 minutes. The second slip took 23.845 minutes. The next took three seconds exactly. Earth scientists concluded the membrane was not fixed, and eddies and currents changed the density and transit time. Their naïveté blinded them to a physical reality known by the more learned portion of the galaxy: after the speed of light, travel time through the membrane at a given place was a constant.

The engine was sputtering a "Please, help me. I'm dying!" message which fell on ignorant, but innocent, Human ears. To Human eyes, it was performing perfectly: the ship was appearing at the exact coordinates and in the same orientation as when it disappeared into the membrane. After ten apparently successful slips, there was no reason not to give a thumbs-up to the mission.

"Galaxy Quest," Mission Control said, "you are a go for the mission. Let me say on behalf of myself and the rest of the planet, 'Good luck and Godspeed.'"

"Mission Control," Miriam said, "thank you for the honor and privilege you have entrusted us with in becoming the representatives of all humanity to the galaxy. I could say, 'We will not let you down.' But we will undoubtedly fall short to some, no matter the outcome. I could ask you to keep a candle burning in the window for us, but we cannot see those beacons of love from the other side of the membrane. So I say simply, we cast off from Earth, but will be bound to you always by the tightest ropes of all, our shared humanity. Farewell."

"Nick, initiate the engine." She cued Wagner's "Ride of the Valkyries" on the ship's sound system. If it was powerful enough to launch Brunnhilde and her sisters' off a mountaintop on their ride to Valhalla, it might be enough to sustain them and keep their little spaceship upright and afloat in the vast galaxy. "We're on our way."

Not a whisper or hum accompanied the slip sequence as the prayer-consecrated vessel of Human hopes and expectations, *Galaxy Quest*, disappeared.

CHAPTER 31

Each member of *Galaxy Quest's* crew was completely versed and trained in the theory and operation of every system: the response of the smallest toggle switch, the meaning of every warning light, and how to unclog the toilet. Each also remained a specialist.

Miriam, Commander and Exobiologist, was designated as first to greet and establish relations with aliens. Chuck, as both Defense Expert and Medic, would be second to greet and would cover their retreat. The only expectation of Nick was to keep the engine running and the lights on.

"Let's take one last look at the sun from dark space and verify the return coordinates before we get going."

Nick entered the sequence to rotate the habitat pod's portals to face the sun. The sun appeared as Richard had described: a thin, bright tip which dimmed to black as it flared out.

"We're not in Kansas anymore," Chuck said, hovering at a portal. Squinting, blinking, and spinning to make himself dizzy, he burned the sun's features and colors to into his memory and hooked that to all of his childhood emotions of home and family. He was unsure of his ability to recognize the sun's dark space image sufficiently to discern it from a group of three. It was the first he had ever seen. But as the soldier and pathfinder of the crew he would have to try if circumstances demanded.

"OK. Let's hit the road. Nick, commence acceleration. Let's start at half-gravity, five meters per second to burn in the systems. If something breaks, hopefully we won't be so far from Earth that we can't limp home. Increase by one meter per second per second every six hours until we get to full gravity."

The crew's body weight returned, along with a queasy feeling in their stomachs. Gravity and anxiety were both stressing their guts.

The navigation display in front of Nick showed an image of the galaxy. A small picture of the *Galaxy Quest* sat on a star labeled "Sun." A pen twirled around his thumb. "Do we have a heading or destination?"

Miriam was more secure with command with her feet firmly planted on a hard surface. With hands wringing behind her back like Captain Bligh on a calm day on the *Bounty,* she paced slowly up one aisle and down another. At one of the brushed aluminum navigation subsystem consoles she stopped to drag her fingertips along its cool, smooth side.

"Quane said the closer we get to the center of the galaxy, the more civilized it's supposed to be. Back home, the brain trust decided we should head straight for the center of the galaxy and see what popped up along the way. The nearest stars along that heading are Barnard's Star in Ophiuchus, Ross 154 in Sagittarius, and Gliese 667 in Scorpius. Gliese 667 is a triple star system with two known planets—possibly more. It sounds pretty darn interesting to the astrophysics crowd, even if there is no life."

Miriam stopped at the networking command console and peered over Chuck's shoulder to verify the happy gossip stream between *Galaxy Quest's* computers.

"Unless there are any disagreements, that's our heading. If Quane was right about space travel being shorter in the gravitational dimension, it should take us about three months to get there. Half of the trip is accelerating and the other half is decelerating. But now we are free to make our own decisions.

Let's use all these fancy computers and telescopes to see if they agree with that plan."

The crew quarters were furnished identically, like modest hotel rooms. Reflected on wall and ceiling were two twin-sized beds, two padded armchairs, two student desks, and two private baths with showers. Toilets operated in gravity or weightlessness. Lamps were wall mounted.

Each astronaut was allowed an unlimited number of pictures, posters, and wall decorations to individualize their surroundings. Miriam chose only one poster—Albert Einstein's mustachioed and white-haired face leaning in with furrowed brow and concerned eye like a grandfather ready to impart his singular understanding of life, the universe, and everything else to his young, wide-eyed grandchild. The caption read, "Imagination is more important than knowledge. For knowledge is limited to all we know and understand, while imagination embraces the entire world, and all there ever will be to know and understand." When she read the quote she often replaced "world" with "universe."

Nick had an original Pokémon Illustrator card, written in Japanese, in a tiny vacuum-sealed plastic container hanging from a thumbtack over his door as a good luck charm. Only six officially existed; he had the seventh. One other poster stated simply, "And God said, let there be light," under which was written Maxwell's equations of electromagnetism. The next line stated, "And God said, let there be matter," under which was the equation for the Higgs boson. The final line was, "And God saw it was good."

Chuck had a simple, letter-sized white piece of paper with three hand-printed Winston Churchill quotes in blue ballpoint ink:

"Sometimes doing your best is not good enough. Sometimes you must do what is required."

"If you're going through hell, keep going."

"I may be drunk, Miss, but in the morning, I will be sober and you will still be ugly."

There was no special reason for selecting the last quote other than it made him smile.

Five hours later, they all came to the same conclusion: Gliese 667 was the most interesting first stop.

The crew adapted to the daily rituals of a ship on course and in motion. They worked in staggered, overlapping shifts. Each worked half of their shift with first one, then the other crew member. The schedule intended to create personal space for both friendship and privacy. Days passed in businesslike fashion.

Chuck spent his spare time working out to stay in shape. Resistance weights were too expensive a luxury to lift from Earth, so he had to be content with hundred-rep rounds of pull-ups, sit-ups, push-ups, burpees, and box jumps. To relax and clear his mind, he drilled his martial arts katas.

Nick spent his time reviewing electronic schematics, drawing manga, and playing video games.

Miriam maintained the ship's log, a private diary, and read.

The ship and crew ran smoothly for the first month. Once a week they had a scheduled movie night complete with butter-flavored microwave popcorn. Once a week there was a sit-down dinner and the assigned *chef du jour* concocted something new and hopefully palatable by combining ingredients from their boring menu into a culinary masterpiece. The grand prize was naming the dish after its inventor and promoting it vigorously on the talk show circuit when they returned to their well-deserved heroes' welcome. Miriam was well in first place with a concoction of macaroni and cheese, barbecued brisket, and chipotle sauce christened "Miriam's Mess."

Once she stumbled on the men in the middle of a fart contest in the common area. She did not stay long; it was potently obvious they had gorged themselves on beans as fuel for their butt trumpets.

Halfway into the second month, they started the deceleration sequence and began living on the ceiling. The second month also saw the crew becoming restless and in need of something to break the boredom. Chuck inevitably beat Nick in Madden NFL. Nick always beat Chuck at Mario Kart. Both men beat Miriam at everything. Badly.

At the beginning of the third month, a trickle of events began which would soon sweep them up in a deluge of human missteps, alien jurisprudence, and galactic coincidences.

Chuck was in the second half of his shift and Nick was in his first half. Miriam had just woken up and was sitting at her desk to start the day's log, still in her sleepwear. Her intercom buzzed.

"I see some irregular readings from the engine," Nick said. "I've never seen them before. I'm not sure if it's a serious problem."

"Thanks." Vivaldi's *Four Seasons* was playing on Miriam's personal speakers. "I was starting today's ship's log. I'll note it. Keep monitoring. I'll be up soon. Cut back deceleration by two meters per. See if that helps."

"Reducing deceleration by two meters per second per second. See you soon."

Miriam finished the log, dressed, and made her way up to the control room. Nick sat at the engine command console scribbling in a notebook and Chuck was at the next console, reading aloud what he saw on his panel.

"Readings still off?" Miriam put a hand on Nick's shoulder.

"The engine efficiency drifted out of the specified control limits—that's when we called you. We cut back deceleration by two meters per and the trend kept drifting out of bounds. We cut back one more meter per and the trend line became steeper. We were about to accelerate to see what happens. Maybe braking is the problem."

The first hurdle of the trip was coming straight at her; she prayed for the emotional and intellectual strength to clear it. Miriam closed her eyes and tilted her head back. "It's almost like it's overheating."

"It's the efficiency trend that's dropping," said Nick, "like it's burning more and more fuel to keep decelerating at the same rate."

"There's an easy way we could test if the engine is overheating."

The other two astronauts stared at Chuck with surprise. They were not expecting a solution from him. He was the muscle, not the brains.

"If we try accelerating again," Chuck said, "and efficiency does not improve, then we know the problem is not related to braking. To test if overheating is the problem, we should turn it off completely. We give the engine an hour or more to cool down, then try to start it up again at no more than, say, one meter per, and see where the efficiency is. Since we are already moving at speed, a small acceleration should not be too much of a strain."

"I like it," Nick said. "If the efficiency is good, then we know we have to run at less than a continuous duty cycle. If the efficiency is still bad, we have a few choices."

"And those choices are?" asked Miriam.

Nick held up three fingers and counted them off with his other index finger. "Continue on and hope we don't break down completely before we find a service station, try to fix it ourselves, or turn around and try to make it back to Earth."

Miriam's head dropped to her chest and her heart sank at the last choice. She might become the commander of the first failed mission to the galaxy. If they never returned, their fate would be fodder for endless speculation. They could have been captured and imprisoned or marooned on a deserted planet, but breakdown after only three months was too unfair; they had barely gotten their foot out the door.

"Let's run the acceleration test first," Miriam said. "Buckle in."

When deceleration stopped, weightlessness returned. Seatbelts kept them in their chairs. "Initiating acceleration at two meters per. Not enough to feel much gravity, but enough to test the engine."

Miriam did not open her eyes until she heard Chuck state the worst: "Efficiency still out of bounds and climbing."

"Shut it down, Nick," Miriam said.

"Shutdown complete. Now we sit back and wait."

Galaxy Quest's crew sat silent for the next hour. If the engine never started again, they would fly off at fifteen thousand kilometers per second on their current path until they crashed into something, like a runaway truck with the driver asleep at the wheel. Long before that, without the electricity generated by the engine, the batteries would run dead, their entire life support would stop, and the ship would become their tomb. *Galaxy Quest* would become a ghost ship—a galactic *Flying Dutchman*. The three started to mentally compose their final messages for whoever might find their well-preserved, long-dead bodies.

"Time's up. Here goes." Nick pressed the button to engage the start sequence.

Fingers crossed in Miriam's lap. Her eyes were closed; her teeth chewed her lower lip.

Chuck touched a Saint Christopher medal through his shirt that his grandmother had given him before he left for SCaTS training. She had the medallion of the Patron Saint of Travelers blessed and told him if he was ever in trouble to touch the medal, say a small prayer, and Saint Christopher would be there to help Chuck find his way. Lacking any particular religious convictions, he took the medal and wore it because he'd promised he would. This was the first time he ever thought he needed its help.

"Nothing," Nick said quietly. "The engine's dead."

CHAPTER 32

In the year 50,000 BQ, Nitram the Average, from the planet Rebroz near the center of the galaxy, was trolling around his solar system. Rebrozians were scaly, chameleon-like creatures standing erect and averaging five foot one and three sixteenths inches in height. Nitram's height was exactly the average. In his wide lipless mouth was a trifurcated tongue. Each section of his tongue terminated with a set of tiny, razor-sharp teeth. A dozen stiff bristles randomly dotted the top of his head. Some Rebrozians decorated their bristles with everything from baubles to bagels. The average Rebrozian did not. Nitram's bristles were bare.

Nitram's eyes twisted about independently on the ends of stubby stalks as he scanned a display. He worked as a mid-level materials acquisition technician for the perfectly unremarkable Galactic Salvage Company, Limited. His job was to roam GSCL's solar system and vicinity for any materials of value. Stray meteors, dead satellites, or broken-down spaceships, occupied or not, occupants dead or not. His drab ship was medium sized and in the middle of its mechanical life expectancy. The ship had a lumpy appearance, as if the intent was to form it from clay but the sculptor gave up before completion. The company logo painted on the outside of the ship unpretentiously identified his employer. Nitram had an average eye for evaluating the worth of the space flotsam he gathered.

Medium-range radar pinged, not too loudly—an alert to an object Nitram should consider investigating. A dead satellite, roughly his own size, floated in the dim illumination of his floodlight. The object was familiar. He churned through a pile of magazines until he found what he was looking for in a recent copy of *Scientific Rebrozian*. The article was an exposé about Dr. AtZ's life, his failed experiments to find dark matter, and his ultimate suicide. Included in the article was a picture of his last experiment.

The object outside the viewport matched the magazine picture exactly, down to a red repair tag wired to a piece of its plumbing. Nitram's bristles fluttered: he was not going to be average anymore.

A reflection caught his average eye. Closing in quickly on Dr. AtZ's experiment was a sleek, polished, and well-maintained ship—the sculptor had taken this one to conclusion. The company logo, emblazoned on the ship in a color and font that seared the optic nerve of lower species, announced to well-above-average species that it was a ship of the line of the Pan Galactic Salvage Company, Unlimited. Aboard were three highly paid employees, all with superior eyes for evaluating materials: Gion BicButtai, Gion Smalbarys, and Gion JaJa. An articulated arm was reaching out of their cargo bay to snatch the satellite.

Nitram turned from the viewport and whipped the magazine away. The pages fluttered as it flipped end-over-end until it slammed into a wall. For the first time in his life, Nitram regretted his mediocrity.

"I wish I was the one who recovered Dr. AtZ's experiment and got the reward," he said.

Suddenly, with all the razzle-dazzle of a heartfelt wish granted by a fairy godmother, a bright light strobed through the portal. When Nitram looked out to see what had happened, the well-above-average ship was gone.

Dr. AtZ's dead experiment hovered, unscathed.

It was Nitram's for the taking.

When incessantly questioned at the multiple hearings regarding the loss of the extremely valuable salvage ship of the Pan Galactic Salvage Company, Unlimited, and the three highly paid employees with superior eyes for evaluating materials, Nitram denied an encounter with any other ship. He repeated the same boring story—he was minding his own business, searching in his usual way with his average eyes, when he saw several, he guessed nine, bright flashes out of the corner of his eye. When he looked in the direction of the flashes, he saw the lost experiment and went to fetch it. There was no other ship.

In spite of an exhaustive search of nearby planets' moons and asteroids, no trace of the lost salvage ship was ever found. It was almost as if they had traded places with Dr. AtZ's experiment.

Nitram delayed returning the experiment to its rightful owners, the government of Rebroz, until he had quietly invested his life savings in the companies that manufactured its components. In a few decades, the engines were perfected and mass-produced. And the value of those companies expanded a thousandfold. Nitram's investments in the future of galactic space travel compounded quickly into an above-average fortune; ensuring his chronologically distant progeny would be some of the richest individuals in the galaxy.

In the year 35 B.Q., Gruseltmira, an heir to the Nitram the Average family fortune, was born.

CHAPTER 33

"The engine's broken." Nick stared blankly at the controls in front of him. He let his arms float where they wanted. They were officially castaways.

Chuck pounded the console in front of him with the side of his fist. His training refused to admit defeat, but his training never included repairing alien technology in the depths of space without any chance of rescue. It seemed Saint Christopher couldn't reach across the membrane to help either.

"We have one option left. Let's go fix it." Miriam was determined to stay positive and maintain morale until—if it came to it—they all died with dignity, humanity, and grace.

"Nick and I will take the walk," Miriam said. "Chuck, stay behind and monitor. We may want you to run diagnostics periodically while we're at the engine."

Miriam put a hand on Nick's shoulder and squeezed a little. "Time to prove how much you really know about alien technology."

"I'll do my best." Nick avoided her eyes; unsure if his best would be good enough.

Earth-side scientists had understood the engine ran equally well if either end was the intake or the exhaust. When switching from acceleration to deceleration, intake and exhaust simply switched sides. The ship did not have to flip end-over-end to reverse its inertia. The only logical rationale for mounting the plate near one end of the axle was simply the ease of removing a habitat pod. Health and safety experts were comforted knowing that aliens were unconcerned whether the habitat was near the intake or exhaust. It meant no toxins or tissue-damaging radiation occurred in those vicinities of the engine.

The final airlock door opened. Miriam and Nick stared into pure blackness, thick and deep and so dense it was hard to believe it did not have substance. Miriam pushed her hand out of the door to prove it was not solid, not a black boulder or blast panel blocking the airlock. This was not the ISC illuminated by Earthshine, moonshine, and sunshine. This was a lone Human vehicle in the galactic desert—a black, airless, uninhabitable desert. She braced and thrust herself into the black as a skydiver jumping out of an airplane door against the force of the onrushing wind.

Waist high out of the airlock, she searched the outside surface of the ship nearest her with her helmet-mounted floodlight. Inside the nearest compartment were six tethers, all long enough to reach the furthest end of the engine by the longest route. One she clipped to her belt and passed another to Nick.

"Ready?"

"You bet I am." Nick was cowering at her feet, fumbling to attach the tether. He gave her a shaky thumbs-up.

"Good." Miriam looked down at him between her feet. "Because I'm not."

Miriam dissolved into the black. When the soles of her boots disappeared, he grabbed the edge of the door and lifted himself into the heavy, solid nothing.

"Man, it's black." Nick's voice was a reverent whisper.

As their eyes adjusted, they first focused on the brightest points of light. The black holes of the Milky Way leaking the most energy across their super thinned gravitational membranes. Miriam pointed them out to Nick. Soon, fainter points of light—photons leaked into dark space by ordinary stars—excited the rods and cones on their retinas.

The starlight was cold and distant and provided less illumination than a handful of pinhead-sized dots of glow-in-the-dark paint on a bedroom ceiling. Miriam shivered involuntarily in spite of her suit's precisely maintained environment.

"Stay close," Miriam said. His hand was clutching the back of her suit.

The two spacewalkers had every available light turned on but could not see the slightest thing unless it was close enough to bounce the light back. It was not like shining a flashlight on Earth and seeing a "beam" of light. Here, there was no air, water vapor, or dust to scatter light back to the human eye, or illuminate a wider area.

Miriam focused her light on a spot of the ship and made a mental note of what she saw. If she turned her lights to a new area, the first was lost, devoured by the hungry, oily blackness. Her retinas retained an image of the previous area, but soon dissolved, like a mirage, replaced by the next area.

Thankfully, a habitat designer had the foresight to install running lights. They were arranged simply: eight lines ran radially on the face of each side of the wheel and divided it into eight, equally-sized wedges. Each light was located in a recess beneath a handhold which doubled as a clip-on point for tethers. The liquid black devoured the photons they dispensed. They did not make the ship brighter, or help the astronauts see anything around them, and were only visible if on an unobstructed line of sight by the human eye.

Handholds, spaced like the rungs of a painter's ladder, allowed them to swing along the side of the habitat pod. When they reached the point where the habitat met the engine, they unclipped their tethers from their belts and threaded them through the last illuminated habitat handhold and reattached them to their belts.

Miriam and Nick panned their suit lights along the engine's smooth side. There was nothing to hold onto.

"Miriam," Nick said, "I'll hold onto this last rung with one hand and your tether with the other. Jump lightly, and when you get to the end of the engine tell me. I'll stop paying out your tether and pull you back to the edge."

"How will you get there without flying off into space?"

Nick handed her his tether. "Hold on to this. There is plenty of slack. When you have a grip on the edge of the engine, just pull me up to you."

The plan worked easily and they positioned themselves where they could shine their lights into the end of the dead stardrive. The inside was a twisted mass of chimney brushes with bristles at all angles to each other. Every bristle and visible surface was caked with red dust. The dust appeared solid and hard, but Earth scientists had quickly learned that when touched, it instantly turned to powder. None had deciphered whether the dust was the catalyst for the reaction of burning dark matter, or the product. Since no one knew for certain if cleaning the dust would make the engine perform better or not at all, all votes were for leaving it in place.

"See anything, Nick?" Miriam said.

"I'm not sure I know what I'm looking for. Back off from the opening. I am going to ask Chuck to start at minimal acceleration and watch what happens."

"Has anyone ever seen anything happen during testing?"

"Not that I know of," said Nick. "No moving parts, no glowing plasmas, no heat."

"Then what do you expect to see now?"

"I hope if it looks like nothing is happening when it's working properly, I might see something happen now that it's broken. Maybe an arc or spark, or something. I don't want both of us to get sucked in, zapped, or blown into space, so please pull back."

"I'm not budging. Two sets of eyes are better than one. I'm going to slide around to ninety degrees from where you are to get a different view. Don't do anything till I get there." Miriam used her hands to shuffle around the lip of the engine.

"Before the test," Nick said, "turn off all your external lights. We might actually see something in this perfect blackness."

When Miriam reached her position, she turned off her lights. Knowing she was ready Nick turned off his lights. Both gasped at the oppressive strength of weightless darkness. They could not have been more blind than if someone had painted their helmets flat black, stuffed them into vats of coal tar, and dropped them down the deepest mine shaft.

Miriam panicked; she did not know if her eyes were open or closed. The more she blinked, the less sure she became. She could not touch her eyes through the helmet for physical confirmation.

"Nick, I can't tell if my eyes are open or closed."

"It's OK." He chuckled. "Happened to me, too. It's easy. Look around. If you can see the black holes and stars in the Milky Way, your eyes are open. OK now?"

Miriam was relieved that Nick could not see her blush.

"Chuck," Nick said, "initiate engine start. Lowest possible acceleration."

"Starting at zero point one meters per in three, two, one." Chuck pressed the ignition. "Anything?"

The response was delayed as four eyes strained to see anything against the perfect black.

"Nothing," said Nick. "Shut it down, Chuck. I want to try one more thing."

After a brief pause, Chuck said, "Shut down complete. What's next?"

"I'm going to break a little of the red stuff off one of the bristles," said Nick. "Then we'll try the same startup."

Touching the bristles was tantamount to treason to the earth SEs assigned to understanding how the stardrive worked. They only analyzed loose samples acquired from the inner walls. Breaking dust off a bristle bordered on the sacrilegious.

"No! Stop! You can't. We don't know what it will do."

"The engine is dead. We have to do something."

"All right," Miriam said. "But just a tiny piece."

Following the beam from his helmet lights, Nick slid into the open end far enough to reach a finger thick bristle. Only the toes of his boots were outside. The coating was lumpy and irregular, like the dripped wax from a cheap birthday candle. What seemed red stone turned to fine dust in his fingers and stained his glove. The bare bristle was now only as thick as a pencil lead. "This stuff is crazy. It's crystalline underneath; triangles within triangles within triangles. And it reflects a rainbow of colors."

"Nick, are you all right?" She had scuttled slowly to his position and was stretching to grab the heel of his boot.

"I'm fine. I cleared about a centimeter of dust from the end of one bristle. Coming out now." He floated out of the engine feetfirst.

"Safe!" she called out when Nick filled her lights.

"What?"

"You should see yourself," said Miriam. "Your legs, chest, and arms are all red. It looks like you slid headfirst into second on a Georgia red-clay infield. What a mess. I'm not washing that load."

"Hopefully we'll have enough battery power left to run a washer. We're ready for test two. Chuck, ignite an engine start at lowest possible acceleration."

CHAPTER 34

Hurtling through dark space, alone and unmindful of her imminent introduction to humanity, was Gruseltmira the too-many-greats-great descendant of the Rebrozian Nitram the Average.

Gruseltmira's five-foot-tall body lay supine on a nest of thorny striped, spotted, and psychedelic pillows with colors both within and beyond Human perception. Some of the pillows' sandy filling leaked from miniscule rips and tears and coalesced into glistening stalactites on the floor as she shifted to make herself more comfortable or fluttered the stumps of her rudimentary feathers like a rush of Human goosebumps. The stiff bristles on her head were adorned with jiggly balls of green gel.

Rebrozians were hermaphrodites, but not in the sense that they could sire a child alone, but in the sense that they harbored both sexes. At any moment, they had the ability to begin a process to switch sexes. The process took days to finish, but the starting was completely self-willed.

This private stardrive transport was a museum of her own making. On the wall above her and her pillows was a life-size portrait. Her painted self was standing on a pedestal while the arms and faces of a variety of beings strained to touch the hem of her garment. While their eyes begged for a scrap of her attention, her beaming eyes stared into the great beyond—a galaxy in accord with her imagination, desires, and tastes. How beautifully that utopia reflected from those two painted eyes into Gruseltmira's own eyes.

A golden, jewel-encrusted bust stood on a near table. She admired how perfectly it captured her visionary gaze for a galaxy as totally enlightened and sophisticated as she.

The most contemporary, sublime, and critically acclaimed music of the galaxy echoed off the walls of her small transport. It sounded like braying goats and fireworks punctuating an avalanche of bagpipes.

Gruseltmira was scratching violently on a notepad, which she dropped on her lap in disgust. Reaching up with her stubby, reptilian arm, she pulled a piece of gooey gel off one of the bristles on her head. The glob was snorted into the nostril above her right eye. Her body shuddered at the rush.

"Nothing like a good gellin' to get one's creative juices flowing," she said to her visionary statue. All of her writing was crossed out on the pad. She rubbed the GAASP logo heading the top of the page.

As a member of one of the richest families in the galaxy, she had been raised with the best of everything: the most prestigious education, the brainiest tutors, the snobbiest charm schools, the most athletic personal trainers, and the most irresponsible art instructors. Gruseltmira was galactically urbane, cosmically sophisticated, drug inured, and a medium-tiered lawyer for GAASP, the Galactic Association for the Advancement of Sentient Species.

GAASP's mission statement was "To ensure the legal rights of all species within the galactic fold and especially to protect the new and innocent" from having their Bleen-given rights and personal space trampled by the wiles of the big bad galaxy. Although not explicitly written, GAASP included in its mission the protection of all galactic citizens from the oppressive regulations imposed by StarDrive Engines, Inc.

Galactic law stated that all stardrives were to be registered with the GMVD. The law had been bought and paid for by SDEI, by exorbitant donations to the lawmakers' election accounts and enforced complete control over their sale, refurbishment, and resale. The punishment for violation was a mandatory life sentence on the nearest prison planet.

GAASP's signature achievement—and Gruseltmira's first case—involved twenty-seven missionaries sent to spread the divine word of their invisible, all-powerful Super-Friend in a ship using an unregistered engine. They were the same group Quane had heard of. The ship was confiscated and the passengers taken to prison. The captives vehemently proclaimed their innocence and maintained they bought the device legally and the salesman had assured them he would take care of registration. The detainees did not offer the subtle detail that they had taken the engine by force and driven off the hapless salesman. Had they been mindful of galactic law, they would have first ensured proper documentation had been submitted before they attacked the salesman.

GAASP had used the case as the touchstone argument for adapting the law to require a trial by judge in cases of unauthorized or unregistered stardrive engines.

Gruseltmira stopped rubbing the GAASP logo and redoubled her creative efforts on the messy page. She must come up with a name. The middle head on her tongue absentmindedly chewed the end of her pencil as she closed her eyes to concentrate.

As a GAASP lawyer, Gruseltmira was expected to defend the downtrodden and innocents from the brutish galaxy. But Gruseltmira was not interested in educating a bunch of hayseeds about the gamma-radiation-proof-oil scam or the magic-gravity-bean swindle. She did not care who took advantage of whom.

She saw her role as a cultural ambassador, as the self-appointed epitome of galactic style and grace, and her simple goal was to tame the barbarians by enlightening them. Like a beacon, she would lead them out of their dark, drab lives into the brilliant warmth of galactic civilization. It was her task to be an example of all the novitiates should aspire to become. Sometimes she wished she had a magic bean for these barbarians to nibble and become instantly as sophisticated, glamorous, and erudite as she—even if the effects were short-lived. At least they would experience the euphoric rush of what it was like to be Gruseltmira. They would search her out, knowing that with her guidance, and her guidance alone, their enlightenment might become everlasting. In lieu of a magic bean, she would have to be such an inspiring and affectionate mentor that her charges could not help but want to emulate her, and thus avoid adding to the number of ruffians and boors so prevalent in the galaxy.

One by one, race by race, planet by planet, she hoped to create a small army: an army of cultural appreciation. It was the name they would call themselves that she was trying to conjure on the page in front of her.

She wrote "Gruseltmira's Army of Galactic Music Enthusiasts (GAGME)" and scratched it out.

Then tried "Gruseltmira's Army for Galactic Culture In The Yokels (GAGCITY)," but rubbed it out.

And scribbled "Gruseltmira's Army for Galactic Appreciation in the Newly Discovered to Develop an Interest in Everything (GAGANDDIE)." She circled it as a possibility, but clicked her tongue worms at its lack of a certain vibrant élan. Artistic creativity was more difficult than she expected. She reached for another blob of gel.

CHAPTER 35

Nick and Miriam were waiting for the attempted ignition after breaking off some of the red dust.

"Engine will start at zero point one meters per in three, two, one." Chuck hit the ignition. This time, he did not ask if it worked.

"That's it," Nick said. "We're dead in the water."

"Let's go in and try to rethink this problem." Miriam was scouring her brain for a route to avoid leading her team into the abyss.

Miriam and Nick pulled on their tethers until they reached the habitat and began their hand-over-hand ladder pull to the airlock.

"Commander," said Chuck, "double-time it! I just picked up two bogies on short distance radar scan. They're heading straight for us."

"Triple-A on the way?" joked Miriam. Holding onto one rung, she turned to search for the approaching UFOs.

"Assume hostile," Chuck said, ignoring the joke. "They're coming at us straight off the short end of the engine."

Miriam and Nick alternated between squinting and staring wide-eyed to detect any kind of movement.

"Nothing but motionless points of light out here," Nick said. "If they don't have their own illumination, we wouldn't see them anyway until they were right in front of our lights."

"Try this," Chuck said. "Look straight off the end of the bar. Then concentrate your stare to the side at the width of your hand at arm's length. Use your peripheral vision to 'see' out of the side of your eye. Human peripheral vision is more sensitive to light and movement than looking at something straight on. It's an adaptation that helped us avoid being eaten on the savannah."

"I see them!" Miriam yelled, tickled by her newly discovered talent. "They're right where you said. Faint. Weaving back and forth, like they're homing in on us."

"Exactly how I see it, Miriam." As a soldier, Chuck had little use for or contact with scientists. They lived in lab coats, deep in the basements of weapons manufacturers or toy companies. The former he blessed when his weapon worked as promised. The latter he ignored; he did not play with toys. But these two were functional: they could take direction and succeed. He made a mental note to reevaluate his assessment of scientists with the probability of revision to the positive.

"Nick, do you see them?"

"Umm, no. I can't quite get it."

"Never mind. Get to the airlock ASAP and observe from there."

The strangers had arrived just as Miriam pushed Nick into the open airlock ahead of her. Their helmets and shoulders bobbed up and down in and out of the airlock opening.

The intruders were lenticular discs the diameter and thickness of a fifteen-foot, above-ground swimming pool. They radiated a soft phosphorescent green. Nick speculated that they might be radioactive. Each disc had three robotic legs on one side and each leg had three joints and terminated with a four-fingered claw, each finger at a right angle to the next.

The discs landed at the farthest end of the engine from the habitat pod and walked along and around its length in a helical path. Each disc swept a bright green laser across the surface.

"What are they doing?" Chuck shut his eyes and concentrated on telepathically transferring the tiniest bit of his military training to his crew.

"They're walking down the engine, toward the pod," Miriam said. "It appears they are scanning its surface."

Chuck fought the urge to suit up and get out the door to engage the machines. By the time he got out there, the worst might have already happened. His crew needed him where he was. Miriam provided the eyes, he provided the strategy, Nick provided...

In minutes, the robotic discs walked to the habitat. One robot climbed to the spot where the electrical cable met the habitat. It disconnected the cable from the habitat and plugged it into a connection on its underside. The other robot disappeared over the astronauts' limited horizon.

"Update," Chuck demanded.

"One robot disconnected the cable from the habitat and plugged it into itself," Nick said. The other disappeared."

"Shut the airlock" Chuck yelled. "Now!" He knew it might already be too late. The robots were executing a basic military maneuver—distract and feint: focus attention on a decoy and allow another to sneak up from behind.

The instant before the hatch closed, they saw the second robot above them. A green light flashed across their eyes in the slit of the airlock door just before it slammed shut. They had been scanned.

CHAPTER 36

Gruseltmira was scribbling acronyms and names for her cultural army when her GAASP pager bleeped. The text message lettering appeared as half-melted geometric symbols.

"High-speed transport to pick you up in five minutes."

This was the first time she was called into emergency service.

"Flock it. I haven't figured out the name of my army yet." She grunted as she rolled off the comfort of her pillows and began a search for her overnight suitcase. GAASP recommended all lawyers have a packed bag ready in the event of emergency calls.

The message arrived as Gruseltmira was returning from a shopping trip to a remote portion of the known galaxy. Gruseltmira had traveled three days to this area because of an advertisement about a new, novel boutique specializing in individually tailored coverings made entirely of kaleidoscopic worms. They had promised "The elite in cutting-edge style. So very *de rigueur.*"

But the boutique was closed. The building was in ruins after an attack from a pack of rabid space-faring sponges that subsisted exclusively on those same kaleidoscopic worms. The entire stock of merchandise had been consumed, digested, and defecated. The sponges died of gluttony. The proprietress was crying into her lawyer's shoulder. He comforted her with talk of making her investment back by converting the rubble into a children's play park. The lawyer insisted there was far more money in selling to children than snobs. The bankrupted owner's sobs decreased in intensity as she mentally calculated the profit margin.

"A wasted trip." Gruseltmira sighed. The whole point of her trek to this edge of civilization was the prospect of extending her winning streak. She had won the last four of her local GAASP office's Best Dressed Pageants.

With this emergency, she might never find a new dress before the next pageant. Gruseltmira triple-locked her habitat to prevent vandalism or outright theft of her most prized possessions. Dejected and resigned, Gruseltmira boarded the high-speed transit determined to make the best of an otherwise bad start to her day.

Little did she know that Humans were involved, or that Smez, the distant Martian ancestors of Humans, had been directly responsible for her family's massive fortune.

CHAPTER 37

Chuck heard the robot's staccato tap dance over the outer surface of the habitat and traced its path with his eyes as it walked from the hub to the airlock where Miriam and Nick had found refuge. He dreaded what he might find when the airlock opened. On Earth, he could walk, slither, or float his way home over any terrain, behind enemy lines, while dragging wounded, if need be. None of those skills were useful now. Without Miriam and Nick to help him fix, maintain, and pilot the ship, the mission was lost. Nothing would scream hopeless failure louder than the inscrutable, uncompassionate silence of infinite space.

The airlock finally opened.

"Wow, that was fun," Nick managed to spit out between belly laughs. Miriam was grunting to inhale between fits. They were spinning slowly and lightly bumping off the walls. Their helmet face shields were raised, but they were still fully clothed in their suits.

The airlock was filled with a pink fog. The airlock walls were the color a five-year-old girl might pick for her bedroom and the astronauts would have fit in as giant, color-coordinated dolls. The weightless pink cloud swirled casually into the control room.

Chuck's mental gears were grinding. Did they not understand the seriousness of the situation? Did the alien destroy their minds? If they had found some alien drugs, he desperately wanted to join in.

Chuck frowned; his hands grabbed each other behind his back and tilted his head to look down his nose at his crewmates. The posture was the same one his father assumed before a good dressing-down for some action of Chuck's that was either boneheaded or downright dangerous. His tone was fatherly and stern.

"You're taking this breakdown and threat of pirates awfully well."

Miriam coughed to compose herself, stiffened, posed with military formality, and then sputtered another laugh.

"I'm sorry, Chuck. You're right. It's a very serious situation; we're lost in space, broken down, and now possibly hijacked by alien robots. Nick got dirty with the red dust when he was examining the engine." Miriam clamped her lips shut but could not help spewing a chuckle.

"I tried to brush him off." She sputtered once, bit her lip, and covered her mouth.

"Then the dust got on her and I tried to brush it off of her." Nick smiled after throwing a quick glance at Miriam. Her head was turned to the wall, both hands were over her mouth and her back was convulsing.

"Then it got back on me, and pretty soon it was like in the book, *The Cat in the Hat Comes Back*, when all the cats try to clean up a little pink spot and wind up spreading it all over until everything is pink." Nick was laughing again.

Miriam struggled to get the words out between her gasps for breath. "I said, 'Vroom,' and we couldn't stop laughing."

Tears were rolling down Miriam's and Nick's cheeks. They hugged their stomachs as they rolled over and around, gently bouncing off the airlock walls. Squeaks and squeals echoed off the walls in the small space as the two pink astronauts tumbled.

Their unbridled joy was infectious. Chuck relaxed and smiled. One minute he had feared they were dead, the next he wanted to punish them for not taking their near miss with death more seriously.

"You both look like a pink nightmare," he said. "You're acting like a couple of deranged Easter bunnies. Make sure you wipe your feet before coming in—I just vacuumed."

"Yes, Dad," Miriam and Nick responded. When they finally calmed down and sighed away the last bit of joy, they began the process of doffing their spacesuits.

"Did anyone ever figure out why Richard was the only one nearly killed by this dust, but it's perfectly harmless to everyone else?" Chuck waved his hand in the cloud and created a weak vortex of swirling dust.

"It's one of the strangest mysteries in inoculation science," Miriam said. "It seems that Richard's body actually developed a vaccine to the dust, even though it almost killed him. That vaccine turned out to be extremely contagious. But since the vaccine targets the dust, there are no side effects. It's like any other vaccine floating around in our bodies, whether against polio, tuberculosis, or influenza. They are harmless to anything except those targeted diseases."

Nick was floating upside down relative to Chuck's perspective and had finished pulling his suit's legs off his feet. Miriam was sideways to both men and was wrestling to get her suit off her right foot.

"We know so little about the human body," she said, "cancer, the common cold, the placebo effect. Our first accidental brush with space opened so many new doors for medical research. The amount we will learn is staggering... Oof."

Chuck watched Miriam and Nick suddenly fall into the wall on his right. His right shoulder slammed onto a console.

"We're accelerating." Chuck jogged back to the control panel. Nick was close behind. Miriam was writhing on the floor, trying to get her suit off her foot.

When Miriam managed to catch up to Chuck, he was frowning at a display and rubbing the back of his neck. "Miriam, your last message said something about one of the robots disconnecting the electrical cable. Did it disconnect it from the habitat?"

"Yes, and plugged it into itself. They must be giving us a jump." Miriam leaned over Chuck's shoulder. Nick was purposefully examining consoles one at a time and entered data into a handheld tablet.

"Did it plug anything into the habitat's connector?"

"No," Miriam said. "Why?"

Nick finished his calculations and swiped his fingers across the tablet as he spoke. "The discs are taking us somewhere, for sure. But without the engines plugged into the batteries, we only have twelve hours of power left. I hope they're giving us a jump and not just a tow, or this will be a ghost ship by the time it makes port."

The last hint of warm pink joy drained from Miriam's face and was replaced by cold gray seriousness. Her light and loose shoulders dropped as she deadlifted the weight of command and the situation.

"Nick, sort essential and nonessential systems. Write an algorithm to define a duty cycle for each to maximize battery lifetime."

"Don't we want to shut off all nonessential systems," Chuck said, "and balance the rest for maximum battery life?"

"If turning off all the lights only buys us a few minutes, I'd rather keep some lights on. I want to fight and die with my eyes open, not hiding blind in a cave."

"Chuck, have you ever taken on a robot in your SCaTS training?"

Miriam was making her own calculations on her tablet. Quick, heavy footsteps distracted her. She turned and saw Chuck double-timing it to the airlock.

Stuffing himself into his spacesuit, his hands were shaking with the excitement of a chance to test his training: engaging an alien in space. He scoured his mental combat file for robots, but there were no entries. With an imaginary pen filled with make-believe ink, he wrote a note "To Ed: Add robots to training."

"Hurry," Chuck yelled from his locker. "Tell me every detail about the robots: every scratch, dent, loose wire, and seam."

Miriam and Nick were still yelling their recollections to Chuck through the closed internal airlock hatch when the final door opened to admit him into open space.

When they took their spacewalk, *Galaxy Quest* was moving at a constant velocity—anything in that frame of reference was effectively weightless. Now their ship was accelerating. Chuck's body experienced a force indistinguishable from gravity. From the direction of the gravitational force and knowing that the habitat was mounted near one end of the engine, Chuck deduced *Galaxy Quest* was flying in a the direction where the habitat was leading, with the long part of the engine trailing. The discs were at the corner where the habitat met the engine on the trailing side.

Chuck approached the open hatch and leaned out. Had he been on Earth, he could have been standing at an open window with his stomach on the sill and gravity pulling his head, hands, and body down. The deep space blackness was a minor inconvenience for him, since he had endured continuous weeks of training while blindfolded. Using the lights on his spacesuit was a little like cheating: like squinting, grimacing, and scrunching one's nose to get a tiny glimpse of anything out of the edge of the blindfold.

Chuck found the loose tethers that Miriam and Nick had jettisoned in their hurry to get into the airlock. Now, like ropes hanging from a cliff, they pointed in the opposite direction from the spaceship's heading. He tugged the lifelines in and made a Hula-Hoop-sized coil at his feet and clipped the end of one tether to his belt.

The calculated the sum of his body weight and spacesuit, if on Earth, was close to 385 pounds. He clambered to a standing position on the sill of the open hatch and reached for a firm handhold above him, on the inside of the airlock. The exertion of his first space pull up was equivalent to an ordinary, sweat-suited terrestrial one. They were accelerating at half a G.

"Chuck! Are you there?"

Flinching at the outburst, he instinctively reached to cover his ears but only slammed the sides of his helmet.

"Miriam, stop shouting."

"Sorry," she whispered.

"My fault. Stealth mode took over. I should have been communicating my position."

The airlock hatch was centered on the outer rim of the control-room half of the habitat pod. If the habitat pod were a tire, the hatch would have been an off-centered square patch of black gum on the tread. Chuck would have to climb out of the hatch and down eight feet to the edge of the habitat. From there, he could peer over the edge and get a look at the hijackers.

Chuck stood on the sill of the hatch, this time with his head outside. He secured a carabiner onto a handhold above the hatch, then snapped his tether into it. The lifeline slipped smoothly both ways across the metal loop. He gripped both lines—the one going from his belt up and the one coming down from the carabiner—together with both hands and stepped off the ledge. The ropes did not slide in his gloves; he hung firmly.

He let go of the tethers with one hand—still no move-ment. Slowly loosening his grip, the lines began slipping through his hand and his weight pulled him downward on his first space rappel. His boot toes tapped against the habitat for footholds and his free hand clung to every ledge until there was nothing left to grab and his helmet light was below the edge of the habitat. He squeezed the lines to halt his descent.

The robots were standing on the engine thirty feet away.

"I see them. They're motionless. They have not responded to my presence, my lights, or our communications. But I don't know how I could tell if they had responded. I'm moving in. I'll be on radio silence from here."

"Good luck," Miriam said softly.

From his position, he would have to move sideways to the acceleration. His feet would be hanging down. His motion to the robots would be swing, catch the next rung, and swing again—like a playground jungle gym, or his favorite part of a training obstacle course. The only risk was in swinging too hard and banging, and maybe cracking, his helmet against the habitat above him.

Halfway to the robots, Chuck stopped, secured his tether to a handhold with his second carabiner, and gripped the ropes. The inside of his helmet fogged from the exertion. The whir of his spacesuit's air conditioning unit increased in pitch and as suddenly as it appeared, the condensation was gone. The aliens had not moved a millimeter from the positions he had memorized. They were standing on the engine near the habitat: two discs, fifteen feet across, feet hidden under them, so he could not see how they held onto the smooth metal surface. They were stable standing sideways to the acceleration and did not flinch at the lights playing over them.

Chuck resumed his swing to the robots. At the last rung before the habitat ended, with the robots directly below him, he clipped in the last carabiner and hung from the tether. His helmet lights illuminated the articulated robotic legs. It was unclear how they were holding onto the smooth surface with four-toed metallic claws. Could he make them lose their grip?

Above him was a tool crib. Redundancy planned for an identical crib in the same position on the other side of the pod. If a few tools went missing forever from this crib, they had more. He opened the hatch and examined his choices. His first choice was a ten pound adjustable wrench. Not much of a weapon in a weightless environment, but a reasonable projectile dropped from a height at half-gravitational acceleration. He held the end of the wrench with two fingers and his arm extended down toward the robots. Closing one eye, he targeted the projectile to take out the nearest leg of the closest robot—the one plugged into the engine—and dropped it.

The wrench hit the leg right at the knee, bounced off, banged into the engine, and caromed off into space. The leg did not budge; the robot did not respond. It was like throwing a plastic spoon at a bulldozer. Chuck repeated the attack with a twenty-five-pound battery-powered ratchet with the same result. There was nothing of substance left in the toolbox.

All he had left was the 385 pounds of him and his suit—193 pounds in half-gravity.

Chuck aimed, adjusted his position, and released his grip on the tether. His feet landed hard on the nearest robot's leg—a direct hit. It was like landing on concrete from a second-story window. He rolled off after the impact to transfer his momentum and avoid two broken legs. His body jerked hard at his waist when he reached the end of his rope.

Facing away from their heading and the lights at the center of the galaxy, he was immersed in the claustrophobic blackness. Chuck shook his head inside his helmet and blinked hard; he had not passed out, nor had his eyes popped out of his head. He waved his hand in front of his lights to verify his eyes were indeed open. The instant his hand left the light, his hand and the light disappeared into darkness.

Chuck reached around to find the tether. The ship was at the other end, and he would have to go through the robot's legs to get there. There was one last course of action. He shinnied up the tether until he was near the belly of the robot attached to the electrical cable. The climb was easy, but a check of his remaining air verified that the workout in half-gravity was more strenuous than if he had been weightless. There was enough air left for one attempt to wrest control of the cable from the robots. If he failed, he would have to abandon the mission and retreat.

The knurled connector's housing was the size of gallon milk jug and screwed onto a mating fitting on the belly of the robot. Three times, with ever-increasing grip and torque, he tried to budge the cable connection. He grit his teeth, shut his eyes, and strained his arms until he felt the first pop in his shoulder warning him that if he continued, he would dislocate his shoulder. Nothing moved: neither the connection, nor the robots.

"Galaxy Quest, I'm coming home." Chuck swallowed hard and croaked out the words that his pride, dedication, ability, and training had promised he would never have to say. "There's nothing I can do. The robots are in control."

Miriam's head fell forward; her chin touched her chest. She forked her fingers into the hair above her forehead. "Come back in one piece. That's an order."

CHAPTER 38

The high-speed transport was already populated when Gruseltmira boarded. The entire interior surface was covered with gel-filled, purple velvet padding designed to conform to any body type while accelerating in any direction. The transport was not donut-shaped like Quane's or *Galaxy Quest's* habitats, which wrapped completely around, but sat on its engine like a saddle. There were only two rooms: the large, padded room for passengers and the cockpit, which only fit two small or one large pilot. The passenger cabin was lit by glowing, softball-sized spheres held in place by finger-width tubes. It was sleek, bright, clean, and still had that new transport smell—something between sour milk and gasoline. The passengers floated in listlessly, waiting for the acceleration to settle them on one cushion or another.

"Welcome," a young Rebrozian said. "Please sit here, next to me."

With one hand gripping the nearest cushion, she pulled Gruseltmira into the transport. "Quickly, we have to be going." To the pilot, his spikey back visible in the open cockpit door, she said, "We're all here. Go!"

The pilot waved a fin in acknowledgment without turning around. The acceleration quickly climbed out of Gruseltmira's comfort zone. None of the other fourteen passengers were enjoying the strong gravity. There were two pairs and one triple; the rest were all single representatives of their species. Gruseltmira judged their dress as plain and their appreciation of culture as nonexistent. What else could one expect if they deliberately lived in this backwater of space?

"So sorry for the rush," Gruseltmira's host said. "GAASP thinks this could be the one—the first real test that we can bring some amount of justice to the galaxy. I admit I am excited. I didn't want to miss this opportunity, so I asked the pilot to step on it. I know the pressure is stressful, but if getting there early will help make a success of this first case, it will be so worth it." Gruseltmira detected a wheeze in her neighbor's breathing. She was going to respond, but only managed a belch as she gasped from the weight on her chest.

"I haven't introduced myself. My name is Schone. I'm just a minor law clerk in the local GAASP office. Actually, I am the only law clerk in the local office. But I know you—you are Gruseltmira. I read all about you."

Schone was Rebrozian, like Gruseltmira, but a younger, more-attractive version. Her tongue had not yet bifurcated. Her skin had not reached the age when scaled replaced her pure white downy feathers.

"Headquarters called, said it was an emergency and I should round up witnesses for the trial." She tilted her head toward the other travelers behind them. "Because your GPS indicated you were in the area, I was told to pick you up and rush straight out to the confiscated engine with the new species on board." Her feathers rippled with excitement. Her talons were swirling in front of her as if assembling an invisible puzzle.

"This is such a perfect test case. An unknown race came upon an engine somehow, managed to get it running, but it broke down. We know about where they came from, if their heading was true. There is no record of life in that area. Some fragmented and unsubstantiated data about an ancient race called Smez."

Schone's deep blue eyes were firmly planted in her skull, not on herky-jerky stalks like Gruseltmira's. In the future, when Humans finally became galactically cosmopolitan, they often philosophized on the strange fact that Rebrozians were the first known case of butterflies metamorphosing into bugs, or swans becoming ugly ducklings.

"Isn't this exciting?" Schone bubbled. "GAASP fought hard to get the law changed from a mandatory prison sentence for illegal ownership or operation to trial by a judge. Now we will finally test our defense of a naïve people, ignorant of galactic law, against the big stardrive engine conglomerate. I can't wait to hear what you think about all of it."

Schone clasped her talons across her downy chest, ruffled her feathers once, and stared expectantly.

Gruseltmira finally took the time for a closer look at the clerk while her wormy tongue *click-clacked*. "What have you read about me, exactly?"

CHAPTER 39

There was a new entity on board *Galaxy Quest* since Chuck's return from his unsuccessful attempt to dislodge the robot hijackers. Silence. It enveloped each astronaut like a cocoon. Hopelessness filled their mouths and stopped up their throats.

They had checked the charts, determined their heading, and reviewed the maps. No star was reachable within *Galaxy Quest*'s remaining battery lifetime. There was no one to call. There was nothing to do, nothing to say.

Miriam calmed herself with the knowledge that there was no greater measure of dedication as a scientist than to die in the pursuit of pushing back the curtain of the unknown.

Chuck believed he would receive accolades as a dedicated soldier on a mission with an extremely low probability of success.

Nick wished he had never bought that box of cereal with the cheap, colored glasses as a prize.

No one asked for an update on remaining battery life. They had individually synchronized their watches t the instant of the final estimate. Thirteen and a half hours passed. They had one hour left.

Nick assumed his lightheadedness was the first indication of the failure of the air purification system. Then he noticed a pen rising off the console in front of him.

"We've stopped accelerating! We're here…wherever that is."

Charged with a sudden burst of hope, they all swam to the nearest viewport for a glimpse of their destination. Miriam and

Chuck had reached ports looking upon nothing but dark space. The only interesting object in Nick's field of view was the long end of the engine.

Had Nick oriented himself properly, unaffected by the impending hush of the galactic hiccup that was the sum of his life, he might have realized that if he was truly looking at *Galaxy Quest*, he should have seen the short end of its engine. Had he been able to focus, his eyes watering with self-pity, he would have also noticed the surface he saw was polished and unblemished.

A second habitat pod had stopped accelerating, matched *Galaxy Quest's* velocity, and docked itself to the Humans' habitat pod. Ten minutes after *GQ's* acceleration stopped, it started again and gravity resumed in the same direction as before.

Thirty minutes later, there were three loud knocks on their airlock door. Nick jerked up to standing as if shot with a bolt of electricity. "Are they trying to break in?"

Chuck did not lift his cheek from his fist. His elbow rested on his armrest. The console, where one of his weapons was hidden, was two feet—or one second—of his reaction.

"If they wanted in," Chuck said calmly while shifting his position to enable quick access to his secreted weapon, "they wouldn't knock."

Three more times the knocks echoed around *Galaxy Quest's* control room. The robot discs were too big to squeeze into the airlock. Did they want to talk, zap them, or offer first aid?

The crew suited up. As far as they knew, dark space was still on the other side of the door.

Miriam poised her hand over the airlock's Open button.

"As first Human ambassadors to the galaxy, let's not screw this up...like so many of our encounters with new peoples. Let's not decimate them with smallpox; let's not shoot the heathen first and ask questions later; and since it seems we might soon be prisoners, let's present the best of the Human race, not the worst. Maintain your dignity, even when enduring the impossible. Make your species proud."

Pressing the button and smiling her best keynote-speaker smile, she said, "It's time to meet the galaxy."

The airlock slid open.

An empty room greeted them: no robots with death rays, no space vacuum, no welcome committee, no armed guard, and no native maidens with leis.

They saw a short, well-lit corridor similar to an airplane's passenger boarding bridge. The airlock at the other end was open. They could not see what was on the other side of the door.

Miriam's mind echoed the sing-song rhyme of three other well-known characters entering a wondrous and dangerous new land. "Lions and tigers and bears, oh my." As expected, the second door on the alien side slammed shut forcibly behind them. The corridor made a hard, short, right turn.

An LSD-induced hallucination would have been preferable to the reality ahead of them. They could wake from the former comfortably strapped to a bed in an insane asylum, but they would have to deal with the latter.

The Humans entered a circular room like an old operating theater. Around them, from floor to ceiling, were tiered rows of spectators oscillating, flagellating, and gyrating while displaying a myriad of colored skins and wings. None wore spacesuits. The Humans heard a cacophony of squawks, buzz, and whistles on the speakers in their helmets.

Chuck scanned each creature, evaluating which of them might be armed as guards or executioners. Next, he scanned for anything he could use as a weapon. He settled on ripping off an appendage from a feeble-looking being in the first row. It had thin arms covered with a tough exoskeleton and might work as a knife if the other aliens' flesh were soft.

Miriam focused on one species at a time, imagining the taxonomy, evolution, and anatomy of each, but the instant she fixed on one, another came into view. None wore breathing apparatuses or pressure suits. Had they been selected or invited because they were the only ones that could survive in this environment? Did they have to pay to get a seat here? What were they expecting to see, a circus or execution?

Nick still wished he had never, ever bought the box of cereal with the cheap, colored glasses as a prize.

Miriam signaled that she was going to remove her helmet. The other two shook and waved their arms in attempts to stop her decision. The action stirred some loose dust off Nick's arms but did not deter Miriam. The removal of her helmet sent another small puff of dust outward, toward the audience.

Smiling formally, and in the sweetest voice she knew, Miriam said, "Greetings. We are from Earth. We are here in peace, friendship, and brotherhood…"

Before she finished, alien backs were jamming each other out of the exits. Nine aliens, all in the lowest, nearest row were motionless.

Nick and Chuck removed their helmets.

"Nice job," said Nick. "You scared them to death. Was it your breath?"

Miriam, flustered, stomped her foot. "What did I do? I didn't do anything wrong! A lot of them were uglier than me, and I didn't scream and run away. Is my hair all that bad?" She pushed some body back into her hair. "These damn helmets."

The door slammed shut moments before he got there. Chuck's responsibility now was for the safety of the crew with no time to waste evaluating Miriam's faux pas; he thought only of escape.

"Check every door and panel," Chuck ordered. "Miriam, take the first level. Nick, take the second level. I'll take third.

Miriam, take the fourth level when finished with the first, and so on."

"What are we looking for?" Miriam said.

"Another way out. A loose panel or a hidden door."

Chuck pressed and hammered every square foot of wall on his level. Nick copied his actions.

The dead aliens commanded Miriam's attention. She hoped to get a reaction of some kind to prove that they were not really dead—and she did not really kill them. If there was the least sign of life, she could try to comfort the being, if not cure it. Without detailed knowledge of alien anatomy, though, there was no chance of actual healing. She gently touched them one by one and waved her hand in front of anything resembling eyes. None moved or responded. Limbs and tentacles remained limp and unresisting.

Convinced they were truly corpses, Miriam moved listlessly to join the others in the search for a way out; dejected for kicking to the gutter her guiding principle for interaction with animals—*Primum non nocere*: First do no harm.

The three methodically moved around the room, pressing, pushing, and pounding every seam and wall panel. When they were nearly to the top level, the airlock door they first entered opened again. Miriam and Nick stopped pounding and started for the exit.

"Stop," said Chuck. "It may be a trick to draw us off. We may be getting near a way out that they don't want us to find. Keep working the wall."

They found no hidden exit or secret panel. Reluctantly, Chuck admitted the only way to go was back to the ship. At least they would have time for a last meal of Miriam's Mess before the batteries died.

The doors shuddered as they closed behind them with a sigh of relief. Chuck checked the controls on *Galaxy Quest*.

"Good news! They're charging our batteries."

Miriam flopped in a chair next to Chuck. Her face was in her hands and her knees were on her elbows. "What happened? How did I kill those aliens?"

"You got the looks that kill." Nick smirked with satisfaction at the other two, proud of his pretty sweet joke.

Miriam glared. She didn't know it, but had finally managed to look fierce. Nick wilted under her stare and walked off quickly to find something to do far away. He promised himself to never lighten up the situation again.

"Miriam." Chuck put a hand on her shoulder. "I don't know what happened, but I do know we made a pretty bad first impression."

CHAPTER 40

"Tell me what you read about me," Gruseltmira stared unblinking at Schone.

Before she could answer, the transport's intercom crackled to life.

"Incoming message," the pilot said, "for someone named Schone."

Gruseltmira watched her young attendant squat outside the cockpit and fit a set of headphones and mouthpiece. The conversation agitated her as it went on; arms flapped, feathers ruffled, and finally her down flattened and flushed a dull gray. She leaned heavily on the cushions as she staggered back and flopped back in her place.

"Nothing too important, I hope." Gruseltmira fidgeted with her skirt. It looked and smelled like burnt alien newsprint and released thin wisps of smoke. Her blouse of overlapping wooden slats was reminiscent of a shagbark hickory tree. "Now, where were we?"

"I'm afraid GAASP's first big trial has already blown up in our faces." Schone was doing her best to sidestep Gruseltmira's self-absorption and stared into her lap. "Initial, unsubstantiated accounts report that the new aliens, arrested for illegal possession and operation of an unregistered stardrive engine, committed a terrorist act at their introductory hearing."

Schone nudged the unresponsive Gruseltmira; frowning as she raked her stare over the dress of her nearest neighbor. "Gruseltmira, did you hear me?"

"Yes," Gruseltmira said with a huff. "What's so important about GAASP blowing up unsubstantial accounts in the faces of new aliens? She—" Gruseltmira pointed at the object of her derision. "—should be arrested for the un-regal effrontery of those earrings."

"No, that's not what I said." Schone pulled a pendant out from beneath her breast feathers. It was modestly expensive and her best piece of jewelry: three brilliant yellow crystal gems set in polished platinum. Flickering sparkles reflected into Gruseltmira's eyes.

When Schone had captured Gruseltmira's attention, she relayed what she had been told. Police drones had captured aliens operating an unregistered stardrive engine. The aliens were taken to a hearing ship to explain themselves and enter a plea for their trial. Eyewitnesses said the aliens entered the welcome room filled with greeters, waved their appendages, and shook some Flock off their spacesuits. One of them removed its space helmet to observe, verify, and satisfy itself on the success of the attack. Nine innocent members of the gallery were confirmed dead; sixteen were in critical condition. All the rest were under observation in hospital.

Closed-circuit camera recordings showed these new aliens unaffected by Flock. The first alien to remove its helmet said something, but without translation, it was unknown if it was a warning, a plea, or an ultimatum. It just stood there, pondering the devastation. The other two aliens removed their helmets after the attack. The first one checked the dead, presumably to finish them off if they were still alive. Then they all performed a search of every inch of the room walls. It was assumed they were searching for an escape, but when the airlock to their ship opened, they ignored the exit and continued the search. Eventually they made their way back to their ship and have been locked in ever since. The police are listening to their conversation to create a translation matrix for the trial.

Acceleration of the Human ship quadrupled to get them to Schone, Gruseltmira, and a proper trial for the original charge of registration violation, and now for the additional charge of terrorism.

No one understood how these new aliens indifference to the intense toxicity of Flock. Even the most radical anti-Bleen factions never used Flock as a weapon because it would kill them long before they could disperse it. The best minds speculated that the aliens had some kind of temporary antidote or invisible shield to delay the effects of Flock and were probably now dead and rotting back on their ship. No one knew what to do next. This had never happened before.

"The rendezvous," Schone said, "is in thirty-six hours at the rogue planet, Altair Five." Schone put her head back on the seat cushion and closed her eyes. The strain of breathing in the heavy gravity was giving her a headache.

"I wouldn't want to be in their shoes." The mention of shoes reminded Gruseltmira of clothes, and her thoughts returned to her favorite topic. "So, exactly what did you read about me?"

CHAPTER 41

"Acceleration quadrupled," Nick said. "We are at 2 G's. Wherever they're taking us, they want us there in a hurry."

Nick's announcement was not a revelation to the gasping Miriam. Chuck nodded and waved nonchalantly.

"Remind me to go on a diet when we get back." Miriam groaned with every step and sighed with every breath. She penguin-waddled her away around the console room to check the other instruments, arms at her side, tablet left behind. Movement at twice her body weight was exhausting, but she was too uncomfortable to sleep. A systems evaluation, even though routine, was at least a constructive distraction.

Nick barely stirred. Lifting his tablet to evaluate the latest data or work on his latest app was like holding a five-pound weight. Physical exercise was not any part of his regular Earthly regimen.

Chuck worked with the added weight as if it were another test. He strained at the last reps of his daily calisthenics, but always finished.

The smell and taste of food was an attractive idea. But the accompanying sensation of stuffing food into an oppressed abdomen was not. Sleep was fitful, since breathing and movement was difficult. All that was left was simple talk about life, friends, coincidence, and why they were here, exploring a space Humans never knew existed. Miriam always drew the conversation back to their first encounter with the gaggle of aliens and why they ran away at the sight of them.

"We had all our shots," Nick mumbled.

"Maybe it was a bacterium. Maybe it was a gas we exhale." Miriam wheezed twice and coughed to shake the weight off her lungs. "Maybe they had an anaphylactic reaction to our dander."

When the ship flipped to deceleration, their mood changed. The ceiling became the floor. The end of the ride was approaching, and the resolution of their situation.

They were strangers in a strange land filled with bizarre natives exhibiting alien and possibly incomprehensible customs. Early human explorers were killed, tortured, or eaten because they unwittingly violated some local taboo. But those taboos were among the same species, sharing the same genetic material and planet—merely differentiated by culture, arrogance, and ignorance.

How would these entirely alien peoples respond to the killing of their citizens? There was no shared DNA, no shared tribal experience. Would they see the incident as accidental, or intentional? Galactic society might decide Humans were no more than a poisonous vermin, a cancer. A rock was overturned and out came the Human plague. Exterminate!

The Humans' weighty conversation allowed the galactic police to eavesdrop and build a conversational matrix around Human speech patterns and their stored digital library of movies and television shows. The Humans' jailers had three questions that they hoped would the prisoners conversation would answer: How long could Humans withstand the effects of Flock? Would the Humans discuss the success or failure of their attack? And, most importantly, would the Humans detail the plan for their next attack? All this was useful evidence for the prosecution.

CHAPTER 42

Schone trapped, took a deep breath and answered Gruseltmira. "I read all about you in the newspapers and magazines. For the longest time, you were the topic of conversation for me and my friends. We read all about the ancient history of your family, including the rumors about Nitram the Average. We studied the schools you attended and the enormous parties you gave. There was not much published since then. It was as if you dropped off an arm of the galaxy. Your name came up again when I started clerking at GAASP."

Gruseltmira's tongue flicked and snapped randomly at nothing in particular. Schone noticed her boredom, but had to discover Gruseltmira's proudest career achievement and continued probing.

"You prefer argument to research. High-profile cases to low-profile cases. You have an above-average dismissal rate, though marginally above-average, and have the most wins in your office's Best Dressed Pageants."

"The honor I am most proud of." Gruseltmira was beaming with pride and her tongue worms stuck straight out and twisted into a braid.

"The dismissal rate?"

"No, silly, the record number of pageant wins." Her eyes spun around on their stalks and blinked as she pictured each champion dress in her imagination.

Schone's feathers fluttered in a single wave from her head to her foot; flushed with excitement at the discovery of

Gruseltmira's vanity button. Schone was intelligent and driven, but did not have Gruseltmira's money, education, or connections. Perhaps Gruseltmira's coattails could tow her out of the choking quicksand of her current dead-end clerical position. Maybe those same coattails could drag her into the limelight of a galactic celebrity. Front row center, next stop.

"I must say, I have never seen such an unbelievable dress. And you pull it off so well." As she gingerly touched Gruseltmira's skirt, her feathers ruffled slightly.

"This old thing?" Gruseltmira pinched and pulled on the skirt as if to punish it. "This is so last month—just a rag I wear when absolutely everything else is at the cleaners." The dress was, in reality, her current favorite.

"You certainly are intelligent and perceptive," Gruseltmira said and offered a blob of gel to Schone, who politely refused. Gruseltmira shrugged and snorted it up. Her tongue clicked three times from the rush.

"As long as we are talking…" Gruseltmira wiggled her shoulder into Schone's. She took a quick look around to see if anyone was listening and tipped her head. "I'd like your opinion." Her hand was over her mouth to prevent eavesdropping. "How would you defend the newcomers if you were in charge, especially now that they committed an act of terror?"

"Really? You want my opinion?" Her feathers fluffed with satisfaction; her plan was working.

"Let's see," Schone said while tapping her cheek. "If I were in charge of the defense, I would first try to understand the newcomers. Why were they operating an unregistered stardrive engine? What did they pay, and who was the salesperson? If this is their first encounter with travel around the galaxy and the salesperson never advised them of their legal responsibilities, how could they have known they were supposed to register it?"

Schone laid her feathers down flat and aligned them in a fine herringbone pattern to make her look precise and professional. "But that was before they Flocked up the hearing." Her brow furrowed. "No registration is of small importance compared to the charge of terrorism. What did they hope to gain by Flocking a gallery of greeters at a hearing gathered to help them?" Shone leaned in to ensure she had Gruseltmira's attention.

"We haven't heard if they are dead. If not, are they immune to Flock? No one else in the galaxy is. If they are immune to Flock and have no knowledge of the galaxy, why would they even think to use it as a weapon against other people?" Schone leaned back, closed her eyes, and combed her breast feathers slowly with her talons.

"The terrorism charge, though more extreme, is not much more complicated to defend than the unregistered engine charge. I would try to convince the judge, based on their immunity to the Flock, that they had no idea it was extremely toxic to every other life-form. The real terrorists duped them into a suicide mission."

"Hmmm." Gruseltmira stroked her chin. "Exactly in line with what I was thinking." She was actually thinking about where she would get another dress to wear for the next Best Dressed Pageant. This bothersome trial would be a lot easier if she enlisted Schone to do most of the work.

"I could use a talented young individual like you on my team," said Gruseltmira. "You can see the big picture and appreciate what is and is not important, much like myself. Would you like to get out of a dingy, lonely office and become my assistant attorney?"

CHAPTER 43

Altair Five was a small sunless planet floating alone and cold in empty space. The planet had lost its sun 45,500 years BQ—or, more correctly, its sun had let the planet go. An explosion on its nearest neighboring planet nudged Altair Five out of stable orbit. Gradually, the planet's orbit became more eccentric as it passed closer and closer to its star, increasing velocity with every pass. Finally, it achieved a velocity great enough to break free and Altair Five flew off into space. The explosion that destroyed Altair Four doomed Altair Five to aimless wandering among the expanses of space.

Altair Five had one artificial, alien-made moon for company. The orbiting satellite was a police outpost manned by two officers. Several factors made this remote outpost attractive for the trial of the Humans. The planet was equidistant from the robot-driven ship housing the defendants and the high-speed transport carrying their defense attorney and trial witnesses. The station had rooms large enough to hold a trial and provide lodging for witnesses and visitors if the trial dragged on. The station had once been a manufacturing facility for now-obsolete computer circuits based on crystalline elements.

When the facility was running at full capacity, personnel entered the manufacturing area through a gauntlet of stations designed to verify the workers were cleansed of particles damaging to the sensitive microscopic electronic structures. In the prehistoric galactic days when computer chips were made out of crystalline wafers, a single particle left at the bottom of a stack would adversely affect the operation of the devices many levels above, not unlike the way the fairy-tale princess was bruised by a pea placed twenty mattresses below her. Though computers based on crystalized elements had become obsolete centuries ago, the apparatus for cleaning workers to make those computer chips was still operational and indispensable to blow the Flock off of the Humans.

The most important reason for conducting the trial at such a remote location was to prevent Humans from Flocking up the proceedings. The body count would remain limited and the post quickly sterilized by crashing it—and the dead or dying inhabitants—onto the frozen surface of Altair Five.

Transcripts of the recorded and interpreted conversation from *Galaxy Quest* were forwarded to the police outpost for analysis before the Humans, lawyers, and trial witnesses arrived for trial.

A loud, repetitive buzz indicated the arrival of a legal document of utmost importance. The noise echoed down the undecorated corridors. Evidence of paw, claw, cup, and foot scuffs decorated the flat-finished, off-white walls. The noise ricocheted around unfurnished conference rooms and off sloppily patched walls. Sooty shadows were the only remnants of missing wall hangings. The sound bounced into the sparse officers' quarters and found the intended recipients: two four-foot-long, brown-shelled cannoli strapped upright to metallic cylindrical cradles.

The bottom end of each cannolo was pale gray and glistened with slime. Saucer-sized glistening puddles had formed on the floor below them. A spiral pattern covered their top ends. The lines, wider near the shell, thinned and tapered to a dot at the center. One of the cannolo's spirals was alternately red and white; the other sported a spiral of black and white. Even the daftest resident of the planet Allunac could immediately identify who was in charge. On Allunac, black and white spirals were considered superior in status, intellect, and mating preference to the inferior red and white spirals.

The black and white spiral quivered in a frequency too low for Human ears. "Frants, get that."

The red and white spiral vibrated back, "No, Villem, it's your turn. I'm not finished with my nap. Besides, you went to bed before me because I had to finish up all your work."

"Finishing all my leftover food was your work?" Villem's spiral vibrated. "Go. That's an order."

"I'll get right on it, your Majesty," Frants' spiral twitched back impudently. A gray slimy end extended from his hard shell, tested, then stuck itself to the floor. His red and white spirals unwound and stretched to their full three-foot length. In the traditional culmination of a waking Allunac stretch, he whipped and snapped each three-foot-long tentacle once. Finally, his glossy-red turtle head rose over the edge of his lumpy brown shell like the dark-red sun climbing over Allunac's horizon. The whole endeavor took ten minutes.

Yellow-green eyes blinked three times and he licked the remainder of Villem's food off his lips. "This'd better be worth my loss of nap time." He snapped his toothless beak.

Frants slithered onto a flat, three-wheeled scooter. He wrapped his tentacles around the handles and twisted the throttle. The battery-powered vehicle lurched forward and soon hit its maximum speed of three miles per hour. He squinted hard against the wild wind as he sped off to receive the ultra-important correspondence and silence the alarm. Without a scooter, it would have taken a week to slither to the communications room.

The document was a transcript of a recorded conversation from a new species called "Humans." An introductory paragraph detailed the events leading to their trial. Frants and

Villem examined and highlighted important passages. Plans for the accused had changed radically after their brazen Flocking of innocent bystanders.

Villem highlighted several passages for the judge assigned to the case.

> Suspect Miriam: GREETINGS. WE ARE FROM EARTH. WE ARE HERE IN PEACE AND FRIENDSHIP.

Many pages passed without highlight.

> Suspect Miriam: I KNOW I WASN'T THE UGLIEST ONE IN THE ROOM. WHAT HAPPENED?

> Suspect Nick: HEY, YOU GOT THE LOOKS THAT KILL. The word "kill" was double underlined.

> Suspect Chuck: MIRIAM, STOP BEATING YOURSELF UP. I DON'T KNOW WHAT HAPPENED. BUT I DO KNOW WE MADE A PRETTY BAD FIRST IMPRESSION.

Many more pages passed without highlight.

> Suspect Nick: WE HAD ALL OUR SHOTS.

> Suspect Miriam: MAYBE IT WAS A BACTERIUM? MAYBE IT WAS A GAS WE EXHALE? MAYBE THEY HAD AN ANAPHYLACTIC REACTION TO OUR DANDER?

"I don't know about you, but I don't see anything here that says they planned anything." The effort of reading and highlighting passages had taxed him considerably. Frants was a top Allunac athlete. A year earlier, he had won a gold medal at the Allunac World's Fittest Competition. He religiously kept his body in tip-top shape. But this exertion was way beyond his limits. His red tentacle was a limp, wet rope against his shell. The tip of his white tentacle massaged his closed eyes.

"I don't understand how they can still be alive," said Villem. Frants' conversation had woken him from a drooling nap. "The discomfort of acceleration worried them more than the Flock." A black tentacle wiped his dull black head. The size of the lumps on his shell indicated he was much older than

Frants, and the dull sheen on his head indicated he was in poor shape. His white tentacle wiped the remaining frothy drool off his chin.

"Do you think they have some antidote to the Flock? We could ask them, kind of secret-like. If they told us, we could probably make lots of money selling it."

"Not me. I'm not going anywhere near them." Villem curved his tentacles in broad loops with the tips in balls and pressed against his shell. The posture resembled a loving cup trophy and was an Allunac demonstration of defiance. "We'd better make a lot of overtime because of all this."

"Look. They're here." Frants pulled his head back into his shell reflecting his disappointment with the trial proceeding.

The Human vessel materialized into light space close to the police satellite with the robot drones still attached. Minutes later, the transport carrying Gruseltmira, Schone, and the other travelers appeared. Frants and Villem obeyed the request from the GAASP transport and extended a bridge to their ship. Fortunately, the mechanical systems were not under the same physical restrictions as Allunacs and the docking happened in less than five minutes.

Schone led the little group, followed by Gruseltmira. The rest of the transport passengers floated behind, gabbling, confused, and tired. Weightlessness was a refreshing relief after the crushing acceleration.

The officers were waiting for them on their scooters. Though Villem was a big shot on Allunac because of his coloration, to the rest of the galaxy, he was just a drab, lowly tubeworm.

"Welcome," Villem said. Without leaving his scooter, he flourished his tentacles listlessly into figure eights—feigning Allunac hospitality.

"Show us the layout of your facility," Schone said brusquely without making eye contact.

"Certainly. I drew this map especially for you." He held out a crookedly drawn map of the satellite's layout on a brown, wrinkled, torn, and stained paper. Irregular boxes were labeled "Big," "Mine," "Cold," "Hot," and "F's."

"We'll figure it out. And bring in our bags." Schone crumpled and tossed the useless map over her shoulder.

"Gruseltmira, when do you want to interrogate the prisoners? Do you want to speak to them in person, or remotely?"

"Since I will be mentoring you at this trial, let me ask how you would handle the prisoners." A broken bit of bark on her dress commanded her attention. She couldn't remember if it was new, or if it had been there all along.

"I would much prefer talking to them in person," said Schone. "I get to know my clients better that way—observe how they act and feel."

"We think a lot alike." Gruseltmira was thinking less about the trial than how susceptible Humans would be to her sophistication. The best way to determine their level of sophisticated taste would be to sit before them in all her galactic splendor and gauge their reaction.

Schone turned to Frants. "We need the aliens on board as soon as possible for their interview."

"Really?" Frants said. His beak yawned. His tentacles were in a spiral over his head. "I was about to take a nap."

"As soon as possible."

"All right," Frants said. When Schone turned to leave, he twisted his tentacles into two coil shapes—the most obscene and insulting gesture an Allunac could flip. Regular naps were in his job description and in the union contract. It might take a whole day to clean up the mess she made. *Throwing paper on the floor, indeed.*

CHAPTER 44

"Hey. We're back in light space." Nick was floating at a viewport with his nose flattened against the window.

The others looked and saw it was true. After they'd adjusted to the dim lights of dark space, the sudden intensity of real starlight was stunning. Instead of a concentration of dull pinpoints in one direction—toward the center of the Milky Way—the distribution of stars was uniform in all directions and all were as bright as the black hole gravity wells in dark space. Outside the window, they saw a beat-up metallic sphere, a couple of city blocks in diameter, illuminated by running lights and floodlights playing over its surface. There was another spaceship. A sleek habitat hugged the cylindrical engine like a saddle. A barely visible, flat black disc of an Earth-sized planet framed the sphere and spaceship.

A voice like the screech of a splintering green tree branch shrieked out of *Galaxy Quest's* intercom. "Humans, you are under arrest." Villem filled his speech with authority. Perhaps, eventually, this species would be treated as even lesser than Allunacs. If not, at least he would have fun dominating them while he could.

The Humans, petrified, glanced at one another, first in surprise to hear an alien speaking perfect English, and second, shocked to hear they were under arrest.

Miriam held her hand up to silence the other two. "May I ask whom I am talking to?"

"You may ask," Villem said, "but I am not obliged to tell you."

"What is the charge for our arrest?"

"I am not here to tell you that, either. Proceedings are underway and you will learn everything soon enough."

"May I ask how you can speak our language?"

"I am really exceeding my instructions by talking to you in such a friendly manner," said Villem. "For now, it is enough for you to know you are being held. Await instructions." The communication clicked off.

"Wait! What?" Miriam blurted to the deaf walls of the habitat.

Villem had used the conversation to verify that the translation algorithm worked both ways and to rattle their cage. It was fun being the species in charge for a change; besides, what they said afterward might yield a confession. His head pulled into his shell for a quick nap.

"We sure stepped in it now." Nick floated away, body listless, ignoring the data offered by the consoles around him.

Miriam turned to Chuck for tactical advice, but he was busy by other consoles halfway across the control room, violently searching one, then another, and then moving to the next. He ripped off cover panels and whipped them with a careless backhand into the weightless control room, the spinning rectangular Frisbees bouncing and banging off walls and consoles. If he'd had a sledgehammer, the consoles would have been reduced to scrap. Miriam floated up behind him.

"Damn solid state," he muttered. "Where are the wires?"

"Chuck?" She said evenly and tapped his shoulder. He spun around the opposite shoulder, assuming a strike position. His face flared with a dare to beat him in a fight to the death. In the fraction of a second it took to recognize Miriam, he just as quickly relaxed.

Miriam jerked her hand away as if the tip of her finger was about to be bitten by the knife-edged jaws of a sprung bear trap.

"What are you looking for?"

"I'm looking for a small coil of wire or plastic to hide in my hand," he said, "just long enough to go around an alien's neck. Plastic would be best because it would not set off any metal detectors." He was not ready to admit he had hidden real weapons on board.

"No weapons," Miriam said.

"We don't fight?" Chuck asked.

"Where would we go? Where are we now? We killed nine aliens. We have to answer for that. Hopefully we can convince someone of our innocence—or, we were ignorant of the effects of our actions. I know you are in charge of security, but I don't see how fighting gets us anywhere."

Chuck frowned. Statesmanship and politics never trumped a strong defense.

Nick had floated by to see what they were up to. "Hopefully they understand the concept of mercy."

"If they didn't," Miriam said, "why would they bother to learn our language, keep us alive, and go to the trouble of putting us on trial? I have to believe a positive outcome is possible."

Chuck touched his medal through his shirt.

Nick suddenly flew off to the hatch for the living quarters. He just made it when the other two heard him retch.

Miriam found a spot on the other side of the hub, out of Chuck's view, and sobbed quietly into her hand.

CHAPTER 45

Frants listened to the translation of the Humans' conversation through a hard rod held against his shell. The shell amplified the vibrations and directed them to his internal eardrum. The Humans clearly sounded convinced of their innocence.

Maybe GAASP was right. New races were not trying to break the law; they simply did not know the law. Too bad there might not be an execution this time. He would have to wait until they caught the one everyone was looking for: Quome... Qane... That trial and execution promised to be a spectacle, a real barnburner. Now he had to get those nasty Humans over here and make sure they did not Flock up the station and make more work for him.

Frants hailed *Galaxy Quest*. "Humans, you will please remove all of your clothes and leave them on your ship. One at a time, you will cross the bridge. We will provide new garments on this side."

"Does it matter who goes first?" In spite of Miriam's objective scientific outlook on animal and human physiology, she was still prudish when it came to displaying her own body in front of the opposite sex. As hypocritical as she knew it was—she could look at the naked male and female form objectively—she felt stressed if someone saw her in the nude. There was no checkbox for that on Internet dating sites.

Frants turned to Villem and shrugged by twisting his tentacles into a pretzel shape. Villem shrugged back and yawned.

"No," Frants said. "I do not care. What I care about is one of you leaves when I say, and the next one waits until I say."

Chuck had no problem stripping and was the first to float boldly over the bridge.

"Next," Frants said.

Nick tried to emulate Chuck's machismo but his thighs were only as thick as Chuck's biceps.

Called finally, Miriam stripped as ordered and floated along the tunnel to the other ship. The first room was narrow, not wide enough to hold both arms out straight. Arrayed on each wall, compressed air nozzles pointed in every direction. Frants ordered her to move to the middle of the room and hold onto railings attached to the walls. Suddenly, hurricane-force winds blasted her. The hair on her head buffeted as if she was riding a motorcycle at 80 miles an hour with no helmet. Ten seconds later, it stopped, and then two seconds later, it started up again. Frants repeated this pulsed air shower ten times before directing Miriam to the next room.

This room was a duplicate of the first, except for a mesh net hanging from the left wall instead of nozzles. This time, air blew continuously from only one direction. She was ordered to turn completely around or the process would not stop.

The third room had banks of lights on both walls, and all she had to do was slowly pass between them.

The last room was all white. The only furnishing was a hook from which a body-length cloth hung. She wound it around her like a bath towel, just below her armpits, as instructed. When the two fabric ends met, they melded together to make a comfortably fitting wrap.

The final portal was a double door with a vertical seam down the middle. A rectangular opening the size of a piece of paper in landscape mode, centered vertically, with half of the opening in the right-hand door and half in the left.

"You will insert both of your upper appendages into the opening," Frants ordered.

"And if I do not?"

"You will never leave this room."

Chuck and Nick must have agreed, or they would still have been there. Miriam trusted their lead and complied with the order. An elastic band tightened around her wrists. When the doors swung open, she saw the wrist cuff was tethered to a small, robotic car magnetically attracted to the floor. The car rolled forward with Miriam in weightless tow.

Barefooted, bare-shouldered, bound at the wrists, and chained to an unmanned vehicle, she found her crewmates similarly dressed, tethered, and floating near a rectangular table as wide as the room. A thick piece of transparent material divided the table down the middle.

"The gang's all here," Chuck said. "Looks like we can get on with the show. Feeling clean and refreshed, Miriam?"

"Like a spring day after a rain shower. What next, I wonder."

"See the window?" Chuck pointed with his restricted wrists to a dark window covering half of one wall. "Just like an interrogation room. Whoever is on the other side is there to watch our reactions during questioning."

Miriam leaned her head toward Chuck and talked out of the side of her mouth, minimizing lip movement. "See any way out?"

"We tested the bands." Chuck spoke normally, without attempting to disguise the conversation. "The more we struggled to free each other, the tighter the bands became. I tried once to pull my car off the floor—I thought I could use it like a track-and-field-hammer throw to break the window—but it wouldn't budge. Our only way out is by way of our captors. You were right, Miriam; we have to convince them we are actually very nice people and whatever we did or said, we meant no harm."

Frants and Villem reviewed the particle data acquired from the air showers. The Humans were Flock clean. Not a single trace of the deadly dust was detected on any of them at any point in the air showers.

Schone and Gruseltmira found their way to the guards' station. Frants and Villem, belted into their chairs, were asleep in front of the one-way glass.

"Wake up!" Schone said. "Are they clean of Flock?"

Frants blinked slightly and pointed weakly to the data summary on one screen. "Not a single Flock molecule," he said. It was way past Frants' naptime and he was getting cranky. Villem was already sleeping; drool was bubbling over the top of his shell.

"Are you ready to meet your next case?" Schone asked Gruseltmira.

"Why not?" said Gruseltmira. "They look harmless to me." Gruseltmira squirted herself liberally with her perfume atomizer. Schone blinked hard as the mist burned her eyes.

CHAPTER 46

Gruseltmira erupted into the interrogation room from a door on the opposite side of the table with the transparent window. A thin yellow fog swirled around her. "Hello, hello, hello. I'm so very happy to meet you." She pranced, pirouetted, and finally plopped into her chair like a pile of wet cement.

The Humans heard, "Gobble, spit, gibble, gobble, spit, gibble, gobble, spit, gibble, hiss, planknish, jibbelty-jab," and recoiled at the sight of Gruseltmira. Her mouthful of worms occasionally spit droplets of brown ooze on the window separating the Humans from the aliens as she talked. The wiry bristles on top of her head were adorned at the tips with variously colored balls. They rocked back and forth, side to side, and around and around at her slightest nod. The loose dress covering her scaly body was a patchwork of greasy rags, rusted metal, and shiny silk. She smelled like the strange brew at the bottom of a trash can in a sweltering summer. Miriam swallowed hard to counter her gag reflex. Chuck clenched his jaw to prevent laughing at Nick, who mimed gaging himself by putting his index finger in his mouth.

Gruseltmira noticed the Humans' response to her entrance and took it as an immense compliment: the sight of true grace and style had taken their breath away.

Schone was smaller and attractively birdlike. Her eyes were fixed on the front of her head and did not move. Her tongue was in one piece. She wore a simple white tunic.

Schone dumped a shoebox of components on the table in front of her. There was a crazy assortment of bent wires and straps terminated with cups, balls, and nails. Some were plush and furry, while others resembled hard iron and might have been more at home at the Spanish Inquisition. Shone stirred the tangled pile of devices with her talon to spread them out and pushed them to the Humans through a small slot under the glass. The Humans waited for instructions.

"Chinkle lobishty spit ack ack ack," Schone said to the perplexed Humans, repeating the words while pointing with great exaggeration to the instruments on the Humans' side of the glass.

Nick leaned his ear closer to the table. He heard something coming from the instruments. "Place a translator by your auditory receptor," said a voice from the nearest unit.

"English is coming from these things. I think they are communicators." Nick grabbed a headset, like stereo headphones, and pushed his ear to the cup.

Chuck grabbed a headset with small rubber cups. Miriam tried a unit that had three orange balls hanging from a thin chain.

Schone said, "Do you understand me now?"

The Humans all nodded.

"Good. Let me introduce ourselves. This is Gruseltmira, your defense attorney. My name is Schone. I am her assistant. Do you understand?"

The Humans nodded again. The alien vocalization of grunts and spits translated instantly into common English. What the translators could not correct was the visual disconnect between the movements of the alien mouth and the words in the headphones. It was like watching a poorly dubbed Japanese science fiction movie.

"Say something," Schone said, "so we can make sure the translators work both ways."

"We understand you perfectly," said Miriam, a little too loud. She was unsure what part of the headpiece to talk into and thought yelling at the glass would help. "May I ask how you can speak our language?"

"We have computers to translate languages instantaneously." Schone's jaw moved up and down like a child's sock puppet, but the sound of her words did not match the rhythm of her mouth. "You hear our language translated; we hear yours. While you were in your ship, we listened to your conversation and downloaded all of your video data files. The translator created a matrix to convert your speech into any known language in the galaxy and vice versa. These headphones connect wirelessly to any translation computer in the area."

"Let's get to it then," Gruseltmira hated not being the center of attention of a captive audience.

"My name is Gruseltmira," she said, "and I am your defense attorney in these proceedings. All three of you are under arrest for the ownership and use of an unregistered stardrive engine. Thanks to GAASP and my considerable effort and influence, this offense no longer carries a mandatory sentence of life imprisonment." Gruseltmira paused to let the gravity of their situation and her personal stature sink in.

She expected some acknowledgment of GAASP's hard work—if not a standing ovation, at least a courteous "Thank you." The efforts to change the law had come from a dedicated batch of GAASP lawyers. Gruseltmira's contribution in total was as the celebrity spokesperson. She took the success of the campaign as validation of her abundant charisma.

"M-mandatory life imprisonment?" Miriam stammered. Her face turned white. Her heart felt like it was climbing up her throat. The crew of *Galaxy Quest* might have the dubious galactic distinction of being the first Human beings arrested, tried, and imprisoned. Humans make it into galactic history at last!

Chuck's wrists were beginning to bleed from his attempts to break his restraints. The possibility of a SCaTS soldier faced with the prospect of cutting off arms, feet, or legs to escape an enemy had been broached in training. For obvious reasons, it could not be practiced. The decision to amputate was given to the soldier based on his evaluation of his situation. The restraints were too wide and soft for a quick section. Chuck aborted the attempt at escape; he would bleed to death before freeing himself.

Nick was dry heaving on his cart. Miriam thought she heard him whining, "There's no place like home," between gags.

"I just told you," Gruseltmira said, "this charge does not carry a mandatory death sentence anymore—thanks to GAASP. I think I can safely say none of you will get more than life imprisonment for this charge." Gruseltmira folded her scaly arms across her flat chest in smug satisfaction.

Miriam stared at Gruseltmira's dress to avoid cringing in disgust. Gruseltmira noticed the Human's was fascination with her attire. Maybe their appreciation of elegance and style was more developed than she had thought. Gruseltmira felt sorry for these Humans and was starting to become fond of them, in a pet-like way. The one called Miriam was clearly so overcome by Gruseltmira's radiant beauty she could not bear to look directly at her.

"What is GAASP?"

"GAASP stands for the Galactic Association for the Advancement of Sentient Peoples. GAASP's mission is to defend the rights of peoples, like you, who are new to the galaxy, and to educate them about basic laws and customs. GAASP is here to assure people like you have a smooth integration into galactic culture and to protect you from exploitation by unscrupulous agents who might try to cheat you—like selling you an unregistered engine."

Miriam locked on Gruseltmira's yellow-green eyes. Quane had deliberately sold them an unregistered engine and knew the consequences. Miriam's heart free-fell into her stomach; they had been duped into buying junk.

"As I said," Gruseltmira continued, "you will be on trial for the crime of operating without registration. You are also charged with a second crime: terrorism, murder, and mayhem for your recent attack on a group of innocent bystanders at your initial hearing for the first crime. Punishment is slow, painful death."

Nick was banging his naked heels together while he heaved. The veins on Chuck's neck were throbbing as he strained to lift his car off the floor. Miriam moved closer to the glass in spite of her revulsion at her lawyer and turned her empty, restrained palms up to plead for their lives.

"Please understand we did not know we broke any laws regarding the engine. We had absolutely no intention of harming anyone. We still do not know what happened or how we hurt those people. How soon is our trial? When and how do we prepare?"

The balls on Gruseltmira's head waved back and forth as she chuckled, her tongue-snakes jerking, at the comical Humans. "The trial starts now. As soon as we can get to the courtroom. This was the preparation."

For the second time in her life—and again without knowing it—Miriam managed to look fierce. "What?" she yelled. "How can you defend us when you don't know the facts? You don't know who we are or where we come from. You don't even know our names."

"Yes," Gruseltmira said. The balls on her head bopped forward every time she nodded to count the facts. "We know the facts. The facts are that you were operating an unregistered engine and you attacked a room full of innocent bystanders. We know you call yourselves Humans and your names are

Miriam, Chuck, and Nick. There is only one thing I don't know and must ask before we leave for the courtroom."

Schone raised her talon to interrupt Gruseltmira. "We listened to your conversations. We know about you and the Smez. We know you are a backward, primitive race and know nothing about galactic law, politics, or religion. And we know you are too ridiculously ignorant to pull off a terrorist attack like this unless you were duped by a terrorist organization. If we thought you were at all dangerous, you would have already been executed."

Miriam looked to her crewmates for support and ammunition against the alien slander. The Human race was not barbaric; it had art, medicine, and science.

Nick, exhausted and weak from vomiting, floated at the end of his tether. His eyes were closed and his heels tapped weakly together. His lips opened and closed, fishlike…paused, then repeated.

Chuck, weary from the unsuccessful attempt to escape his restraints, simply stared at Miriam. Both men had removed their headpieces. Intellect and muscle was not going to free them. Statesmanship was all they had left.

"There is just one important question I have to ask," said Gruseltmira. The headphone even translated her insistence.

"Ask."

"As I am the organizer of a society for the appreciation of galactic style and culture and I would like to know your opinion of this dress."

Miriam's fists clenched, her knuckles turned white. Chuck saw the rising anger. The Humans were facing imprisonment at best, a slow-death sentence at worst, and their lawyer was more interested in interrogating them about her dress than the case. Chuck put his bleeding, restrained hands over Miriam's. She shot a glance at him nearly as intense as Chuck's was to her when she had surprised him searching for a weapon. He closed his eyes slowly and exaggerated the act of taking of a long, slow breath. He lifted the fingers of one hand off hers. Then slowly, one at a time, his fingers closed on her fists, counting down: five...four...three...two...one, and nodded his head with each count. Miriam's grip relaxed. Her face calmed.

"It is possibly the most unspeakable thing I have ever seen," Miriam said through gritted teeth.

The galactic fashionista congratulated herself for her luck at finding these Humans. The Human liked it so much she could not speak the words! They were ignorant of laws and protocols, but when faced with true beauty, they could not look at it nor speak comfortably about it. Gruseltmira's tutelage would change all that. Gruseltmira mirrored her pose in the portrait in her habitat. She was glimpsing the start of her cultural army.

Schone nudged Gruseltmira out of her daydream. "Time to go."

Gruseltmira and Schone walked ahead of the prisoners, held to the floor by magnetic boots. The Humans were dragged into the courtroom by their shackles and magnetic cars. A rush of screams and cries greeted their ears as they entered the room.

The bedlam set off an alarm caroming off walls to the officers' quarters, signaling the need for the Allunacs' presence as officers of the court to restore order.

"They've obviously heard of me," Gruseltmira whispered to Schone.

"Where are the lions?" Chuck said to Miriam. Nick was floating, dazed, like a limp windsock.

"Gristle-myra, can you tell us what is happening?" asked Miriam. "What do you expect from us?"

"My name is Gru-selt-mir-a," she said. "The trial is about to begin. I expect when this is all over and you are freed, you will join my cultural army and help me infuse the galaxy with sophistication and style and make the entire galaxy finally fit to live in."

Miriam paused to consider whether a galaxy full of Gruseltmiras would be worth living in. "If you get all of us out of here in one piece, I promise we will join your army. Maybe you would even consider making us captains."

Gruseltmira's feather stumps on her back wiggled with excitement. The balls on her head clacked as she danced a little jig. These Humans were everything she could have hoped for but had to find a way to get an acquittal. If only she could inspire Schone to do all the work. With Schone's brains and her own good looks, there was no way they could lose.

The courtroom was the size and shape of a high school gymnasium. The bleachers thundered with stamping feet and a roar of voices. The quintet stopped in the middle of the courtroom under a single white spotlight. Its glare prevented the Humans from seeing exactly how many and what kind of beings surrounded them. Their instinctive reaction was to shield their eyes with their hands to get a better look around. Tugging on the restraints pulled their weightless faces to the floor. To prevent a face-first collision with the floor, they pushed off with their hands and wound up summersaulting erect. The audience cheered even louder at the Humans' acrobatic entertainment. A second alarm bounced off the shells of the two Allunacs extending their slimy feet to the floor and unbuckling themselves from their cradles.

Gruseltmira had specifically requested the spotlight. The strong light emphasized the subtle juxtaposition of fabrics, textures, and colors only the most cosmopolitan intellect could possibly appreciate and lesser intellects could not help but admire.

"Court is in session, the Honorable Judge Minot presiding," a disembodied voice announced.

"This is Judge Minot," a second, sonorous voice announced. "Court, come to order." An unseen gavel banged until there was silence. "I see the defendants are ready. Is the defense ready?"

"Yes, your Honor," Gruseltmira said.

Miriam tapped Schone on the arm and whispered, "Where is the judge? I can't see him."

Schone whispered back, "She's on remote and can see us and hear us, but we can't see her. It was an emergency trial and she could not get here in time."

"Let's get on with it then," Judge Minot said. "I see these aliens are charged with operation of an unlicensed stardrive engine. This used to carry a mandatory, immediate sentence of life imprisonment. Now we have to have a trial—all because of those damned GAASP lawyers." Minot's voice was snide. "Galactic Association for the Advancement of Savage Peoples is more like it. Senseless Peoples is even better. How about Sordid Peoples? I bet GAASP originally wanted to make it Saintly Peoples..."

Schone interrupted the judge's rant. "Gruseltmira is a GAASP attorney and I am a GAASP clerk, your Honor."

"Oh, great," said the judge. "Now I have to listen to you bleeding hearts spouting all your liberal nonsense about how these primitive yokels deserve a chance to explain themselves. Ignorance of the law is no excuse for criminal activity.

"If GAASP had its way, even those damned anti-Bleen terrorists would be able to get off by saying, 'I didn't know I was doing a bad thing when I bombed the store. Eww, I didn't know someone was going to get hurt. Eww, eww, I thought were just playing a fun game,'" she whined sardonically.

Gruseltmira hung her head; the balls did not clack. Judge Minot had not complimented her dress. The dress alone should have convinced the judge to grant an acquittal, if Gruseltmira would only have been so kind as to share the name of her tailor.

Schone saw Gruseltmira's distress and took over. "Your Honor, we are not here to argue the merits of the new law. We are simply here to defend our clients."

"Right you are," Minot said. "This rabble is also charged with terrorism, murder, and mayhem." There was a long pause. "Wait a minute. Is this correct? They Flocked a hearing?"

"Yes, your Honor." Gruseltmira curtsied deeply as an excuse to spread her dress for the judge's appreciation.

"That's impossible," Minot said. "Something's wrong here. Hang 'em. Hang 'em, I say, before they get away and terrorize the rest of the galaxy. Is this some new kind of weapon?"

"Not as far as we know." Schone rubbed Gruseltmira's back sympathetically. "All of the samples from the hearing room confirm it was Flock dust."

"This is the craziest thing I ever heard," said the judge. "Well, let's get on with this. I have an appointment to present my posterior to Nibor of Xof in a couple of hours and I can't be held up by this trial. How do the defendants plead?"

Schone saw Gruseltmira slipping into depression because of the slight to her dress. "Should we start with the first charge?"

"First, second, fifth," said Minot, "I don't care. I have to get out of here. Let's go!"

Schone nudged Gruseltmira. "Tell her not guilty to the charge of operating an unlicensed stardrive engine."

"Not guilty," Gruseltmira repeated and twirled her dress coquettishly from side to side to reflect more light into the judge's eye.

"You know the new law. I have to hear it from the defendants. Defendants...Hum-enz, you seem to be called, or Smez, or whatever. I can't make this out. Are you guilty or innocent?"

Gruseltmira crumpled into a pile on the floor; her dress had never lost a case before.

Blood seeped from Miriam's fingernails digging into her palms; the trial was going bad quickly. Their lives, their mission, the hopes and dreams of humanity would be saved or broken in the next few moments. "What do I do?" she gasped to Schone.

"Answer the judge," Schone said. "Are you guilty or innocent of operating an unlicensed stardrive engine?"

"Innocent," Miriam said. "We did not know the law. We never saw a stardrive before. We didn't even know aliens existed before one came to sell us one. We didn't know we had—"

"All right, all right," said Minot. "The defendants say they are not guilty of the first charge. What do they say to the second charge?"

"Not guilty. We know something bad happened at our first meeting, but don't know what or why. We were hoping for some help because our engine died, and then the robots came. They started it back up, and then we found ourselves at the other ship. Some people died when I tried to introduce—"

"Enough," said Minot. "The defendants plead not guilty to the second charge. Big surprise. Hum-enz, you are lucky GAASP has taken an interest in this case. I'm not so lucky. If it weren't for GAASP, I would be out of here and you already sentenced."

Nick was comatose, trying to sleep his way out of a bad dream. Chuck, still without a translation headset, was only listening. He squinted through the spotlight to see what kinds and how many aliens he might be up against. His wrists had stopped bleeding.

"To the first charge of operating an unregistered stardrive engine," the judge said, "you were caught in possession of one so old it had been scrapped for junk and was unregistered. Do you deny this fact?"

"No, but—"

"No buts. GAASP, your turn to cross-examine."

Schone nudged Gruseltmira and whispered, "Ask Miriam where and when they found it."

Gruseltmira blinked hard. "Where and when did you find this engine?"

"About seven years ago. An alien visited our planet and sold it to us."

"And how much did you pay for—" said Gruseltmira.

"What?" interrupted Minot, "You actually paid for this piece of junk?"

"We didn't know it was junk. To us, it was amazing alien technology. We hoped it would let us travel to the stars."

"Stars, shmarz," said Minot. "You would have been better off if you had stayed where you were."

"So it seems." Miriam lowered her eyes.

"Well, come on, GAASP," Minot said. "Get on with it."

Gruseltmira, flustered by the chaos and interruptions, found a last bit of gel and snorted it. "What were you thinking? I mean, how much did you pay for the junk engine?"

"Two hundred thousand genomes," Miriam said.

The courtroom exploded in a roar of shouts. Minot's hammering gavel could barely be heard above the din. Miriam took the opportunity to swim out of the spotlight. When her eyes had adjusted, she saw strange and exotic figures in the gallery. Some were like those at the first hearing; others were different. Something was vaguely familiar about one of them. A third alarm for reinforcements echoed off Frants and Villem's shells as they boarded their scooters.

"Hum-enz," Judge Minot said after shouting down the courtroom, "that is a lie!"

"What is a lie?" Miriam said.

"All of it," the judge said. "Every last bit. Your species must be dumber than a box of Shishishishtarian rocks if you paid anything at all for the junk engine. You should have made whoever it was pay you to take it away. Even if you were really stupid enough to buy it, there is absolutely no way to convince me your planet could have half that number of genomes available to sell. Two hundred thousand? Impossible!"

"But Judge, we did pay that. Two hundred thousand is only a fraction of our planet's diversity."

"Inconceivable. Any planet with so many plants and animals would have gone stark raving mad with the distraction. Not to mention that you would need nearly as many individual habitats to support such diversity."

"It's true. All of it—the habitats, the diversity. At last count, Earth has nearly nine million individual species. We have five hundred thousand genome files on board our ship right now."

Pandemonium thundered through the courtroom. Schone ducked and shielded her head with her hands at the outburst. Gruseltmira stopped futzing with her dress. The Humans froze at the courtroom's overreaction to simple facts. Earth believed it had made a shrewd deal for a stardrive engine, only to find out Quane had screwed them royally.

"Lies," said Minot. "No new genomes have surfaced or become available in the last seven years. If you really paid two hundred thousand genomes—an enormous sum by any measure—surely some of them would have surfaced for common use by now. I'd bet your claim of five hundred thousand is a booby trap to help you escape. Unless there are any other facts to support your claim that you purchased the engine, we have to find you guilty as charged."

Miriam suddenly remembered what she thought she saw in the gallery—there was someone who could provide a witness for the defense.

"Your Honor. There is someone here who can help us explain and prove what I say is true."

Miriam squinted and found her target. "There!" she said, pointing as best as she could with her bound hands to a hooded creature. "Quane! Tell them. Tell them you know us, we bought the engine from you, and what we paid!"

Frants and Villem pushed the door open into a roaring bedlam. The courtroom seethed with alien bodies; some were trying to leave, others crowded on an individual in the gallery. Unaccustomed to disturbance, Frants and Villem's attempts to restore order were easily rebuffed by the belligerent crowd. Before this, their greatest conflict had been over which one of them left the coffee kiosk dirty. A dense ball of moving flesh slowly made its way from the gallery to the courtroom floor, holding an alien overhead. Frants and Villem snapped their tentacles at random while they pulled their heads into their shells. They snapped and popped at nothing in particular like two broken party noisemakers. Had Dante seen the melee, he might have used the courtroom scene as an engraving to represent his Eighth Circle of Hell.

The captive almost escaped the mob's grasp by virtue of his weightlessness. He separated from the mob and floated beyond their reach. Suddenly, a whiplike flagella shot from the crowd, wrapped around his waist, and reeled him back into the mob's clutches. It was an Yndi of Senoj who lassoed the floating alien. Evolution decided Yndi males needed this adaptation as a way to snatch their favorite food from the air and attract a prospective mate. By snapping near a prospective lover's face without hitting her, he made himself known. If overt lust caused him to miss his mark and strike her face, she was instinctively programmed to turn and eat him. The errant suitor was instinctively programmed to allow her to consume him.

The ball of alien flesh pulsed forward into the spotlight. Chuck had pulled Miriam and Nick in by their restraints. Their hands gripped and their shoulders touched. Schone's soft, warm feathers pressed against Chuck's bare left shoulder and Gruseltmira's rough, stinking skin scraped his right. The mob advanced toward the huddled group in a wave. The alien tsunami deposited its gift at the Humans' feet before it retreated and dissolved. A tattered, hooded mass shivered and panted from fright and exhaustion. Its legs had been crudely tied to Nick's truck to prevent his escape, weightless or otherwise. The smell of Gruseltmira revived Nick from his coma like a deep whiff of smelling salts.

"Hum-enz," Judge Minot said after once again restoring order, "is this the creature that sold you the stardrive engine? Your answer is extremely important. Take your time."

Miriam had known him for only a few hours, seven years before. She slowly approached the huddled alien and reached out her hand. "Quane?" she asked tentatively.

"Who?" The creature trembled under its cloak without looking. "I am Wyruk. I do not know any Quane." Wyruk was grinning from ear to ear under his hood.

"Why are you tormenting me? Judge, please help me. They lie! I have never seen any of them before. I am an ordinary citizen. I came here to see justice served on these terrorists and thieves. I have nothing to do with them."

Wyruk cringed as his Human accuser approached to get a better look. She slowly reached out and pulled back his hood. Wide, diagonal stripes with a tint of gray crossed his otherwise red face. His black onyx eyes were not as shiny as she remembered; his shoulders were broad and he sported a thin goatee. This devil, Dia'Bolos, was different than the alien she had met. Miriam interrogated her memories. It had been over seven years and did not know how his race aged or if Quane was young or old when they had last met.

"Your Honor. I was wrong. This is not who I thought he was. From a distance and in the bad lighting, he looked similar to a creature I met once whose name was Quane. In the better light and without his hood, I cannot unequivocally identify him."

"Are you absolutely certain?" The judge's voice was patient. "Take your time."

"Yes, I am certain." The shame of her mistake, obvious to Chuck, was missed by the judge.

"The accused may leave," Minot said. Her voice was filled with disappointment. This might have been her biggest case ever. Wyruk untied his ankle and slunk toward the gallery. "So, you know Quane?"

Schone punched Gruseltmira in the back of her head. "Don't let her answer that. Ask for a recess."

Gruseltmira, discombobulated by all the confusion and searching her dress for the tiniest scratch, shook herself awake and jumped in front of Miriam just as she was about to speak. Whatever she started to say was gagged back down her throat by the sudden scent of her gargoyle lawyer.

"Judge," Gruseltmira said, "in light of these new developments, I request a recess to consult with my clients. These facts are new to us and we need time to—"

"Denied," Minot growled. "Answer the question: do you know Quane?"

Miriam looked to her lawyer for guidance, but Gruseltmira only had eyes for the stain on her dress.

Schone whispered, "Answer."

"Yes, I know Quane."

"Now we're getting somewhere," Minot said. "I might get out of here in time. So, you know Quane. Just exactly what larceny were you planning? Was he behind this terrorist attack?"

"We did not plan any attack. I know him because he is the one who sold us the engine."

"Quane? Quane sold it to you? Ha, ha, ha!" The judge roared with laughter. "Ha, ha, ha!" Miriam made a mental note to challenge linguists to develop an algorithm to translate laughter.

"Hum-enz," Minot coughed to catch her breath, "did you know Quane is on the Ten Most Wanted list for crimes committed against the galaxy? He is a swindler and cheat. He's sold almost everything to just about everyone in his miserable life. Once he sold a four-armed Schlarn an insurance policy on a fifth arm, in case the Schlarn decided he needed to grow another one, or one got cut off and he needed a replacement. Lately, the complaints are about his selling junk stardrive engines to anyone he can, which are mostly idiots like you. Tell me, how did he convince you to buy?"

"He gave one of us a test drive to prove it worked." Miriam hung her head in shame. "He said it was a stolen museum piece and it was a collector's item."

The judge's uproarious laughter was so contagious the gallery, including Wyruk, shared the joke and all had an enormously good laugh. Frants and Villem poked their sleepy heads out of their shells to see what they had missed.

"You Hum-enz didn't invent stupid," the judge said, "but you sure perfected it."

Miriam blushed.

"GAASP," Judge Minot said, "congratulations. Flawless defense. I commend you on your presentation. I find the defendants innocent of the first offense: operating an unregistered stardrive engine. Let's move on." Her voice relaxed; she would make her appointment with the Nibor.

"On the second charge, terrorism, murder, and mayhem, how do you plead?"

CHAPTER 47

Wyruk had heard enough, skulked out of the courtroom, and boarded his small ship. Wyruk had lied; he knew Quane well.

The living quarters of his habitat was packed with a myriad assortment of counterfeit, illicit, and contraband items ready for black-market sale. He smirked at the irony that Quane was a wanted criminal while the authorities had just set Wyruk free. If the police had found his cargo, Wyruk would have spent ten years in courts on twenty different planets for possession of stolen goods, illegal transport of hazardous waste and explosives, restricted weapons technology, and Shnacuoilitian pornography. All of that punishment combined, though, was only a tenth of what he would have received for the three chained and caged Xcrutians he was carrying. His combined sentences would have found him tied to a planet sweeping through a pulverizing storm of meteors, wallowing in a lake-sized waste pit of a Shiel herd, eaten and digested through the nineteen stomachs of a two-horned Trazom, toasted on a planet engulfed in the atmosphere of a red giant, and finally, just for spite, his remains would be injected into the black hole at the center of the galaxy.

A small antenna extended to eavesdrop on communications from the courtroom while he hid in the membrane. Quane and Wyruk were from the same planet, the same race of Dia'Bolos, and were ten years different in age; Wyruk being older. His wide stripes were individual, but predictive of age.

Wyruk was the source for the junk Quane sold and he laundered the illegal profits. It was a safe and lucrative arrangement. Victims identified Quane as the perpetrator while Wyruk, unidentified in the background, took three-fourths of the earnings and overcharged for the engines. The result was Quane's enormous debt to Wyruk; he planned to dispose of the debt and recoup his losses by selling tickets to Quane's excruciating and bloody death. Afterward, he would sell the snuff video to the rest of the galaxy. But all that changed with the discovery of Earth.

The trove of Earth's genomes nearly blinded him. He slapped Quane silly for settling on a price too quickly. The planet was overflowing with genomic riches far above anything ever seen and he could have had it all but was obviously too simple-minded to negotiate.

Quane had been on a random walk around the galactic backwater for so long he did not know if he was coming or going, and could not pinpoint Earth's location even under Wyruk's not-so-subtle threats of bodily harm. His broken GPS—the one Wyruk sold him, on credit—did not record, so there was no chance of backtracking the trail to Earth.

Finding Earth became his obsession. The potential profit was immense. He scoured police communications to intercept any report of illegal engine operations ignoring all other business. He bribed, bought, and traded information until his bank account drained to pennies. With barely a week of finances left, he heard the thrilling news of the terrorist attack by aliens who were driving without registration. Even if they were not the Humans he was seeking, the spectacle and distraction of a terrorist trial was easily worth the price of admission. Praise Bleen he was within a distance to arrive in time.

His ears were still buzzing as he left the courtroom: nine million genomes. One of them had mistaken him for Quane.

This had to be the people with the genome hoard. Quane had warned Wyruk about the bungling, accident-prone nature of these Humans, predicting they would leave nothing but destruction in their wake.

The plan was simple. Their engine had been confiscated, so they had no way to travel about the galaxy. He would present himself as a benefactor of species development. Maybe forge a GAASP credential and offer a deal on several factory-certified stardrives. His offer would include full registration, a prepaid maintenance plan, and delivery to their home planet—which he would arrange personally. If they were going to buy engines anyway, why not buy them from honest old Wyruk? He would follow them to their planet, take all the genomes, and then destroy Earth so he would have the only copies.

Had he waited in the courtroom and listened to the rest of the testimony regarding the Earthlings' deadly Flock attack, Wyruk would have learned the Humans possessed something of far greater value than any number of Earth's genomes.

CHAPTER 48

"On the second charge," said Judge Minot, "terrorism, murder, and mayhem, how do you plead?"

Miriam's shoulders drooped. One charge was lifted, but one remained—potentially the most devastating: murder. Her attention had been strained and exhausted maintaining composure against the Alice in Wonderland trial: the abhorrent Gruseltmira, the hallucinogenic gallery of spectators, and the Kafkaesque maze of alien law.

Overcome by the realization her entire race was made a galactic laughingstock by a conniving cheat, Miriam sighed deeply. If she was lucky enough to have the chance, would she—could she?—stand in front of a worldwide telecast, digital-eye-to-digital-eye, and admit they had been swindled, skunked, fleeced, and taken to the cleaners? Would her race feel ashamed by their naïveté, recoil from galactic travel, and retire forever to their singular planet?

"Not guilty," Miriam said with head bowed.

"GAASP," said Minot, "why are they not guilty?"

Gruseltmira fingered the small hole in the hem of her dress, torn slightly in the recent chaos. A tear formed in her eye.

Schone stood up. Her feathers fluttered once and flattened.

"Human," Schone said, "tell us your version of the events when several innocent members of the galaxy, sent as an emissary to hear your side of the story, were killed by the Flock dust you dispersed."

Miriam took two deep, cleansing breaths and stared at her bound wrists. "What I recall is that we entered the room with our spacesuits on. I indicated to my crew members that I was going to remove my helmet because I wanted to greet the people in the room eye-to-eye."

"Then what happened?" said Schone.

"One of the crew," Miriam tilted her head in Chuck's direction, "waved his arms to stop me, but I took off my helmet anyway. I didn't think any of them would understand what I was saying, and I wanted to appear friendly."

"Do you know what Flock is?" Schone put a talon under Miriam's chin and lifted her eyes.

"I have never heard of Flock."

"Have you ever been inside an engine?" Schone asked. Gruseltmira was trying to heal the wound to her dress by rubbing it with her spit. "Have you ever touched the red dust, called Flock, which coats the filaments inside?"

"Yes." Miriam squared her shoulders and stiffened her spine. Assertiveness returned to her voice. "Just before the robots came, our engine stopped working. We went out to attempt a repair. We had a lot of dust on our suits when we returned to the ship." There was no need to recount the childish "dust-up" in the airlock.

"Did you," said Shone, "or any of your crew feel the least bit sick, dizzy, or tired after removing your suits?"

"No."

"Did you know that the red dust—what we call Flock—is the most toxic substance known to the galaxy?"

"No."

"Did you know that you had enough Flock on your suits to kill every living organism on a small planet?"

"I-I-I," Miriam stammered, "I had no idea."

"How is it then—" Schone said.

Judge Minot interrupted. "Why are you are immune to the effects of Flock when the rest of the galaxy is not?"

"I do not know," said Miriam.

"Could it be you developed an antidote to Flock? Was this attack staged as a display to prove the efficacy of that antidote?"

"No. Definitely not."

"Are you agents of a drug cartel determined to sell the antidote to the highest bidder, even if it is anti-Bleen terrorists?" Her voice had a determination as if she thought she was on to something.

"Honestly…" Miriam's body went slack in an unconscious, physical plea of innocence and readiness to accept the inevitable. "I have absolutely no idea what you are talking about."

With eyes closed and head lowered, she mumbled, "We are simple explorers. We came in peace. We only wanted to meet new life, discover new civilizations. We wanted to go where no Human has ever gone before."

"Judge," Schone said, "we rest our case. We claim the Humans are innocent of the charges of terrorism, murder, and mayhem because they were ignorant of the implication of their actions. If they were immune to the deadly effects of Flock, why would they assume Flock could be used as a weapon against anyone else in the galaxy?"

"Umm," said Minot.

"And," Schone said, "if these Earthlings really were terrorist agents able to Flock at will, why would they use a piece of beat-up junk that failed and allowed us to apprehend them? The anti-Bleens are well funded. If the Humans were working for them, they surely would have been driving a working device that at least would have made it to the primary target."

"Umm," said Minot.

"Your Honor, live tissue samples from them may lead our scientists to an antidote to Flock. I propose all charges be dropped if the Humans agree to let our scientists run some tests."

"Why shouldn't we imprison them and take whatever we want?"

Schone looked at Gruseltmira for support but she was still toying with the ripped part of her dress.

"That is not galactic justice, your Honor," said Schone. "Set them free after their tests and let them become ambassadors of the galaxy to their planet. Let them spread the word that the galaxy is a kind place, a forgiving place, a place that puts justice above material wealth. And you, Judge Minot—you will be revered as Minot the Compassionate, Minot the Wise."

No one could see Judge Minot check her watch because of the one-way transmission. She had just enough time to make her appointment.

"Hum-enz, Smez, Earthlings," Minot said, "or whatever you call yourselves, will you agree to submit DNA samples for study as the condition for your freedom?"

"As long as it does not kill, maim, or disfigure us," Miriam said.

"Officers of the court, you will see the sentence is carried out."

Frants and Villem were napping peacefully while floating in a dark corner under the bleachers.

"Officers of the court!" Minot yelled.

Schone whipped a pen at the nappers and hit Frants near the top of his shell. Startled, he unfurled his tentacles with a whiplike snap and accidentally jostled Villem awake.

"Yes, sir!" Frants blurted out.

"Officers of the court," Minot said, "you will see that the sentence carried out."

"Sentence," Frants said. "Carried out. Yes, sir." Frants twisted his tentacles into a double pretzel. Villem blinked hard and returned the shrug. They had no idea what the judge was talking about, but agreement would get them back to their naps sooner than asking a lot of fool questions.

"GAASP," Minot continued, "ensure the Hum-enz fulfill the sentence or I will have them imprisoned for life. I will also imprison both of you for life for contempt of court. Do I make myself perfectly clear?"

The threat of life imprisonment and having to wear bleak, uncomfortable prison garb woke Gruseltmira from her funk about her dress. She suddenly recalled the Human's promise to join her cultural army if freed.

"I will personally oversee that the sentence is carried out," Gruseltmira said. "GAASP is especially interested in initiating these Humans into galactic society and culture."

"I don't care if they are initiated into the cult of the Inverted Pisht," Minot said. "Just make sure they submit to any and all tests. I sent a message to the Galactic Office of Flocking Research with a copy of the court order authorizing any tests they deem necessary. Damn. I'm running late. Case closed."

As swiftly as the Humans were dropped into a trial for their lives, it was over. The spotlight was extinguished. The spectators evaporated. The dim, gray room was filled with nothing but the Humans, Gruseltmira, Schone, and two lightly snoring Allunacs.

Schone and Gruseltmira hugged each other and squealed with joy. One by one, they hugged the Humans. Miriam finally recalled the name for Gruseltmira's odor—chou...better known as stinky tofu sold at Chinese night markets.

"What happens next?" Miriam rasped, coughing, eyes burning from Gruseltmira's stench.

"You may go back to your habitat," Gruseltmira said. "You will have to wait for the tests to be completed. Besides, you no longer have an engine. It was impounded."

Nick thrashed at his bindings. His eyes were wide and violent. "We are stranded here?" he yelped. "Forever? I'll go crazy. I can't. I won't." Writhed and twisting he thrust himself at the aliens, arms out, teeth bared as if he were going for their necks. His tether was short. When he reached the end, the line went taut, his hands stopped short, and his momentum succeeded in flipping himself head over heels.

Chuck pulled Nick in by his tether and brought his face inches from his own. "Cool it. We're all in this together."

"OK, OK." Nick went limp in Chuck's grasp and looked away. "I get it. I'm fine."

PART 3

CHAPTER 49

Two boring weeks passed as the crew waited anxiously for the tests to begin. No one came. No one asked for a drop of saliva or blood. They admitted to each other they should count their blessings after being acquitted on all charges. But, humans being humans—and since these were three particularly high-strung, driven, and ambitious humans—living in the status quo was akin to being in prison, no matter how benign. They were selected for this mission precisely because of their innate drive to explore. Yet, here they were locked in a *Twilight Zone* waiting room.

The only communication between the Humans and their jailors happened on the eleventh day. Miriam was tapping the tip of her pen on the next line of the ship's log, desperate for something new to write besides "Another day of waiting." Chuck was napping after a workout. Nick was trying to beat his best time at a Sudoku program he had written to generate puzzles beyond fiendish.

Their music—the song, "Can't Find My Way Home," by Blind Faith—was interrupted by static. Before anyone could get up to inspect the media player, a twangy guitar, twinkling piano, and chopping beat blasted from the intercom speakers. Chuck Berry's "Johnny B. Goode" played continuously, in an endless loop, for over six hours, and as suddenly as it began, it stopped. When *Galaxy Quest's* music returned, Sam and Dave were in the middle of belting out, "Hold On, I'm Comin'."

Dominating the crew's discussion night and day was whether they should admit to the Human race in general, and Richard Winn in particular, that Quane was nothing more than a smarmy con man, only interested in swindling a gullible planet. To hear Richard reminisce about his time with Quane, some thought he might lobby for his beatification, or at least a statue on the National Mall. Richard insisted on Earth honoring Quane as the one who freed Earth from the shackles of the solar system and provided not only the key but the door to the renaissance of human exploration.

Fourteen days after their court dismissal, there was a loud knock on the door.

Before Miriam opened the door, she took a deep breath and consciously and deliberately steeled herself for the possible shock at the sight and smell of Gruseltmira. In spite of all her preparation, she still gulped hard. Gruseltmira was covered in something like bubbling tar and smelled equally strong. She entered the room with an arrogant swagger. Sharp, fine-tipped stars—looking more dangerous than decorative—adorned the bristles on her head. A spiked choke collar and barbed-wire bracelets finished her ensemble.

Miriam coughed; her throat constricted reflexively. She turned her head to blink the tears out of her burning eyes and gasped to clear her lungs. Nick and Chuck had moved themselves to positions where they could hear and see but did not have to sample Gruseltmira's aura.

"Gruseltmira, will the tests start soon? We are excited and anxious to continue our exploration of the galaxy."

"Call me Gruseltmiro." His voice was low and slow. No Human could have perceived that Gruseltmira had changed his-her sex since their last meeting. "The tests are over. You are free to go."

"When were we tested?"

"You were tested continuously since you returned here," Gruseltmiro said. "Can't your tiny brains remember anything?"

"No one came." Miriam rubbed her arms but could not find signs of needle marks. "Nothing was taken."

"We took what we needed without you knowing. At random intervals, we spiked your air and water with varying levels of Flock. We accessed your habitat and took samples of your exhalation, excrement, and the cells washed off in your bath."

He fidgeted impatiently. "I know it is way beyond your understanding but we conduct what we call 'double blind' experiments. The testees do not know they are being tested and the tester does not know what is being tested. The director administers changes at intervals decided by the senior staff. The senior staff evaluates the data and presents the conclusions."

Nick raised his eyebrows and Chuck smiled. Both waited for her reaction. Would she be more insulted by the slur that Human scientists did not understand how to conduct an experiment, or that she and her crew had been treated as lab rats?

"We are not as backward as you think." Miriam pumped her index finger at Gruseltmiro. "I am a scientist, too, and understand the principle of a blind experiment." Miriam was defensive of the Human race, but as a scientist, she was curious, even though she was one of the rats. "What were the results?"

"I am not at liberty to discuss results. Samples were shipped by high-speed transport to the Office of Flocking Research. You are free to go."

"Where can we go without an engine?" Miriam grimaced like she had been kicked out of a plane at thirty thousand feet without a parachute, or any clue of what country or continent she was over.

"Where you go is your affair," Gruseltmiro flipped his talons loosely. "GAASP will provide you with a used, but perfectly operational, stardrive."

"You are giving us a new engine? That is extremely generous of you."

Nick pumped his fist in the air in celebration and Chuck rubbed his medallion through his shirt with his eyes closed.

"No," Gruseltmiro sighed. "Not a new one—a used but working one. A generous citizen donated it; not from interest in your welfare, but because they needed an enormous tax write-off. Thanks to all the GAASP fundraisers, bake sales, hundred-thousand-kilometer Runs for Aliens, donation buckets outside Al Katy distributors, and advertising pleas for stardrive donations, GAASP manages to help brutish peoples like you.

"Along with this used engine, you will get a shuttle so you can land on the surface of the planets you visit, an amount of food GAASP decided upon based on what we learned of your metabolism, a Galactic Positioning System so you won't lose your way the galaxy, and a translation computer. Keep using those headphones and you will be able to talk to the galaxy, and the galaxy will talk back."

"Thank you very much." Miriam was beaming with gratitude for her good fortune and most generous friend. In spite of her revulsion, she moved to shake his hand and hug him. "How can we ever repay you?"

"Well," he scratched his chin with a talon and rolled his eyes in thought. "GAASP is funded by grants, charities, and generous donors like you. Any donation, big or small, in appreciation for what you have received might greatly affect the next new alien species' integration into galactic society. Your gift may provide for both legal representation and material assistance."

Gruseltmiro had changed sex deliberately for this meeting. He knew Gruseltmira would blow the deal. She would trade everything for the Humans agreeing to join her idiotic cultural army. The Humans only had the genomes to offer in payment. Legally, they belonged to them until they transferred the data, willingly, to a beneficiary. With the funds from his trust and the black-market sales from this haul, he would write his own ticket. He would buy females, not be one.

Miriam scratched her head. One eyebrow went up. "If we give you all of our genomes, what will we have left to barter? We hoped to continue our voyage of discovery and visit all of the places Quane talked about: presenting our posteriors to the Nibor of Xof, pounding our Ballwangts in honor of the Inverted Pisht, touching the Sanx of the Bleating Galb, seeing the tricolor dawn over the falls on Shnacuoility…"

"All of those sites are programmed into your GPS," he said. "You have a reliable engine, plenty of supplies, and, if you donate all of your genomes, I'll throw in several thousand planetary credits, which you crudely refer to as *money*. Will you be any worse off than you were? As GAASP sees it, we gave you a lift up. You are off to a really good start." The Humans did not know that several thousand planetary credits were less than shuttle fare between the dreary, mining moons of Noipe.

Miriam had no counter arguments. Shortly after they started the expedition, they were fighting for their lives. GAASP came to the rescue and defended them successfully against theft and murder charges. GAASP now donated the equivalent of a new car, with supplies, a tankful of gas, and highlighted maps to get them where they wanted to go. To refuse a request for payment of legal services rendered would be very bad manners.

"We are immensely grateful for all GAASP and you have done for us," Miriam said. "Our only wish is to make friends and continue our exploration of the galaxy. Please accept our offer of all the genomes in our library as a donation to GAASP so they can continue the fine work of promoting the integration of new planets into the galaxy."

Gruseltmiro wrung his talons together. His tongue worms were snapping at his pointed stars. "Show me to your data computer and I'll take care of the transfer."

"Nick, transfer the genome file to Gruseltmiro." Miriam could not wait to hand off the alien stench to someone else so she could find fresh air to breathe.

Nick squirmed and held his breath as long as possible to minimize the amount of Gruseltmiro's fumes he inhaled. It didn't help that Gruseltmiro leaned over his shoulder to help direct the transfer.

Pleased with his new wealth, Gruseltmiro relaxed and became cordial to his new friends. "This is a great day for you. I almost envy the adventures you are going to have. I wish I could go back to a time when I didn't know anything about the galaxy and could discover it again, like it was new." He slapped Nick on the back so hard he inhaled; his eyes teared and he put his head down on the console so Chuck and Miriam would not see him gag.

"Your engine arrived days ago. I was ordered not to mate it to your habitat until the Flock tests were completed. It will be mated to your habitat immediately."

"Do you think you will continue to explore the galaxy?" he said shaking his head slowly, "or return home?" He nodded lightly. The galaxy did not need these Earthlings rumbling around and polluting things.

"We haven't decided but whatever our decision we will forever be grateful for GAASP's help." Miriam presented her hand in sincere friendship and Human gratitude. Gruseltmiro ignored the offering, turned, and headed for the airlock.

"Wait," Nick yelled and flew toward the airlock holding his nose. "Why did you play the song, "Johnny B. Goode," over and over for us a couple of days ago? Where did you get it?"

The song was translated from a pitted golden disc attached to a spindly spacecraft picked up by the police drones in the Earthlings' solar space. The first technicians hearing it went into a euphoric trance. The military swooped in and was testing it on prisoners as a truth serum. So far, no race was immune to the song's effects other than these Earthlings.

These were powerful, dreadful beings if they were resistant to the effects of Flock and the song. What other weapons or immunities were they hiding, or just plain ignorant of? Gruseltmiro did not want to touch them and find out.

"No matter," Gruseltmiro said. The airlock slammed in Nick's face.

CHAPTER 50

Wyruk hammered his bony red fist on his console. "What are they waiting for?" he asked the illuminated buttons. "Why don't those Humans leave? GAASP's donated engine arrived ten days ago. Why hasn't it been attached to the habitat?"

He finished his food and water two days earlier and was running on minimum power to conserve his batteries, but they were nearly dead. It was already thirteen days since the trial ended. The antenna was still inside light space to monitor transmissions. Wyruk heard nothing but mundane chatter on the police bands and government channels. Nothing indicated the Humans were held on additional charges, or why they were still here.

Wyruk had to get supplies and charge his batteries. The nearest stores were two days away, one way. If he missed the Humans' departure, he would have to chase them around the galaxy to catch up with them. But if he waited much longer, he would starve. "These Humans are a real pain in the klaarn," he mumbled. He locked in a GPS map to the nearest stores and flew away at his maximum survivable acceleration.

Thirty minutes after Wyruk disappeared into dark space, the court order for the restraint of the Humans was lifted and they were free to leave. The engine was inserted smoothly into the Human habitat. Only a tiny fraction of the stardrive's buffed, mirrored surface was visible. Plastered over every square inch were illegible glyphs that translated to: "This is a GAASP-donated engine." The phrase repeated in as many languages as the detailers could manage to squeeze across its surface and still ensure legibility at a reasonable distance.

Schone spent a week on *Galaxy Quest* instructing the Humans on the new engine's updates, operation of the planetary shuttle, and how to program the GPS system. Schone's demeanor changed slowly but perceptively during the training. Her normally smooth, downy surface became more and more irregular. Patches lifted and settled randomly over her body. The disheveled feathers, unsettled attitude, and avoidance of eye contact was noticed by Miriam; she had not seen an appearance so bedraggled since she laid eyes on Quane's ragged dog costume.

Miriam waited for the right moment and pulled Schone aside. Chuck was busy checking off an inventory of their new supplies on a clipboard. Nick was obsessed with how many weightless pens he could spin at exactly the same rate, at the same time, and in the same plane. Three were spinning and he lightly puffed on the fourth to speed it up to match the others. His fingernails were growing back.

"Schone, you seem to be taking our departure a little too emotionally." Miriam placed her hand comfortingly on Schone's shoulder. "We will miss you very much, too, and will never be able to repay your help and generosity."

Schone blinked hard and, for the first time in days, looked directly into Miriam's eyes. Her feathers were fluttering faster; her feet shuffled side to side while trying to dip her shoulder out from under Miriam's hand.

"I won't miss you at all," Schone said. "I have one question."

The soft shoulder shuddered when Miriam removed her hand. "What do you want to know?"

"How could you be so irresponsible as to send a dangerous sound out into the galaxy without testing it first? Were you trying to knock us out before you Flocked us? Paving your way to take over this corner of the galaxy?"

Miriam stared dumbfounded at Schone, her mind racing to understand and formulate an answer to the question. She had a vague recollection of what was on the golden record sent out into space on Voyager I more than forty years ago: music, animal sounds, and images of human beings going about their business. The record was an attempt to introduce Earth to the universe and present Earth as a vibrant planet with a vigorous society and ecology. A society with nothing better to do than scratch grooves on metal discs, glue them to archaic junk, and toss them into the impossible vastness of space like a scrawled message in an indecipherable language on a piece of single-ply toilet paper in a leaky bottle. Human vanity assumed any beings intercepting the craft would be advanced enough to decipher the message—after pitting by a heavy barrage of micro-meteorites—and be so enthralled with the mystery and wonder of Earthly life they would drop whatever they were doing, or whoever they were fighting, and hustle straight away to the party they were missing.

Humanity never assumed the finders of the record might be perfectly disinterested in investigating the home planet of a beat-up, technologically backward, inoperable spacecraft possibly thousands of years old. By the time the satellite was intercepted, all of those pictures and sounds might have been nothing more than a time capsule, a postcard from a long-dead planet: "Having a wonderful time. Wish you were here." The only thing of value would be a few scraps of the satellite's metal that, with some conditioning, might be useful as a gift wrap.

"No." Miriam raised her brow, tucked her elbows at her sides, and opened her palms—begging for understanding. "We meant no harm. It was a simple invitation to come and visit the sights and sounds that all of us love of Earth."

Schone's feathers smoothed as she made her way to the exit. She closed her eyes and said quietly but firmly, "Please go home and stay there."

CHAPTER 51

Miriam did not inform Nick and Chuck of Schone's recommendation. The record had not been a malicious ploy to take over the galaxy, but another simple case of humanity's best intentions being misunderstood. Miriam grabbed the clipboard from Chuck's hands and swept her hand through Nick's five spinning pens.

"Now that I have your attention," Miriam slapped her hands together and rubbed vigorously. "We are free to go wherever we want in the galaxy. The way I see it, we can either fly straight back to Earth, or we can engage in a bit of exploration. Since there are three of us, it can't be a split vote. Whoever loses has to accept the decision of the other two."

From their stares and smirks, Nick assumed they had already, secretly, made their decisions. Way beyond ready for a soft bed draped in drier-sheet-perfumed bedding, Nick dreamt of daily pizza delivery: breakfast, lunch, and dinner. His nose flared at the recalled aroma of baked sausage, onions, and mushrooms bathing in a bed of bubbling, salty cheese. The nerdy side of him, however, did not lack curiosity, or a desire to be as brave as Chuck or as stalwart as Miriam.

To the floor in a quiet, resigned monotone, he said, "I vote we explore."

Nick straightened, looked the other two straight in the eye, and lifted his index finger, where dried blood dotted the red, chewed down cuticle. "But just one planet," he said sternly, "and just long enough to collect souvenirs to prove we really made it into the galaxy. After that, we head straight back to Earth, no matter what."

Miriam had experienced enough excitement for a lifetime: breakdowns, arrest, trials, and murder, all on a galactic scale, and was ready to return to Earth. She had assumed Nick was even more ready to return home.

Chuck was a soldier used to taking orders and challenging his mind and body to the most grueling tests his superiors could imagine. His training had been untested on this trip, but he was more than willing to return to Earth and a regular regimen with real weights, a strict paleo diet, and pizza delivery: breakfast, lunch, and dinner. If this nerdy tech could take a side trip to wherever, he would not refuse the dare. Rubbing his chin, he raised a brow, and nodded. "I agree with Nick. The mission was to explore, and we haven't seen squat yet."

Tears of admiration for Nick's bravery and Chuck's determination filled Miriam's eyes. This was going to be a successful mission after all. "That makes three. Let's head to the Nibor of Xof. The judge was keen to get there, Quane recommended it to Richard, and it's reasonably close. Then we head straight to Earth and a heroes' welcome."

Nick entered the coordinates for Xof and plotted their trajectory. "Engaging engines at one gee in five, four, three, two, one, engage." One Earth gravity pushed them to the floor. "It looks like the Nibor of Xof is located on a planet called Petell. Two weeks to get there."

As if induced by galactic karma, a nervous organ, stumbling drums, and an unsure guitar bumbled confusedly for minutes until they finally settled and organized into the Boston song "Long Time." Miriam was lip-synching the words, Nick played air guitar, and Chuck was drumming a console with his index fingers.

The crew kept busy on the trip with the operational procedures and test sequences for the new engine and shuttle. The food GAASP provided was palatable and nutritious enough, as long as they did not bring up cheeseburgers and fries. Miriam had each person write their own version of events from launch to the breakdown to the release from custody. This was a first for human history. The compiled document could be used as a learning tool for the next batch of human explorers: basic rules, regulations, and considerations when flying about the galaxy. Landing on an alien planet and interacting with the natives would add greatly to the handbook.

They had been gone only four months, but the intensity of events had crowded out memories of their relatively mundane lives on Earth. There was a subtle understanding among *Galaxy Quest's* crew that they might never be able to go home again—not physically, but emotionally and intellectually. Friends and strangers would buy the space explorers drinks, nod, and slap their backs heartily at the moderately exaggerated tales of aliens and space flight, but there was no yardstick of the right dimension to compare terrestrial experience to what *Galaxy Quest's* crew lived through. The only humans they could ever commiserate with were themselves, like soldiers after intense and lengthy combat. The bizarre was the norm in the galaxy; Earth's most aberrant behavior was feebly infantile in contrast. Future trips would add to the human encyclopedia of galactic knowledge, but it would never seem as strange as this first foray into the unknown.

"We've arrived," Nick waved his arm in a long arc. "Presenting: the first soil humans will set foot upon outside of the solar system: the planet Petell." He attempted a deep bow like a tuxedoed master of ceremonies in a circus introducing the first trapeze act. His motion in weightlessness only made him tumble headfirst into a console.

Petell, from space, was a patchwork of browns and greens, lit by a dark-yellow sun. There were no expansive oceans or white polar caps.

Nick piloted the shuttle. Miriam confirmed via the GPS computer that Petell maintained an atmosphere compatible with Human life, but with a stifling temperature and humidity: something like combining the heat of Death Valley with the humidity of the Amazon. To save weight and keep room for souvenirs or new friends, they decided to leave their bulky spacesuits behind. They also hoped to avoid another accidental Flocking of innocents if some particles remained lodged into some small fold or cavity of their spacesuits. They had showered vigorously and washed their clothes three times.

"Halow!" an overly excited voice blared out of the shuttle's speakers. "Halow, halow. Who is there?"

"Hello," Miriam used her syrupy-sweetest "Can I please have more research money?" voice.

"We are Humans. We would like to visit your planet, please, and see the Nibor of Xof."

"Humans, you say," the voice on the speakers said. "I never heard of you. We are always interested in meeting new people. We can even take you to the Nibor. I'll enter the landing coordinates into your navigational computer. See you soon."

Miriam turned from the microphone with a pleased expression on her face. Friendly natives! Things were looking up for her and her intrepid crew. They might actually discover something or someone that would not see them as a threat or danger.

The shuttle set down on a grassy meadow near a pond. Miriam stood and placed her hands on the shoulders of the men still sitting at the pilot and co-pilot controls.

"Let's do our best to not maim or kill the next alien we see," she said with eyes closed and head bowed in prayerful sincerity.

They stepped into the sultry air. The heat and humidity dropped on their shoulders like a ten pound bag of wet cement and weighed on them as they stepped down the three shallow stairs of the shuttle. Sweat soaked their shirts after the minor exertion. The dark-yellow sun flickered like glowing campfire embers. Miriam raised her hand to block the sun from her face, but her face was not cooled. The cloudless sky was a light green. The smell was of damp compost. Gravity was slightly less than Earth's.

The ankle-high grass was dotted randomly with thorny bushes as tall as they were and as wide as their outstretched arms. Small puddles of shade, hiding from the high noon sun, huddled under the bushes. No mountains or hills broke the hot, shimmering horizon. Chuck squatted, pulled a few leaves of grass, stood, and dropped them. They fell on his shoes without a whisper of breeze moving them. Nothing chirped, buzzed, or croaked.

"Do you think it is real water?" Nick's voice was weak. His lungs were reluctant to draw the steamy air.

"I don't know," said Miriam, panting. "In this gravity and with this vegetation, I would say it is. We see it in empty space and frozen on moons in our solar system."

Intense training allowed Chuck to ignore the oppressive atmosphere. He was poking at the water in the pond with a thin stick. "It's clear like water. It splashes like water." He sniffed at the wet end. "It even smells like water."

"Don't step in it," Nick joked. He had found some small stones and was flinging them sideways, skipping them off the pond's surface.

"And don't taste it!" Miriam said." You don't know what toxic elements might be dissolved in it. Arsenic, for example."

Chuck whipped the stick out to the center of the pond. It made a thin whirring sound until it struck the water with a feeble splash. He froze at the sight of something moving in the direction of the drowning stick. He stepped slowly and quietly backward until he felt his crew with his stretched hands.

"Over there. It looks like we have company." He tilted his head toward something across the pond.

On the other side of the pond, two figures stood, gesturing wildly as if in strong argument. They looked like average-sized Humans. They wore pointed hats, long robes, and long scraggly beards down to their knees. One was dressed in satiny blue with white markings. The other's clothing was a copy of the first, but was red with white markings. The sound of the stick striking the center of the pond distracted them from their discussion and they scanned the Human's side of the pond with their hands shading their eyes. Once they saw the visitors, they jumped excitedly and started racing toward them—running on the surface of the water. Each creature twisted a small stick in tiny figure eights at the water in front of their sprinting feet.

"I saw them first," said the one dressed in red.

"No, you didn't," said the one dressed in blue. "I saw them first."

"You couldn't see my klaarn if it was hanging in front of your face," said the red one.

"I bet you didn't see this," said the blue one as he pointed his stick at the water. A small wave picked itself up as if to trip his competition.

"You have to be faster than that." Red pointed his stick at the water in front of Blue. The water parted all the way to the leafy bottom of the pond.

The blue alien jumped over the void, somersaulted in midair, and landed solidly on the surface of the water on the other side of the obstacle without missing a step. Blue was frowning as they reached the shore by the Humans because he could not retaliate.

"I beat you." Red smirked at his adversary with smug superiority—like a child who ate all the cookies left on Santa's plate on Christmas morning after convincing his sibling to stay in bed while he checked to see if the coast was clear.

"No you didn't." Blue stomped his feet and pounded his fists on the air. "I touched first."

The aliens were more interested in their argument than the Humans.

Miriam pushed her way around the turnstile of Chuck's protective, outstretched arm. Nick fidgeted behind Chuck's left arm—he longed to touch the aliens and see if they were real, but could not brave leaving the protective space. Miriam held out her hand to separate and distract the aliens.

"Excuse me. Did one of you contact us about our coming to your planet?"

"Yes," the red-dressed alien said. "That was me."

"No it wasn't." Blue pushed Red backward. "I contacted them. You couldn't contact my klaarn if it was hanging in your face!"

"Well," Red's face was nearly as red as his clothing. "You couldn't contact your own klaarn if it was hanging in *your* face!"

"That doesn't make any sense." Blue folded his arms across his chest and turned his back on Red. "You're an idiot."

"I'm not the idiot." Red turned his back to Blue and folded his arms in front of him. "You are."

Blue spun and twisted his stick at Red's back. "Let's see who's the idiot…"

Up close, their dress was identical but for the color. The white markings on their pointed hats were easily identified as stars, crescent moons, and comets with expanding tails. Shiny metallic covers over one ear were translators. Their bell-sleeved robes extending from their necks to the ground were decorated with unrecognizable glyphs. Their curved, tapered noses nearly touched their curved, tapered chins as they argued. Their bushy gray eyebrows wriggled like fat caterpillars struggling to get off their faces. Except for the color of their robes, they were perfectly identical clones, down to the wrinkles in their faces, the twists of their beards, and hairs sticking out of their ears.

291

They were stereotypical images of the legendary magician, Merlin.

"Stop! Stop, you two." Miriam's patience with these petulant aliens, in spite of a desire to maintain a level of propriety in the presence of their new hosts, was wearing thin. The two froze in mid-argument and stared at her.

"I would like to get some answers."

"I'll answer anything you want," said Red.

"No you won't. You don't know anything." Blue stepped his leg over Red's and shouldered Red backward.

"I know more than you." Blue, fought to get his leg in front of Red. "I was the one who said they must have some Al Katy."

"No you didn't." Red pushed Blue's shoulders back. "I said, 'Hey, look! They're poking with sticks and throwing stones. They must be on Al Katy.'"

"I said it first!" Blue pushed Red's chest.

"If you said it first, then you're an idiot because it's obvious they are not on Al Katy. So you were wrong." He puckered his face and thrust out his tongue.

"No. You were wrong because you said it first." Blue's fists were pumping the air above him.

Their noses touched, their chins battled, and their spittle sprayed into each other's mouth. Their arms waved clenched fists at nothing and everything.

"Stop!" Miriam barked. "I will point to the one I want to talk and the other must be quiet. Can you do that?"

"I can but he can't." Blue pointed at Red behind his robe so only Miriam could see.

"No he can't," said Red, hip-checking Blue sideways.

"I will point and only one will speak," said Miriam. "If you understand, just nod."

Red nodded. Blue glanced at Red and nodded faster. Then Red nodded faster still until they looked like toy bobbleheads on a car's dashboard while it drove on a fiendishly pot-holed street.

"Stop it!" Miriam stepped up to them and touched Red's chest with an index finger. "Red, what is this place?"

"This is the planet Petell." Red smiled proudly at being Miriam's favorite. "It's a wonderful place. Everyone loves everything about this place. Except for him. Everyone hates him."

Blue was quivering. His eyes were bulging; his face was turning red. His head seemed to grow like a balloon ready to pop. Red detected his partner's discomfort and deliberately drew out his explanation to torture him.

"You, Blue," Miriam said, "how did you walk on water? Is it magic of some kind?"

Blue smirked at Red for receiving a more important question. "Let me show you." Blue wiggled his flimsy stick at the pond.

A rope of water climbed out of the pond and twisted into swirls and squiggles, ornate and well defined, in midair above the surface of the pond as if the sculpted water was solid.

Chuck relaxed. These aliens were more entertaining than threatening. The three watched the magic show with amazement.

Red could not contain himself. While everyone was watching Blue's demonstration, he wiggled his stubby stick behind his robes. Blue's sculpture fell into the pond like rain and out of the pond grew a small castle complete with battlements, an operating drawbridge, and pennants flying. Blue stomped the ground at the interruption then raised a giant aqueous hand out of the water and squashed Red's castle—all without saying a word, as requested.

"How did you do that?" Miriam pushed her sweat-drenched hair off her face.

The magicians were jumping and grunting to gain her attention.

Doing her best to avoid moving her lips, she said quietly to Nick, "Whose turn is it?"

"Red's," Nick whispered back, imitating Miriam's ventriloquist act.

"Red, how are you manipulating the water? Is it magic?"

He waved the question away as if he was answering an ignorant child. "There is no such thing as magic. We have a Quantum Probability Identifier and Extractor: a QtPIE."

"A what?" Miriam pointed to Blue.

"A QtPIE. You must know there is a quantum probability for any occurrence—that a single water molecule can hover in midair, for instance. Or, if you completely dissolve a sugar cube in a glass of water, there is a quantum probability that all of the sugar molecules will wind up at their original positions at the same time and reform the sugar cube. You just have to find the one probability, extract it, and make it a reality."

Nick's eyes rolled during his mental calculation and the fingers of his left hand typed something on the palm of his right hand. "That computation is statistically astronomical. As close to infinity as you can get, yet you manipulated trillions and trillions of water molecules instantly."

"This entire planet," Blue continued, "is one giant computer wired and programmed to identify the quantum probability of an event and make it happen. Moving all that water around used only a tiny fraction of QtPIE's potential—like, one electron, compared to all the water molecules in this pond."

Red was fuming at missing his turn because Nick had directed his question at Blue. His eyebrow caterpillars were close to climbing down his nose. Miriam relieved his rage. "Red, continue."

"The heat you feel is not from the sun, but from the heat generated by a billion billion circuits buried beneath your feet running trillions of trillions of calculations per second. One, ten, a trillion, a trillion trillion water molecules can be levitated and arranged by anyone with access to the computer. These wands are the interface to the computer and enable the effect you thought was magic. We can walk on water, fly through the air, and make castles out of water. All the plants and animals you see here were imported from other planets and selected especially because they thrive in these temperatures."

"This is fantastic." Nick couldn't wait to get a QtPIE for himself. He would buy the smallest tabletop version and astound the legerdemain community with impossible magic tricks. "A QtPIE can manipulate matter into any form instantaneously?"

"There are rules—" Red quickly continued.

"Sorry. Blue," Miriam interrupted, "your turn again."

Blue held up a finger. "The first rule is one even quantum physics cannot ignore: QtPIE cannot change elements into other elements. There is no turning lead into gold."

Blue held up two fingers. "The second rule is we can only manipulate the atoms and molecules of one thing to change it into another thing that shares similar atoms. We can turn a plant into another plant, or an animal into another animal, or a rock into a different-shaped rock, but not a rock into a plant." He bent and picked a blade of grass and held it in middle of his wrinkled, frail palm. A quick wave of the wand morphed it into a small broad leaf.

Red was hopping from foot to foot and waving his arms in the air to get her attention. His sweat was dripping on the grass at his feet. Miriam called on him.

"The third rule is that mass must be conserved: the successor must have no more molecules than the predecessor. We can change a blade of grass into another blade of grass or into a leaf of different shape, but cannot change a blade of grass into a tree. We can, however, turn a tree into a blade of grass like this." He extended his wand and turned the nearest shrub into a blade of grass with a faint puff of smoke. "The smoke was the excess molecules leftover after some of the bush's molecules changed into the smaller grass."

Blue was tapping a foot and shaking his head. "I wasn't supposed to do that anymore," said Red sheepishly. "We lose more trees that way."

Miriam selected Blue to continue. "Do you have something like a small bit of metal? A tool or small part?"

The Humans patted themselves down, searching their persons for an object like a magician's audience. Chuck jogged to the shuttle and brought back a small adjustable wrench. "Will this do?" he tried to wipe the sweat off his brow with his sleeve, but was so drenched it deposited as much sweat as it sopped up.

"Hold it in your open hand." Blue waved his wand. The wrench turned into a thin sheet of foil draped loosely over Chuck's hand and nearly touched the ground. The wand waved again and the sheet folded itself into an ornate origami crane. The wrench changed into a coiled spring, a small vase with a metal flower, and finally back into its original shape.

"I have one more trick I think you'll really enjoy." Blue beamed. The grin became a scowl after Miriam indicated Red should continue.

Red bounced up and down and rubbed his hands with excitement. "Take the wrench apart, into as many pieces as possible and put all the pieces in your pocket."

Chuck disassembled the wrench into three pieces—the handle, the jaw, and the worm screw—and fit them into his breast pocket.

"Now," said Red, "lightly shake the pocket."

Chuck shook the pocket with the three rattling wrench pieces. Red put his index finger in the center of his forehead, closed his eyes, and waved his wand over the rattling pocket. The rattling stopped.

"Open the pocket and take out the wrench," Red said.

Chuck reached in and pulled out the wrench, fully assembled, and tested it. It worked perfectly.

Red bowed deeply. "Thank you. I'm here every night this week. Tell all your friends to come by and catch the show."

Nick grabbed the wrench out of Chuck's hand and operated it: open, close, open, close. "You can take raw bits of metal," Nick stared at the tool, "put them in a box, shake the box, have individual parts form to precise tolerances, and self-assemble into a finished, operating machine—instantly."

"Exactly," Blue said. "As long as the bits have the same, or more, mass as the parts they are to become. There is a quantum probability that the bits will form themselves into parts and assemble themselves into a finished device. It is an infinitesimally infinitesimal probability, but it does exist. It's what we call quantum manufacturing. We have to have a clear idea what we are making so we can visualize it for the computer. It cannot be too complicated, or something we know nothing about. That is the fourth rule."

"How come you're not manufacturing everything for the entire galaxy?" Nick's eyes were glassy, his voice distant. He was dreaming about the millions of dollars he would make on Earth—with even a cigar box-sized QtPIE—as a magician and manufacturer of precisely machined parts. With his knowledge of semiconductors, he would be able to visualize and create circuits on an atomic level and sell them for thousands of dollars apiece. He almost laughed out loud at how ridiculous he was in once thinking 3D printing was a really nifty technology.

"Unions." Red sighed. "The StarTeam's union—those who pilot the ships to deliver the raw materials and ship the finished parts to the rest of the galaxy—went on strike in solidarity with the manufacturing unions until the galaxy agreed to make it illegal for us to make the smallest part for sale to anyone…except for our own personal use."

"We get a few black-market contracts," Blue said, "and orders for single parts to fix some out-of-date, antique machine. Mostly we cater to the tourist trade: Those coming to see the Nibor."

"The Nibor of Xof," Miriam said. "I almost forgot. We came to see the Nibor. Can you two take us there?" Since she addressed them both, they both felt free to talk.

"I know the way," said Red.

"I know a better way," said Blue.

"You don't know anything." Red pushed Blue.

"Oh, yeah?" Blue pushed Red harder. "You wouldn't know it if my klaarn was in your face."

"You wouldn't know it if…"

Miriam let them fight. They seemed to enjoy it. "Which way?"

"This way," said Blue. "Follow me."

"No," said Red, "follow me. He'll just get you lost."

"I won't," said Blue. "You will."

They were both going in the same direction. Pushing and shoving like rivalrous siblings, the guides did not follow a path or discernable signposts, trail blazes, or cairns. There was only grass, bushes, and the stifling heat.

"I can't get over how much you both resemble the iconic image of magicians from our planet," Miriam said to distract them. "Especially one we call Merlin."

"Our translational computers examined your digital records when you were in range," Red said. "We changed ourselves into something we thought you would like."

"We can change into something else if you prefer." Blue transformed into a teenage boy with unruly hair, round glasses, and a zigzag scar on his forehead.

"That is so stupid." Red turned himself into a tuxedoed gentleman with a black mustache and a fanned-out deck of cards.

"You're stupid," said Blue. "I can do better than that—"

"Are there any more like you here?" Miriam said. "Blue, you answer please." She would go insane if she spent any time in the company of a whole city of these magicians.

"No more," said Blue. "We are all that's left. Our home planet was called Altair Four. The first QtPIE computer was built there many centuries ago. It was christened Altair Five. The plan was to build and sell them to the rest of the galaxy. They built Altair Five, this planet, and three more QtPIEs as demonstration models—and for quick sale once the galaxy understood the capabilities."

"The galaxy wasn't interested in instantaneous manufacturing, Red?" Miriam wiped away the sweat stinging her eyes. There was nowhere to wipe her hand dry: her clothes were soaked.

"They lined up from here to the center of the galaxy," said Red, "fighting for the chance to buy a QtPIE. They bought and sold places in line. It turns out the sellers got the best deal. The night before the Grand Opening and Display, The Great Accident happened: Altair Four exploded."

"The whole QtPIE exploded?" Nick's manufacturing facility might have to be located on a desert island, depending on how much radiation and fallout a QtPIE explosion might produce.

"The whole QtPIE," said Blue, "and everyone with it. The explosion was so powerful it sent our home planet, Altair Four, out of orbit, and with it the satellite moon used as the QtPIE's manufacturing facility. Our best guess is a faulty breaker overheated and fused causing a cascading failure that overloaded and overheated the entire computer. The QtPIE went into thermal runaway, meltdown, and finally exploded. Obviously, that put the kibosh on anyone spending quadrillion planetary credits to buy a QtPIE. Who would spend money on a ticking bomb? Insurance premiums went through the roof."

The magicians put their arms over each other's shoulder. Miriam thought she saw tears in their eyes, but it might have been sweat.

"The manufacturing unions," said Red, "saw the time was right to kill, once and for all, the promise of quantum manufacturing. Some lobbied the government to outlaw QtPIEs as dangerous and unstable technology; some went on strike until planets agreed not to buy QtPIEs and throw hard-working, middle-class people out of jobs; and some decided to take matters into their own hands. Thugs attacked the QtPIE planets, causing permanent damage to the computers. Just before they reached us here, the unions won the strike and laws were passed to keep us from interfering with their jobs."

"How come you could not stop them from vandalizing the QtPIEs using your powers?" said Nick.

"The fifth rule of QtPIE's," said Blue, "is that it cannot cause harm to another animal. We cannot change the tiniest bacteria into something else. The QtPIE defenders did their best to diffuse the vandals' bombs and turn their weapons into smoke—at least, the ones they could see. The enemy just needed to sneak one bomb past the defenses. Even minor damage puts a QtPIE into a safe mode, which slows it down so much it takes forever for it to add two numbers. This is the last fully functioning QtPIE in the galaxy. The galaxy has added this planet to their list of Historic Sites Deserving of Preservation. We are a museum piece."

The aliens gestured animatedly and mouthed an alien language. They nodded to each other and Red finished by pointing to Blue.

"It is our turn to ask you a question," Red said.

"Yes," Miriam said, "anything."

There was a long pause as if Blue were getting up the nerve to ask the question. "Are you Smez?"

The term was familiar to Miriam, but could not put her finger on where she had heard it recently. So much had happened. She recalled the old joke where the first line is: "Memory is the second thing to go." "What's the first?" is the response. "I can't remember," is the punch line.

"Where have I heard Smez before?"

"At the trial," Chuck said. "Remember? The judge called us 'Smez.'"

"Why do you ask?" Miriam said.

"After Altair Five became operational," Blue said, "but before it exploded, a race of creatures, which according to somewhat faded pictures in our historical records looked very much like you, contracted Altair Five for a special project. The Smez wanted our ancestors to build a bomb—a very precise bomb to explode at a very precise moment in time in a very precise place. The time was in the long past."

Red continued, "The Smez knew the GPS coordinates, the time, and the size of the bomb they needed. They were attempting to change the future by altering the past."

"But," said Nick, "that's an unresolvable paradox. If they changed the past so they did not live in the future, they could not have hired your ancestors to make the bomb in the first place. Or if changing the past meant the QtPIE never existed..." Nick trailed off, lost in the convolutions of the conundrum.

Blue nodded. "The Altarians detailed the paradox to the Smez in no uncertain terms. But the Smez adamantly persisted.

They claimed that was the exact outcome they wanted. They wanted to sacrifice themselves and their existence to guarantee some major event in their past did not occur. They never said what the event was. They demanded to witness the bomb being conjured and would judge its success or failure by their personal dissolution or continuation. Success meant they would vanish, as if they never existed."

Red continued the story. "The Altarians argued for months about the moral, philosophical, and physical problem proposed. Nothing like it had ever been attempted. By a single vote majority, the Altarians agreed to the Smez's proposal and drew up a contract specifying they would do as asked, but could not guarantee a result. If the bomb worked as desired, the Smez would likely vanish. If history were unchangeable, the Smez would remain. The contract stipulated the Smez to pay in advance, nonrefundable. The Smez agreed."

"What happened?" Nick was walking next to the aliens with his arm around both staring at whichever one was talking. His eyes were wide, desperate for the outcome.

Blue still had his arm around Red. "It was very complicated. The QtPIE can only transform already existing matter, so they could not send a bomb back in time. The bomb had to be built from matter already in the GPS vicinity at time specified. The Smez assured them enough matter of the proper type would exist at the coordinates provided. The Smez gave the Altarians details about the amount and type of materials available at the time and place and how to construct the bomb. They drew up detailed blueprints and held classes for the Altarians on the chemistry and physics underpinning the bomb's workings. The Smez were determined to supply the Altarians with every detail necessary to complete the mission. The Altarians were drilled until they repeated their lessons in their sleep."

"To guarantee success," Red said, "the ten best Altarian students simultaneously and independently accessed the QtPIE to generate a bomb at the given coordinates."

Nick was shaking both of the magicians so hard their hats were jiggling on their heads; he was near to fainting from the heat and mental excitement. "Did it work? What happened?"

"Nothing," Red said with a tone of shame at his ancestors' greatest failure. "Not the slightest thing happened. The Smez stood right where they were. Not a hair on their heads or a cell of their bodies changed. The Altarians huddled. Each stated confidently they had connected with the QtPIE and were convinced they created the bomb as specified. The Smez left, dejected and mumbling that the Altarians were a bunch of charlatans."

"Do you have any records of what was at those coordinates?" Miriam said. Nick let go of the magicians and slowed until he was the last of the group.

"A salvage ship from the Pan Galactic Salvage Company, Unlimited," Blue said.

"You forgot the best part," Red said, "about the one excommunicated Altarian."

"I was getting to it," Blue said. "One Altarian admitted after the Smez left that he might have failed in his mission because during the melding with QtPIE, all he could think about was the letters of the scientist's name that created the device: D-R-A-T-Z. He became the scapegoat for the QtPIE's failure and was banished from Altarian space forever. Legend has it he went insane, screaming in fear of thick black rubber wheels flying around his head."

"Here we are, the Temple of the Nibor of Xof. I told you I knew the best way," Blue stuck out his tongue at his Red twin.

The group rounded a stand of small bushes and six Human eyes beheld the Temple of the Nibor of Xof.

CHAPTER 52

The Smez—via the Altarians, via a planet-sized computer called QtPIE—had acted as Nitram's benefactor and granted Nitram's wish. The Smez had hired the Altarians to create a bomb to destroy Dr. AtZ's experiment. They knew the GPS coordinates and exact time Dr. AtZ's experiment was discovered. The wanted the QtPIE computer to use matter from the device to create the bomb that would destroy itself. Their intent was to prevent the experiment from ever being found and galactic stardrive engines from ever being developed. Then, no Dia'Bolos salesman would visit Mars and sell their Smez ancestors a broken-down machine that would ultimately leave them marooned far from their original planet.

Hundreds of Smez generations grew up indoctrinated into the cult of hate involving the salesman who sold them the engine. Hundreds more generations lived and died with enmity toward any alien with something to sell until another salesman, named Quane, visited them on their new planet, which they had christened Mars Lost. The alien's visit was well publicized and the populace drove him out with every weapon at their disposal. They would have killed him had they caught him.

Unknown to ordinary Martians Lost was that a stardrive had been secretly purchased, and only a decade after they were marooned. The sale was kept top secret by a cabal of Smez scientists, intellectuals, and politicians dedicated solely to the repatriation of their ancestral planet. This ultrasecret group called themselves Mars Sons. Inclusion in Mars Sons was limited. Indoctrination was often fatal.

Mars Sons preferred Martians Lost remained ignorant of the plan to purchase another stardrive engine to scour the galaxy for the whereabouts of Mars. If and when Mars was found, Martians Lost would be offered the option of staying on Mars Lost or returning to their home planet. Mars Sons made blood oaths to return to Mars if found, no matter the condition. The group debated whether any ordinary Martians Lost would agree to return. Mars Lost was and had been their home for generations.

The Smez Mars Sons stumbled upon Altair Five in their quest for their lost planet. When they learned of the QtPIE computer's capability, they hatched their plot. All involved in the top-secret plan fully understood and accepted they might destroy all the lives, history, and culture created on Mars Lost, and most likely themselves, as well. They were zealots looking for a do-over. They wanted a reset. They were trying to click their heels and return home.

There were three probable outcomes: If the QtPIE experiment succeeded, the Smez who contracted the QtPIE would either vanish as if they never existed, or, genetics being what it is, they might become the current progeny of their ancestors and be living back on their home world. In either case, they would have no memory of a future that did not happen. The third outcome was the QtPIE would fail and nothing at all would happen to them or their history. The last outcome was exactly what happened.

What the Mars Sons failed to consider in their well-laid plan was that GPS had developed and become more precise over the centuries. What used to be pinpointed to the nearest several meters could now be defined within a couple of centimeters. They also forgot to consider that all the stars had moved relative to the original recorded coordinates where Dr. AtZ's experiment was recovered. The shift was tiny but significant.

In the end, the QtPIE worked perfectly but narrowly missed the intended target. Instead of destroying Dr. AtZ's experiment, it obliterated the state-of-the-art, well-maintained, polished-and-professional, materials acquisition ship of the Pan Galactic Salvage Company, Unlimited, along with three, highly paid and experienced employees, who all had an expert eye for evaluating materials: Gion BicButtai, Gion Smalbarys, and Gion JaJa.

Each flash Nitram the Average saw was a fraction of the matter from the ship organizing into a bomb, exploding, reorganizing, and exploding again, and again, and again, nine times, until there was nothing left of the ship and the Gion brothers but a thin cloud of atoms.

Nitram recovered the experiment. Stardrive engines were developed by the same conglomerates as before. The same junk salesmen roamed the galaxy looking to make a quick buck selling junk to gullible planets. The Smez were marooned, as they had been destined. The galactic timeline remained undisturbed for just about every being in the galaxy with one familial exception: the ultimate status of Gruseltmira. In the timeline where the Pan Galactic ship is not destroyed and it recovers the satellite instead of Nitram, Gruseltmira winds up running a small Al Katy kiosk along the approach to the Temple of the Nibor of Xof.

Denise Ratz never learned that her permanently lost tire was the result of a wayward spell.

Nitram vowed to never admit to anyone he once wished to be more than average, or that his wish was granted by his fairy godmother. It would be a secret he would take to his grave. He would never have to be average again. He would have fame and fortune. To avoid suspicion and nagging questions about his newfound above-averageness, Nitram would still act like his same old average self. It is easier for the above-average to act as if they were average than the average to act like hot shots.

CHAPTER 53

"I thought the Nibor of Xof was going to be a little bit more impressive," Chuck whispered to Nick.

"It reminds me of an old Mayan temple, but in way worse shape," Nick whispered back.

The Temple of the Nibor of Xof was a crumbling, pyramidal stone structure with weeds and trees growing from nearly every crack. It was two stories high, square, and built in layers. Each of the eight layers was smaller in width than the one below, poorly centered, and arranged as if piled up by a giant child stacking blocks.

A stone path, ten feet wide and two football fields long, led straight to the base of the temple and to a black, crooked entrance. The stone path had less upkeep than the temple. Stones were missing, sunken, or tilted.

Each side of the path to the temple was crowded with vendor stands. The stands were shabby and poorly assembled. Some had flimsy covers to shade the vendors from a sun without heat. Stained and frayed pennants, flags, and banners, sparkling and raggedy, hung listlessly or were propped with sticks or wires to make them stand out and be legible. Their messages, some which resembled fractal patterns, were indecipherable to the Humans. The proprietors were as stagnant as the flags. Three Humans and two magicians were the only customers today.

"I guess it's a slow day," Chuck said to Miriam.

It was the vendors who had deliberately removed or disoriented the paving stones to cause distracted visitors to trip and fall in front of their stand. The owners would rush to the stranger's aid while offering a thousand apologies and ten thousand curses to the lazy, nonexistent, groundskeepers. Once the strangers had been helped to their feet, they were directed to view the proprietors' incomparable wares all for sale at a price not to be beaten anywhere else in the galaxy.

The Humans stepped slowly and carefully behind the magicians. They had barely dodged the gauntlet of the galactic legal system and did not want to test the possible Kafkaesque maze of the galactic medical establishment. The doctors out here had never seen a Human and would not know where to start treatment.

Baubles and trinkets covered several tables. Some items looked like broken Christmas ornaments and others like burnt, melted plastic. The Humans had no gauge of any of the items' true value on Earth or in the rest of the galaxy. They could be broken junk, or a Christie's auction record-breaking sale. Nothing was from Earth, so every scrap was significant—a cultural find worthy of square footage, enclosures, alarms, and spotlights in any of Earth's finest museums. Even on Earth, the once-broken and discarded toy of an ancient Egyptian peasant became the centerpiece and icon of a major city's museum of fine art display.

Miriam giggled to herself at the thought of returning with a ship full of useless trash and brandishing it to the world with elaborate claims about them being irreproducible examples of the finest artistic and scientific efforts the galaxy had to offer. She imagined creating an elaborate story regarding each piece but would be long gone before they understood she had punked them.

"Don't touch that!" yelled Red.

Nick was reaching for two twirling, swirling beetles scrambling about in a small box. Chuck reacted to Red's alarm and nearly broke Nick's wrist.

"Yeow! What the—"

"Thank your friend," Red said. "Their bite is poisonous."

"What are they?" Nick asked, rubbing his sore wrist.

"A joke gift," Blue responded. "The idea is to give a pair to someone on a special occasion in a hidden compartment below a decoy gift—something the recipient really needs or wants. Usually, they are presented to someone the giver does not like very much. Overnight, they mate and multiply a thousandfold, burst out of the box, and fill the recipient's house with thousands of poisonous, biting invaders. Great fun.

"You'll love this," said Blue. "This is the gravity bean swindle. No matter what you see, don't buy it. It's a hoax."

The Humans stared at a creature the size and shape of a twin mattress. The scrolling, indecipherable display on the mattress' table suddenly displayed English as the Humans approached.

GRAVITY BEAN—Here, for a limited time only—IMPRESS YOUR FRIENDS—FOOL YOUR ENEMIES.

The Humans watched the mattress pick a small bean from its stock and nibble timidly at the end with its cottony mouth. The mattress suddenly launched into the air, flipped, and landed easily, upright on its edge.

GUARANTEED TO WORK—FIRST TIME—EVERY TIME rolled across the display.

Nick grabbed Miriam's arm. "Let me have some of the money Gruseltmiro gave you," he said.

Blue grabbed his arm. "Don't believe it," Blue whispered. "The beans are a fake. The alien expels a gas jet out of its bottom naturally. It has nothing to do with the beans it sells. Females have far more gas than the males and can jet themselves higher and do more flips than the males. That's why they're best at the swindle."

"What's going on there?" Miriam pointed to several small creatures running in circles in a roped-off section of grass away from the stands. They were blindfolded and swinging spiked clubs randomly in the air and were miniature versions of Schone, the mattress, and several of the aliens they saw at their trial.

"A birthday party," said Blue. "They're playing quantum piñata. The piñata appears randomly and in different places. One time it could be filled with riches, the next with angry, stinging wasps, and the next with rocks."

The small version of Schone shrieked as she hit the hog-shaped, glistening piñata square in the middle. The spikes sank in and she yanked, exposing the surprise within. The contestants removed their blindfolds to gaze on their plunder.

"Poor things." Miriam put her hand over her mouth in disgust. "It looks like they won several pounds of Human sewage."

"On the contrary," said Red, "they just won the very expensive and rare ingredient of the Kick Your Klaardid drink—Sleen." The parents of the partiers had rudely elbowed the youngsters out of the way and were on their knees greedily scooping up the slimy mess into pockets, folds, and discarded party favors.

"Look." Blue tugged hard on Red's robe. "Al Katy!"

On a low table were broken, shallow paper boxes filled with rows of white, silver, and gold foil-wrapped squares roughly the size of a business card. The proprietor of the display resembled a squat, green-and-yellow-striped sloth. It sat cross-legged on a partially inflated ball, deathly still and unblinking. A badge fixed to its chest alternated between English and another language written like hen's feet and chicken scratch—the native language of the magicians. The

English version of the badge read "Gion Worfin." Gion Worfin's translator was a diamond tiara with chinstrap.

"Al... Katy... Al... Katy... here," the sloth mumbled. Another Gion would have been shocked at the zealous effort Worfin was expending to entice the new customers into buying. "All... colors... one... credit... each..."

While Red and Blue argued over which saw the Al Katy stand first, the humans fingered the wares. Nick picked up a gold square, examined both sides, shook it by his ear, shrugged, and dropped it on the table. Not as interesting as a QtPIE.

"What is Al Katy?" Miriam asked the sloth.

Gion Worfin had bored, tired yellow eyes. "What... do... you... want... it... to... be? You... are... going... to... see... the... Ni—"

"The Nibor of Xof," Miriam interrupted.

"—bor... of... Xof?"

"Yes, the Nibor of Xof." The slower the sloth spoke, the faster Miriam spoke.

"Then... you... might... want... the... gold..."

"The gold. OK. We'll take five. How much?"

"Count me out, Miriam," said Chuck. "I'm on duty."

"Four." Miriam held up four fingers. "We'll take four."

"You... might... like... the... black..." Gion Worfin moved a striped, clawless paw in a slow-motion wave over another box. "If... you... feel... you... are... import—"

"Important?" Miriam said.

"—ant... you... might... like... the—"

"We are not important."

"—white... The... silver... is... good... too... if... you—"

"We'll take all of them," Miriam said in a rush, exasperated by the impossibly slow-talking alien. "Red! Blue! Take what you want. My treat. Pick one for Nick and me, please."

Red and Blue snatched one silver and one gold sample each for themselves, hoping Miriam did not see, and picked two black samples for Miriam and Nick.

"That... will... be... seven... galactic—"

"Credits," Miriam said, fishing out of her pockets the galactic credits given as a donation from GAASP and held the papers at arm's length to Gion's chin.

"Take what we owe. Whatever you want."

Gion Worfin blinked slowly and took two of the bills. "Change... I... owe... you... change... Wait... here—" Gion's legs unfolded and it slipped off the ball.

"Keep it." Miriam was shaking with frustration. Chuck covered his mouth to hide his laughter.

"—and... I'll... get... it... for—"

"Keep it!" Miriam spun and hurried away from the Al Katy booth, shuddering once from head to toe as if shedding water. She took one deep, slow, cleansing breath.

"What now?" Miriam asked the magicians.

"Carefully unwrap your Al Katy." Red opened his Al Katy with a solemnity bordering on reverence. Blue's hands shook with greedy excitement.

Inside the opened foils were small squares the size, thickness, and stiffness of a postage stamp. They reflected a spiraling rainbow of colors like a thin oil slick on water when tilted them in the sunlight.

"Next, place the Al Katy in your mouth." Blue held a corner gingerly with his fingertips and ceremoniously laid the thin square on his tongue.

"Do not break, chew, or swallow it," said Red, repeating Blue's reverent motion.

Miriam and Nick placed their Al Katies gently on their tongues. Chuck watched closely for their reaction. He would have to wait to see if he would be preventing harm to them or preventing them from harming others.

The magicians continued walking toward the temple with the humans behind. The Al Katies were cool on the Humans' tongues, the endothermic reaction powered by body heat. A tickle, like a weak electrical current, passed over Nick's tongue. Miriam's skin erupted in goose bumps. Red and Blue walked with a swagger and a look of smug arrogance on their faces.

A hot wind blew through Miriam. Her shoulders fell back. She felt two, then three, then six inches taller. Miriam burned with her own importance, proud of being the commander of the first human mission of exploration of space. She showered in the intense self-satisfaction that she had saved them all from a death sentence; her shrewd judgment and reasoning convinced the aliens of her crew's innocence. It was because of her charismatic personality that the aliens had become so generous when granting them their freedom. It was not arrogant or conceited for her to feel she was the most important member of the crew; it was a simple fact.

Nick suddenly knew he had been predestined to find the colored glasses that made human space flight possible. Even with similar glasses, no one else would have seen what he saw. He was more important than Quane, or even Richard Winn. Without Nick's keen eye, the engine would have remained an enigma, Quane a circumstance, and Richard a historical side note. It was not arrogance or conceit that he felt toward Miriam and Chuck, but sympathy. It was not their fault that he was the one-eyed man in the kingdom of the blind.

Chuck noticed their change in posture and demeanor. Whatever the drug was doing, at least it wasn't making them violent. Pompous fools rarely attack anyone.

For the first time in history, three Humans crossed the portal of the Temple of the Nibor of Xof.

The musty stone room was lit only by thin knives of light squeezing though cracks in the walls and the open door. The room was empty; there were no pews, altar, icons on the wall, or statues gazing to the sky with open arms. Chuck expected the shaded, stone room to be cool. On Earth, a cave was cooler because it was shielded from the burning sun. Here, heat was created within the planet. That meant the chamber of the Nibor contained the heat generated by the QtPIE belowground and was hotter inside than out. Chuck utilized his training and consciously slowed his bodily functions to prevent himself from fainting. He could not tell if the thick, musky, sweaty stench had been in the room before they entered or was caused by their Human presence.

Nick stood in the middle of the room with his fists on his hips, his chest out, head tilted back. "Nibor," he said, "we are here to present our posteriors."

Miriam held her open palms to the ceiling. "Nibor of Xof," she said, "our posteriors await you."

There was no response, only silence. Nick grunted. "This was such a waste of my time. This Nibor is no big deal." He poked Chuck in the ribs with an elbow and winked. "Maybe we should drop our pants for it."

"Don't you dare present your posteriors," said a voice in their heads, "and don't you dare drop your pants."

"Are you the Nibor of Xof?" asked Miriam.

"Who else would be in my temple? I am the Nibor of Xof, the Oracle Supreme, the Grantor of Humility, and the Healer of Souls. Thanks for coming, Miriam and Nick, but there's really nothing I can do for you."

"You must have heard of our coming," said Nick. "Our reputation preceded us. That's how you know our names."

"What? No. I can read your minds and talk to you through the Al Katy. So stop yelling and think your questions."

"You were recommended as a must-see in the galaxy," Miriam thought. "We were told to present our posteriors to the Nibor of Xof."

"Yes, I am a major point of interest in the galaxy," Nibor thought, "to the important, but not to beings as insignificant as you. Why would you want to present your trivial, insignificant, unimportant rumpuses to my almighty influence?"

"How important," Nick thought back, "do our posteriors have to be?"

"Way more than yours," the Nibor thought. "Only the most important patooties make the pilgrimage for an audience. They are the ones most in need of my service."

"What service?" thought Miriam.

"I grant them a swift kick in the wazoo," thought the Nibor.

"Important people make a pilgrimage to you," thought Nick, "just to get a kick in the ass?"

"Exactly," thought Nibor. "I punt their little heinies right through their arrogant little brains."

"But why?"

"They deserve it," thought the Nibor. "The more important they are, the more they need it. Sometimes a swift kick in the keister is by far the best motivation to change a bad habit, or one's outlook on their current situation."

"I still don't get it," thought Miriam.

"Listen," thought the Nibor. "I don't know where you are from, but a lot of beings in the rest of the galaxy spend an awful lot of time, money, and effort trying to improve. Some want to be kinder and more caring toward others so they will feel better about themselves. Some want to be better looking to make them think they are better than others; only then can they feel compassion toward the less fortunate. Some want to be rich for the simple reason that then they could afford to be compassionate. And some want all of the above so they can be famous for all of their compassion, looks, and money.

"They chase the traditions of Bleen, pound their Ball-wangts in honor of the Inverted Pisht, and touch the Sanx of the Bleating Galb in the hopes that adherence to some superstitious ritual, or spending a klaarn-load of cash, will somehow absolve them of their past transgressions and free them to pursue their renewed, purified selves. They present their offerings, beat their chests, wail, and gnash their teeth. Then they turn their backs and leave the altars of their weekly epiphanies feeling cleansed and rededicated. They promise they won't stray from the new, shiny, perfect path.

"It all works for a while, but they soon slip back into their old ways and they wind up repeating their penitence over and over and over again.

"I, the Nibor of Xof, the Motivator Supreme, give them what they really need, what they are really looking for: the one-time motivation to stay on their chosen path forever. My motivation is a swift boot in the caboose. The more self-important they are, the more they need motivation, so the harder the kick."

"Why would anyone willing subject themselves to such abuse?" Miriam thought.

"There is no 'willingly,'" thought the Nibor. "No one knows what happens here. They must be on Al Katy to enter and let me view their level of self-importance. The instant I boot their tukhuses, I use the Al Katy to wipe their memory. I have to be quick about it because sometimes the Al Katy flies right out of their mouths when I connect. In the end—Get the pun? It's one of my favorites—they all leave, permanently and subconsciously motivated to change their lives forever. None have ever returned for a refresher."

"We respectfully decline the honor of your motivation," Miriam thought.

The Nibor's laughter echoed in the Humans' heads. "I would not have told you all of this," the Nibor thought, "if I was going to motivate you. You are not nearly self-important enough for my services. Time for you to go—I have a top political figure coming soon. I expect to wallop his arse all the way out to the Al Katy stand on a fly."

"What if we tell someone," Nick thought, "and spread the word about what really happens here?"

"Good luck with that," the Nibor thought. "Now kiss off." The Nibor broke the connection and overloaded their Al Katy devices.

Miriam and Nick blinked stupidly as if they had just woken from a hypnotic trance. Chuck shook Nick by the shoulders and slapped his cheeks lightly until he woke and grabbed Chuck's wrist to stop. Chuck slapped Miriam's hand until she pulled it away and rubbed her eyes. "What happened?"

"Soon after you took those things, the both of you started strutting around like a king and queen on parade in front of your subjects. When we got inside here, you called the Nibor a couple of times then just stared around. Your lips were moving but you said nothing."

Nick shrugged. Miriam spit her dead Al Katy into her hand. "I didn't see or hear anything. Did you, Nick?"

"Nope. I lost all track of time. How long were we in there, Chuck?"

"Ten, maybe twelve minutes."

"I guess we can scratch this one off the list of major attractions," Miriam said. "We must have come at the wrong time; maybe it's out of season. Let's get out of here and back to Earth."

The magicians were just outside the temple opening. Blue was poking Red with his wand and Red was throwing stones at Blue, trying to knock his hat off.

"What's so special about the Nibor?" Miriam asked the magicians.

"Don't know," said Blue. "Some ask the same question. Others are rubbing their backsides and say they are changed forever, telling everyone that it was the most motivating and transformative experience of their lives."

Blue and Red argued continuously on their walk back to the shuttle. Miriam was too spent to stop them from fighting. She was proud of her crew, proud of their accomplishments. Although small in the galactic experience, in human terms, three naïve Earthlings had made it through a major breakdown of an alien technology that they completely misunderstood; with alien help, they fought a legal battle against imprisonment or death; and ultimately, they set foot on an alien planet that was a giant computer which allowed the residents to perform magic. Not a bad story for the history books.

There was just one tiny thing to try before leaving for Earth.

"Red is it possible for a Human to access the QtPIE?"

"Why not?" said Blue, "All you need is a wand. Here, use mine."

"She asked me." Red pushed Blue's wand away and held out his wand.

"She knows my wand is better than—"

"Stop," Miriam said. "Red, please give me your wand. Chuck? Nick? Would you like to try Blue's wand?"

"Definitely!" Nick jumped and yanked the wand from Blue's hand.

Red guided her hand with the wand. "Concentrate clearly and exactly on what you want to happen. Start with something simple." He placed a small blade of grass on her open hand. "Turn this into a smaller piece of grass. Same shape, but smaller."

Miriam waved, twisted, and whipped the wand, but nothing happened. She turned to see how Nick was doing and saw he had made a small woven basket out of some longer grasses. Chuck elbowed Nick for a turn.

"I told you my wand was better," said Blue.

"I'm no good at this." Miriam handed the wand to Chuck.

Elevating several gallons of water, he created a scaled image of *Galaxy Quest*. A model of their shuttle buzzed around the glimmering *Galaxy Quest*.

"Nicely done." Nick patted Chuck's shoulder. Red and Blue applauded.

"It's all in the wrist," Chuck bowed deeply at the waist.

The watery sculpture exploded into a rain of droplets when a figure burst from the center. A frail, devilish-looking creature with wide, diagonal stripes with a tint of gray on his otherwise red face flew over the pond straight at them. His black marble eyes were weary, his shoulders were broad, and he sported a thin goatee and wore a hooded gray robe. He landed gently on the pond's shoreline with a twist of his wand.

CHAPTER 54

"So, I finally caught up with you." Wyruk walked slowly toward the group. His wand pointed at them and twirled in a slow circle.

Chuck jumped between the surprise guest and his crew and assumed a wrestling stance. He stared at Wyruk's slowly moving hand and calculated if he could reach the wand before Wyruk could react. QtPIE Rule Five ensured Wyruk would not attack him directly and turn him into a frog, but he could trap him in a waterspout.

Red and Blue grabbed their wands out of the Humans' hands, jumped behind Chuck, clutched his shirt, and shut their eyes.

Miriam recognized the creature from the trial. "Wyruk, what are you doing here?"

"I'm here for some measure of justice." Wyruk pointed a boney finger at her. "You falsely identified me as that despicable criminal, Quane."

Wyruk knew less about justice than revenge. Revenge would have to wait. To get his share, or all, of the Human planet's genomes, he was willing to play his part. First make them feel guilty for causing him pain, then twist the guilt into a sympathetic decision to let him sell them the next round of engines. If they let him follow them to Earth, then he could steal all of Earth's genomes.

"I could not see well in the bad lighting. From a distance, you looked so much like the alien who called himself Quane."

Miriam stepped ahead and placed her hand on Chuck's forearm to lower his defenses. Avoiding an action that might cause a human or animal to harbor a grudge against her was always high on her mind. "What can I do to show you how sorry I am?"

Wyruk fingered the point of one of his horns with one hand and hid his mouth in his other hand to hide his smile. "I don't know if there is payment of any kind sufficient enough to repair the damage to my reputation and pride."

"I have some galactic credits." Miriam brought out the crushed lump of bills left in her pocket. "I don't know how much they are worth. You can have them all. We don't need them anymore. We are heading back to our planet."

Wyruk's tail wagged and corkscrewed with excitement at the shock of his outstanding luck. Elaborate lies were concocted to dissuade them from continuing their exploration so he could follow them back to Earth. Threats of legal action or physical harm were designed to send them home with their tails between their legs. But now they were returning home of their own volition.

"So you were going to run away, were you? Without letting me have the slightest restitution for your crimes against me?"

Miriam stepped forward and extended the cash toward Wyruk. "Take this. Unfortunately, we have nothing left to offer other than to say we are truly sorry."

Without lowering his wand, Wyruk snatched the money, turned sideways, and bent to count the money. Red and Blue peeked around Chuck's back.

"Nothing else?" Wyruk asked. "Any genomes?"

"We donated them all to GAASP," Miriam said, "as payment for their legal services."

"You what? I suppose you handed them over to the lawyer instead of sending them in to the corporate offices."

"We gave them to our lawyer, Gruseltmiro." Miriam hung her head. The joy of returning to Earth was once more dissolving into regret of another bad decision; they had been played for fools once again.

Wyruk shook his head. "You idiots that lawyer of yours just made off with a small fortune. GAASP will never see a decimal of that payment."

Red and Blue, reassured Wyruk had not come to punish them, came out from behind Chuck's back and ran up to Wyruk.

"Mister Wyruk," said Red, "do you want me to make some more black-market parts?"

"I'll do it," said Blue. "You always say my parts are better."

"Shut up you two!" Wyruk said. The magicians froze under Wyruk's icy glare.

When Wyruk turned to address the Humans, the magicians escaped in a cloud of smoke. Wyruk's smile was as wide as his face. "They made a couple of parts for me in the past. The parts have been out of production for years. I admit I sold them as original equipment instead of after-market parts." He winked at the Humans. "I was down on my luck and needed a few credits. You won't turn me in, will you?"

Miriam did not know where to go or whom to tell even if she felt like filing a complaint against Wyruk. "No. We will not tell. Besides, we are heading back to Earth. No one there will care about you cheating a few customers."

Wyruk's smile curved up toward his horns and he stroked his shabby goatee. "It seems you Humans are definitely interested in flying around the galaxy, but you won't get far from your home planet with this one GAASP engine. True, it is much better than the piece of galdickity Quane sold you."

Wiggling his wand at the ground, he levitated to eye level with the Humans. A finger curled to draw the Humans into a huddle. He put a hand on Nick's and Chuck's shoulders while his eyes darted around to all three. His breath was cool and smelled of roses. "Wouldn't it be wonderful to see Humans piloting a whole fleet of spaceships? An armada of Humans exploring the galaxy in a free exchange of culture and technology?"

Wyruk lifted his arm off Nick's shoulder and traced an arc across the sky with his wand. The arc spread and the Humans viewed the conjured mirage as if on a movie screen. "I can see it now; statues raised to Miriam, Nick, and Chuck, the first Human emissaries to the galaxy, and Earth's genomes traded in every system known to galactic-kind." Wyruk laughed so hard he choked, lowered his wand, and the vision disappeared.

"How do we make that happen?"

"I can sell you any number of stardrives," Wyruk nodded. His expression was serious and professional. "All much better than the thing GAASP gave you."

"So *you* want to sell us engines now?" Miriam pulled out of the huddle no longer knowing whom to trust. Lately, even her best judgment was letting her down. "Can we see and inspect these engines of yours?"

"I absolutely insist on that." Wyruk levitated to Miriam, smiled comfortingly, and put his arm around her neck. His breath smelled like new mown hay. "I will not allow one credit or genome to pass hands until you have inspected and tested every operational system at least twice."

Chuck and Nick moved to hear what the devil was proposing. "My plan is simple. I follow you to your planet. Then I take a number of pilots to where I have the engines. Your pilots will inspect them, select the ones they think are best, and the test drive will be the return to Earth. Once back at Earth, your engineers can re-examine and select some, all, or none for purchase. Only then will I ask for payment. That is how confident I am you will appreciate my merchandise." His enormous smile radiated confidence. His breath smelled like sweet wine.

His actual plan was even simpler: Follow the Humans to Earth, then threaten them with total destruction if they did not give him all their existing genome sequences. Once he had the genomes, Earth would be obliterated and he would own the only copies.

"I need to discuss this with my crew."

"I understand." Wyruk bowed and floated backward.

"I don't see how it can be a bad deal," said Nick.

Chuck held up his hand to stop the conversation, took off his headset, and motioned for them to do the same. After setting the translators on the grass, he led Miriam and Nick five steps away. Chuck stood with an unobstructed view of Wyruk and did not take his eyes off him. "That's better. Go ahead, Nick."

"We can send all of our best engineers. Select the best ones, bring them back to Earth, and still have the right to refuse any or all of them. When we get one or two really good ones, we head out into space and find some new engine showrooms." Nick was wringing his hands and licking his lips, hoping to be one of those best engineers. "I vote to accept Wyruk's offer."

"Our recent experience proves we know nothing about any alien's intentions," Chuck said. "Quane was a cheat and he threatened Earth with poisoning from the fallout of a destroyed engine. It could have been a bluff, and Wyruk could just be another devilish cheat. Is he a threat? There's no way to know. I can't pass a stranger I don't know or understand. I vote to reject Wyruk's offer." Wyruk was stacking softball-sized balls of water.

"Up to me again," said Miriam. "I agree with Nick, the proposal of getting a bunch of engines delivered is enticing. I also agree with Chuck; we can't allow the possibility of admitting a Trojan horse through the only defense we have, which is the secret of Earth's location."

Wyruk was stacking water balls into a pyramid.

"I'm sorry," said Miriam, "but we have to refuse your offer."

"Unfortunate for me. But when you decide to get serious about buying stardrives, look me up. Everyone knows my name." He smiled. "Let me walk you to your ship and say good-bye so you understand there are no hard feelings."

After the crew boarded the shuttle, Miriam turned to apologize again.

"Here," said Wyruk, offering his wand. "Take this as a souvenir of our meeting."

Miriam held out her hands and accepted the gift like she was being bequeathed with an ancient samurai sword. "Thank you." She bowed slightly. "I sincerely hope that the next time we meet, I will be able to pay my debt to you in full."

"You will," he said under his breath without the slightest smile. "You will."

Wyruk watched the Human shuttle launch, climbed into his shuttle, and activated the homing beacon hidden in the wand. He faced the three Xcrutians. "Sorry my friends but your fun is delayed. Be patient, for instead of three measly little Humans to pull apart, you will be able to feast on a whole planet. When you wipe out the Earthlings, the entire planet and all its genomes will be mine."

CHAPTER 55

On the return voyage, Miriam, Nick, and Chuck made a pact, unless they could not dodge answering a direct question, they would never reveal Quane had deliberately swindled Earth. His connivance might have left them marooned and dead in the desolation of dark space, but they would maintain their confidence out of respect for Richard Winn, his reputation, and his absolute conviction that Quane should be honored as the greatest influence on the Human race—more important to human history than any religious figure, conqueror, or despot.

Each day closer to Earth, the crew became more agitated with the anticipation of their arrival. Their appearance would be sudden and unanticipated, since they could not radio ahead. It was a given that they would be honored as heroes and would never have to buy their own drinks in any bar, ever. They daydreamed about television interviews, book contracts, science fiction conventions, and a worldwide lecture circuit.

Before *Galaxy Quest* launched, a bill was introduced designating Richard as a North American International Landmark. American and Canadian park services breathed sighs of relief when the bill failed. The park services had no clue how to administer a person. Charge admission to visitors? Affix a plaque to him? The house he grew up in was on a fast track for becoming a national monument. His elementary, middle, and high schools were in the process of being renamed and erecting statues and plaques to honor their most famous graduate.

Miriam, Nick, and Chuck would be the most renowned explorers in modern history. They had blazed a trail for humans to follow to the stars and back. They had met the natives and found some friendly and had established English as a translatable language. They performed magic and made it back alive. Their most ambitious mission goal—buying more engines for human use—would have to be accomplished on the next mission. All three agreed there was not enough money or fame to entice them to ever venture into space again. They would content themselves with a comfortable life of accolades, applause, and retelling of stories—with a calculated amount of exaggeration.

Weightlessness informed them the GPS had found Earth's coordinates and was automatically preparing to cross the membrane. Each astronaut hogged a viewport to claim the first sight of their big blue home. Each was tearing up with gratitude to whatever fate or guiding hand had returned them safely home. The first shock was the incredible brightness from the sun's intense reflection off the blue, white, and green planet.

"I see it," Chuck yelled. "What a sight! Right where we left it and as beautiful as ever. Man, it's bright."

"Is that South America or Africa?" Nick asked.

"Africa," Chuck said. "See Madagascar just to the left? We're upside down. Miriam, do you see?"

"Did any of the instruments indicate we were followed?"

"I never saw any signals," Nick said.

Chuck heard Miriam's tone and read her body language. She was tense and stared, unblinking, out her viewport. This was bad.

"I count five starships. Did we accidentally bring an invasion fleet back with us?"

Miriam's daydreams of thick red carpets at her feet, rose petals in her hair, and cheering, loving, teary-eyed faces melted into a nightmare of being pilloried by those same faces scowling with derision. Had she been in such a hurry to get back to Earth and her coronation that she damned Earth with her carelessness?

To Chuck, well trained in human psychology and ferreting out an enemy's thoughts even through the firewall of their military's indoctrination, Miriam was an open book with fifty-point lettering. He put his arm around her, waiting for the expected reaction. She broke down into fitful sobs.

"Calm down." Chuck touched his hidden medallion just in case. "You brought the three of us back alive. You did it on your nerves and feelings. You brought us back from the abyss of being lost or imprisoned in space forever. No matter what happens, I will honor you as my captain."

Nick, clueless about the exchange, but hearing how it ended, added, "Miriam, you're the best. We could not have gotten back here without you. Hey, did you see all those other stardrive ships out there? What's going—"

"Galaxy Quest, is *that* you? Please come in." It was Richard Winn's voice.

The sound of Richard's voice and Chuck's consolation was a lifeline to Miriam drowning in an ocean of self-pity. "Mission control," Miriam said in her best command voice, "Galaxy Quest reporting, mission accomplished. Crew is alive and well. Ship undamaged."

The speaker was drowned in static. Then, after repeated, unheeded demands for silence, it became apparent the background static was nothing less than hundreds of unrestrained cheers and applause at the recovery of *Galaxy Quest* and its crew.

"On behalf of everyone on the planet," Richard said, "congratulations on your historical accomplishment."

"Thank you all for keeping the faith," said Miriam. "Not much penetrates the membrane, but we are here to attest that prayers are the exception. It was your prayers and wishes that kept us going and brought us back safely."

"You even brought some friends." Richard groaned as he adjusted his back.

"If you mean the five other ships I see, we don't know who they are or why they are here."

"That's strange because they know you by name. Earth has been trying to find out why they're here and what they want for two months now. The only response we get is they will not talk to anyone but one of you three. That's why they brought me here—Mission Control thought Quane or some friend of his might be in one of the ships.

"The aliens have been popping in and out of light space. We detected them all over the solar system, but they spend most of their time near the inner planets, Mercury, Venus, and Mars, like they're looking for something. We identified five ships that are almost always around and at least twenty more popping in once, or multiple times. They appear and disappear for no reason, don't answer our calls, and won't tell us what they're doing or what they want. We pick up something like communication, but we have no means of translating."

"Have they made any threats?" Miriam crossed her fingers, folded her arms across her chest, closed her eyes, and prayed.

"They don't talk to us," said Richard. "No one knows how we could possibly defend ourselves in any case. Our biggest nukes would be nothing more than popguns. These aliens can disappear at will. In the end, we might do more damage to ourselves than them with all the nuclear fallout. Some insist that is precisely their plan: taunt us to throw nukes at them that they dodge, and we poison ourselves with the fallout."

"Wait, Miriam," Richard said. "I'm getting a communication. I'll patch it through to you."

"…Grrr, this spot is never going to come out…" Gruseltmira said.

"Psst. You're on," Schone whispered.

"I know," Gruseltmira said. "Miriam, Nick, Chuck, is that you? I recognized the engine we donated you—hard to hide all the markings. You were going to join my galactic cultural army, remember?"

"Gruseltmira," Miriam said. "Of course we remember you. How could we possibly forget you and all that GAASP has done for us? But why are you here, and what can we do for you? Did you come all this way just to enlist us into your army?"

"Silly, that comes later. I have some very exciting news. Did you know I completely ran out of clothes waiting for you? I wore each outfit exactly once and now have nothing left to wear. I am so lucky you arrived or I would have had to leave Schone in charge and she would have to give you the incredible news."

There was a long silence. "Miriam," Gruseltmira said, "who is in the ship the just appeared? It's not one of ours. Is it a friend of yours? Do they have any clothes to fit me?"

"The last person we saw before we left for Earth was Wyruk."

"Wyruk?" said a voice rumbling like a mountain of steel drums falling over. "Wyruk is in that ship? Ships Two and Three, after him! No shooting. I want him alive."

"You there, Humans," said the rumble. The voice was deep and thick, as if coming from the diaphragm of a hippopotamus or a whale. "Humans, did you know you were consorting with one of the galaxy's five Most Wanted criminals? He's guilty of slavery, counterfeiting, extortion, murder, and treason—just to start. What exactly was your business with Wyruk?"

"Wyruk offered to sell us some more engines," Miriam said, "but we refused. He must have followed us."

"We scanned his ship," the booming voice said. "Did you know Xcrutians were aboard?"

"No. What are they?"

"Vile creatures. They live to torture others and consume their pain. Once they feed, they start to multiply. Transporting just one Xcrutian is a capital crime. Wyruk has three. Wyruk came here for a reason. He must have wanted something of great value. He takes whatever he wants and leaves no witnesses. Xcrutians would have exterminated Humans. Xcrutians pay well for new planets. Lucky for you we were here."

"Are you the police? Are we in trouble?"

"We are higher than police," said the voice. "You are not in trouble. GAASP vouched for you. They told us your story. You are bumbling simpletons."

Ouch. Thanks to Miriam, the galaxy now thought of Humans as feckless chumps. She almost preferred thieves, murderers, and makers of mayhem. At least Humans would get some respect from the galactic riffraff; now they were a galactic laughingstock.

"When can we meet to tell you the wonderful news?" Gruseltmira said.

"Can we meet on Earth?" Miriam said. "We really want to breathe some fresh air and set foot on our own planet again."

"No, we can't. Our shuttle is not gravity worthy. And the news cannot wait."

"OK, then, come over ASAP. Let's get this over with." Miriam expected it was some news about Gruseltmira's newest dress or her galactic army. Once she got to Earth, she would clear Gruseltmira's smell out of her nose forever—by scrubbing public toilets, if need be—and drink until she could no longer recall her face... If that was possible.

Gruseltmira and Schone floated into *Galaxy Quest's* control room. Three aliens trailed behind. The first alien was Miriam's mental image of an Xcrutian: a hulking mass of teeth, muscle, scales, spikes, and weapons. The creature could barely fit through the Human-sized hatch. The hulk was followed by an extremely rotund, sleepy, rat-faced, hairy alien squeezed into a too-small spangled suit. The last alien was a skinny, twitchy version of the fat rat, but with loose-fitting clothes. Only the fat alien did not wear a translation headset.

Gruseltmira lit up at the sight of the three Humans—three sets of fresh eyes unfamiliar with her latest ensemble. A brand-new audience for her once-worn clothes.

"I am so glad to see you all." Gruseltmira managed a slow, weightless twirl with arms and legs outstretched to fully display her latest creation.

"Miriam, Chuck, Nick, how wonderful that you finally made your way home. I thought you might have gotten lost. We guessed you might come straight here after the trial. You took a little detour? Did some shopping, I hope." She glanced down at their clothes and winced. "Obviously, not for clothes."

Gruseltmira's dress looked like she had poked her head through an enormous crumpled napkin, complete with jagged rips. Instead of balls decorating the ends of the wiry bristles on her head, various-sized insects had been impaled there. Some appeared to be still alive and squirming to free themselves. Schone was just behind, trying to avoid Gruseltmira's spinning appendages. She wore the same simple clothes as their first meeting.

"Gruseltmira, Schone it is wonderful to see you, and we welcome you aboard our humble habitat." Miriam resisted the urge to float over and give them both a hug. Gruseltmira pulled a bug off her head and popped it in her mouth. The bug released a sickening sulfurous smell when the toothed snakes of her trifurcated tongue ripped the insect apart. The Humans grasped at any available handhold and pushed as far away from the stench as they could. Nick vowed to never chew with his mouth open again.

Miriam tried to be gracious. "What a fabulous dress you are wearing, Gruseltmira. You have undeniably outdone yourself this time."

"Oh, this old rag? It's nothing." Gruseltmira was satisfied that she had been noticed for her most important feature.

"Schone, will you introduce your friends?" Miriam had to stop Gruseltmira from talking and spreading her stench.

"This big lunk," said Schone, scratching the hulk behind his ear, "is the personal bodyguard of the other two. Let me introduce the Chairman of the Galactic Association of Stardrive Manufacturers and Engineers—" Schone waved toward the skinny, twitchy rat. "—and this is the Chief Financial Officer and Operations Lawyer." She indicated the fat sleepy rat.

"This bodyguard doesn't have a name. It can't speak or even think. It has telepathic sense for threats. If it sensed you had the tiniest idea to harm its owners, you would already be stains on the walls. If there are no threats, it turns into a cuddly pet... Don't you, baby?

"GASME is the division of StarDrive Engines, Inc. that oversees manufacturing."

"This is so exciting." Gruseltmira's breath smelled like something between burnt fireworks and rotten eggs.

Miriam directed Gruseltmira and Schone to the seats near the navigation consoles, the two businessmen in front of them and Nick, Chuck, and she found seats facing the rat-faced aliens—as far away from Gruseltmira as possible. The oversized one could not fit the seat belt across his lap, so he held one strap in each of his short, frail arms. The buckle was too long for the skinny one to make snug. He held himself against the seat by pulling on the seat belt like a horse's reins. Both of their puny legs stuck straight out. The bodyguard floated nearby like a statue.

Chuck kept the bodyguard in his vision, alert to the slightest threatening motion. He ignored Miriam's suggestion of seat assignment and picked one two seats over, near a hidden weapon. His seat belt was folded, unbuckled, across his lap and his feet pressed against the console. He tensed his legs so his hips strained at the belt. At the slightest provocation, he was ready to grab his hidden pistol and launch out of his seat. He expected to get off one clean shot at the monster.

Chuck tested the bodyguard's telepathic sense starting with light images of throwing harmless projectiles at the monster and finishing with vicious attacks. The monster ignored those thoughts. Then he imagined tugging lightly on the fat rat's whiskers. The bodyguard's muscles flexed slightly, it changed its grip on its weapon, and fixed its eyes on Chuck. The bodyguard did not care what happened to it, as long as its masters were secure.

Miriam said, "What is so important that GAASP and representatives from the stardrive manufacturers want to visit Earth and talk to us? What can we do for you that all our Earth-based representatives cannot?"

"We are here for a very important reason." The fat rat opened his eyes for the first time. His voice was thin and his sentences were punctuated by high-pitched wheezes.

"The results of the tests...*wheeze*...performed after your trial were astounding to the medical and stardrive engine communities. It seems you Humans...*wheeze*...are completely impervious to a Flocking. Your metabolism can tolerate Flock at levels that would kill entire planets...*wheeze*...

"We hired the best medical scientists to create an antidote or vaccination...*wheeze*...to being Flocked, using your biological samples." The fat rat reached into the pocket of his vest, pulled out a plastic fork, and used it to scratch his chin.

"The most successful formulation only offered a temporary resistance. Over time, it actually heightened intolerance and…*wheeze*…in one case, caused the death of a patient after she heard the word 'Flock.'

"I am authorized on behalf of GASME to offer you any compensation…*wheeze*…no matter how ridiculous it might seem to you, for the secret to your Flocking immunity. Name your price. Your wish is my…*wheeze*…command. Please, give us your secret."

The fat rat's eyes fluttered closed as if completely exhausted from his short monologue.

For the first time since the alien's arrival, Chuck took his eyes off the bodyguard to look at Miriam. Nick, obsessed with the idea of pizza and beer, woke up at the line, "Your wish is my command." Was there delivery to space?

"We have no secret," Miriam said. "We have no special immunity. To us, it was just dust. We don't know why we are immune." She noticed a small drop of drool at the corner of the sleeping fat rat's mouth and raised her voice. "We said this all at our trial. We did not know the dust was toxic."

The rat did not stir from his slumber.

"The only Human we know who was affected by the dust is Richard Winn. It crippled him. Others he came in contact with were sickened. But not as much as he was." No matter how loudly she yelled, Miriam could not wake the rat.

Miriam turned to her crew and shrugged. Nick used his left hand to cover his right hand pointing at the fat rat.

"I never heard of this Richard Winn," the fat rat wheezed, now wide-awake. "Can you tell me more about him?"

"Captain Winn was the first Human to take a ride with the alien, Quane, who sold us the first engine and we were arrested for using it.

"He had been on an engineering crew assigned to understand and assess the physical principles behind the engine's operation. After poking around inside, he wound up with a bunch of red dust all over his spacesuit. Shortly after, Richard became critically sick. The illness was highly contagious, but in an unusual way. The doctors, nurses, and visitors who interacted with him immediately after his first symptoms also became ill, but not as severely as Richard. The farther one was removed from Richard, the milder the reaction.

"There was also a diminished response with time. The first to treat Richard were severely affected. Those who were in contact with him days later did not become as sick. Weeks later, people in contact with him only complained of a minor cold."

The fat rat's drool was dripping off his chin and creating rivulets across his wide belly.

"Richard never recovered," Miriam yelled. The fat rat was asleep again. "But everyone else did as if they were immune to the effects of the dust." Miriam yelled, "Do you hear me?"

"I hear you." The fat rat opened his eyes. "Why...*wheeze*...do you keep increasing your volume?"

"I am trying to wake you up. You fall asleep whenever I start talking."

"I am a somno-linguist," he said. "I can only translate... *wheeze*... while I am sleeping. If I understand you correctly...*wheeze*...you have no secret formula, antidote, or special protection from Flock. Correct?" His eyes drooped and fluttered closed.

"We knew nothing about the dangers of Flock until we accidentally spread the dust around at the first meeting with the aliens gathered to meet us."

"Please...*wheeze*...excuse us."

The fat rat turned to the skinny rat. The skinny rat removed his headset. They squeaked and gesticulated animatedly at each other for several minutes. The bodyguard turned his attention to Miriam.

"Miriam," Chuck yelled to distract her quiet examination of the rats. She was mentally dissecting the creatures to find out how they metabolized and what organs might be adapted for a somno-linguist. "What do you think they want?" The bodyguard quickly lost interest in Miriam.

"I don't know. You heard it all. What do you think is going on?"

"As I see it, they need us for something." Chuck was determined to keep her focus on him. "We are immune to Flock. That is significant to them. You got us this far—don't let us down now. Think. Was there anything in Richard's transcripts to shed any light on what they might want?"

Every astronaut was required to memorize Richard Winn's transcripts of his meeting with Quane. No one could know what miniscule fact might be of life-saving importance. Miriam closed her eyes, slowed her breathing, and concentrated and uncovered an item she thought humorous when she first heard it.

Gruseltmira and Schone were whispering quietly. The Chairman of GASME and the Chief FOOL were squeaking loudly.

"Does this have anything to do with the lobster-like beings currently making your engines?"

The rats stopped squeaking. They and Schone and Gruseltmira looked stunned, as if a flash bomb had exploded.

"Bingo," Chuck whispered. "Go for it!"

Miriam made it up as she went; speaking slowly and deliberately to not get too far ahead of her thoughts. The skinny rat had the most expressive face and she directed her attention to him.

"The lobster creatures build your engines."

The skinny rat squeaked and his body winced and twitched with every word. His eyes refused to fix on her. "Yes," the skinny rat squeaked; twitching and wincing at every word. "Lobsters. Manufacture. Engines."

"They make all of your stardrives?"

"Yes." The rat spasmed. "All."

"Lobsters make all of your engines... No one else makes them...because..." The pause allowed her mind time to connect the dots and reach the logical conclusion.

It was so obvious!

Chuck high-fived Nick and gave Miriam a wink. Her face glowed with her epiphany.

"They make all of your engines because they are immune to Flock." This was the fixed point Earth was going to use to leverage themselves from galactic chumps into galactic players. The lock was in her hands and the combination in her mind. It was going to be enjoyable opening the door to the riches of the galaxy for all humanity.

"You are here because Humans are also immune to Flock."

The little rat twitched and shook like it had stuck its finger in a live socket.

"You *need* us," Miriam continued, "because of our immunity."

Schone's feathers were fluttering like there was a strong breeze. Gruseltmira stared at Miriam as if she was an incredibly gorgeous gown at an impossible price.

Chuck read Miriam's face, knowing she had solved the puzzle. He elbowed Nick to make him aware of the development, but saw Nick's unblinking eyes and knew he had solved it minutes before.

"You need Humans to build and service your engines because...because... Because you want to break the monopoly the lobsters currently have on building your stardrives!"

"Yes," Chuck said. Maybe he could buy a Saint Miriam medal.

The twitchy rat was shaking so hard he seemed to be holding the reins to a galloping, runaway stallion.

"Yes," the rat squealed. "Contract. Terms. Negotiable."

"I have to present this offer to all of Earth's representative governments. I cannot decide this alone."

"Please…" The twitchy rat twitched. "Consult. Respond. Negotiate."

"What if the answer is no?"

"No, please!" Gruseltmira cried. "Don't let the answer be no." She looked more dejected than if her favorite dress had been soiled—or even worse, ignored.

Schone put her arm around Gruseltmira's shoulder. "We did not tell you that Gruseltmira and I no longer work for GAASP. We quit when we heard the results of your biological tests. We convinced the Stardrive Engine Consortium that we knew you and they should hire us as the liaisons to negotiate the contract between the consortium and Humans. If you say no, we are out of jobs. Gruseltmira will be nearly penniless, since her trust fund pays only enough to buy one new outfit every month." Schone gently stroked the stumps of Gruseltmira's rudimentary back feathers.

"Those genomes you gave me were worthless," Gruseltmira sobbed and buried her face in Schone's shoulder.

"We gave those genomes to GAASP," Miriam said.

"Yes, yes," Gruseltmira stammered. "I was going to cash them in and give GAASP the money directly and save them the bother of doing the exchange. Besides, I knew if I went to the black market, I could triple my money… I mean, the money I was going to give to GAASP on your behalf." She tapped her headset with a talon. "There must be a flaw in these translators."

"There was something wrong with the genomes?"

"No. Half of the batch you gave me has been around for five years. Some drug cults grew up around a few of them and a new company is launching an ad campaign to promote the very best one—Kuckrooch, I think it's called. The other half was worthless junk to be sold as toys or joke gifts."

"If you accept the offer," Schone said, "you, your planet, and your solar system will be one of the richest in the galaxy. Salesmen will appear overnight, endlessly offering you every cheap trinket and priceless rarity. Politicians, intellectuals, and tourists will come begging for favors, information, and selfies. Earth will become a galactic node for commerce and culture. We really, really urge you to accept."

"Where would you build the manufacturing facilities?" Miriam said.

"GASME searched," Schone said, "and decided Mars would be ideal. There would be factories on the planet's surface, and in orbit. A sub-assembly site might be built on your moon, for easy Human access. The consortium would fully fund construction, and your planet would receive a commission on all engine sales. That would naturally be above and beyond the workers' salaries. Earthlings could buy them at cost."

CHAPTER 56

"Houston, this is Commander Miriam Wu of the *Galaxy Quest*. Please see what you can do with getting as many of Earth's leaders on a conference call."

"They have all been on a hot button since the first ships arrived and on hold since the minute you called," Richard said.

"Open the call, then."

"*Galaxy Quest*," said President Burke. "On behalf of all Americans and every citizen of Earth, let me be the first to officially welcome you back, congratulate you on a mission well done, and say how happy we are that you arrived safe—"

"Mr. President," Miriam interrupted, "we really don't have time for this. We need an answer concerning an offer of staggering importance."

"Invite all your friends down to Earth," Burke said, "and we will give them a welcome they will never forget. We'll have a banquet at the White House with the most important heads of state, complete with a ticker tape parade and—"

"No, sir. I need an answer now."

"All right," the president said, stung by the rebuff. "Can you tell me something about this offer?"

"Are all of the other world leaders on the line?" Miriam asked.

"Russia, here."

"China, here."

"India, here."

Another ten countries, including England, Germany, Brazil, and Saudi Arabia, had added their names before Miriam stopped the roll call.

"Enough. I am here with the chairman of the Galactic Association of Stardrive Manufacturers and Engineers and their Chief Financial Officer and Operations Lawyer. Their offer is to the entire Human race.

"I'll try to explain. When Captain... Sorry, *General* Richard Winn became ill from the red dust that the aliens call Flock, he woke a long-dormant Human gene that in some manner protects Humans from the deadly effects of Flock. How it originated is anyone's guess. But his exposure was like a booster shot for typical Human vaccinations. How and why this happened is not important.

"What we have been told," Miriam continued, "and have seen with our own eyes, is only one other creature in the galaxy shares the resistance. Flock is instantly deadly to every living being at infinitesimal levels and never loses potency. The Flocking reaction with dark matter is the fundamental principle enabling stardrive propulsion used on every spaceship by every alien in the galaxy.

"The other species, the lobsters Richard reported, holds a monopoly on the manufacture of stardrive engines. As you can imagine, the royalties are huge and they command enormous salaries."

Urgent, muffled whispers erupted from Earth's side of the conversation.

"I trust this is not a union shop," the president said. "I will not interfere with union rights if it means depriving hard-working lobsters of a living wage and putting food on the table. I am not a job killer," the president said pompously to satisfy a specific constituency. The image of lobsters sitting down to a dinner table underwater was a bit hard to grasp.

"That's not important, Mr. President," Miriam said. "What is important is we are the only other species in the galaxy with the same Flocking immunity. The businessmen here on our ship want to build a manufacturing plant on Mars and on the moon. They will fully fund the construction, pay Earth a commission on each engine, and pay the Human workers to build them." Miriam glanced at the skinny rat to see if she had spoken correctly. The rat twitched and nodded.

"They are asking your permission to make Earth and the Human race one of the richest planets in the galaxy."

"This is momentous," the president said. "It means many jobs. But there are also many legal considerations. Specifically regarding Martian and lunar sovereignty as regards spheres of influence and rights and treaties—"

The Russian president cut in. "The Russian people will allow the aliens to build factories on sovereign Russian soil on Mars and the moon and provide ten thousand of the highest skilled Russian working cla—"

The Chinese premier interrupted. "The People's Republic of China grants rights to build on Chinese national soil on Mars and the moon and provide twenty thousand highly skilled Chinese labor—"

"This is the prime minister of Great Britain. We will provide thirty thousand of the world's most elite and best-trained workers—"

"Stop, now!" the president yelled. "We can't go selling Mars and the moon without a little reasoned thought, and guarantees that—"

"Russia offers its rights to Venus as well as Mars and the moon and fifty thousand of the best scientists and engineers Earth has to offer if the aliens build factories on Russian territory."

"China offers one hundred thousand skilled workers plus all rights to build manufacturing facilities on any Chinese soil on Mercury, Venus, Earth, the moon, or Mars."

"Two hundred thousand workers and the aliens can build on any planet, even underwater, within the United Kingdom's territorial boundary."

"India will allow factories to be built anywhere within its borders on Earth—"

"Stop!" yelled the American president. "Miriam, I'll be right back."

"Are you really here with Earth's best interests at heart?" Miriam shivered with a feeling of déjà vu.

"Most definitely," the GASME chairman said and twitched. Especially if those interests meant the consortium would make an enormous profit and break the lobster monopoly. How many times had the lobsters held up production with the taunt, "Go ahead, find someone else to make your engines. Go ahead and try"?

The consortium had done just that. Humans appeared intellectually and physically adaptable. They were not quite as durable as the lobsters, but they made up for it in numbers, creativity, and dexterity.

"Miriam, this is the president of the United States. I am authorized to say that Earth is willing to negotiate a contract to allow manufacturing facilities on Mars and the moon and other planets as agreed upon. But, before I do, I need to ask some questions."

"Ask," the twitchy rat said. The Chief FOOL had multiple rivulets of drool dripping off the edge of his stomach.

"First," said the president, "we need some kind of leasing agreement to guarantee a minimum level of employment for many years to come."

"Define," squeaked the twitchy rat, "level. Many years."

"We were thinking," said the president, "about one million workers for the next one hundred years." The president was bluffing. The agreed upon numbers were half those amounts.

The GASME chairman allowed a momentary feeling of remorse for being responsible for converting Earth into a single-resource galactic economy. Humans would be doomed to live and die supporting their engine-manufacturing industry. The industry would be extremely lucrative for them and would generate well over 50 percent of their galactic wealth. Ultimately, dependence on that revenue stream to satisfy their thirst for galactic goods and services would force Human political and social structures to wrap a protectionist blanket tightly around the industry. Other Human industries and businesses attempting to reach for the stars or improve the earth would have to fight for the financial crumbs falling from the stardrive industry's table. But the moment was fleeting.

The wild card in all of these negotiations was how the lobsters would react to losing at least half of their monopoly.

"Send..." Squeak, twitch. "Contract..." Twitch, squeak. "Lawyers..." Twitch, squeak, twitch. "Negotiate..." Squeak, twitch, squeak. "Terms."

Miriam was exhausted and hungry. Nick was sleeping, and Chuck was gazing far away.

The rats unbuckled themselves and floated to the hatch back to their shuttle. Gruseltmira was beaming and squealing with joy. Schone's down was as soft and white as a cloud. They floated toward Miriam.

Schone grabbed Miriam's hand. "You will never regret this. No one on your planet will be poor again. They will have anything—*anything*—they want in the galaxy. Gruseltmira and I will fight for your best interests."

Miriam nearly passed out from Gruseltmira's breath.

"You know, Miriam, I think this might be the start of a beautiful friendship."

EPILOGUE

Richard Winn had, by far, the greatest number of monuments and memorials named after him than any other person alive or dead. Referendums routinely populated nearly every North American federal, regional, state, county, and city election to rename their respective jurisdiction after the most famous Human being of all time. An office of three full-time accountants could barely keep tally of the proposed or approved christenings of parks, fountains, streets, bridges, malls, statues, stadiums, schools, or breakfast cereals in Richard's name. Frustrated cartographers were bleary-eyed from trying to keep up with the latest landmark and street renaming.

Richard's hometown lobbied successfully to rename the town Winn City.

Comedians mused that citizens might eventually vote to have a country, region, state, county, and city named after the famous astronaut. It would be a Winn-Winn-Winn-Winn-Winn situation. Whoever lived on Winn Street would have hit the jackpot.

Miriam Wu faced similar adulation. China still regarded her as one of their own and treated the most famous Chinese woman of all time with the status of a rock star. Universities, streets, and parks were named after her. Her hometown was renamed Wuville. Statues and fountains were raised in her honor. A cultivated species of rose was christened, *Miriamus Heroica*.

Fedor, Nancy, Nick, and Chuck all shared lesser acclaim, accolades, and awards. Nick launched a signature brand of sunglasses. Chuck managed a chain of fitness clubs called Beast Mode. Nancy wrote children's books about living in space. Fedor went fishing.

Richard, Miriam, Nick, Chuck, Fedor, and Nancy became the six most popular given names for many years. In some cities, entire classrooms populated with twenty-five children shared only six names. It was only natural for parents to endow their children with the aspirational hope associated with a famous name.

All of the honors, awards, and accolades bestowed by humans were bestowed only on humans—Quane being the obvious exclusion. Richard lobbied hard for some kind of memorial to his friend and mentor. Approval was on a political fast track until *Galaxy Quest's return*. Suddenly, all progress toward any type of remembrance halted. The reasons were never fully explained and vexed Richard until the day he died.

No homage was ever made to the principal players in the story of Human expansion into the galaxy. Not a statue, not a plaque, not even a memorial urinal honored their effort and sacrifice. No thing, no act, no word honored the true heroes of Human history, the enabler of Human inoculation against Flock, and the foremost influence in making Earth one of the wealthiest planets in the galaxy: The Smez.

ACKNOWLEDGEMENTS

First and foremost, I'd like to thank my daughter, Rebecca Rose Tabat, for whispering the answer to a single question that has bothered me since childhood: How will we humans really find our way off Earth and explore the galaxy? That seed of an idea found fertile soil in my compost pile of a brain and grew into this story.

Next, I have to thank my wife, Charlene, and my son, Chuck, for their patience and understanding while I lived off-planet for the many days, months, and years it took to finish *Welcome to the Galaxy*. Fortunately, they were not the least bit jealous of my small fling with Gruseltmira.

Finally, a very heartfelt thank you to all of you readers. I often wished this story had revealed itself to an experienced writer who could have made this book into a classic. I did my best. I hope my puddling effort was acceptable.

Made in the USA
Coppell, TX
16 April 2020

20313375R00197